PENGUIN  CLASSICS

FANTÔMAS

After *Fantômas* was published in 1911 to wild popularity and success, PIERRE SOUVESTRE, an already well-known journalist and novelist, and MARCEL ALLAIN, his secretary and writing partner, went on to publish twenty sequels to the original. After Souvestre's death in 1914, Allain wrote another eleven books in the Fantômas series and launched several other pulp fiction series on his own. Allain passed away in 1969, having written over four hundred novels throughout his career.

JOHN ASHBERY was born in Rochester, New York, in 1927. He is the author of more than twenty books of poetry, including *Chinese Whispers; Your Name Here; Can You Hear Bird; And the Stars Were Shining; Hotel Lautréamont; Flow Chart; Self-portrait in a Convex Mirror*, which received the Pulitzer Prize for Poetry, the National Book Critics Circle Award, and the National Book Award; *Some Trees*, which was selected by W. H. Auden for the Yale Younger Poets Series; and *Where Shall I Wander*, which was a finalist for the National Book Award. John Ashbery is a Charles P. Stevenson, Jr. Professor of Languages and Literature at Bard College. He lives in New York.

MARCEL ALLAIN
AND
PIERRE SOUVESTRE

Fantômas

With an Introduction by
JOHN ASHBERY

PENGUIN BOOKS

PENGUIN BOOKS

Published by the Penguin Group

Penguin Group (USA) Inc., 375 Hudson Street, New York, New York 10014, U.S.A.

Penguin Group (Canada), 10 Alcorn Avenue, Toronto, Ontario, Canada M4P 2Y3
(a division of Pearson Penguin Canada Inc.)

Penguin Books Ltd, 80 Strand, London WC2R 0RL, England

Penguin Ireland, 25 St Stephen's Green, Dublin 2, Ireland (a division of Penguin Books Ltd)

Penguin Group (Australia), 250 Camberwell Road, Camberwell, Victoria 3124, Australia
(a division of Pearson Australia Group Pty Ltd)

Penguin Books India Pvt Ltd, 11 Community Centre, Panchsheel Park, New Delhi – 110 017, India

Penguin Group (NZ), cnr Airborne and Rosedale Roads, Albany, Auckland 1310, New Zealand
(a division of Pearson New Zealand Ltd)

Penguin Books (South Africa) (Pty) Ltd, 24 Sturdee Avenue, Rosebank, Johannesburg 2196, South Africa

Penguin Books Ltd, Registered Offices:
80 Strand, London WC2R 0RL, England

Fantômas with an introduction by John Ashbery first published in the United States of America by
William Morrow and Company, Inc. 1986
Published in Penguin Books 2006

Introduction copyright © John Ashbery, 1986
All rights reserved

ISBN 978-0-14-310484-1
CIP data available

Printed in the United States of America
Set in Adobe Sabon

146122990

Contents

Introduction

Stretching his immense shadow
Across the world and across Paris
What is this gray-eyed specter
Rising out of the silence?
Fantômas might it be you
Lurking on the rooftops?
—ROBERT DESNOS,
"Complaint of Fantômas"

From the moment it was published in February 1911, *Fantômas* (and the thirty-one sequels which immediately followed it) was a phenomenon: a work of fiction whose popularity cut across all social and cultural strata. Countesses and concierges; poets and proletarians; Cubists, nascent Dadaists, soon-to-be surrealists: Everyone who could read, and even those who could not, shivered at posters of a masked man in impeccable evening clothes, dagger in hand, looming over Paris like a somber Gulliver, contemplating hideous misdeeds from which no citizen was safe. Plastered on billboards, on kiosks and *colonnes Morris*, on walls of corridors in the Métro, his image multiplied throughout the city. In short order five Fantômas films directed by the incomparable Louis Feuillade further celebrated the exploits of the "king of the night," his mistress Lady Beltham, his mysterious daughter Hélène, and his implacable foes, Inspector Juve and the daredevil young reporter Jérôme Fandor (soon to become romantically involved with Hélène). There have been endless reprints of the novels, frequent remakes of the films until as recently as the mid-sixties (though none bears comparison with Feuillade's), not to mention theatrical adaptations, photonovels, and translations into umpteen foreign languages, including Czech, Greek, and Serbian. (The present translation is a modernized version of one published in 1915 by both Stanley

Paul in London and Brentano's in New York.) In France, the Fantômas phenomenon is a live issue even today: Coauthor Marcel Allain was an honored guest at a conference of intellectuals at Cerisy in 1967, two years before his death, and at least two serious literary reviews have published special Fantômas issues (*La Tour de Feu* in December 1965 and *Europe* in 1978). I am particularly indebted to the latter for information given here; in addition, a 1951 book entitled *Les Terribles* by Antoinette Peské and Pierre Marty has valuable material on Fantômas and on kindred spirits like Maurice Leblanc's Arsène Lupin and Gaston Leroux's Chéri-Bibi. It would seem that the *empereur du crime*, whose fate was naturally left in doubt at the end of each novel, is still alive and well and living in Paris.

Fantômas was the chance creation of two inspired hacks, both of whom had studied law before turning to the French equivalent of Grub Street. Pierre Souvestre was born to a well-to-do family at the manor of Keraval in Brittany in 1874; after being admitted to the bar he apparently grew bored with that profession and entered the new field of automotive journalism, first at a magazine called *L'Auto* and then with another called *Poids Lourds* ("heavy trucks"), while also serving as drama critic for the newspaper *Le Soleil*. In search of a secretary, he happened on Marcel Allain, a clever young man almost ten years his junior who amazed him by producing a seventeen-page article on a new truck (the "Darracq-Serpolet") about which he knew nothing, in the space of two hours. So their collaboration began, and soon Allain was made managing editor of *Poids Lourds* as well as ghostwriter of a column by Souvestre in *L'Auto*; shortly both joined the editorial staff of the newly created theatrical review *Comoedia*. The withdrawal of an advertiser from *L'Auto* left the magazine with a number of blank pages which the resourceful authors rapidly filled with a "Hindu" serial called *Le Rour*. This proved so successful that they supplied a pseudonymous parody of it for yet another vehicular journal, *Le Vélo* ("the bike"). That sequel, entitled *Le Four* ("the oven," or, in popular parlance, "the flop"), brought them to the attention of the publisher Arthème Fayard, who commissioned them to write a series of five fantastic novels having a common theme. The day after meeting with Fayard they put their heads together and came up with a lot of ideas but no title; later, in the Métro, Allain seized on the name *Fantômus*. Souvestre wrote it down in a notebook and subsequently showed it to Fayard, who misread it *Fantômas*—doubtless a lucky accident, for *Fantômus* doesn't seem quite to make it, while *Fantômas* is somehow pregnant with mystery.

Thanks to a blockbusting publicity campaign, the first novel was an instant success and the sequels, frequently dictated by the authors to save time and sometimes produced in the span of a couple of days, were awaited with an impatience rivaling that with which upper-class Frenchmen of the time of Louis XV awaited the arrival of the first green peas in spring. Feuillade's films of 1913–14 fanned the craze; then Souvestre died suddenly of Spanish influenza in 1914, the war arrived a few months later, and Allain was off to the trenches. He survived to produce eleven more Fantômas novels on his own as well as an immense amount of ephemeral fiction on other themes (some six hundred novels as well as innumerable stories and articles), eventually marrying Souvestre's widow. He died in 1969 three weeks short of his eighty-fourth birthday, apparently still an amused and adventurous spirit, content with his singular career and active almost to the end of his life as a pulp writer and compulsive driver of the cars he collected.

What is most surprising about the Fantômas tales is the gap between their crude narratives, appropriately garbed in hackneyed prose, and the deep impression they left on the work of poets and painters. As early as 1912 Apollinaire founded the *Société de Amis de Fantômas* (SAF); in 1914 he wrote in the august *Mercure de France* of "that extraordinary novel, full of life and imagination, lamely written but extremely vivid. . . . From the imaginative standpoint *Fantômas* is one of the richest works that exist. . . ." And Cocteau later wrote of "the absurd and magnificent lyricism of *Fantômas*." It is true that Apollinaire and Cocteau were, in the words of one critic, "always afraid of missing the boat." But what of more reserved spirits such as Max Jacob, an active member of the SAF who wrote poems about Fantômas; of Blaise Cendrars who called the Fantômas

series "the modern *Aeneid*"; of Desnos whose "Complaint of
Fantômas," quoted above, was set to music by Kurt Weill?
(What, one wonders, has happened to the score? Was it a Gallic
version of Weill's "Ballad of Mackie Messer"?) To say nothing
of Aragon, Colette, Raymond Queneau, and Pablo Neruda, all
of whom are reported to have been fans of the beastly hero, as
were the painters Picasso, Juan Gris, and Magritte.

It is all somewhat puzzling, since a case can easily be made
against the "absurd and magnificent lyricism" of the novels.
Fantômas was a late-blooming *fleur du mal* on a vine whose
roots extended back to the mid-nineteenth century and beyond,
if we want to include the Gothic period and such ancestors as
Melmoth and Manfred. But Fantômas isn't just a personage, superhuman or not, but a place, an atmosphere, a state of mind:
this tradition too goes back to Eugène Sue's *Mystères de Paris*
(1842–43) and to Ponson du Terrail (1829–71), whose hero Rocambole gave the French language the adjective *rocambolesque*,
still used to describe anything farfetched. In Hugo's *Les Mis-
érables* we have the reverse prototypes of Fantômas and Juve in
Jean Valjean, the long-suffering convict-hero, and the evil Inspector Javert; while Maldoror in Lautréamont's *Les Chants de
Maldoror*, a proto-surrealist *chanson de geste*, has often been
seen as a forerunner of Fantômas, though it is unlikely that Allain and Souvestre had ever heard of him. As the century drew to
a close the genre of the novel of terror, often with Paris as the
important backdrop, reached new heights with such writers as
Maurice Leblanc (Arsène Lupin), Gaston Leroux (Chéri-Bibi),
and the amazing, recently rediscovered, and aptly named Gus-
tave LeRouge, author of such gory treats as *The Mysterious Dr.
Cornelius* and *The War of the Vampires*. (LeRouge, who wove a
strain of science fiction into his incredible and interminable novels, seems to have had a love-hate affair with America, which he
never visited but often used for his settings; his energetic young
American villains are the exact antitheses of America's Nick
Carter, also immensely popular in France at the time, and perhaps prefigure one of Fantômas's alter egos, the American detective Tom Bob in *Le Policier Apache*—"the hoodlum policeman,"
but published in England as *Slippery as Sin*.)

It is safe to say that any of the above writers were superior to
Messrs. Allain and Souvestre, even as purveyors of popular en-
tertainment. For all their crimes, Arsène Lupin (who, one critic
has said, used the same tailor as Fantômas) and Chéri-Bibi had
their sympathetic, Robin Hood side; even Leroux's Phantom of
the Opera is a not-inhuman monster. LeRouge's villains are
certainly beyond redemption, but the dreamlike atmosphere of
his narratives lightens the terror. But with Fantômas, terror almost becomes monotonous. He really has no redeeming traits;
greed and vengeance are his chief motivations, despite a knee-
jerk paternal attachment to the ambiguous and ultimately un-
convincing Hélène. His sadism seems especially directed
toward women, and it doesn't matter whether they are young or
old, virtuous or wicked, marchionesses or streetwalkers. But of
course men aren't spared either. In *The Daughter of Fantômas*,
the eighth novel in the series, Fantômas is off to South Africa
with Juve in hot pursuit; once there he does away with his
daughter's elderly female guardian and almost simultaneously
provokes the lynching of Jupiter, a black "noble savage," having meanwhile infected the luxurious ocean liner *British Queen*
by injecting rats with plague germs and watching its five hundred passengers die ghastly deaths.

In an article titled "The Morality of Fantômas" in the review
Europe, Louis Chavance summarizes the case against the anti-
hero. The enduring popularity of the novels for literati and just
plain folks is justified "neither by the clarity nor the vigor of
their style, which, in its density, resembles a layer of volcanic
ash into which one sinks to the ankles; nor by their imagination
nor their extremely simple construction, wherein a single 'cli-
max' per volume (the phantom hansom cab; the singing foun-
tains of the Place de la Concorde) constitutes the central point
around which the other events turn; nor by the extremely con-
ventional and simplistic characters, including that of Fantômas
himself . . . which is ultimately reduced to his penchant for
atrocities and his morality: that of a *petit bourgeois* who
prefers crime to bowling."

Chavance explains that our fascination with Fantômas is due
to the surrealists' having welcomed him into their cénacle,

though given his low opinion of the series, he offers no very good explanation for their having done so. He also attributes the success of the stories in part to the exploits of the *bande à Bonnot*, a gang of anarchist criminals whose crimes horrified and fascinated the French, and in whom he sees the germ of the Fantômas series—but eleven of the novels had already appeared by the time the Bonnot gang burst on the scene in December 1911. Still, Chavance alone among the contributors to *Europe*'s Fantômas symposium raises an interesting issue: given their shortcomings, what is the secret of the fascination these books have had for so many of the great creators of our time? Why not, indeed, the far more promising LeRouge, who seems to have been ignored by the intelligentsia, except for Cendrars, who managed to strike up a friendship with the self-effacing author?

Well, LeRouge was too much on the way to being a *surréaliste sans le savoir* to have satisfied the populist longings of that group: we must remember how Breton carried *encanaillement* to the point of eulogizing (in *Nadja*) a forgotten Hollywood serial about a giant octopus, starring Ben Wilson and Neva Gerber. The prose, the plots, the personages of what has come to be known as the *geste de Fantômas* were constructed of the requisite industrial-strength fustian. And besides, Fantômas was more than the sum of the thirty-two novels of the original series. He was, first of all, an image: the unforgettable one of the masked man with a dagger brooding over Paris, inspired perhaps by Félicien Rops's famous engraving, "Satan Sowing Tares." The artist, an Italian named Gino Starace, continued to provide lurid cover illustrations for each sequel, and no doubt contributed in large part to their success. (Some notable examples were his covers for *The Marriage of Fantômas*—a group of gendarmes laying hands on a woman in a white bridal gown and a black mask; *The Gold Stealer*—two men stripping gold from the dome of the Hôtel des Invalides; and *The Severed Hand*—a bloody hand clutching the roulette wheel of a casino.) The films of Feuillade extended the repertory of images, and are if anything more like the novels than the novels themselves. Indeed, Feuillade's later serials based on different sources (*Judex*,

Les Vampires, Barabbas) are not only superior to his Fantômas films, which were made at a time when he was still learning the tricks of his trade, but develop their atmosphere, so that in watching them one keeps expecting the characters from Fantômas to appear. Actually Feuillade was but one of a number of filmmakers working this vein. Stills from Monca's *The Prey* and Gance's *The Madness of Dr. Tube* partake of a similar ambience of exotic terror at odds with the reassuring naturalism of the settings: humble estaminets, the concierge's loge, the writing rooms of grand hotels, vast Parisian department stores such as the Galeries de Paris where Fantômas substitutes sulfuric acid in the atomizers of the perfume counter, trains, ocean liners, industrial suburbs, or elegant faubourgs.

The authors' uncanny sense of *genus loci* is one of the principal ingredients of the novels' potent charm. If the five principal characters—Fantômas, Juve, Fandor, Lady Beltham, and Hélène—remain hieratically frozen in their relation to one another, like figures in a romanesque frieze, they are nonetheless constantly on the move, traversing the landscapes of the world by every available means of locomotion. The effect is not unlike that of a passacaglia, whose fixed underlying motive allows for ornamentation above that can all but obscure it. In Fantômas what we savor most are the details and decor including subordinate characters and subplots, while the basic situation remains the same. The atmospheres and landscapes, particularly those of Paris, are brushed with remarkable sensitivity, and these extensions of the personage of Fantômas and of his friends and foes are the real characters in the epic. The facility with which Fantômas can become an object was noted by Max Jacob in one of two Fantômas prose-poems in his collection *The Dice Cup*: "On the burnished silver knocker of the door, darkened by time, by the dust of time, was a kind of chiseled Buddha with a too-high forehead, with pendulous ears, with the look of a sailor or a gorilla: it was Fantômas." And this physicality was transmitted into film by Feuillade so flawlessly that what one critic has written about the Fantômas films could apply equally to the novels themselves. Feuillade, in the words of Francis Lacassin, "had discovered before Antonioni the secret of grisaille. He had understood that nothing is more beautiful than a certain suburban poetry that emanates from disjointed paving stones, from working-class districts, from a dismal suburb, silent and deserted, from vacant lots beyond which, at a distance, the blurred profiles of buildings under construction are silhouetted against the sky."

It is possible that French place names are more suggestive than those of other countries; at any rate the names of Paris streets have a life of their own in fiction and in real life. Crimes are named after them: thus the first of the Bonnot gang's bloody exploits has gone down in history as *"l'attentat de la rue Ordener,"* conferring a kind of immortality on an otherwise undistinguished thoroughfare. French newspapers keep their readers abreast of late-breaking developments in *"le drame de la rue Raynouard"* or *"l'affaire du Boulevard Saint-Jacques"* until it seems that the places themselves are actually actors in the events described. No doubt the earliest readers of Fantômas shuddered delightedly at the thought that dire acts were being committed in the next street or one they walked along to work every day, its sober façades a seeming denial of fantastic goings-on behind them. Frequently it is enough for the authors to name a place, in Paris or elsewhere in France, or even in London (though not in locations with which they were obviously unfamiliar, such as Durban) for the magic to start. Space that extends and amplifies the human figure, meanwhile mingling it with printed words and mundane objects, was an invention of the Cubists, the exact contemporaries of Fantômas, and it is not at all surprising that Juan Gris should have painted a *Fantômas Still-Life.*

But one shouldn't analyze too closely the charms of this superb charade, as flimsy as they are durable. Lacassin is surely close enough when, speaking again on the films, he observes that their dreamlike quality almost makes us forget their extraordinary realism. "Perhaps the most beautiful scene in *Fantômas,*" he writes, "isn't the struggle with the boa constrictor and the latter's deathpangs, nor the gunfight among the wine-barrels nor the masked criminal slipping into a cistern, but simply that in which a policeman is expertly unscrewing the grill of a ventilating duct, holding on to the fastened side of the plaque and experiencing from time to time the resistance of the screws, then carefully placing them beside the piece of metal once it has finally been removed. In this marvelous poetic anthology, each of us has at our disposal beforehand an image that is destined to thrill us. And for each of us it will never be the same one."

Suggestions for Further Reading

Cocteau, Jean. *Opium*. Paris: Stock, 1930. (English translation by Margaret Crosland and Sinclair Road.) New York: Grove Press, 1958.

Europe, nos. 590–591, June–July 1978.

Fauchereau, Serge. *La Révolution cubiste*. Paris: Denoël, 1982.

Jacob, Max. *Le Cornet à dés*. Paris: Gallimard, 1945.

Lacassin, Francis. *Louis Feuillade*. Cinéma d'aujourd'hui, no. 22. Paris: Seghers, 1964.

Marty, Pierre, and Antoinette Peské. *Les Terribles*. Paris: Chambriand, 1951.

Tour de feu, La, nos. 87–88, December 1965.

Fantômas

THE GENIUS OF CRIME

"Fantômas."

  "What did you say?"

  "I said: Fantômas."

  "And what does that mean?"

  "Nothing. . . . Everything!"

  "But what is it?"

  "Nobody. . . . And yet, yes, it is somebody!"

  "And what does the somebody do?"

  "Spreads terror!"

Dinner was just over, and the company was moving into the drawing room.

Hurrying to the fireplace, the Marquise de Langrune took a large log from a basket and flung it onto the glowing embers on the hearth; the log crackled and shed a brilliant light over the whole room; the guests of the marquise instinctively drew near to the fire.

During the ten consecutive months she spent every year at her château of Beaulieu, on the outskirts of Corrèze, that picturesque district bounded by the Dordogne, it had been the immemorial custom of the Marquise de Langrune to have a few of her personal friends in the neighborhood to dinner every Wednesday, thereby obtaining a pleasant respite from her loneliness and keeping up some contact with the outside world.

On this particular winter evening the good lady's guests included a few regulars: President Bonnet, a magistrate who had retired to his small property at Saint-Jaury, in the suburbs of Brives, and the Abbé Sicot, who was the parish priest. A more occasional guest was also there, the Baronne de Vibray, a young and wealthy widow, a typical woman of the world who spent the greater part of her life either in motoring, or in the most exclusive drawing rooms of Paris, or at the most fashionable watering places. But when the Baronne de Vibray put herself out to pasture, as she racily phrased it, and spent a few weeks at Querelles, her estate close to the château of Beaulieu, nothing pleased her more than to take her place again in the delightful company of the Marquise de Langrune and her friends.

Finally, the younger generation was represented by Charles Rambert, who had arrived at the château a couple of days before. A charming lad of about eighteen, he was treated with warm affection by the marquise and by Thérèse Auvernois, the marquise's granddaughter, who, since her parents' death, had lived at Beaulieu.

The strange and even mysterious words spoken by President Bonnet as they were leaving the table, and the personality of this Fantômas about which he had been rather vague in spite of all the questions put to him, had excited the curiosity of the company, and while Thérèse Auvernois was gracefully dispensing the coffee to her grandmother's guests, the questions were renewed with greater insistence. Crowding round the fire, for the evening was very cold, Mme. de Langrune's friends showered fresh questions upon the old magistrate, who secretly enjoyed the interest he had inspired. He cast a solemn eye upon the circle of his listeners and prolonged his silence, the more to capture their attention. At length he began to speak.

"Statistics tell us, ladies, that of all the deaths that are registered every day, fully a third are due to crime. You are no doubt aware that the police discover about half of the crimes that are committed, and that barely half of those result in convictions. This explains how it is that so many mysteries are never cleared up, and why there are so many mistakes and inconsistencies in judicial investigations."

"What is the conclusion you wish to draw?" the Marquise de Langrune inquired with interest.

"This." The magistrate proceeded: "Although many crimes pass unsuspected, it is nonetheless obvious that they have been committed; now while some of them are due to ordinary criminals, others are the work of enigmatical beings who are difficult to trace and too clever or intelligent to let themselves be caught. History is full of stories of such mysterious characters; the Iron Mask, for instance, and Cagliostro. In every age there have been bands of dangerous creatures, led by such men as Cartouche and Vidocq and Rocambole. Now why should we suppose that in our time no one exists who emulates the deeds of those mighty criminals?"

The Abbé Sicot raised a gentle voice from the depths of a comfortable armchair, where he was peacefully digesting his dinner.

"The police do their work better in our time than ever before."

"That is perfectly true," the president admitted, "but their work is also more difficult than ever before. Criminals who operate in the grand manner have all sorts of things at their disposal nowadays. Science has done much for modern progress, but unfortunately it can be of invaluable assistance to criminals as well; the hosts of evil have the telegraph and the motorcar at their disposal just as authority has, and some day they will make use of the airplane."

Young Charles Rambert had been listening to the president's dissertation with the utmost interest and now broke in, with a voice that quivered slightly.

"You were talking about Fantômas just now, sir—"

The president cast a cryptic look at the lad and did not reply directly to him.

"That is what I am coming to, for, of course, you have understood me, ladies. In these days we have been distressed by a steady increase in crime, and among the causes we shall henceforth have to count a mysterious and most dangerous creature, to whom the baffled authorities and general rumor have for some time now given the name of Fantômas. It is impossible to say exactly what or to know precisely who Fantômas is. He often assumes the form and personality of some particular and even well-known individual; sometimes he assumes the forms of two human beings at the same time. Sometimes he works alone, sometimes with accomplices; sometimes he can be identified as

such and such a person, but no one has ever yet gotten to know
Fantômas himself. That he is a living person is certain and cannot be denied, yet he is impossible to catch or to identify. He is
nowhere and everywhere at once, his shadow hovers above the
strangest mysteries, and his traces are found near the most inexplicable crimes and yet—"

"You are frightening us!" exclaimed the Baronne de Vibray
with a little forced laugh, and the Marquise de Langrune, who
for the past few minutes had been uneasy at the idea of the children listening to the conversation, cast about in her mind for an
occupation more suited to their age. The interruption gave her
an opportunity, and she turned to Charles Rambert and
Thérèse.

"You must find it very dull here with all of us grown-up people, my dears, so run away now. Thérèse," she added with a
smile to her granddaughter who had risen obediently, "there is
a splendid new puzzle in the library; you ought to try it with
Charles."

The young fellow realized that he must comply with the desire of the marquise, although the conversation interested him
intensely; but he was too well bred to betray his thoughts, and
the next moment he was in the adjoining room, sitting opposite
the girl and deep in the intricacies of the latest fashionable game.

The Baronne de Vibray brought the conversation back to the
subject of Fantômas.

"What connection is there, President, between this uncanny
creature and the disappearance of Lord Beltham, of which we
were talking at dinner?"

"I should certainly have agreed with you and thought there
was none," the old magistrate replied, "if Lord Beltham's disappearance had not been accompanied by any mysterious circumstance. But there is one point that deserves your attention:
the newspaper from which I read an extract just now, *La Capitale*, points it out as important. It is said that when Lady
Beltham began to be uneasy about her husband's absence, on
the morning of the day following his disappearance, she remembered noticing just as he was going out that he was reading

a particular letter, the peculiar, square shape of which surprised her. She had also noticed that the handwriting of the letter was very heavy and black. Now, she found the letter in question upon her husband's desk, but all of the writing had disappeared, and only the most minute examination resulted in the discovery of a few almost imperceptible stains which proved that it really was the identical document that had been in her husband's hands. Lady Beltham would not have thought very much about it if it had not occurred to the editor of *La Capitale* to interview detective Juve, the famous inspector of the Criminal Investigation Department, you know, who has brought so many notorious criminals to justice. Now, Juve became extremely excited over the discovery and description of this document; and he did not attempt to hide from the interviewer his belief that the strange nature of this unusual epistle was proof of the intervention of Fantômas. You probably know that Juve has made it his special business to pursue Fantômas; he has sworn that he will take him, and he is after him body and soul. Let us hope he will succeed! But it is no good pretending that a more difficult task can possibly be imagined.

"However, it is fair to infer that when Juve spoke as he did to the representative of *La Capitale*, he did not think he was going too far when he declared that the disappearance of Lord Beltham was no accident, and that perhaps the blame should be laid at Fantômas's door; and we can only hope that at some not distant date, justice will not only throw full light upon this mysterious affair but also rid us forever of this terrifying criminal!"

President Bonnet had convinced his audience completely, and his closing words cast a chill upon them all.

The Marquise de Langrune thought it time to change the subject.

"Who are these people, Lord and Lady Beltham?" she inquired.

"Oh, my dear!" the Baronne de Vibray answered, "it is perfectly obvious that you lead the life of a hermit in this remote country home of yours, and that news from the world of Paris does not reach you often! Lord and Lady Beltham are among the best known and most popular people in society. He was formerly attached to the British Embassy, but left Paris to fight in the Transvaal. His wife went with him and showed magnificent courage and compassion there in charge of the ambulance and hospital work. They then went back to London, and a couple of years ago they settled once more in Paris. They lived, and still live, in the boulevard Inkermann at Neuilly-sur-Seine, in a delightful house where they entertain a great deal. I have often been one of Lady Beltham's guests; she is a most fascinating woman, distinguished, tall, fair, and endowed with the charm that is peculiar to the women of the North. I am very distressed at the trouble that is hanging over her."

"Well," said the Marquise de Langrune conclusively, "I believe that the gloomy prognostications of our friend the president will not be justified in the end."

"Amen!" murmured the abbé mechanically, roused from his gentle slumber by the closing words of the marquise.

The clock chimes ten, and the marquise's duties as hostess did not make her forget her duties as a grandmother.

"Thérèse," she called, "it is your bedtime. It is very late, darling."

The child obediently left her game, said good night to the Baronne de Vibray and President Bonnet, and last of all to the old priest, who gave her a paternal embrace.

"Shall I see you at the seven o'clock mass, Thérèse?" he asked.

The child turned to the marquise.

"Will you let me accompany Charles to the station tomorrow morning? I will go to the eight o'clock mass on my way back."

The marquise looked at Charles Rambert.

"Your father really is coming by the train that reaches Verrières at six fifty-five?" And when Charles assented she hesitated a moment before replying to Thérèse. "I think, dear, it would be better to let our young friend go alone to meet his father."

But Charles Rambert put in his plea.

"Oh, I am sure my father would be delighted to see Thérèse with me when he gets out of the train."

"Very well, then," the kind old lady said; "arrange it as you please. But, Thérèse, before you go upstairs, tell our good steward, Dollon, to give orders for the carriage to be ready by six o'clock. It is a long way to the station."

Thérèse promised, and the two young people left the drawing room.

"A pretty couple," remarked the Baronne de Vibray, adding with a characteristic touch of mischief, "You mean to make a match between them someday, Marquise?"

The old lady threw up her hands protesting.

"What an idea! Why, Thérèse is not fifteen yet."

"Who is this Charles Rambert?" the abbé asked. "I just caught a glimpse of him the day before yesterday with Dollon, and I racked my brains wondering who he could be."

"I am not surprised," the marquise laughed, "that you did not figure it out, for you do not know him. But you may perhaps have heard me mention a certain M. Etienne Rambert, an old friend of mine, with whom I shared many a dance long ago. I lost touch with him completely until about two years ago, when I met him at a charity function in Paris. The poor man has had a rather checkered life; twenty years ago he married a woman who was perfectly charming, but who is, I believe, very ill with a distressing malady: I am not certain, but I think she even may be insane. Quite lately Etienne Rambert has been compelled to send her to an asylum."

"That does not tell us how his son comes to be your guest," President Bonnet urged.

"It is very simple: Etienne Rambert is an energetic man who is always on the move. Although he is at least sixty he still occupies himself with some rubber plantations he owns in Colombia, and he often goes to America: he thinks no more of the voyage than we do of a trip to Paris. Well, just recently young Charles Rambert was leaving the *pension* in Hamburg where he had been living in order to perfect his German; I knew from his father's letters that Mme. Rambert was about to be put away, and that Etienne Rambert was obliged to be absent, so I offered to let Charles stay here until his father should return to Paris. Charles came the day before yesterday, and that is the whole story."

"And M. Etienne Rambert joins him here tomorrow?" said the abbé.

"That is so—"

The Marquise de Langrune would have offered more information about her young friend had he not come into the room just then. He was an attractive lad with refined and distinguished features, clear, intelligent eyes, and a graceful figure. The other guests were silent, and Charles Rambert approached them with the slight awkwardness of youth. He went up to President Bonnet and mustered sudden courage.

"And what then, sir?" he asked in a low tone.

"I don't understand, my boy," said the magistrate.

"Oh!" said Charles Rambert, "have you finished talking about Fantômas? It was so amusing!"

"For my part," the president answered dryly, "I do not find stories about criminals 'amusing.'"

But the lad did not detect the shade of reproach in the words.

"But still it is very odd, very extraordinary that such mysterious characters as Fantômas can exist nowadays. Is it really possible that one man can commit so many crimes, and that any human being could escape discovery, as they say Fantômas can, and be able to foil the cleverest devices of the police? I think it is—"

The president's manner grew steadily more chilly as the boy's curiosity waxed more enthusiastic, and he interrupted curtly.

"I fail to understand your attitude, young man. You appear to be hypnotized, fascinated. You speak of Fantômas as if he were something alluring. It is out of place, to put it mildly," and he turned to the Abbé Sicot. "There, sir, that is the result of a modern education and the state of mind produced in the younger generation by the newspapers and even by literature. Criminals are given halos and proclaimed from the housetops. It is astounding!"

But Charles Rambert was not the least impressed.

"But it is life, sir; it is history, it is the real thing!" he insisted. "Why, you yourself, in just a few words, have romanticized this Fantômas to an extent that makes him absolutely fascinating! I would give anything to have known Vidocq and Cartouche and Rocambole, and to have seen them closeup. Those were men!"

President Bonnet contemplated the young man in astonishment; his eyes flashed lightning at him and he burst out:

"You are mad, boy, absolutely mad! Vidocq—Rocambole! You mix up legend and history, lump together murderers with detectives, and make no distinction between right and wrong! You would not hesitate to put the heroes of crime and the heroes of law and order on one and the same pedestal!"

"You have said the word, sir," Charles Rambert exclaimed; "they all are heroes. But, better still Fantômas—"

The lad's outburst was so vehement and spontaneous and sincere that it provoked unanimous indignation among his listeners. Even the indulgent Marquise de Langrune ceased to smile. Charles Rambert perceived that he had gone too far, and stopped abruptly.

"I beg your pardon, sir," he murmured. "I spoke without thinking; please forgive me."

He raised his eyes and looked at President Bonnet, blushing to the tips of his ears and looking so abashed that the magistrate, who was basically a kind-hearted man, tried to reassure him.

"Your imagination is much too vivid, young man, much too vivid. But you will grow out of that. Come, come: that's all right; boys of your age do talk without knowledge."

It was very late now, and a few minutes after this incident the guests of the Marquise de Langrune took their leave.

Charles Rambert accompanied the marquise to the door of her own private rooms, and was about to bid her a respectful good night before going on to his own bedroom, which adjoined hers, when she asked him to follow her.

"Come in and get the book I promised you, Charles. It should be on my writing table." She glanced in that direction as she entered the room and went on, "Or in it, perhaps; I may have locked it away."

"I don't want to trouble you," he protested, but the marquise insisted.

"Put your light down on that table," she said. "Besides, I have got to open my desk, for I must look at the lottery tickets I gave to Thérèse a few weeks ago." She pushed back the roll top of her Empire desk and looked up at the young fellow. "It would be a piece of good luck if my little Thérèse won the first prize, eh, Charles? A million francs! Wouldn't that be worth winning?"

"I'll say!" said Charles Rambert with a smile.

The marquise found the book she was searching for and gave it to the lad with one hand while with the other she smoothed out various papers.

"These are my tickets," she said, and then broke off. "How stupid of me! I have not kept the number of the winning ticket announced in *La Capitale*."

Charles immediately offered to go downstairs again to fetch the newspaper, but the marquise would not let him.

"It is no good, my dear boy; it is not there now. You know— or rather you don't know—that the abbé takes away the week's newspapers every Wednesday night in order to read all the political articles." The old lady turned away from her writing table, which she left wide open, conducted the young man to the door, and held out a friendly hand. "It is tomorrow morning already!" she said. "So now good night, dear Charles!"

In his own room, with the lights out and the curtains closed, Charles lay wide awake, a victim of nervous excitement. He turned and tossed in his bed. In vain did he try to banish from his mind the words spoken during the evening by President Bonnet. In his imagination Charles saw all sorts of sinister and dramatic scenes, crimes and murders. Hugely interested, intensely curious, craving for knowledge, he generally was given to concocting plots and trying to unravel mysteries. If for an instant he dozed off, the image of Fantômas took shape in his mind, but never twice the same way. Sometimes he saw a colossal figure with bestial face and muscular shoulders; sometimes a wan, thin creature, with strange and piercing eyes; sometimes a vague form, a phantom—Fantômas!

Charles slept, and woke, and dozed again. In the silence of the night he thought he heard creakings and heavy sounds. Suddenly he felt a breath over his face—and then nothing! And suddenly again strange sounds were buzzing in his ears.

Bathed in cold sweat Charles started and sat upright in bed, every muscle tense, listening with all his concentration. Was he dreaming, or had he really awakened? He did not know. And still, still he was conscious of Fantômas—of mystery—of Fantômas!

Charles Rambert heard the clock strike four.

A TRAGIC DAWN

As his cab turned by the end of the Pont Royal toward the Gare d'Orsay, M. Etienne Rambert looked at his watch and found, as he had anticipated, that he had a good quarter of an hour before his train was due to leave. He called a porter, and gave him the heavy valise and the bundle of rugs that formed the whole of his hand luggage.

"Where is the baggage office, my man?" he inquired.

The porter led him through the famous paneled hall of the Gare d'Orsay, and M. Etienne Rambert made certain that his trunks had been properly registered for Verrières, the station at which he had to get off for the château of Beaulieu.

Still accompanied by the porter, who had conceived a respectful admiration for him because of the authoritative tone in which he demanded information from the various railway employees, and who scented the probability of a big tip, M. Etienne Rambert proceeded to the ticket office and booked a first-class seat. He spent a few minutes more at the book stall where he selected an imposing collection of illustrated magazines and then, his final preparations completed, he turned once more to the porter.

"The Luchon train," he said; "where is it?" and as the man only made a vague gesture and growled something wholly incomprehensible, he added: "Lead the way, and I will follow."

It was now just half past eight, and the station showed all the bustle inseparable from the departure of main-line trains. M. Etienne Rambert hurried onward, and reaching the platform from which all the lines begin, was stayed by the porter who was laden with his baggage.

"You want the express, sir?"

"No, the slow train, my man."

The porter showed some surprise but made no remark.

"Do you like the front or the back of the train?"

"The back, if I have a choice."

"First class, isn't it?"

"Yes, first class."

The porter, who had stopped a moment, picked up the heavy valise again.

"Then there isn't any choice. There are only two first-class carriages on the slow train, and they are both in the middle."

"They are corridor carriages, I suppose?" said Etienne Rambert.

"Yes, sir; there are hardly any others on the main-line trains, especially first class."

In the growing crowd Etienne Rambert had some difficulty following the porter. The Gare d'Orsay has little or none of the attractiveness of the other stations, which cannot fail to hold a certain fascination for any imaginative person who thinks of the mystery attaching to all those iron rails reaching out into the distance of unknown countries. It is less noisy than the others also, for between Austerlitz and Orsay the traction is entirely electric. And further, there is no clearly defined separation between the main and the suburban lines.

On the right of the platform was the train that was to take Etienne Rambert beyond Brives to Verrières, the slow train to Luchon; and on the left of the same platform was another train for Juvisy and all the small stations in the suburbs of Paris.

Very few people were heading for the train to Luchon; but a large crowd was pressing into the suburban train.

The porter who was piloting M. Etienne Rambert, set the baggage down on the footboard of a first-class carriage.

"There is no one for the slow train yet, sir; if you get in first you can choose your own compartment."

M. Etienne Rambert acted on the suggestion, but he had hardly set foot in the corridor when the guard, also scenting a generous tip, came to offer his services.

"It really is the eight-fifty you want, sir?" was his first inquiry. "You are sure you are not making a mistake?"

"No," Etienne Rambert replied. "Why?"

"A great many first-class passengers do make a mistake," the man explained, "and confuse the eight-fifty with the eight-forty-five express."

As he spoke the guard took the baggage from the porter, who had remained on the platform, and the porter, after being generously remunerated for his trouble by M. Rambert, hurried away to look for other travelers.

"The eight-forty-five is the express, isn't it?" M. Rambert inquired.

"Yes," the guard answered; "it runs right through without stopping at all the small stations, which this train does. It goes in front of this one and gets to Luchon three hours earlier. There it is on the side there," and he pointed through the window in the door on the far side to another train on the next rails, in which a number of travelers were already taking their seats. "If you prefer to go by that one, sir," he went on, "there is still time for you to change; you are entitled to take your choice since you have a first-class ticket."

But after a moment's consideration, Etienne Rambert declined the suggestion.

"No, I would rather go by the slow train. If I take the express I would have to get out at Brives, and then I should be twelve or thirteen miles from Saint-Jaury, which is my destination; whereas the slow train stops at Verrières, where I've already telegraphed to say I will arrive tomorrow morning."

He walked a little way along the corridor, assuring himself that the various compartments were still empty, and then turned to the guard:

"Look here," he said, "I am awfully tired, and I mean to get some sleep tonight; consequently I should like to be alone. Where shall I most likely be undisturbed?" The inquiry carried an implicit promise of a handsome tip if nobody did disturb him.

"If you'd like to settle down here, sir," the man answered, "you can draw down the blinds at once, and I'll most likely be able to find room for any other passengers elsewhere."

"Good," said M. Rambert, moving toward the compartment indicated. "I will smoke a cigar until the train starts, and immediately afterward I will try to get some sleep. By the way, sir, since you seem so obliging, I wish you would call me tomorrow morning in time for me to get out at Verrières. I am desperately tired and quite capable of not waking up."

The guard touched his cap.

"You can rest assured, sir, and sleep without the least anxiety. I won't fail."

"Thank you."

When his baggage had been stowed away, and his rugs spread out to make the seat more comfortable still, M. Etienne Rambert repeated his appeal, for he was an old traveler and knew that it does not do to rely too much upon the promises of chance attendants.

"I can rely upon you, can't I? I may sleep as soundly as I like, and you will wake me at Verrières?" And the more to assure himself, he slipped a franc into the guard's hand.

Left alone, M. Rambert continued his preparations for the night. He carefully drew down the blinds over the door and over the windows of the compartment that gave onto the corridor, and also lowered the shade over the electric light, and then, in order to enjoy the last few puffs of his cigar in peace, he opened the window over the other door and leaned his elbows on it, watching the final preparations being made by the travelers in the express on the other line.

The departure of a train is always a picturesque sight, and M. Rambert leaned forward inquisitively to note how the passengers had installed themselves in the two compartments that he could see from his place of vantage.

There were not many people in the train. As a matter of fact, the Brives and Luchon line is not much used at this time of year. If the number of passengers in the express was any criterion, Etienne Rambert might reasonably expect that he would be the only one on the slow train. But there was not much time for observations and reflections of this kind. On the platform for the express, which he could glimpse through the compartments, people were rushing to make their farewells. The passengers had gotten into their carriages, and the friends who had come to see them off were standing alone upon the platform. There was the sound of safety locks being fastened by porters, and the noise of pushcarts being wheeled along bearing articles for sale.

"Pillows! Rugs! Sweets! Papers!"

Then came the whistle of the guard, the shriller scream from the electric engine, and, slowly at first but steadily, more rapidly as the engine got up speed, the express moved along the platform and plunged into the tunnel on its way to Austerlitz.

Meanwhile, the guard on the slow train was doing wonders. Shamelessly resolved to assure perfect quiet to "his" passenger, he managed, without unduly compromising himself but yet without leaving any doubt about it in any mind, to insinuate discreetly that M. Rambert's carriage was reserved, so that that gentleman might count upon an entirely undisturbed night.

A few minutes after the express had gone, the slow train drew out in its turn and disappeared into the darkness of the underground tunnel.

At the château of Beaulieu young Charles Rambert was just finishing dressing when a gentle tap sounded on the door of his room.

"It is a quarter to five, Charles. Get up at once!"

"I am awake already, Thérèse," Charles answered with some pride. "I shall be ready in two minutes."

"What? Up already?" the girl exclaimed from the other side of the door. "Marvelous! I congratulate you. I'm ready too; I will wait for you in the dining room. Come down as soon as you are dressed."

"All right!" the young man answered.

He wasted no time getting ready, the more so because it was none too warm in his room; at this early hour it was still quite dark. Taking his light in one hand he opened his door carefully so as to make no noise, tiptoed along the landing, and down the staircase to join Thérèse in the dining room. The girl was a competent housekeeper already, and while waiting for the young fellow she had gotten a hasty meal together.

"Let us eat breakfast quickly," she suggested; "it isn't snowing this morning, and if you like we might walk to the station. We have plenty of time, and it will do us good."

"It will warm us up anyway," Charles replied. He was only half awake, but he sat beside Thérèse and dutifully ate the meal she had made.

"Do you know that it is truly wonderful of you to get up so punctually?" Mme. de Langrune's granddaughter remarked. "How did you manage it? Last night you were afraid you would sleep late as usual."

"It was not very difficult for me to wake up," Charles answered. "I hardly closed my eyes all night."

"But I promised to come and knock at your door myself, so you could have slept without worrying."

"That's so, but to tell you the truth, Thérèse, I was too nervous and excited at the thought of Papa arriving this morning."

They had both finished breakfast, and Thérèse got up.

"Shall we start?" she asked.

"Yes."

Thérèse opened the hall door, and the two young people went down the flight of steps leading to the garden. Thérèse had thrown a big cloak over her shoulders, and she inhaled the pure morning air with keen delight.

"I love going out in the early morning," she declared.

"Well, I don't like it at all," Charles confessed with characteristic candor. "Good Lord, how cold it is! And it is still pitch dark!"

"Surely you are not going to be frightened?" said Thérèse teasingly.

Charles made an irritable movement of vexation and surprise.

"Frightened? What do you take me for, Thérèse? I don't like going out in the early morning because it is cold."

She laughed at him while they were crossing the lawn toward the outbuildings, through which she meant to get out onto the main road. As they passed the stables they came across a groom who was leisurely getting an old brougham out of the coach house.

"Don't hurry, Jean," Thérèse called out as she greeted him. "We are walking to the station, and the only important thing is that you should be there to bring us back."

The man touched his cap and the two young people passed
through the park gate and found themselves upon the main road.

It was still very dark, with just a wan reflection in the distance
vaguely outlining some cloud shapes to the east giving some
promise of the day. No sounds broke the silence of the fields, and
as they walked briskly along, Charles and Thérèse could hear
their footsteps ringing on the hard surface of the frozen ground.

"You must be happy to be going to meet your father," said
Mme. de Langrune's granddaughter half-questioningly. "It is a
long time since you have seen him, isn't it?"

"Three years," Charles answered, "and then just for a few
minutes. He is coming home from America now, and before
that he traveled in Spain for a long time."

"He traveled the whole time you were a child, didn't he?"

"Yes, always: either in Colombia, looking after his rubber
plantations there, or in Spain, where he has a good deal of
property too. When he was in Paris he used to come to the
school and ask for me, and I would see him in the parlor—for a
quarter of an hour."

"And your mother?"

"Oh, Mamma was different. You know, Thérèse, I spent all
my childhood that I can remember at school. I liked the masters
and had good friends, and was very happy there. To tell the
truth I did not look forward to the holidays, when I had to go
to my parents' house. I always felt like a stranger with them;
my real home was the schoolroom, where I had my desk and
my own concerns. And then, you know, when one is a child one
doesn't understand things much; I didn't feel as if I had any
family, hardly."

"But you loved your mother very much?"

Thérèse asked the question quite anxiously, and it was obvious she would have thought it dreadful if her companion had
not had a true affection for his mother.

"Oh, yes, I loved her," Charles answered; "but I hardly
knew her either." And as Thérèse showed her surprise he went
on, telling her something of the secret of his lonely childhood.
"You see, Thérèse, now that I am a man I have guessed lots of

things that I had not even a suspicion of then. My father and mother did not get on well together. They were what you call an ill-matched couple. They were both good people, but their characters did not mix well. I always saw Mamma silent and sad, and Papa active and on the go, and outgoing and talking at the top of his voice. I half-believe he frightened Mamma! And then my father was constantly away, whereas Mamma hardly ever went out. When a servant took me to the house on Thursdays, I was taken up to say good morning to her, and I invariably found her lying on a sofa in her room, with the blinds down, almost in the dark. She would just touch me with her lips and ask me one or two questions, and then I was taken away again because I tired her."

"Was she ill, then?"

"Mamma has always been ill. I suppose you know, Thérèse, that three months ago—wait, it was just when I had taken my degree and went to Germany—she was sent to an asylum? I believe my father had wanted her to undergo intensive treatment of this kind long before, but she would not."

Thérèse was silent for a few minutes.

"You have not been very happy," she said after a while.

"Oh, it was only after I grew up that I felt unhappy. When I was a little boy I never thought of how sad it is to have no real father or mother. The last four or five years it has hurt me, but when he came to see me once at school, Papa told me he would take me with him as soon as I had taken my degree and grown up. Last October, after my examination, he wrote and told me to be patient a little longer, that he was winding up his business and coming back to France. That has brightened my hopes these last few months, and will also make you understand why I am so happy this morning at my father's coming. I feel like I am about to begin a new life."

Day was breaking now: a dirty December day, with the light filtering through heavy gray clouds that drifted along the ground, hid the horizon, clung to the low hills, and then suddenly dispersed in long wisps driven by a keen breeze that whipped along in gusts and drove clouds of dust along the hard frozen ground.

"I have not been very happy either," said Thérèse, "for I lost my father when I was a baby: I don't even remember him. And Mamma must be dead as well."

The ambiguous turn of phrase caught Charles Rambert's interested attention.

"What does that mean, Thérèse? Don't you know if your mother is dead?"

"Yes, oh yes; Grandmamma says so. But whenever I ask for particulars Grandmamma always changes the subject. I will echo what you said just now: When you are little you don't know anything and are not surprised at anything. For a long time I took no notice of her sudden reticence, but now I sometimes wonder if something is not being kept back from me—whether it is really true that Mamma is no more in this world."

Talking like this Thérèse and Charles had walked at a good pace, and now they came to the few houses built around the Verrières station. One by one, bedroom windows and doors were being opened; peasants were making their way to the sheds to lead their cattle to the pastures.

"We are very early," Thérèse remarked, pointing to the station clock in the distance. "Your father's train is due at six-fifty-five, and it is only six-forty now; we still have a quarter of an hour, and more, if the train is late!"

They went into the little station and Charles, thankful for some relief from the cold, stamped his feet, making a sudden din in the empty waiting room. A porter appeared.

"Who is making such a racket?" he began angrily, and then, seeing Thérèse, broke off short. "Ah, Mademoiselle Thérèse," he said with the familiar yet perfectly respectful cordiality that marks country folk, "up already? Have you come to meet somebody, or are you going away?"

As he spoke, the porter turned a curious eye upon Charles Rambert, whose arrival had caused quite a sensation two days before in this little spot—with only a few exceptions no one but those belonging to the neighborhood ever came by train.

"No, I am not going away," Thérèse replied. "I have come with M. Rambert, who is here to meet his father."

"Ah-ha, to meet your papa, sir: Is he coming from far away?"

"From Paris," Charles Rambert answered. "Is the train signaled yet?"

The man drew out a watch like a turnip and looked at the time.

"It won't be here for at least another twenty minutes. The work on the tunnel makes it necessary to be careful, and it's always late now. But you will hear when the bell rings: That will be when the train is coming over the level crossing; it will pull into the station three minutes after that. Well, Mademoiselle, I must get on with my work," and the man left them.

Thérèse turned to Charles Rambert.

"Shall we go onto the platform? Then we can watch the train come in."

So they left the waiting room and began to walk up and down the entire length of the platform. Thérèse watched the jerky movements of the hands of the clock and smiled at her companion.

"Five minutes more, and your father will be here! Four minutes more! Ah! There it is!" and she pointed to a slope in the distance where a slight trail of smoke rose white against the blue sky, now cloudless. "Can't you see it? There is the steam from the engine coming out of the tunnel."

Before she finished speaking the quivering whir of the bell echoed through the empty station.

"Ah!" said Charles Rambert. "At last!"

The two porters who, with the stationmaster, constituted the entire railway staff at Verrières, came bustling along the platform, and while the bell continued its monotonous whirring, they pulled forward their hand trucks in preparation for any possible luggage. Puffing portentously, the engine slackened speed, and the heavy train slowed down and finally stopped, bringing the station of Verrières, which but a moment ago was so still, to noisy life.

The first-class carriages had stopped immediately in front of Charles and Thérèse, and on the footboard stood Etienne Rambert, a tall, elderly man of distinguished appearance, proud bearing, and great energy, with extraordinarily keen eyes and an unusually high and intelligent forehead. Seeing Thérèse and Charles he seized his baggage and in an instant had sprung onto the platform. He dropped his valise, tossed his bundle of rugs onto a bench, and gripped Charles by the shoulders.

"My boy!" he exclaimed; "my dear boy!"

Although in years past he had paid so little attention to his child, it was obvious that the man was making a great effort to restrain his emotions, and was genuinely affected now that he saw him again as a young man.

Nor on his part did Charles Rambert remain unmoved. As if the sudden grip of this man who was almost a stranger, and yet was still his father, had awakened a world of memories within him, he turned very pale and his voice faltered as he replied:

"Papa! Dear Papa! I am so glad to see you!"

Thérèse had drawn tactfully aside. M. Rambert still held his son by the shoulders and stepped back a pace, the better to look him over.

"Why, you are a man! How you have changed, my boy! You are just what I hoped you would be: tall and strong! Ah, you are my son all right! And you are quite well, yes? You look tired."

"I did not sleep well," Charles explained with a smile. "I was afraid I would not wake up in time."

Turning his head, M. Rambert saw Thérèse and held out his hand.

"How do you do, my little Thérèse?" he exclaimed. "You have changed too since I saw you last. I left a little imp of a child, and now I behold a grown-up young lady. Well! I must be off at once to pay my respects to my dear old friend, your grandmother. All's well at the château, eh?"

Thérèse shook hands warmly with M. Rambert and charmingly thanked him.

"Grandmamma is very well; she told me to ask you to excuse her if she did not come to meet you, but her doctor says she must not get up so early."

"Of course your grandmamma is excused, my dear. Besides, I have to thank her for her kindness to Charles, and for the hospitality she is going to extend to me for a few days."

Meanwhile the train had gone on again, and now a porter came up to M. Rambert.

"Will you take your luggage with you, sir?"

Recalled to practical matters, Etienne Rambert contemplated his trunk, which the porters had taken out of the luggage compartment.

"Good Lord!" he began, but Thérèse interrupted him.

"Grandmamma said she would send for your heavy luggage during the morning, and that you could take your valise and any small parcels with us in the brougham."

"What's that? Your grandmamma has taken the trouble to send her carriage?"

"It's a long way to Beaulieu, you know," Thérèse replied. "Ask Charles if it isn't. We came on foot, but the walk would be too tiring for you after a whole night in the train."

The three had reached the station yard, and Thérèse stopped in surprise.

"Why, how's that?" she exclaimed; "the carriage is not here. And yet Jean was beginning to get it ready when we left the château."

M. Etienne Rambert was resting one hand on his son's shoulder and contemplating him with affectionate scrutiny every now and then. He smiled at Thérèse.

"He may have been delayed, dear. I tell you what we will do. Since your grandmamma is going to send for my luggage there is no need for me to take my valise; we can leave everything in the cloakroom and start for the château on foot; if my memory serves me right—and I have a very good memory—there is only one road, so we shall meet Jean and can get into the carriage on the way."

A few minutes later all three set out on the road to Beaulieu. M. Rambert walked between the two young people; he had gallantly offered his arm to Thérèse, who was more than a little proud of the attention, which proved to her mind that she was now regarded as a grown-up young lady. On the other side of his father Charles answered the incessant questions put to him.

M. Etienne Rambert enjoyed the walk in the quiet morning

through the peaceful countryside. With tender, almost melancholy emotions he recognized every turn in the road, every bit of scenery.

"Just imagine my coming back here at sixty years of age, with a great son of eighteen!" he said with a laugh. "And I remember as if it were yesterday the good times I have had at the château of Beaulieu. Mme. de Langrune and I have plenty of memories to talk over. It must be forty years since I came this way, and yet I remember every bit of it. Say, Thérèse, isn't it a fact that we shall see the front of the château directly after we pass this little stand of trees?"

"Quite true," the girl answered with a laugh. "You know this country very well, sir."

"Yes," said Etienne Rambert; "when one gets to my age, little Thérèse, one always does remember the happy days of one's youth; one remembers recent events much less distinctly. Most likely that means, my dear, that the human heart declines to grow old and refuses to preserve any but pictures of childhood."

For a few minutes M. Rambert remained silent, as if absorbed in somewhat melancholy reflections. But he soon recovered himself and shook off the tender sadness evoked by memories of the past.

"Why, the park enclosure has been altered," he exclaimed. "Here is a wall that used not to be here. There was only a hedge."

Thérèse laughed.

"I never knew the hedge," she said. "I have always seen the wall."

"Must we go on to the main gate?" M. Rambert asked. "Or has your grandmamma had another gate made?"

"We are going in by the outbuildings," the girl answered; "then we shall find out why Jean did not come to meet us." She opened a little door half hidden among the moss and ivy that clothed the wall surrounding the park, and, making M. Rambert and Charles pass in before her, cried: "But Jean *has* gone with the brougham, for the horses are not in the stable. How was it we did not meet him?" Then she laughed. "Poor Jean! He is so muddle-headed! I would not be surprised if he went to meet us at Saint-Jaury, as he does every morning to bring me home from church."

The little group, Etienne Rambert, Thérèse, and Charles, was now approaching the château. Passing beneath Mme. de Langrune's windows, Thérèse called merrily up to them.

"Here we are, Grandmamma!"

There was no reply.

But at the window of an adjoining room appeared the figure of the steward, Dollon, making a gesture, as if asking for silence.

Thérèse, in advance of her guests, had proceeded but a few yards when Mme. de Langrune's old servant rushed down the stone flight of steps in front of the château, toward M. Rambert.

Dollon seemed distraught. Usually so respectful and so deferential in manner, he now seized M. Rambert by the arm and, imperiously waving Thérèse and Charles away, drew him aside.

"It is awful, sir," he exclaimed; "horrible. A terrible thing has happened. We have just found Mme. la Marquise dead—murdered—in her room!"

THE HUNT FOR THE MAN

M. de Presles, the examining magistrate in charge of the court at Brives, had just arrived at the château of Beaulieu, having been notified of the tragedy by the police sergeant stationed at Saint-Jaury. The magistrate was a young, fashionable, and rather aristocratic man of the world, who regarded it his burden to be tied down to work that was mechanical rather than intellectual. He was essentially modern in his ideas, and his chief ambition was to get away as quickly as possible from the small provincial town to which he had been exiled by the whim of bureaucratic authority; he was sick of Brives, and now it occurred to him that a crime like the present one would give him an opportunity of displaying his gifts of intuition and deduction, prove his superiority, and so might enable him to get another appointment. After Dollon had received him at the château, the magistrate had first of all inquired as to who was in the house at the time. From the information given him he was satisfied that it was unnecessary to subject either Thérèse or Charles Rambert to immediate examination, both of the young people being much too upset to be able to reply to serious questions, and both having been taken away to the house of the Baronne de Vibray. It was also clear that M. Rambert senior, who had only arrived after the crime, could not furnish any pertinent information.

"Tell me exactly how you discovered the crime, M. Dollon," he said as the steward, pale and trembling, accompanied him down the corridor to the scene of the murder.

"I went this morning as usual, sir," the steward replied, "to say good morning to Mme. de Langrune and receive her orders for the day. I knocked at her door as I always do but got no answer. I knocked louder, but still there was no answer. I don't know why I opened the door instead of going away; perhaps I had some kind of presentiment. Oh, I shall never forget the shock of seeing my poor dear mistress lying dead at the foot of her bed, steeped in blood, and with such a horrible gash in her throat that for a moment I thought her head was severed from the trunk."

The police sergeant corroborated the steward's description.

"The murder certainly was committed with peculiarly horrible violence, sir," he remarked. "The body shows that the victim was struck with the utmost fury. The murderer must have gone mad over the corpse from sheer blood lust. The wounds are shocking."

"Knife wounds?" M. de Presles asked.

"I don't know," said the sergeant uncertainly. "Your worship can form your own opinion."

The magistrate followed the steward into the room where Dollon had taken care that nothing had been touched.

The furniture and general arrangement of Mme. de Langrune's room recalled the character of the old lady. It was large and quietly furnished with old wardrobes, armchairs, chairs, and old-fashioned tables. It was evident that she had had no liking for modern styles but preferred to have her own room stamped with the rather severe yet comfortable character of former days.

The whole of one side of the room was filled by the marquise's bed. It was large and raised upon a kind of dais covered with a carpet of subdued tones. At the foot of the bed, on the right, was a large window, half open despite the keen cold, no doubt for hygienic reasons. In the middle of the room was a round mahogany table with a few small objects upon it, a blotting pad, books, and so on. In one corner a large crucifix was suspended from the wall with a prie-dieu in front of it, the velvet of which had been worn white by the old lady's knees. Finally, a little further away, was a small escritoire, half open now, its drawers gaping and papers scattered on the floor.

There were only two ways of entering the room: one by the door through which the magistrate had come and which opened on to the main corridor on the first floor, and the other by a door communicating with the marquise's dressing room; this dressing room had one large window, which was shut.

The magistrate was shocked by the spectacle presented by the corpse of the marquise. It was lying on its back on the floor, with the arms extended; the head was toward the bed, the feet toward the window. The body was almost naked. A gash ran almost right across the throat, leaving the bones exposed. Buckets of blood had saturated the victim's clothes, and on the carpet round the body a wide stain was still slowly spreading.

M. de Presles stooped over the dead woman.

"What an appalling wound!" he muttered. "The medical evidence will explain what weapon it was made with, but no doctor is required to point out the violence of the blow or the fury of the murderer." He turned to the old steward who, at sight of his mistress, could hardly restrain his tears. "Nothing has been moved in the room, eh?"

"Nothing, sir."

The magistrate pointed to the escritoire with its open drawers.

"That has not been touched?"

"No, sir."

"I suppose that is where Mme. de Langrune kept her valuables?"

The steward shook his head.

"The marquise could not have had any large sum of money in the house: a few hundred francs perhaps for daily expenses, but certainly no more."

"So you do not think robbery was the motive of the crime?"

The steward shrugged his shoulders.

"The murderer may have thought that Mme. de Langrune had money here, sir. But anyhow he must have been distracted, because he did not take the rings the marquise had laid upon the dressing table before she got into bed."

The magistrate walked slowly round the room.

"This window was open?" he asked.

"The marquise always left it like that; she liked all the fresh air she could get."

"Might not the murderer have gotten in that way?"

The steward shook his head.

"It is most unlikely, sir. See, the windows are fitted outside with a kind of grating pointing outward and downward, and I think that would prevent anyone from climbing in."

M. de Presles saw that this was so. Continuing his investigation, he satisfied himself that there was nothing about the furniture in the room, or in the dressing room, to show that the murderer had been through them, except the disorder on and around the little escritoire. At last he came to the door that opened on to the corridor.

"Ah!" he exclaimed. "This is interesting!" And he pointed to the inner bolt on the door, the screws of which were wrenched half out, showing that an attempt had been made to force the door.

"Did Mme. de Langrune bolt her door every night?" he asked.

"Yes, always," Dollon answered. "She was very nervous, and if I was the first to come to bid her good morning I always heard her unfasten that bolt when I knocked."

M. de Presles made no reply. He made one more tour of the room, minutely considering the situation of each article.

"M. Dollon, will you kindly take me where I can have the use of the table and inkstand, and anything else I may need to get on with my preliminary inquiry?"

"Your clerk is waiting for you in the library, sir," the steward replied. "He has everything ready for you there."

"Very well. If you don't mind, we will join him now."

M. de Presles followed Dollon down to the library on the ground floor, where his enterprising clerk had already established himself. The magistrate took his seat behind a large table and called to the police sergeant.

"I shall ask you to be present during my inquiry, sergeant. The first investigations will devolve upon you, so it will be well for you to hear all the details the witnesses can furnish me with. I suppose you have taken no steps as yet?"

"Beg pardon, sir, I have sent my men out in all directions, with orders to interrogate all vagrants and to detain any who do not give satisfactory account of their whereabouts last night."

"Good! By the way, while I think of it, have you sent off the telegram I gave you when I arrived—the telegram to police headquarters in Paris asking for a detective to be sent down?"

"I took it to the telegraph office myself, sir."

His mind made easy on this score, the young magistrate turned to Dollon.

"Will you please take a seat, sir?" he said and, disregarding the disapproving looks of his clerk, who had a particular predilection for all the long circumlocutions and red tape of the law, he omitted the usual questions as to name and age and occupation of the witness, and began by questioning the old steward: "What is the exact plan of the château?"

"You know it now, sir, almost as well as I do. The passage from the front door leads to the main staircase, which we went up just now, to the first floor where the bedroom of the marquise is situated. The first floor contains a series of rooms linked by a corridor. On the right is Mlle. Thérèse's room, and then come guest chambers which are not occupied now. On the left is the bedroom of the marquise, followed by her dressing room on the same side and after that there is another dressing room and then the bedroom occupied by M. Charles Rambert."

"Good. And the floor above: How is that arranged?"

"The second floor is exactly like the first floor, sir, except that there are only servants' rooms there. They are smaller, and there are more of them."

"What servants sleep in the house?"

"As a general rule, sir, the two maid servants, Marie the housemaid and Louise the cook, and also Hervé the butler; but Hervé did not sleep in the château last night. He had asked the mistress's permission to go into the village, and she had given it to him on condition that he did not come back that night."

"What do you mean?" inquired the magistrate, rather surprised.

"The marquise was rather nervous, sir, and did not like the idea of anyone being able to get into the house at night; so she was always careful to double lock the front door and the kitchen door herself every night. She went round all the rooms too every night, and made sure that all the iron shutters were properly fastened, and that it was impossible for anyone to get into the house. When Hervé goes out in the evenings he either sleeps in the village and does not return till the following morning, which is what he did today, or else he asks the coachman to leave the yard door unlocked and sleeps in a room above the stables, which is usually unoccupied."

"That is where the other servants sleep, I suppose?"

"Yes, sir. The gardeners, the coachman, and the keepers all live in the outbuildings. With regard to myself, I have a small cottage a little farther away in the park."

M. de Presles was silent for a few moments, lost in deep thought. The only sound in the room was the irritating squeak of the clerk's quill pen as he industriously wrote down all the steward's replies. At last M. de Presles looked up.

"So, on the night of the crime the only persons sleeping in the château were Mme. de Langrune, her granddaughter Mlle. Thérèse, M. Charles Rambert, and the two maids. Is that so?"

"Yes, sir."

"Then it does not seem likely that the crime was committed by anyone living in the château?"

"That is so, sir—and yet I do not believe that anybody could have gotten into the château; only two people had a key to the front door—the marquise and myself. When I got to the house this morning I found the door open, because Mlle. Thérèse went out early with M. Charles Rambert to meet M. Rambert senior at the station, and she opened the door with the keys that the marquise had given her the night before; but she told me herself that when she left to meet the train at five o'clock the door was shut. Mlle. Thérèse had put her keys under her pillow, and my bunch never left my possession."

"Is it not possible," the magistrate suggested, "that someone may have gotten in during the day, hidden himself, and have committed the crime when night came? Remember, M. Dollon, the bolt inside Mme. de Langrune's bedroom door has been wrenched away; that means that the murderer entered by that door, and by force."

But the steward shook his head.

"No, sir, nobody could have hidden himself in the château

during the day; people are always coming to the kitchen, so the back door is under constant supervision, and all yesterday afternoon there were gardeners at work on the lawn in front of the main entrance; any stranger would certainly have been seen. And finally, Mme. de Langrune had given orders, which I always attended to myself, to keep the door to the cellars locked. So the murderer could not have hidden in the basement, and where else could he have hidden? Not in the rooms on the ground floor: there was company to dinner last night, and all the rooms were used more or less; the marquise or one of the guests would certainly have discovered him. So he would have had to be upstairs, either on the first or second floor. That is most unlikely—it would have been very risky; besides, the big house dog is fastened up at the foot of the staircase during the day, and he would not have let a stranger pass him. Either the dog must have known the man, or perhaps some meat was thrown to him; but there are no traces to show that anything of the sort was done."

The magistrate was extremely perplexed.

"Then the crime is inexplicable, M. Dollon. You have just told me yourself that there was no one in the château but Mme. de Langrune, the two young people Thérèse and Charles, and the two maids: certainly none of those can be the guilty person, for the way in which the crime was committed and the force of the blows show that the criminal was a man—a professional murderer in fact. Consequently the guilty party must have gotten in from outside. Come now, have you no suspicions at all?"

The steward raised his arms and let them fall in utter despair.

"No," he replied at last, "I do not suspect anybody! I cannot suspect anybody! But, sir, as far as I am concerned, I feel certain that although the murderer was not one of those who occupied the château last night he nevertheless did not come in from outside. It was not possible! The doors were locked and the shutters were fastened."

"Nevertheless," M. de Presles remarked, "inasmuch as someone has committed a murder, it must necessarily be so; either that someone was hidden inside the château when Mme. de Langrune herself locked the front door, or else he got in during the night. Do you not see, M. Dollon, that one or other of these two hypotheses must be correct?"

The steward hesitated.

"It is a mystery, sir," he declared at last. "I swear to you, sir, that nobody could have gotten in, and yet it is perfectly clear also that neither M. Charles nor Mlle. Thérèse, nor either of the two maids, Marie and Louise, could be the murderer."

M. de Presles sat rapt in thought for a few minutes and then asked the old steward to fetch the two women servants.

"Come back yourself," he added, as the old man went away; "I may require further details from you."

Dollon left the room, and Gigou, the clerk, leaned forward toward the magistrate: tact was not M. Gigou's most shining quality.

"When your inquiry is finished, sir—presently—we shall have to pay a visit to the mayor of Saint-Jaury, in accordance with the usual procedure. And then he cannot do less than invite us to stay to dinner!"

"NO! I AM NOT MAD!"

Two days after the crime, on Friday, Louise the cook, who was still terribly upset by the dreadful death of her dear mistress in whose service she had been for fifteen years, came down to her kitchen early. It was scarcely daybreak, and the woman was obliged to light a lamp to see by. With her mind anywhere but on her work, she was mechanically getting breakfast for the servants and for the visitors to the château when a sharp knock at the back door made her jump. She went to open it and uttered a little scream as she saw the cocked hats of gendarmes silhouetted against the wan light of the early morning.

Between the gendarmes were two miserable-looking specimens of humanity. Louise had opened the door only a few inches when the sergeant, who had known her for many years, took a step forward and gave her a military salute.

"I must ask your hospitality for us and for these two fellows whom we have found tonight, prowling about the neighborhood," he said.

The dismayed Louise broke in.

"Good heavens, sergeant, are you bringing thieves here? Where do you expect me to put them? Surely there's enough trouble in the house as it is!"

The gendarme Morand smiled with the disillusioned air of a man who knows very well what trouble is, and the sergeant replied:

"Put them? Why, in your kitchen, of course," and as the servant made a sign of refusal, he added: "I am sorry, but you must; besides, there's nothing for you to be afraid of; the men are handcuffed, and we shall not leave them. We are going to wait here for the magistrate who will examine them."

The gendarmes pushed their wretched captives in before them, two tramps of the shadiest appearance.

Louise, who had gone mechanically to raise the lid of a pot beginning to boil over, looked round at his last words.

"The magistrate?" she said. "M. de Presles? Why, he is here now—in the library."

"He is?" exclaimed the sergeant, jumping up from the kitchen chair on which he had seated himself.

"He is, I tell you," the old woman insisted, "and the little man who generally goes about with him is here too."

"You mean M. Gigou, his clerk?"

"Most likely," muttered Louise.

"I leave the prisoners with you, Morand," said the sergeant curtly; "don't let them out of your sight. I am going to the magistrate. I have no doubt he will wish to interrogate these fellows at once."

The gendarme came to attention and saluted.

"You can trust me, sergeant!"

It looked as if Morand's job was going to be an easy one; the two tramps, huddled up in a corner of the kitchen opposite the stove, showed no disposition to escape. The two were utterly different in appearance. One was a tall, strongly built man, with thick hair crowned by a little jockey cap. He was enveloped in a kind of overcoat that might have been black once but now was of a greenish hue, the result of the inclemency of the weather; he gnawed his heavy mustache in silence and turned his somber, uneasy gaze on everyone, including his companion in misfortune. He wore hobnailed shoes and carried a stout cudgel. He was more like a piece of the human wreckage one sees on the street corners of large cities than a genuine tramp. Instead of a collar, there was a brightly colored handkerchief round his neck. His name, he had told the sergeant, was François Paul.

The other man, who had been discovered at the back of a farm just as he was about to crawl inside a stack, was a typical country tramp. An old soft felt hat was crammed down on his head, and a shock of rebellious red and gray hair curled up all round it, while a hairy beard entirely concealed all the features of his face. All that could be seen of it was a pair of sparkling eyes incessantly moving in every possible direction. This second man contemplated with interest the place into which the police had conducted him. On his back he bore a heavy sort of duffel bag in which he stowed articles of the most varied description. Whereas his companion maintained a rigid silence, this man never stopped talking. Nudging his neighbor every now and then, he whispered:

"Say, where do you come from? You're not from these parts, are you? I've never seen you before, have I? Everybody round here knows me: Bouzille—my name's Bouzille." Turning to the gendarme he said: "Isn't it true, M'sieu Morand, that you and I are old acquaintances? This is the fourth or fifth time you've pinched me, isn't it?"

Bouzille's companion deigned to give him a glance.

"So it's a habit of yours, is it?" he said in the same low tone. "You often get nabbed?"

"As to 'often,'" the garrulous fellow replied, "that depends on what you mean. In wintertime it's not so bad to go back to the clink, because of the rotten weather; in the summer it's better to go free, and then, too, in the summer there isn't so much crime; you can find all you want on the road. Country people aren't so particular in the summer, while in the winter it's quite another thing. So they have done me down tonight for Mother Chiquard's rabbit, I expect."

The gendarme, who had been listening with no great attention, chimed in.

"So it was you who stole the rabbit, was it, Bouzille?"

"What's the good of your asking me that, M'sieu Morand?" protested Bouzille. "I suppose you would have left me alone if you hadn't been sure of it?"

Bouzille's companion bent his head and whispered very low:

"There has been something worse than that: the job with the lady of this house."

"Oh, that!" said Bouzille with a gesture of complete indifference. But he did not proceed. The sergeant came back to the kitchen and said sternly:

"François Paul, forward: the examining magistrate will hear you now."

The man stepped toward the sergeant and quietly submitted to being taken by the arm, for his hands were fastened. Bouzille winked knowingly at the gendarme, now his sole remaining confidant, and remarked with satisfaction:

"Good luck! We are getting on today! Not too much 'remanded' about it," and as the gendarme, severely keeping his proper distance, made no reply, the incorrigible chatterbox went on merrily: "As a matter of fact, it suits me just as well to be committed for trial, since the government gives you your board and lodging, and especially since there's a really beautiful prison at Brives now." He leaned familiarly against the gendarme's shoulder. "Ah, M'sieu Morand, you didn't know it— you weren't old enough—why, it was before you joined the force—but the lockup used to be in an old building just behind the law courts. Dirty! I should say it was dirty! And damp! Why once, when I did three months there, from January to April, I came out so ill with rheumatism that I had to go back into the infirmary for another two weeks! God!" He went on after a moment's pause during which he sniffed the air around him, "Something smells pretty good here!" He unceremoniously addressed the cook who was busy at her work: "Mightn't there perhaps be a bit of a handout for me, Mme. Louise?" And as she turned around with a somewhat scandalized expression he continued: "You needn't be frightened, lady, you know me very well. Many a time I've come and asked you for any old thing, and you've always given me something. M'sieu Dollon, too: whenever he has an old pair of shoes that are worn out, well, those are mine; and nobody ever refuses a crust of bread."

The cook hesitated, touched by the recollections evoked by the poor tramp; she looked at the gendarme for a sign of encouragement. Morand shrugged his shoulders and turned a patronizing gaze on Bouzille.

"Give him something, if you like, Mme. Louise. After all, he is well known. And for my own part I don't believe he could have done it."

The tramp interrupted him.

"Ah, M'sieu Morand, if it's a matter of picking up trifles here and there, a wandering rabbit perhaps or a fowl that's tired of being lonely, I don't say no; but as for anything else—thank you kindly, lady."

Louise had handed Bouzille a huge chunk of bread which he immediately interned in the depths of his enormous bag.

"What do you suppose that other chap can have to tell the authorities? He didn't look like a regular! Now, when I get before the gentlemen in black, I don't want to contradict them, and so I always say, 'Yes, my lord,' and they are perfectly satisfied; sometimes they laugh and the president of the court says, 'Stand up, Bouzille,' and then he gives me two weeks, or twenty-one days, or a month, as the case may be."

The sergeant came back alone and addressed the gendarme.

"The other man has been discharged," he said.

"As for Bouzille, M. de Presles does not think there is any need to interrogate him."

"Am I to be kicked out then?" inquired the tramp with some dismay as he looked uneasily toward the window, against which the rain was lashing.

The sergeant could not restrain a smile.

"Well, no, Bouzille," he said kindly, "we must take you to the lockup; there's the little matter of the rabbit to be cleared up, you know. Come now, get moving! Take him to Saint-Jaury, Morand!"

The sergeant went back to the library to place himself at the magistrate's disposal; through the torrential downpour of rain Bouzille and the gendarme wended their way to the village; and left alone in her kitchen, Louise communed with herself and put out her lamp, for despite the shocking weather it was getting lighter now.

"I've a kind of idea that they would have done better to keep that other man. He was a shady-looking fellow!"

The sad, depressing day passed without any notable incident.

Charles Rambert and his father spent the afternoon with Thérèse and the Baronne de Vibray, addressing large black-edged

envelopes to the relations and friends of the Marquise de Langrune, whose funeral had been fixed for the day after next.

A hasty dinner had been served at which the Baronne de Vibray was present. Her grief was distressing to witness. Despite
outward appearances, this woman had a very kind and tender
heart; as a matter of course she had designated herself the pro-
tector and comforter of Thérèse, and she had spent the whole of
the previous day with the child at Brives, ransacking the local
shops to find mourning clothes.

Thérèse was terribly shocked by the dreadful death of her
grandmother whom she had adored, but she displayed unexpected strength of character and controlled her grief so that she
might be able to look after the guests whom she was now enter-
taining for the first time as mistress of the house. The Baronne
de Vibray had failed in her attempt to persuade Thérèse to
come with her to Querelles to sleep. Thérèse was determined
not to leave the château and what she termed her "post of
duty."

"Marie will stay with me," she assured the kind baronne,
"and I promise you I shall have sufficient courage to go to sleep
tonight."

So her friend got into her car at nine o'clock and went back
to her own house, and Thérèse went up at once to bed with
Marie, the faithful servant who, like Louise the cook, had been
with her ever since she had been born.

After having read all the newspapers, with their detailed and often inaccurate account of the tragedy at Beaulieu—for everyone
in the château had been besieged the previous day by
reporters—M. Etienne Rambert said to his son simply, but with
a marked gravity:

"Let us go upstairs, my son: it is time."

At the door of his room Charles deferentially offered his
cheek to his father, but M. Etienne Rambert seemed to hesitate;
then, as if making a sudden resolution, he entered his son's
room instead of going on to his own. Charles kept silent and refrained from asking any questions, for he had noticed how lost
in sad thought his father had seemed since the day before.

Charles was very tired. He began to undress at once. He had taken off his coat and waistcoat, and was turning toward a mirror to undo his tie when his father came up to him; with an abrupt movement M. Etienne Rambert put both his hands on his son's shoulders and looked him straight in the eyes. Then in a stifled but peremptory tone he said:

"Now confess, unhappy boy! Confess to your father!"

Charles went ghastly white.

"What?" he muttered.

Etienne Rambert kept his eyes fixed upon him.

"It was you who committed the murder!"

The ringing denial that the young man tried to utter was strangled in his throat; he threw out his arms and groped with his hands as if to find something to support him in his faintness; then he pulled himself together.

"Committed the murder? I? You accuse me of having killed the marquise? It is terrible, hateful, awful!"

"Alas, yes!"

"No, no! Good God, no!"

"Yes!" Etienne Rambert insisted.

The two men faced each other, panting. Charles controlled the emotions sweeping over him once more and, looking steadily at his father, said in tones of bitter reproach:

"And it is actually my own father who says that—who suspects me!"

Tears filled the young fellow's eyes and sobs choked him; he grew whiter still and seemed so near collapse that his father had to help him to a chair, where he remained for several minutes utterly overcome.

M. Rambert paced up and down the room a few times, then took another chair and sat down in front of his son. Passing a hand across his brow as if to sweep away the horrible nightmare that was haunting him, he spoke again.

"Come now, my boy, my poor boy, let us talk it over quietly. I do not know how it was, but yesterday morning when I saw you at the station I had a presentiment of something: you were haggard and tired, and your eyes were drawn—"

"I told you before," Charles answered tonelessly, "that I had

had a bad night: I was overexcited and did not sleep; I was awake the whole night."

"By Jove, yes!" his father burst out. "I can believe that! But if you were not asleep, how do you account for your not hearing anything?"

"Thérèse did not hear anything either," said Charles after a moment's reflection.

"Thérèse's room was a long way off," M. Rambert replied, "while there was only a thin wall between yours and the marquise's. You must have heard; you did hear! More than that— oh, my boy, my unhappy boy!"

Charles was folding and unfolding his hands, and huge drops of cold perspiration beaded his brow.

"You are the only person who thinks I committed such an awful crime!" he said, half as a question.

"The only one?" Etienne Rambert muttered. "Perhaps! For now! But you ought to know that you made a very bad impression indeed upon the friends of the marquise the evening before the crime, when President Bonnet was reading the particulars of a murder that had been committed in Paris by—somebody, I forget who."

"Good heavens!" Charles exclaimed in indignation, "I said nothing wrong. Do you mean to say that just because I am interested in stories of great criminals like Rocambole and Fantômas—"

"You created a deplorable impression," his father repeated.

"So they suspect me too, do they?" Charles inquired. "But you can't make accusations like that," he said, warming up; "you've got to have facts, and proof." He looked at his father for paternal sympathy and encouragement. "Listen, Papa, I know you will believe me when I swear that I am innocent, but do you think other people—"

M. Etienne Rambert sat with his head between his hands, rapt in thought; there was a short silence before the unhappy father replied:

"Unfortunately there is evidence against you," he said at last. "Damning evidence!" he added with a glance at his son that seemed to pulverize him. "Terrible evidence! Consider,

Charles: the magistrates have decided, as a result of their investigations, that no one got into the château on the fatal
night; you were the only man who slept there; and none but a
man could possibly have committed such a horrible crime,
such a monstrous piece of butchery!"

"Someone might have gotten in from outside," the unhappy
lad urged, as if trying to escape from the web that was entan-
gling him.

"No one did," Etienne Rambert insisted; "besides, how
could you prove it?"

Charles was silent. He stood in the middle of the room, with
shaking legs and haggard eyes, seemingly stupefied, incapable
of coherent thought, and vacantly watching his father. With
bowed head and shoulders as though he was straining beneath a
too-heavy load, Etienne Rambert moved toward the dressing
room attached to the bedroom.

"Come here," he said in an almost inaudible voice; "follow me."

He went into the dressing room, and picking up the towels
that were heaped carelessly on the lower rail of the washstand,
he selected a particularly crumpled one and held it out in front
of his son.

"Look at that!" he said in a low, short tone.

And on the towel, thus held in the light, Charles Rambert
saw red stains of blood. The lad started and was about to burst
into some protestation, but Etienne Rambert imperiously
checked him.

"Do you still deny it? Unhappy, miserable boy, there is the
convincing, irrefutable evidence of your guilt! These stains of
blood proclaim it. Something always is overlooked! How are
you to explain the presence of this bloodstained linen in your
room? Can you still deny that it is proof positive of your guilt?"

"But I do deny it, I do deny it! I don't understand! I know
nothing about it!" And once more Charles Rambert collapsed
into the armchair; the unhappy boy was nothing but a human
wreck, with no strength to argue or even utter a word.

His father's eyes rested on him, filled with infinite affection
and profoundest pity.

"My poor, poor boy!" the unhappy Etienne Rambert murmured, and added, as if speaking only to himself: "I wonder if you are entirely responsible—if there are circumstances to plead for you!"

"Do you still accuse me, Papa? Do you really believe I am the murderer?"

Etienne Rambert shook his head hopelessly.

"Oh, I wish, I wish," he exclaimed, "that for the honor of our name, and for the sake of those who love us, I could prove you had congenital, hereditary tendencies that made you not responsible! Why could not I have watched over your upbringing? Why has fate decreed that I should only see my son three times at most in eighteen years, and come home to find him—a criminal? Oh, if science could but establish the fact that the child of a cursed mother—"

"Cursed?" Charles exclaimed. "What do you mean?"

"Cursed with a terrible and mysterious disease," Etienne Rambert went on, "a disease before which we are powerless and unarmed—insanity!"

"What?" cried Charles, growing momentarily more distressed and bewildered. "What is that, Papa? Is my mind going? My mother insane?" And then he added hopelessly: "My God! You must be right! Often and often I have been amazed by her strange, puzzling looks and behavior! But I—I have all my proper senses: I know what I am doing!"

"Was it perhaps some appalling hallucination," Etienne Rambert suggested, "some moment of uncontrollable behavior?"

But Charles saw what he meant and cut him short.

"No, no, Papa! I am not mad! I am not mad! I am not mad!"

In his intense excitement the young fellow never thought of moderating the tone of his voice but shouted out what was in his mind, shouted it into the silence of the night, heedless of all but this terrible discussion he was having with the father whom he loved. Nor did Etienne Rambert lower his voice; his son's impassioned protest wrung the retort from him:

"Then, Charles, if you are right, your crime is beyond forgiveness! Murderer! Murderer!"

The two men stopped short as a slight sound in the passage

caught their attention. A silence fell upon them that they could not break, and they stood dumbfounded, nervous, and overwrought.

The door of the room opened very slowly, and a white form appeared against the darkness of the corridor outside.

Robed in a long nightdress, Thérèse stood there, with hair disheveled, bloodless lips, and eyes dilated with horror; the child was shaking from head to foot; as if every movement hurt her, she painfully raised her arm and pointed to Charles.

"Thérèse!" Etienne Rambert muttered. "Thérèse, you were outside?"

The child's lips moved; she seemed to be making a superhuman effort, and a whisper escaped her lips:

"Yes—"

But she could say no more: her eyes rolled, her whole frame tottered, and then, without a sign or cry, she fell rigid and unconscious to the floor.

"ARREST ME!"

Twelve or thirteen miles from Souillac the main line from Brives to Cahors, which flanks the slope, describes a rather sharp curve. The journey is a particularly picturesque one, and travelers who make it during the daytime have much that is interesting and pleasant to see; but while they are admiring the country, which marks the transition from the severe region of the Limousin to the gentler landscapes on the confines of the Midi, the train suddenly plunges into a tunnel that runs for half a mile or more through the heart of a mountain slope. Leaving the tunnel, the line continues along the slope, then gradually descends toward Souillac. Two or three miles from that little station, which is a junction, the line runs alongside the high road to Salignac, skirts for a brief distance the Corrèze, one of the largest tributaries on the right bank of the Dordogne, and then plunges into the heart of Lot.

Torrential winter rains had seriously affected the railway embankment, particularly near the mouth of the tunnel; a succession of heavy storms in early December had so greatly eroded the ballast that the chief engineers of the company had been hastily summoned to the scene of the damage. The experts decided that major repairs were required near the Souillac end of the tunnel. It was necessary to put in a complete drainage system, with underground pipes through which the water that came off the mountain could escape between the ballast and the side of the rock and so pass underneath. The sleepers, too, had been loosened by the bad weather, and some of them had deteriorated so much that the chairs were no longer fast, a matter all the more serious because the line described a very sharp curve at that precise spot.

Gangs of laborers had been hurriedly requisitioned, but in spite of the fact that an exceptional wage was paid, a local strike had broken out and for some days all work was stopped. Gradually, however, moderate counsel prevailed, and for over a week now nearly all the men had taken up their tools again. Nevertheless, for a month past these various circumstances had resulted in all the trains running between Brives and Cahors being regularly half an hour late. Further, in view of the dangerous state of the line, all engine drivers coming from Brives had received orders to stop their trains two hundred yards from the end of the tunnel, and all drivers coming from Cahors had to stop their trains five hundred yards before the entrance to the tunnel, so that should any work be going on that rendered it dangerous to pass, the train could wait until the work was completed. The order was also issued to prevent the workers on the line from being taken by surprise.

Day was just breaking this gray December morning when the gang of laborers set to work under a foreman, fixing on the down line the new sleepers that had been brought up the day before. Suddenly a shrill whistle was heard, and in the gaping black mouth of the tunnel the light of two lamps became visible; a train bound for Cahors had stopped in accordance with orders and was calling for permission to pass.

The foreman ranged his men on either side of the down line and walked to a small cabin erected at the mouth of the tunnel, where he pulled the hand signal to show the green light, thereby authorizing the train to proceed on its way.

There was a second short, sharp whistle; heavy puffs escaped from the engine, and belching forth a dense volume of black smoke it slowly emerged from the tunnel, followed by a long train of carriages, the windows of which were frosted over by the cold air outside.

A man approached the cabin allotted to the plate layer in charge of that section of the line with the tunnel.

"I suppose this is the train due at Verrières at six-fifty-five?" he said carelessly.

"Yes," the plate layer answered, "but it's late; the clock down there in the valley struck seven several minutes ago."

The train had gone by: the three red lamps fastened at the end of it were already lost in the morning mist.

The man who spoke to the plate layer was no other than François Paul, the tramp who had been discharged by the magistrate at the château of Beaulieu, at precisely the same time the day before, after a brief examination. In spite of the deep wrinkle furrowed in his brow the man seemed to make an effort to appear friendly and to carry on the conversation.

"There aren't many people in this morning train," he remarked, "specially in the first-class carriages."

The plate layer appeared in no way unwilling to postpone for a few moments his tiring and chilly underground patrol; he put down his pick before answering.

"Well, that's not surprising, is it? People who are rich enough to travel first class always come by the express that gets to Brives at two-fifty A.M."

"I see," said François Paul; "that's reasonable—and more practical for travelers to Brives or Cahors. But what about the people who want to get out at Gourdon, or Souillac, or Verrières, or any of the small stations where the express doesn't stop?"

"I don't know," said the plate layer, "but I suppose they have to get out at Brives or Cahors and drive, or else travel by the day trains, which are fast to Brives and slow afterward."

François Paul did not press the matter. He lit a pipe and breathed on his benumbed fingers.

"Hard times, these, make no mistake!"

The plate layer seemed sorry for him.

"I don't suppose you're an independent gentleman, but why don't you try to get taken on here?" he suggested. "They want hands here."

"Oh, do they?"

"That's the fact; this is the foreman coming along now: would you like me to speak to him for you?"

"No hurry," replied François Paul. " 'Course, I'm not saying no, but I should like to see what sort of work it is they're doing here: it might not suit me. I shall still have time to get a couple of words with him," and with his eyes on the ground the tramp slowly walked along the embankment away from the plate layer.

The foreman met and passed him, and came up to the plate layer at the mouth of the tunnel.

"Well, Michu, how goes it with you? Still got the old complaint?"

"Middling, boss," the fellow answered, "just keeping up, you know. And how's yourself? And the work? When shall you finish? I don't know if you know it, but these trains stopping regularly in my section give me an extra lot of work."

"How's that?" the foreman inquired in surprise.

"The engine drivers take advantage of the stop to empty their ash pans, and they leave a great heap of mess there in my tunnel, which I'm obliged to clear away. In the ordinary way they dump it somewhere else: where, I don't know, but not in my tunnel, and that's all I care about."

The foreman laughed.

"You're a good man, Michu! If I were you I would ask the company to give me another man or two."

"And do you suppose the company would?" Michu retorted. "By the way, that poor devil who is going along there, shivering with cold and hunger, was grumbling to me just now, and I advised him to ask you to take him on. What do you think he said? Why, that he would have a look at the work first, and off he went."

"It's a fact, Michu, that it's mighty difficult to come across people who mean business nowadays. It's quite true that I want more hands. But if that chap doesn't ask me to engage him in another minute, I'll kick him out. The embankment is not public property, and I don't trust these rascals who are forever coming and going among the workmen to see what mischief they can make. I'll go and cast an eye over the bolts and things, for there are all sorts of vagrants about the neighborhood just now."

"And criminals, too," said old Michu. "I suppose you have heard of the murder up at the château of Beaulieu?"

"Of course! My men are talking of nothing else. But you are right, Michu, I'll take a closer look at all strangers, and at your friend in particular."

The foreman stopped abruptly; he had been examining the foot of the embankment and was standing quite still, watching. The plate layer followed his glance, and also stood fixed. After a few moments' silence the two men looked at each other and smiled. In the half light of the valley they had seen the outline of a gendarme; he was on foot and appeared to be looking for somebody, while making no attempt to remain unseen himself.

"Good!" whispered Michu. "That's Sergeant Doucet: I know him by his stripes. They say the murder was not committed by anyone belonging to this part of the country; everybody was fond of the Marquise de Langrune."

"Look! Look!" the foreman broke in, pointing to the gendarme who was slowly climbing up the embankment. "It looks as if the sergeant were making for the gentleman who was looking for work just now and hoped he would not find it. The sergeant's got a word for him, eh, what?"

"That might be," said Michu after a moment's further watching. "That chap has an evil, ugly face. One can tell from the way he's dressed that he don't belong to these parts."

The two men waited with utmost interest to see what was going to happen.

Sergeant Doucet reached the top of the embankment at last and hurried past the workers, who stopped to stare inquisitively after the representative of authority. Fifty yards beyond them, François Paul, wrapped in thought, was walking slowly down toward the station of Verrières. Hearing the sound of steps behind him, he turned. When he saw the sergeant he frowned. He glanced rapidly about him and saw that while he was alone with the gendarme, so that no one could overhear what they said however loudly they might speak, they were still close enough so that every sign and movement they made would be clearly visible to whoever might watch them. And as the gendarme paused a few paces in front of him and—most remarkably— seemed to be on the point of bringing his hand to his cap in salute, the mysterious tramp rapped out:

"I thought I said no one was to disturb me, sergeant?"

The sergeant took a step forward.

"I beg your pardon, Inspector, but I have important news for you."

For this François Paul, whom the sergeant thus respectfully addressed as inspector, was no other than an officer of the secret police who had been sent down to Beaulieu the day before from headquarters in Paris.

He was no ordinary officer. As if M. Havard had had an idea that the Langrune affair would prove to be puzzling and complicated, he had singled out the very best of his detectives, the most expert inspector of them all—Juve. It was Juve who for the last forty-eight hours had been prowling about the château of Beaulieu disguised as a tramp, and who had himself arrested with Bouzille that he might carry out his own investigations without raising the slightest suspicion as to his real identity.

Juve made plain his vexation at the overdeferential attitude of the sergeant.

"Pay attention!" he said in a low voice. "We are being watched. If I must go back with you, pretend to arrest me. Slip the handcuffs on me!"

"I beg your pardon, Inspector, I don't like to," the gendarme answered.

In reply, Juve turned his back on him.

"Look here," he said, "I will take a step or two forward as if I meant to run away; then you must put your hand on my shoulder roughly, and I will stumble; when I do, slip the cuffs on."

From the mouth of the tunnel the plate layer, the foreman, and the workers all followed with their eyes the unintelligible conversation passing between the gendarme and the tramp a hundred yards away. Suddenly they saw the man try to get away and the sergeant seize him almost simultaneously. A few minutes later the tramp, with his hands linked together in front of him, was obediently descending the steep slope of the embankment, by the gendarme's side, and then the two men disappeared behind a clump of trees.

"Now I understand why that man was not too keen on being taken on here," said the foreman. "He had a bad conscience!"

As they walked briskly in the direction of Beaulieu Juve asked the sergeant:

"What has happened at the château, then?"

"They know who the murderer is, Inspector," the sergeant answered. "Little Mlle. Thérèse—"

"FANTÔMAS, IT IS DEATH!"

Hurrying back toward the château with the sergeant, Juve ran into M. de Presles outside the park gate. The magistrate had just arrived from Brives in a motorcar that he had commandeered for his personal use during the last few days.

"Well," said Juve in quiet, measured tones, "have you heard the news?" And as the magistrate looked at him in surprise he went on: "I gather from your expression that you have not. Well sir, if you will kindly fill out a warrant we will arrest M. Charles Rambert."

Juve briefly repeated to the magistrate what the sergeant had reported to him, and the sergeant added a few further details. The three men had now reached the foot of the steps in front of the house and were about to go up when the door of the château opened and Dollon appeared. He hurried toward them, with unkempt hair and haggard face, excitedly exclaiming:

"Didn't you meet the Ramberts? Where are they? Where are they?"

The magistrate, who was bewildered by what Juve had told him, was trying to form some coherent idea of the whole sequence of events, but the detective realized the situation at once and turned to the sergeant.

"He got away," he said. The sergeant threw up his hands in dismay.

Inside the hall Juve and M. de Presles ordered Dollon to give them an exact account of the discovery made by Thérèse in the course of the previous night.

"Well, gentlemen," said the old fellow, who was still greatly upset by the discovery of the murderer of the Marquise de Lan-grune, "when I got to the château early this morning I found the two old servants, Marie and Louise, entirely occupied seeing to the young mistress. Marie slept in an adjoining room to hers last night and was awakened about five o'clock by the poor child's in-comprehensible cries. Mlle. Thérèse was bathed in perspiration; her face was all drawn and there were dark rings under her eyes; she was sleeping badly and evidently having dreadful nightmares. She half woke up several times and muttered some unintelligible words to Marie, who thought that it was the result of overexcite-ment. But about six o'clock, just as I arrived, Mlle. Thérèse really woke up and, bursting into a fit of sobbing and crying, repeated the names of her grandmother and the Ramberts and the Baronne de Vibray. She kept on saying, 'The murderer! The mur-derer!' and showing all sorts of signs of terror, but we were not able to get from her a clear statement of what it was all about. I felt her pulse and found she was very feverish, and Louise pre-pared a cool drink, which she persuaded her to take. In about twenty minutes—it was then nearly half past six—Mlle. Thérèse quieted down and managed to tell us what she had heard during the night, and the dreadful interview and conversation between M. Rambert and his son which she had seen and overheard."

"What did you do then?" inquired M. de Presles.

"I was dreadfully upset myself, sir, and I sent Jean the coach-man to Saint-Jaury to fetch the doctor and also to let Sergeant Doucet know. Sergeant Doucet got here first; I told him all I knew, and then I went upstairs with the doctor to see Mlle. Thérèse."

The magistrate turned to the police sergeant and ques-tioned him.

"As soon as M. Dollon told me his story," the sergeant replied, "I thought it my duty to report to M. Juve, who I knew was not far from the château, on his way to Verrières: M. Juve told me last night that he meant to explore that area in the early morning. I left Morand on duty at the entrance to the château, with orders to prevent either of the Ramberts from leaving."

"And Morand did not see them going away?" the magistrate asked.

Juve had already divined what had happened and replied for the sergeant.

"Morand did not see them go out for the obvious reason that they had left long before—in the middle of the night, directly after their altercation: in a word, before Mlle. Thérèse woke up." He turned to the sergeant. "What has been done since then?"

"Nothing, Inspector."

"Well, Sergeant," said Juve, "I imagine His Worship will order you to send out your men at once after the fugitives." He glanced at the magistrate as if asking for his approval, but he only did so out of politeness, for he took it for granted.

"Of course!" said the magistrate; "please do so at once." The sergeant turned and left the hall.

"Where is Mlle. Thérèse?" M. de Presles asked Dollon, who was standing nervously apart.

"She is sleeping quietly just now, sir," said the steward, coming forward. "The doctor is with her and would rather she were not disturbed, if you have no objection."

"Very well," said the magistrate. "Leave us, please," and Dollon also went away.

Juve and M. de Presles looked at one another. The magistrate was the first to break the silence.

"So it is all over?" he remarked. "This Charles Rambert is the culprit?"

Juve shook his head.

"Charles Rambert? Well, he ought to be the culprit."

"Why any doubt?" inquired the magistrate.

"I say 'ought to be,' for all the circumstances point to that conclusion, and yet in my bones I don't believe he is."

"Surely the presumptions of his guilt, his so-called confession, or at least his silence in the face of his father's accusation, may make us sure he is," said M. de Presles.

"There are some presumptions in favor of his innocence too," Juve replied, but with a slight hesitation.

The magistrate pressed his point of view.

"Your investigations formally demonstrated the fact that the crime was committed by some person who was inside the house."

"Possibly," said Jove, "but not positively. The probabilities do not allow us to assert it as a fact."

"Explain yourself."

"Let's not jump to any conclusions, sir," Juve replied, and getting up he added: "There is nothing for us to do here, sir; shall we go up to the room Charles Rambert occupied?"

M. de Presles followed the detective into the room, which was plainly furnished. The magistrate installed himself comfortably in an easy chair and lighted a cigar, while Juve walked up and down, scrutinizing everything with quick, sharp glances, and began to talk:

"I said 'let's not jump to conclusions' just now, sir, and I will tell you why. In my opinion there are two preliminary points in this affair that must be cleared up: the nature of the crime, and the motive. Let us first of all ask ourselves how the murder of the Marquise de Langrune ought to be 'classified' in the technical sense. The first conclusion of any observant person who has visited the scene of the crime and examined the corpse of the victim is that this murder must be placed in the category of professional crimes. The murderer seems to have left the implicit mark of his character upon his victim; the very violence of the blows dealt shows that he is a man of the lower orders, a typical criminal, a professional."

"What do you deduce that from?" M. de Presles inquired.

"Simply from the nature of the wound. You saw it. Mme. de Langrune's throat was almost entirely severed by the blade of some sharp instrument. The breadth and depth of the wound absolutely prove that it was not made with one stroke; the murderer must have gone amok and dealt several blows—striking even after the victim was dead, or at least after her death was a foregone conclusion. That shows clearly that the murderer belongs to the type of individual who feels no repugnance for his horrid work, but who kills without horror, and even without excitement. Again, the nature of the wound shows that the murderer is a strong man. Weak men with weak muscles strike 'deeply' by choice, that is to say with a pointed weapon they aim at a vital organ, whereas powerful murderers have a predilection for blows dealt 'superficially' and for broad, ghastly wounds.

Besides, that is only following a natural law; a weak man finesses with death, tries to make sure of it at some precise point, penetrating the heart or severing an artery; a brutal man does not care where he hits but trusts to his own brute strength to achieve his purpose.

"We have next to determine the sort of weapon with which the murder was committed. We have not got it, at any rate not yet; I have given orders for the drains to be emptied and the pond to be dragged and the shrubberies to be searched, but, whether our search is successful or not, I am convinced that the instrument was a knife, one of those common knives with a catch lock that street thugs always carry. If the murderer had had a weapon whose point was its principal danger, he would have stabbed, and stabbed to the heart, instead of cutting; but he used the edge, the part of a knife that is most habitually used, and he actually cut. When the first wound was made he did not strike anywhere else, but continued working away at the wound and enlarging it. It is a point of primary importance that this murder was committed with a knife, not with a dagger or stiletto, and therefore this is a professional crime."

"And what conclusion do you draw from these facts?" the magistrate proceeded to inquire.

"Merely that it cannot have been committed by Charles Rambert," Juve answered very gravely. "He is a young man who has been well brought up, he comes of very good stock, and his age makes it most improbable that he can be a professional criminal."

"Obviously, obviously!" murmured the magistrate, not a little embarrassed by the keen logic of the detective.

"And now let us consider the motive or motives of the crime," Juve continued. "Why did the man commit this murder?"

"Doubtless for purposes of robbery," said the magistrate.

"What did he want to steal?" Juve retorted. "As a matter of fact, Mme. de Langrune's diamond rings and watch and purse were all found on her table, in full view of everybody; in the drawers that had been broken open I found other jewels, over twenty pounds in gold and silver, and three bank notes in a card case. What is your view, sir, of a professional robber who sees valuables like that within his reach, and who does not take them?"

"It is certainly surprising," the magistrate admitted.

"Very surprising, and goes to show that although the crime in itself is a common, sordid one, the criminal may have had higher, or at any rate different, motives from those that would lead an ordinary thug to commit murder for the sake of robbery. The age and social position and personality of Mme. de Langrune make it unlikely that she had enemies, or was the object of vengeance, and therefore it was very likely she was murdered in order to be robbed—but robbed of what? Was there something more important than money or jewels to be gotten? I frankly admit that although I ask the question, I am at a loss how to answer it."

"Obviously," murmured the magistrate again, still more puzzled by all these logical deductions.

Juve proceeded with the development of his ideas.

"And now suppose we are face to face with a crime committed without any motive, as a result of some morbid impulse, a by no means uncommon occurrence, an obsession or temporary insanity?

"In that case, although, in consequence of the professional nature of the crime, I had previously dismissed the very serious case against young Rambert, I should be inclined to reconsider and think it possible that he might be the culprit. We know very little about the young fellow from the psychological point of view; in fact we don't know him at all; but it seems that his family is not altogether normal, and I understand that his mother's mental condition is precarious. If for a moment we regard Charles Rambert as a hysterical subject, we can associate him with the murder of the Marquise de Langrune, for a man of only medium physical strength, when suffering from an attack of mental alienation, can have his muscular power increased at least tenfold during his paroxysms. Under such influence Charles Rambert might have committed murder with all the fierce brutality of a giant!

"But I shall soon be in possession of absolutely accurate knowledge as to the muscular strength of the murderer," Juve

proceeded. "Quite lately M. Bertillon invented a marvelous dynamometer that enables us not only to ascertain what kind of
lever has been used to force a lock or a piece of furniture, but
also to determine the exact strength of the individual who used
the tools. I have taken samples of the wood from the broken
drawer, and I shall soon have exact information."

"That will be immensely important," M. de Presles agreed.
"Even if it does away with our present certainty of Charles Rambert's guilt, we shall be able to find out whether the murder was
committed by any other occupant of the house—still assuming
that it was committed by some member of the household."

"With regard to that," said Juve, "we can proceed with our
method of deduction and eliminate everybody who has a good
alibi or other defense; it will be so much ground cleared. For my
own part I find it impossible to suspect the two old maidser-
vants, Louise and Marie; the tramps whom we have detained
and subsequently released are too simpleminded to have been
capable of devising the minute precautions that demonstrate the
subtle cleverness of the man who murdered the marquise. Then
there is Dollon; but I imagine you will agree with me in thinking that his alibi clears him of suspicion—more especially as the
medical evidence proves that the murder was committed during
the night, between two and three o'clock."

"Only M. Etienne Rambert is left," the magistrate put in,
"and about nine o'clock that evening he left the d'Orsay station
in the slow train that reaches Verrières at six-fifty-five A.M. He
spent the whole night in the train, for he certainly arrived by
that one. He could not have a better alibi."

"Not possibly," Juve replied. "So we need only trouble ourselves with Charles Rambert," and warming to the subject the
detective proceeded to pile up a crushing indictment against
the young man. "The crime was committed so quietly that not
the faintest sound was heard; therefore the murderer was in the
house. He went to the marquise's room and announced his arrival by a cautious tap on the door; the marquise then opened
the door to him and was not surprised to see him, for she knew
him quite well. He went into her room with her and—"

"Oh, come, come!" M. de Presles broke in. "You are getting

carried away now, M. Juve; you forget that the bedroom door was forced, the best proof of that being the bolt, which was found wrenched away and hanging literally at the end of the screws."

"I was expecting you to say that, sir," said Juve with a smile. "But before I reply I should like to show you something rather peculiar." He led the way across the passage and into the bedroom of the marquise, where order had been restored; the dead body had been removed to the library, which had been transformed into a *chapelle ardente*, and two nuns were watching over it there. "Have a good look at this bolt," he said to M. de Presles. "Is there anything unusual about it?"

"No," said the magistrate.

"Yes, there is," said Juve; "the slide bolt is out, as when the bolt is fastened, but the socket into which the slide bolt slips to fasten the door to the wall is intact. If the bolt really had been forced, the socket would have been wrenched away too." Juve next asked M. de Presles to look closely at the screws that were wrenched halfway out of the door. "Do you see anything on those?"

The magistrate pointed to their heads.

"There are tiny scratches on them," he said, rather hesitatingly, for in his heart of hearts he knew the detective's real superiority over himself, "and from those I must infer that the screws have not been wrenched out by the pressure exerted on the bolt, but really unscrewed, and therefore—"

"And therefore," Juve broke in, "this is a mere blind, from which we may certainly draw the conclusion that the murderer wished to make us believe that the door was forced, whereas in reality it was opened to him by the marquise. Therefore the murderer was personally known to her!

"The murderer was personally known to her," he repeated. "Now, I should like to remind you of young Charles Rambert's equivocal behavior in the course of the evening that preceded the crime. It struck President Bonnet and shocked the priest. I also recall his hereditary antecedents, his mother's insanity, and finally—" Juve broke off abruptly and unceremoniously dragged the magistrate out of the room and into Charles Rambert's bedroom. He hurried into the dressing room adjoining, went down on his knees on the floor, and laid a finger on the middle of the oilcloth that was laid over the boards. "What do you see there, sir?" he demanded.

The magistrate adjusted his eyeglass and, looking at the place indicated by the detective, saw a little black stain; he wet his finger, rubbed it on the spot, and then, holding up his hand, observed that the tip of his finger was stained red.

"It is blood," he muttered.

"Yes, blood," said Juve, "and I gather from this that the story of the bloodstained towel that M. Rambert senior found among his son's things, and the sight of which so greatly impressed Mlle. Thérèse, was not an invention on that young lady's part but really existed; and it forms the most damning evidence possible against the young man. He obviously washed his hands after the crime in the tap water of this washbasin here, but one drop of blood falling on the towel and dripping on to the floor has been enough to give him away."

The magistrate nodded.

"It is conclusive," he said. "You have just proved beyond a shadow of a doubt, M. Juve, that Charles Rambert is the guilty party. It is beyond argument. It is conclusive—conclusive!"

There were a couple of seconds of silence, and then Juve suddenly said, "No!

"No!" he repeated. "It is quite true that we can adduce perfectly logical arguments to show that the murder was committed by some member of the household and that, therefore, Charles Rambert is the only possible culprit; but we can adduce equally logical arguments to show that the crime was committed by some person who got in from outside: there is nothing to prove that he did not walk into the house through the front door."

"The door was locked," said the magistrate.

"That's nothing," said Juve with a laugh. "Don't forget that there isn't such a thing as a real safety lock nowadays—since all locks can be opened with an outside key. If I had found one of the good old-fashioned catch locks on the door, like they used to make years ago, I should have said to you: 'Nobody got in, because the only way to get through a door fastened with one of those locks is to break the door down.' But here we have a lock that can be opened with a key. Now the key does not exist of which one cannot get an impression, and there is no such thing as an impression from which one cannot manufacture a duplicate key. The murderer could easily have gotten into the house with a duplicate key."

The magistrate raised a further objection.

"If the murderer had gotten in from outside he would inevitably have left some traces roundabout the château, but there aren't any."

"Yes, there are," Juve retorted. "First of all there is this piece of an ordnance map that I found yesterday between the château and the embankment." He took it from his pocket as he spoke. "It is an odd coincidence that this scrap shows the neighborhood of the château of Beaulieu."

"That doesn't prove anything," said the magistrate. "To find a piece of a map of our district in our district is the most natural thing possible. Now, if you were to discover the rest of this map in anybody's possession, then—"

"You may rest assured that I shall try to do so with the least possible delay," said Juve gently. "But this is not the only argument I have to support my theory. This morning, when I was walking near the embankment, I found some very suspicious footprints. It is true there are any number of footprints near the end of the Verrières tunnel, where the laborers are at work. But at the other end of the tunnel, where there is no occasion for anyone to be, I found that the earth of the embankment, which was crisp with the frost, had been disturbed, showing that someone had clambered up the embankment; the tips of his shoes had been driven into the earth, and I could see distinctly where his feet had been placed; but unfortunately the soil there is so dry that the footprints were too faint to hope we will be able to identify the person who made them. But the fact remains that someone did climb up the embankment, someone who was making for the railway."

The magistrate did not seem to be impressed by Juve's discovery.

"And pray what conclusion do you think ought to be drawn from that?" he inquired.

Juve sat down in an easy chair, threw back his head, closed his eyes as if he were about to indulge in a long soliloquy, and began to express his thoughts aloud.

"Suppose we were to combine two hypotheses into one; to wit, that the murderer was in the château prior to the crime and left the château directly after it was committed. What should you say, sir, of a criminal completing his deed, then hurrying over the couple of miles that separate Beaulieu from the railway, and catching a passing train, and on his way climbing the embankment at the spot where I found the footprints I mentioned."

"I should say," the magistrate replied, "that you can't jump onto a moving train as you can into a passing tram, and further, that at night none but express trains run between Brives and Cahors."

"All right," said Juve. "I will merely point out that owing to the work on the line at present, all trains have stopped at the beginning of the tunnel for the last two months. If the murderer had planned to escape in that way he might very well have been aware of this."

The magistrate's confidence was a little shaken by these new deductions on the part of the detective, but he submitted yet another objection.

"We have not found any traces roundabout the château."

"Strictly speaking, no, we have not," Juve admitted, "but it is clear that if the murderer walked on the grass, and he probably did so, he walked on it during the night, that is to say, before the morning dew. Now, everybody knows that when the dew rises in the early morning, grass that has been bent down by any passing man or animal stands up again in its original position, thereby destroying all traces; so if the murderer did walk on the lawn when he was getting away, nobody could tell that he had done so. Nevertheless, on the lawn in front of the window of the room where the murder was committed I have observed, not exactly footprints, but signs that the earth has been disturbed at that spot. I imagine that if I were to jump out of a first-floor window on to the soft surface of a lawn and wanted to efface the marks of my boots, I should smooth the earth and

the grass around them in just the same way that the little piece
of lawn I speak of seems to have been smoothed."

"I should like to have a look at that," said M. de Presles.

"Well, that's not difficult to do," Juve replied. "Come along."

The two men hurried down the staircase and out of the
house. When they reached the patch of grass that the inspector
said had been "smoothed over," they crouched down and scrutinized it closely. Just by the side of the grass, even overhanging
it a little, a large rhubarb plant outspread its thick, dentelated
leaves almost parallel with the soil. Juve happened to glance casually at the nearest leaf, and uttered an exclamation of surprise
and gratification.

"God, here's something interesting!" and he drew the magistrate's attention to some little specks of earth with which the
plant was peppered.

"What is that?" inquired M. de Presles.

"Dirt," said Juve, who had swept the top of the leaf with
the palm of his hand, "ordinary dirt, like the rest ten inches
below it."

"Well, what about it?" said the puzzled magistrate.

"Well," said Juve with a smile, "I imagine that ordinary dirt,
or any kind of dirt, has no power to move of its own volition,
much less to jump up ten inches into the air and settle on the
top of a leaf, even a rhubarb leaf! So I conclude that since this
dirt did not get here by itself it was brought here. How? That is
very simple! Somebody has jumped on to the grass there, M. de
Presles; he has removed the marks made by his feet by smoothing the earth with his hands; the earth soiled his hands, and he
rubbed one against the other quite mechanically; the earth that
was on his hands fell off in little balls on to the rhubarb leaf
and remained there for us to discover. And so it is certain—this
is one proof more—that even if the murderer did not get in
from outside, he did at any rate take to flight after he had committed the crime."

"So it can't be Charles Rambert after all," said the magistrate.

"It ought to be Charles Rambert!" was Juve's baffling reply.

The magistrate waxed irritable.

"My dear sir, your everlasting contradictions end by being

rather absurd! You have hardly finished building up one laborious theory before you start knocking it down again. I fail to understand you."

Juve smiled at M. de Presles's sudden irritability but quickly became serious again.

"I am anxious not to be led astray by any preconceived opinion. I put forward the hypothesis that so-and-so is guilty and examine all the arguments in support of that theory; then I submit that the crime was committed by somebody else and proceed in the same way. My method certainly raises the objection that it confronts every argument with a diametrically opposite one, but we are not concerned with establishing any one case in preference to another—it is the truth, and nothing else, that we have to discover."

"And that is tantamount to saying that in spite of the overwhelming circumstantial evidence, and in spite of the fact that he has run away, Charles Rambert is innocent?"

"Charles Rambert is the culprit, sir," Juve replied brightly. "If he were not, whom else could we possibly suspect?"

The detective's placidity and his perpetual self-contradictions exasperated M. de Presles. He held his tongue and was silently revolving the case in his mind when Juve made yet one more suggestion.

"There is one final hypothesis that I feel obliged to put before you. Do you realize sir, that this is a typical Fantômas crime?"

M. de Presles shrugged his shoulders as the detective pronounced this half-mythical name.

"Upon my word, M. Juve, I should never have expected you to invoke Fantômas! Why, Fantômas is the too obvious subterfuge, the cheapest device for investing a case with mock honors. Between you and me, you know perfectly well that Fantômas is merely a legal fiction—a lawyer's joke. Fantômas has no existence in fact!"

Juve stopped in his stride. He paused a moment before replying, then spoke in a restrained voice but with an emphasis on each word that always characterized him when he spoke in all seriousness.

"You are wrong to laugh, sir, very wrong. You are a magistrate

and I am only a humble detective inspector, but you have three
or four years' experience, perhaps less, while I have fifteen
years' work behind me. I know that Fantômas does exist, and I
do anything but laugh when I suspect his intervention in a
case."

M de Presles could hardly conceal his surprise, and Juve
went on:

"No one has ever said of me, sir, that I was a coward. I have
looked death in the eyes; I have often hunted and arrested criminals who would not have had the least hesitation in doing away
with me. There are whole gangs of crooks who have vowed my
death. All sorts of horrible revenges threaten me today; to all
that I am completely indifferent! But when people talk to me of
Fantômas, when I fancy that I can detect the intervention of
that genius of crime, in any case, then, M. de Presles, I am terrified! I tell you this frankly. I am frightened, because Fantômas
is a being against whom it is idle to use ordinary weapons; because he has been able to conceal his identity and elude all pursuit for years; because his daring is boundless and his power
immeasurable; because he is everywhere and nowhere at once
and, if he has had a hand in this affair, I am not even sure that
he is not listening to me now! And finally, M. de Presles, because everyone whom I have known to attack Fantômas, my
friends, my colleagues, my superior officers, have one and all,
one and all, sir, been beaten in the fight! Fantômas does exist, I
know, but who is he? A man can brave a danger he can mea-
sure, but he trembles when confronted with a peril he suspects
but cannot see."

"But this Fantômas is not a devil," the magistrate broke in
testily; "he is a man like you and me!"

"You are right, sir, in saying he is a man; but I repeat, the
man is a genius! I don't know whether he works alone or
whether he is the head of a gang of criminals; I know nothing
of his life; I know nothing of his motives. In no single case yet
has it been possible to determine the exact part he has taken.
He seems to possess the extraordinary gift of being able to slay
and leave no trace. You don't see him; you divine his presence.
You don't hear him; you have a presentiment of him. If Fantômas

is mixed up in this present affair, I don't know if we ever shall succeed in clearing it up!"

M. de Presles was impressed in spite of himself by the detective's earnestness.

"But I suppose you are not recommending me to drop the inquiry, are you, Juve?"

The detective forced a laugh that did not ring quite true.

"Come, come, sir," he answered, "I told you just now that I was frightened, but I never said I was a coward. You may be quite sure I shall do my duty, to the very end. When I first began—and that was not yesterday, not even the day before—to realize the importance and the power of this Fantômas, I took an oath, sir, that some day I would discover his identity and bring about his arrest! Fantômas is an enemy of society, you say? I prefer to regard him first and foremost as my own personal enemy! I have declared war on him, and I am ready to lose my head in the war if necessary, but by God I'll have his!"

Juve ceased. M. de Presles also was silent. But the magistrate was still skeptical, despite the detective's strange outburst, and presently he could not refrain from making a gentle protest and appeal.

"Do please bring in a verdict against someone, M. Juve, for really I would rather believe that your Fantômas is—a creation of the imagination!"

Juve shrugged his shoulders, seeming to arrive at a mighty decision, and began:

"You are quite right, sir, to require me to come to some definite conclusion, even if you are not right in denying the existence of Fantômas. So I make the assertion that the murderer is—"

The sound of urgent steps behind them made both men turn around. A postman, hot and perspiring, was hurrying to the château; he had a telegram in his hand.

"Does either of you gentlemen know M. Juve?" he asked.

"My name is Juve," said the detective, and he took the telegram and tore the envelope open. He glanced through it and then handed it to the magistrate.

"Please read that, sir," he said.

The telegram was from the Criminal Investigation Department and ran as follows:

"Return immediately to Paris. Are convinced that extraordinary crime lies behind disappearance of Lord Beltham. Privately, suspect Fantômas's work."

THE CRIMINAL
INVESTIGATION
DEPARTMENT

"Could you please tell me, does M. Gurn live here?"

Mme. Doulenques, the concierge at 147 rue Lévert, looked at the questioner and saw a tall, dark man with a heavy mustache, wearing a soft hat and a tightly buttoned overcoat, the collar of which was turned up around his ears.

"M. Gurn is away, sir," she answered; "he has been away for some time."

"I know," said the stranger, "but still I want to go up to his rooms if you would kindly go with me."

"You want—" the concierge began in surprise and doubt. "Oh, I know; of course, you are the man from the what's-its-name company, come for his luggage? Wait a bit; what is the name of that company? Something funny—an English name, I believe."

The woman left the door, which she had been holding ajar, and went to the back of the lobby; she looked through the pigeonholes where she kept the tenants' letters already sorted and picked out a soiled printed circular addressed to M. Gurn. She was busy putting on her spectacles when the stranger drew up behind and from over her shoulder got a glimpse of the name for which she was looking. He drew back again noiselessly and said quietly:

"I have come from the South Steamship Company."

"Yes, that's it," said the concierge, laboriously spelling out the words, "the South—whatever you said. I can never pronounce those names. Rue d'Hauteville, isn't it?"

"That's it," replied the man in the soft hat in pleasant, measured tones.

"Well, it's very plain that you don't hurry in your place," the concierge remarked. "I've been expecting you to come for M. Gurn's things for nearly three weeks; he told me you would come a few days after he had gone. However, that's your business."

Mme. Doulenques cast a mechanical glance through the window that looked on to the street and then surveyed the stranger from head to toe; he seemed to be much too well dressed to be a mere porter.

"But you haven't got any handcart or truck," she exclaimed. "You're not thinking of carrying the trunks on your shoulder, are you? Why, there are at least three or four of them—and they're heavy!"

The stranger paused before answering, as though he found it necessary to weigh each word.

"As a matter of fact, I merely wanted to get an idea of the size of the luggage," he said quietly. "Will you show me the things?"

"If I must, I must," said the concierge with a heavy sigh. "Come up with me, it's the fifth floor," and as she climbed the stairs she grumbled, "It's a pity you didn't come when I was doing my work: I shouldn't have had to climb a hundred stairs a second time then; it adds up at the end of the day, and I'm not so young anymore."

The stranger followed her up the stairs, murmuring monosyllabic sympathy and adjusting his pace to hers. Arriving at the fifth floor, the concierge drew a key from her pocket and opened the door of the flat.

It was a small modest place, but quite attractively decorated. The door on the landing opened into a tiny sort of anteroom, from which one passed into a front room furnished with hardly anything but a round table and a few armchairs. Beyond this was a bedroom, almost filled by the large bed, which was the first thing one saw on entering, and on the right there was yet another room, probably a little study. Both the first room, which was a kind of general living room, and the bedroom had large windows overlooking gardens as far as one could see. An advantage of the flat was that it had nothing opposite, so that the occupant could move about with the windows open if he liked and yet have no fear of inquisitive neighbors.

The rooms had been shut up for several days, since the tenant had gone away indeed, and there was a stuffy smell about them, mingled with a strong smell of chemicals.

"I must air the place," the concierge muttered, "or else M. Gurn won't be pleased when he comes back. He always says he is too hot and can't breathe in Paris."

"So he does not live here regularly?" said the stranger, scanning the place curiously as he spoke.

"Oh, no, sir," the concierge answered. "M. Gurn is a kind of commercial traveler and is often away, sometimes for a month or six weeks at a time." The gossipy woman was launching into a long and incoherent story when the stranger interrupted her, pointing to a silver-framed photograph of a young woman he had noticed on the mantelpiece.

"Is that Mme. Gurn?"

"M. Gurn is a bachelor," Mme. Doulenques replied. "I can't imagine him married, with his traveling kind of life."

"Just a little girlfriend of his, eh?" said the man in the soft hat, with a wink and a meaningful smile.

"Oh, no," said the concierge, shaking her head. "That photograph is not a bit like her."

"So you know her, then?"

"I do and I don't. That's to say, when M. Gurn is in Paris, he often has visits from a lady in the afternoon, a very fashionable lady, I can tell you, not the sort that one often sees in this quarter. Why, the woman who comes is a society lady, I am sure: she always has her veil down and passes by my door very quick, and never talks much with me. Free with her money, too: it's very seldom she does not give me something when she comes."

The stranger seemed to find the concierge's words very interesting, but they did not interrupt his mental inventory of the room.

"In addition, your tenant does not keep too sharp an eye on his money either?" he suggested.

"No, indeed: the rent is always paid in advance, and sometimes M. Gurn even pays two terms in advance because he says he never can tell if his business won't be keeping him away when the rent falls due."

Just then a deep voice called up the staircase:

"Concierge. M. Gurn: have you anyone of that name in the house?"

"Come up to the fifth floor," the concierge called back to the man. "I am in his rooms now," and she went back into the flat. "Here's somebody else for M. Gurn," she exclaimed.

"Does he have many visitors?" the stranger inquired.

"Hardly any, sir: that's why I'm so surprised."

Two men appeared; their blue blouses and metal-peaked caps proclaimed them to be porters. The concierge turned to the man in the soft hat.

"I suppose these are your men come to fetch the trunks?"

The stranger made a slight grimace, seemed to hesitate, and finally made up his mind to remain silent.

Rather surprised to see that the three men did not seem to be acquainted with each other, the concierge was about to ask what it meant when one of the porters addressed her curtly:

"We've come from the South Steamship Company for four boxes from M. Gurn's place. Are those the ones?" and taking no notice of the visitor in the room, the man pointed to two large trunks and two small boxes that were placed in a corner of the room.

"But aren't all three of you together?" inquired Mme. Doulenques, visibly uneasy.

The stranger still remained silent, but the first porter replied at once.

"No, we have nothing to do with this gentleman. Get on to it, pal! We've no time to waste!"

Anticipating their action, the concierge got instinctively between the porters and the luggage. So did the man in the soft hat.

"Pardon me," said he politely but peremptorily. "Please take nothing away."

One of the porters drew a crumpled and dirty notebook from his pocket and turned over the pages, wetting his thumb every time. He looked at it carefully and then spoke.

"There's no mistake: this is where we were told to come," and again he signed to his coworker. "Let's get on with it!"

The concierge was puzzled. She looked first at the mysterious stranger, who was as quiet and silent as ever, and then at the porters, who were beginning to get irritated by these incomprehensible complications.

Mme. Doulenques's mistrust waxed greater, and she sincerely regretted being alone on the fifth floor with these strangers, for the other occupants of this floor had gone off to work long ago. Suddenly she escaped from the room and called shrilly down the stairs:

"Madame Aurore! Madame Aurore!"

The man in the soft hat rushed after her, seized her gently but firmly by the arm, and led her back into the room.

"I beg you, Madame, do not make any noise. Do not call out!" he said in a low tone. "Everything will be all right. I only ask you not to create a disturbance."

But the concierge was thoroughly alarmed by the really odd behavior of all these men and again screamed at the top of her voice:

"Help! Police!"

The first porter was exasperated.

"Now we're to be accused of being thieves," he said with a shrug of his shoulders. "Look here, Auguste, just run down to the corner of the street and bring back a gendarme. The gentleman can explain to the concierge in his presence, and then we'll be able to get on with our job."

Auguste hurried off, and several tense moments passed, during which not a single word was exchanged among the three people who were left together.

Then heavy steps were heard, and Auguste reappeared with a gendarme. The latter came swaggering into the room with a would-be majestic air, and solemnly and pompously inquired:

"Now then, what's all this about?"

At sight of the officer every countenance cleared. The concierge ceased to tremble; the porter lost his air of suspicion. Both were beginning to explain to the representative of authority when the man in the soft hat waved them aside, stepped up to the guardian of the peace, and, looking him straight in the eyes, said:

"Criminal Investigation Department! Inspector Juve!"

The gendarme, who was quite unprepared for this announcement, stepped back a pace and raised his eyes toward the man
who addressed him: then suddenly he raised his hand to his
kepi and came to attention.

"Beg your pardon, Inspector, I didn't recognize you! M. Juve!
And you have been in this division a long time too!" He turned
angrily to the foremost porter. "Step forward, please, and let's
have no nonsense!"

Juve, who had thus disclosed his identity as a detective,
smiled, seeing that the gendarme now assumed that the South
Steamship Company's porter was a thief.

"That's all right," he said. "Leave the man alone. He's done
no harm."

"Then who am I to arrest?" the puzzled gendarme asked.

The concierge broke in to explain: she had been much impressed by the style and title of the stranger.

"If the gentleman had told me where he came from I would
certainly never have allowed anyone to go for a gendarme."

Inspector Juve smiled.

"If I had told you who I was just now, Madame, when you
were quite naturally so upset, you would not have believed me.
You would have continued to call out. Now, I am particularly
anxious to avoid any scandal or noise at the present moment. I
rely on your discretion." He turned to the two porters, who
were dumb with amazement and could make nothing of the affair. "As for you, my good fellows, I must ask you to neglect
your other work and go back at once to your office in the rue
d'Hauteville and tell your manager—what is his name?"

"M. Wooland," one of the men replied.

"Good: tell M. Wooland that I want to see him here at the
earliest possible moment; and tell him to bring with him all the
papers he has that refer to M. Gurn. And not a word to anyone
about all this, please, especially in this neighborhood. Take my
message to your manager, and that's all."

The porters had left hurriedly for the rue d'Hauteville, and a
quarter of an hour went by. The detective had requested the
concierge to ask the Madame Aurore to whom she had previously

appealed so loudly for help to take her place temporarily in the lobby. Juve kept Mme. Doulenques upstairs with him partly to get information from her, and partly to prevent her from gossiping downstairs.

While he was opening drawers and ransacking furniture, and plunging his hand into closets and cupboards, Juve asked the concierge to describe this tenant of hers, M. Gurn, in whom he appeared to be so deeply interested.

"He is a rather fair man," the concierge told him, "medium height, stout build, and clean shaven like an Englishman; there is nothing particular about him: he is like lots of other people."

This very vague description was hardly satisfactory. The detective told the policeman to unscrew the lock on a locked trunk and gave him a small screwdriver that he had found in the kitchen. Then he turned again to Mme. Doulenques who was standing stiffly against the wall, severely silent.

"You told me that M. Gurn had a lady friend. When did he used to see her?"

"Pretty often, when he was in Paris; and always in the afternoon. Sometimes they were together till six or seven o'clock, and once or twice the lady did not come down before half past seven."

"Did they used to leave the house together?"

"No, sir."

"Did the lady ever stay the night here?"

"Never, sir."

"Yes, evidently a married woman," murmured the detective as if speaking to himself.

Mme. Doulenques made a vague gesture to show her ignorance on the point.

"I can't tell you anything about that, sir."

"Very well," said the detective; "kindly pass me that coat behind you."

The concierge obediently took down a coat from a hook and handed it to Juve who searched it quickly, looked it all over, and then found a label sewn on the inside of the collar: it bore the one word *Pretoria*.

"Good!" said he, in an undertone. "I thought as much."

Then he looked at the buttons; these were stamped on the underside with the name *Smith*.

The gendarme understood what the detective was about, and he too examined the clothes in the first trunk, which he had just opened

"There is nothing to show where these things came from, sir," he remarked. "The name of the maker is not on them."

"That's all right," said Juve. "Open the other trunk."

While the gendarme was busy forcing the second lock Juve went for a moment into the kitchen and came back holding a rather heavy copper mallet with an iron handle, which he had found there. He was looking at this mallet with some curiosity, balancing and weighing it in his hands, when a sudden exclamation of fright from the gendarme drew his eyes to the trunk, the lid of which had just been thrown back. Juve did not lose all his professional stoicism, but even he leaped forward like a flash, swept the gendarme to one side, and dropped on his knees beside the open box. A horrid spectacle met his eyes. For the trunk contained a corpse!

The moment Mme. Doulenques caught sight of the ghastly thing, she fell back into a chair half fainting, and there she remained, unable to move, with her body hunched forward and haggard eyes fixed upon the corpse, of which she caught occasional glimpses as the movements of Juve and the gendarme every now and then left the shocking thing within the trunk exposed to her view.

Yet there was nothing especially gruesome or repellent about the corpse. It was the body of a man of about fifty years of age, with a pronounced brick-red complexion, and a lofty brow, the height of which was increased by premature baldness. A long, fair mustache drooped from the upper lip almost to the top of the chest. The unfortunate creature was doubled up in the trunk, with knees bent and head forced down by the weight of the lid. The body was dressed with a certain fastidiousness, and it was obviously that of a man of fashion and distinction; there was no wound to be seen. The calm, quiet face suggested that the victim had been taken by surprise while in the full vigor of life and killed suddenly, and had not been subjected to the anguish of a fight for his life or to any slow torture.

Juve half turned to the concierge.

"When did you see M. Gurn last? Exactly, please: it is important."

Mme. Doulenques babbled something unintelligible and then, as the detective pressed her, made an effort to collect her scattered wits.

"Three weeks ago at least, sir: yes, three weeks exactly; no one has been here since, I swear."

Juve made a sign to the gendarme, who understood, and felt the body carefully.

"Quite stiff and hard, sir," he said; "yet there is no smell from it. Perhaps the cold—"

Juve shook his head.

"Even severe cold could not preserve a body in that condition for three weeks, and it's not cold now, but there is this." He showed his subordinate a small yellowish stain just at the opening of the collar, close to the Adam's apple, which, in spite of the comparative thinness of the body, was very pronounced.

Juve took the corpse under the armpits and raised it gently to examine it more closely, but anxious, also, not to alter its position. On the nape of the neck was a large stain of blood, like a black mole and as big as a half-dollar, just above the last vertebra of the spinal column.

"That's the explanation," the detective murmured, and carefully replacing the body he continued his investigation. With quick, clever hands he searched the coat pockets and found the watch in its proper place. Another pocket was full of money, chiefly small change. But Juve looked in vain for the wallet that the man had doubtless been in the habit of carrying about with him, the wallet probably containing some means of identification.

The inspector merely grunted, got up, began pacing the room, and questioned the concierge.

"Did M. Gurn have a motorcar?"

"No, sir," she replied, looking surprised. "Why do you ask?"

"Oh, for no particular reason," said the inspector with affected indifference, but at the same time he was contemplating a large nickel pump that lay on one of the shelves, a syringe holding perhaps half a pint, like those that chauffeurs use. He looked at it steadfastly for several minutes. His next question was addressed to the gendarme who was still on his knees by the trunk.

"We have found one yellow stain on the neck; you will very likely find some more. Have a look at the wrists and the calves of the legs and the stomach. But do it carefully, so as not to disturb the body." While the gendarme began to obey his chief's order, carefully undoing the clothing on the corpse, Juve looked at the concierge again.

"Who did the cleaning in this flat?"

"I did, sir."

Juve pointed to the velvet curtain that screened the door between the little anteroom and the room in which they stood.

"How did you come to leave that curtain unhooked at the top, without putting it right?"

Mme. Doulenques looked at it.

"It's the first time I've seen it like that," she said apologetically; "the curtain could not have been unhooked when I did the room last without my noticing it. Anyhow, it hasn't been like that long. I ought to say that as M. Gurn was seldom here I didn't do the place thoroughly very often."

"When did you do it out last?"

"About a month ago."

"That is to say M. Gurn went away a week after you last cleaned the place up?"

"Yes, sir."

Juve changed the subject and pointed to the corpse.

"Tell me, Madame, did you know that person?"

The concierge fought down her nervousness and for the first time looked at the unfortunate victim with a steady gaze.

"I have never seen him before," she said, with a little shudder.

"And so, when that gentleman came up here, you did not notice him?" said the inspector gently.

"No, I did not notice him," she declared, and then went on as if answering some question that had occurred to herself. "And I wonder I didn't, for people hardly ever inquired for M. Gurn; of course, when the lady was with him M. Gurn was not at home to anybody. This—this dead man must have come straight up here himself."

Juve nodded and was about to continue his questioning when the bell rang.

"Open the door," said Juve to the concierge, and he followed her to the entrance of the flat, partly fearing to find some intruder there, partly hoping to find some unexpected person whose arrival might throw a little light upon the situation.

At the opened door Juve saw a young man of about twenty-five; obviously an Englishman, he had clear eyes and close-cropped hair. With an accent that further made his British origin unmistakable, the visitor introduced himself:

"I am Mr. Wooland, manager of the Paris branch of the South Steamship Company. It seems that I am wanted at M. Gurn's flat on the fifth floor of this house, by order of the police."

Juve came forward.

"I am much obliged to you for inconveniencing yourself, sir. Allow me to introduce myself: M. Juve, an inspector from the Criminal Investigation Department. Please come in."

Solemn and impassive, Mr. Wooland entered the room; a side glance suddenly showed him the open trunk and the dead body, but not a muscle of his face moved. Mr. Wooland came from good stock and had all that admirable self-possession that is the strength of the powerful Anglo-Saxon race. He looked at the inspector in somewhat haughty silence, waiting for him to begin.

"Will you kindly let me know, sir, the instructions your firm had with regard to the forwarding of the baggage that you sent for at this flat this morning?"

"Four days ago, Inspector," said the young man, "on the fourteenth of December to be precise, the London mail brought us a letter in which Lord Beltham, who had been a client of ours for several years, instructed us to collect, on the seventeenth of December, that is, today, four articles marked H. W. K., 1, 2, 3, and 4, from M. Gurn's apartments, One Forty-seven rue Lévert.

He informed us that the concierge had orders to allow us to take them away."

"To what address were you to dispatch them?"

"Our client instructed us to forward the trunks by the first steamer to Johannesburg, where he would send for them. We were to send two invoices with the goods as usual; the third invoice was to be sent to London, Box Sixty-three, Charing Cross Post Office."

Juve made a note of Box Sixty-three, Charing Cross in his notebook.

"Addressed to what name or initials?"

"Simply Beltham."

"Good. There are no other documents relating to the matter?"

"No, I have nothing else," said Mr. Wooland.

The young man relapsed into impassive silence. Juve watched him for a minute or two and then said:

"You must have heard the various rumors current in Paris three weeks ago, sir, about Lord Beltham. He was a very well-known personage in society. Suddenly he disappeared; his wife did everything to give the matter the widest possible publicity. Weren't you rather surprised when you received a letter from Lord Beltham four days ago?"

Mr. Wooland was not disconcerted by the rather embarrassing question.

"Of course I had heard of Lord Beltham's disappearance, but it was not for me to form any official opinion about it. I am a businessman, sir, not a detective. Lord Beltham might have disappeared voluntarily or not: I was not asked to say which. When I got his letter I simply decided to carry out the orders it contained. I should do the same again in similar circumstances."

"Are you satisfied that the order was sent by Lord Beltham?"

"I have already told you, sir, that Lord Beltham had been a client of ours for several years; we have had many similar dealings with him. This last order that we received from him appeared to be entirely above suspicion: identical in form and in terms with the previous letters we had had from him." He took a letter out of his wallet and handed it to Juve. "Here is the order, sir; if you think it proper you can compare it with similar documents filed in our office in the rue d'Hauteville." As Juve was silent, Mr. Wooland, with the utmost dignity, inquired: "Is there any further occasion for me to remain here?"

"Thank you, sir, no," Juve replied. Mr. Wooland made an almost imperceptible bow and was on the point of withdrawing when the detective stopped him once more. "M. Wooland, did you know Lord Beltham?"

"No, sir. Lord Beltham always sent us his orders by letter; once or twice he spoke to us over the telephone, but he never came to our office, and I have never been to his house."

"Thank you very much," said Juve, and Mr. Wooland withdrew.

With meticulous care Juve replaced every article that he had moved during his investigations. He carefully shut the lid of the trunk, thus hiding the unhappy corpse from the curious eyes of the gendarme and the still terrified Mme. Doulenques. Then he leisurely buttoned his overcoat and spoke to the gendarme.

"Stay here until I send a man to relieve you; I am going to your superintendent now." At the door he called the concierge. "Will you kindly go down before me, Madame? Return to your rooms and please do not say a word about what has happened to anyone whatever."

"You can trust me, sir," she murmured, and Juve walked slowly away from the house with head bowed in thought.

There could be no doubt about it: the body in the trunk was Lord Beltham! Juve knew the Englishman quite well. But who was the murderer?

"Everything points to Gurn," Juve thought, "and yet would an ordinary murderer have dared to commit such a crime as this? Am I letting my imagination run away with me again? I don't know, but it seems to me that this murder, committed in the very middle of Paris, in a crowded house where, still, nobody heard or suspected anything, possesses an audacity, a certain impunity, and above all a multiplicity of precautions that are typical of a Fantômas manner!" He clenched his fists and an evil smile curled his lips as he repeated, like a threat, the name of that terrible and most mysterious criminal, of whose hellish influence he seemed to be made conscious yet once again. "Fantômas! Fantômas! Did Fantômas really commit this murder? And if he did, shall I ever succeed in solving this new mystery, and learning the secret of that tragic room?"

A DREADFUL CONFESSION

While Jove was devoting his incomparable skill and marvelous daring to the elucidation of the new case with which the Criminal Investigation Department had entrusted him in Paris, things were marching along at Beaulieu, where the whole machinery of the law was being set in motion for the discovery and arrest of Charles Rambert.

Making a mighty clatter and racket, Bouzille came down the slope and stopped before old Mother Chiquard's cottage. He arrived in his own equipage, and an extraordinary one it was!

Bouzille was mounted upon a tricycle of prehistoric design, with two large wheels behind and a small steering wheel in front, and a rusty handlebar from which all the plating was worn off. The solid rubber tires that once had adorned the machine had worn out long ago and were now replaced by twine twisted round the rims of the wheels; this was forever fraying away and the wheels were fringed with a veritable lacework of string. Bouzille must have picked up this impossible machine for practically nothing at some local market, unless perhaps some charitable person gave it to him simply to get rid of it. He styled this tricycle his "motor," and that was by no means all of his vehicle. Attached to the tricycle by a thick rope was a kind of wicker perambulator on four wheels, which he called his "sleeping car," because he used it to store all the bits and pieces of rags he picked up on his journeys, and also his primitive bedding and the little piece of waterproof canvas under which he often slept in the open air. Behind the sleeping car was a third vehicle, the restaurant car, consisting of an old soapbox mounted on four solid wooden wheels which were fastened to the axles by huge conical bolts; in this he kept his provisions: lumps of bread and fat, bottles and vegetables, all mixed up in agreeable confusion. Bouzille made rather long journeys in this train of his and was well known throughout the southwest of France. Often did the astonished population see him bent over his tricycle, with his pack on his back, pedaling with extraordinary rapidity down the hills, while the carriages behind him swayed and jolted over the potholes and bumps in the road until it seemed impossible that they could retain their equilibrium.

Old Mother Chiquard recognized the cause of the racket. The healthy life of the country had kept the old woman strong and active in spite of her eighty-three years, and now she came to the door, armed with a broom, and hailed the tramp in angry, threatening tones.

"So it's you, is it, you thief, you robber of the poor! It's shocking, the way you spend your time in evildoing! What do you want now, pray?"

Slowly and sheepishly and with head bowed, Bouzille approached Mother Chiquard, nervously looking out for a whack over the head with the broom the old lady held.

"Don't be cross," he pleaded when he could get in a word, "I want to come to an arrangement with you, Mother Chiquard, if it can be done."

"That all depends," said the old woman, eyeing the tramp with great mistrust; "I haven't much faith in arrangements with you. Rascals like you always manage to take advantage of honest folk."

Mother Chiquard went back into her cottage; it was no weather for her to stay out of doors, for a strong north wind was blowing, and that was bad for her rheumatism. Bouzille deliberately followed her inside and closed the door carefully behind him. Without ceremony he walked up to the hearth, where a scanty wood fire was burning, and put down his pack so as to rub his hands together.

"Miserable weather, Mother Chiquard!"

The obstinate old lady stuck to her one idea.

"If it isn't miserable to steal my rabbit, then this is the finest weather that ever I saw!"

"You make a lot of fuss about a trifle," the tramp protested, "especially since you will be a lot better off by the arrangement I'm going to suggest."

The notion calmed Mother Chiquard a little, and she sat down on a bench, while Bouzille took a seat on the table.

"What do you mean?" the old woman inquired.

"Well," said Bouzille, "I suppose your rabbit would have fetched something in the market; I've brought you two fowls that are worth at least half as much, and if you will give me some dinner at twelve o'clock I will put in a good morning's work for you."

Mother Chiquard looked at the clock on the wall; it was eight o'clock. The tramp's proposal represented four hours' work, which was not to be despised; but before striking the bargain she insisted on seeing the fowls. These were extracted from the pack; tied together by the feet and half suffocated, the unfortunate creatures were not much to look at, but they would be cheap, which was worth considering.

"Where did you get these fowls?" Mother Chiquard asked, more as a matter of form than anything else, for she was pretty sure they had not been honestly come by.

Bouzille put his finger to his lip.

"Hush!" he murmured gently, "that's a secret between me and the poultry. Well, is it a deal?" and he held out his hand to the old lady.

She hesitated a moment and then made up her mind.

"It's a deal," she said, putting her horny fingers into the man's hard palm. "You shall chop me some wood first, and then go down to the river for the rushes I have put in to soak; they must be swollen enough by this time."

Bouzille was glad to have made it up with Mother Chiquard and pleased at the prospect of a good dinner at midday; he opened the cottage door and leisurely arranged a few logs within range of the ax with which he was going to split them. Mother Chiquard began to throw down some grain to the skinny and famished fowls that fluttered round her.

"I thought you were in prison, Bouzille," she said, "for stealing my rabbit, and also for that affair at the château of Beaulieu."

"Oh, those are two quite different stories," Bouzille replied. "You mustn't mix them up for anything. As for the château job, every tramp in the district has been run in: I was copped by M'sieu Morand the morning after the murder; he took me into the kitchen of the château and Mme. Louise gave me something to eat. There was another chap there with me, a man named François Paul who doesn't belong to these parts; between you and me, I thought he was a tough-looking customer who might easily have been the murderer, but it doesn't do to say that kind of thing, and I'm glad I held my tongue because they let him go. I heard no more about it, and five days later I went back to Brives to attend the funeral of the Marquise de Langrune. That was some ceremony! The church all lighted up, and all the nobility from the neighborhood present. I didn't waste my time, for I knew all the gentlemen and ladies and took the best part of a few francs, and the blind beggar who sits on the steps of the church called me all the names he could think of!"

The tramp's story greatly interested Mother Chiquard, but another idea still dominated her mind.

"So they didn't punish you for stealing my rabbit?"

"Well, they did and they didn't," said Bouzille, scratching his head. "M'sieu Morand, who is an old friend of mine, took me to the lockup at Saint-Jaury, and I was to have gone next morning to the court at Brives, where I know the sentence for stealing domestic animals is three weeks. That would have suited me just fine now, for the prison at Brives is quite new and very comfortable, but that same night Sergeant Doucet shoved another man into the clink with me at Saint-Jaury, a raving lunatic who started smashing everything up and tried to tear my eyes out. Naturally, I gave him as good as I got, and the row we made brought in the sergeant. I told him the man wanted to throttle me, and he had no choice, for he couldn't do anything with the man, who was crazy, and he couldn't leave me alone there with him. So at last the sergeant took me to one side and told me to hoof it and not let him see me again. So there it is."

While he was chattering like this Bouzille had finished the job given him by Mother Chiquard, who meanwhile had peeled some potatoes and poured the soup on the bread. He wiped his brow, and seeing the brimming pot, gave a meaningful wink and licked his chops.

"I'll poke the fire up, Mother Chiquard; I'm getting really hungry."

"So you ought to be, at half past eleven," the old woman replied. "Yes, we'll have dinner, and you can get the rushes out afterward."

Mother Chiquard was the proud owner of a little cottage that was separated from the bank of the Dordogne by the high road between Martel and Montvalent. Around the cottage she had planted a small orchard, and opposite, through a gap in the trees, was a view of the yellow waters of the Dordogne and the chain of hills that stood on the far side of the river. Living here summer and winter, with her rabbits and her fowls, Mother Chiquard earned a little money by making baskets; but she was crippled with rheumatism and was miserable every time she had to go down to the river to pull out the bundles of rushes that she put there to soak; the work meant not merely an hour's paddling in mud up to the knees, but also two weeks' acute agony and at least a few francs for medicine. So whoever wanted to make a friend of the old woman only had to volunteer to get the rushes out for her.

As he ate, Bouzille told Mother Chiquard of his plans for the coming spring.

"Yes," he said, "since I'm not doing any time this winter I'm going to undertake a long journey." He stopped munching for a second and paused for greater effect. "I am going to Paris, Mother Chiquard!" Then, seeing that the old lady was utterly dumbfounded by the announcement, he leaned his elbows on the table and looked at her over his empty plate. "I've always had one great desire—to see the Eiffel Tower: that idea has been running through my head for the last fifteen years. Well, now I'm going to get my wish. I hear you can get a room in Paris cheap enough so even I can manage it."

"How long will it take you to get there?" inquired the old woman, immensely impressed by Bouzille's adventurous plan.

"That depends," said the tramp. "I must allow at least three months with my train. Of course if I got run in on the way for stealing, or as a vagrant, I couldn't say how long it would take."

The meal was over, and the old woman was quietly washing up her few plates and dishes when Bouzille, who had gone down to the river to fetch the rushes, suddenly called shrilly to Mother Chiquard.

"Mother Chiquard! Mother Chiquard! Come and look! Just fancy, I've earned twenty-five francs!"

The summons was so urgent and the news so amazing that the old lady left her house and hurried across the road to the riverbank. She saw the tramp up to his waist in the water, trying, with a long stick, to drag out of the current a large object that was not identifiable at a first glance. To all her questions Bouzille answered with the same delighted cry, "I have earned twenty-five francs," too intent on hauling in his catch even to turn around. A few minutes later he emerged dripping from the water, towing a large bundle to the safety of the bank. Mother Chiquard drew nearer, greatly interested, and then recoiled with a shriek of horror.

Bouzille had fished out a corpse!

It was a ghastly sight: the body of a very young man, almost a boy, with long, slender limbs; the head was so horribly swollen and torn as to be shapeless. One leg was almost entirely torn from the trunk. Through rents in the clothing strips of flesh were trailing, blue and discolored by their long immersion in the water. On the shoulders and back of the neck were bruises and stains of blood. Bouzille, who was quite unaffected by the ghastliness of the object and still kept up his happy chant "I have fished up a body, I've earned twenty-five francs," observed that there were large splinters of wood, rotten from long immersion, sticking in some of the wounds. He stood up and addressed Mother Chiquard who, white as a sheet, was watching him in silence.

"I see what it is; he must have gotten caught in some mill wheel; that's what has cut him up like that."

Mother Chiquard shook her head uneasily.

"Suppose it was a murder! That would be terrible!"

"It's no good my looking at him anymore," said Bouzille. "I don't recognize him; he's not from around here."

"That's for sure," the old woman agreed. "He's dressed like a gentleman."

The two looked at each other in silence. Bouzille was not nearly so complacent as he had been a few minutes before. The reward of twenty-five francs prompted him to go at once to inform the police. The idea of a crime, suggested by Mother Chiquard, disturbed him greatly, and all the more because he thought it was probably true. Another murder in the neighborhood would certainly vex the authorities and put the police in a bad temper. Bouzille knew from experience that the first thing people do after a tragedy is to arrest all the tramps, and that if the police are at all harried they always contrive to get the tramps sentenced for something else. He had had a previous inclination to establish his winter quarters in prison, but since then he had formed the plan of going to Paris, and liberty appealed to him more. He reached a sudden decision.

"I'll put him back into the water!"

But Mother Chiquard stopped him, just as he was putting his idea into execution.

"You mustn't. Suppose somebody has seen us already? It would land us in a lot of trouble!"

Half an hour later, convinced that it was his unhappy duty, Bouzille left two thirds of his train in Mother Chiquard's custody, got astride his prehistoric tricycle, and slowly pedaled off toward Saint-Jaury.

New Year's Day is a melancholy and a tedious one for everybody who has no particular reason to celebrate. There is the change in the year's date, for one thing, which provokes thought, and there is the enforced idleness for another, coming upon energetic people like a temporary paralysis and leaving them nothing to do but meditate.

Juve, comfortably ensconced in his own private study, was realizing this just as evening was falling on this first of January. He was a confirmed bachelor and for several years had lived in a little flat on the fifth floor of an old house in the rue Bonaparte. He had not gone out today, but though he was resting, he was not idle. For a whole month he had been wholly engrossed in his attempt to solve the mystery surrounding the two cases on which he was engaged, the Beltham case and the Langrune case, and his mind was leisurely revolving around them now as he sat in his warm room before a blazing wood fire and watched the blue smoke curl up in rings toward the ceiling. The two cases were quite dissimilar, and yet his detective's instinct persuaded him that although they differed in details their conception and execution emanated not only from one single mind but also from one hand. He was convinced that he was dealing with a mysterious and dangerous individual, and that while he himself was out in the open he was fighting a concealed and invisible adversary; he strove to give form and substance to the adversary, and the name of Fantômas came again into his mind. Fantômas! What might Fantômas be doing now; and, if he had a real existence, as the detective most firmly believed, how was he spending New Year's Day?

A sharp ring of the doorbell startled him from his chair, and not giving his manservant time to answer it, he went himself to the door and took from a messenger a telegram which he hastily tore open and read:

"Have found in the Dordogne drowned body of young man, face unrecognizable, from description possibly Charles Rambert. Please consider situation and wire what action you will take."

The telegram had been sent from Brives and was signed by M. de Presles.

"Something new at last," the detective muttered. "Drowned in the Dordogne and face unrecognizable! I wonder if it really is Charles Rambert?"

Since M. Etienne Rambert and his son had disappeared so unaccountably, the detective naturally had formulated several hypotheses, but he had arrived at no conclusion that really satisfied his judgment. But though their flight had not surprised him greatly, he had been rather intrigued that the police had not been able to find any trace of them, for rightly or wrongly Juve credited them with a good deal of ingenuity and power. So it was by no means unreasonable for him to accept the death of the fugitives as the reason the police couldn't find them. However, this was a fresh development in the case, and he was about to write a reply to M. de Presles when once more the bell rang sharply.

This time Juve did not move but listened while his man spoke to the visitor. It was an absolute rule of Juve's never to receive visitors at his flat. If anyone wanted to see him on business, he was to be found almost every day in his office at headquarters at about eleven in the morning. To a few people he was willing to give appointments at a quiet and discreet little café in the boulevard Saint-Michel; but he invited no one to his own rooms except one or two of his own relatives from the country, and even they had to be provided with a password before they could obtain admission. So now, to all the entreaties of the caller, Juve's servant stolidly replied with absolute certainty that his master would see no one; yet the visitor's insistence was so great that at last the servant was prevailed upon to bring in his card, though with some fear as to the consequences for himself. But to his extreme relief and surprise, Juve, when he had read the name engraved on the card, said sharply:

"Bring him in at once!"

And in another couple of seconds M. Etienne Rambert was in the room!

The old gentleman who had fled so mysteriously a few days before, taking with him his son over whom so awful a charge was hanging, bowed deferentially to the detective, with the pitiful mien of one who is crushed beneath the burden of misfortune. His features were drawn, his face bore the stamp of deepest grief, and in his hand he held an evening paper, which in his agitation he had almost crumpled into a ball.

"Tell me, sir, if it is true," he said in low trembling tones. "I have just read this."

Juve pointed to a chair, took the paper mechanically, and smoothing it out read, below a large headline, "IS THIS A SEQUEL TO THE BEAULIEU CRIME?" a story similar to the one he had just learned from M. de Presles's telegram.

Juve contemplated M. Etienne Rambert in silence for a few

minutes, and then, without replying directly to his visitor's first question, asked him a question in that quiet voice of his, a wonderfully indifferent tonelessness that concealed the least clue to his inmost thoughts.

"Why have you come to me, sir?"

"To find out, sir," the old man answered.

"To find out what?"

"If that poor drowned corpse is—my son's, is my poor Charles!"

"It is rather you who can tell me, sir," said Juve, impassive as ever.

There was a pause. Despite his emotion, M. Rambert seemed to be thinking deeply. Suddenly he appeared to make an important decision, and raising his eyes to the detective he spoke very slowly:

"Have pity, sir, on a brokenhearted father. Listen to me. I have a dreadful confession to make!"

Juve drew his chair close to M. Etienne Rambert.

"I am listening," he said gently, and M. Etienne Rambert began his "dreadful confession."

ALL FOR HONOR

Society had turned out in force at the Cahors Law Courts, where the session was about to be held. Hooting motorcars and antiquated coaches were arriving every minute, bringing gentry from the great houses in the neighborhood, young landowners and well-to-do country people, prosperous farmers and jovial wine growers, all of them determined not to miss "the trial" that was causing such immense excitement because the principal figure in it was well known as a friend of one of the oldest families in those parts; and because he was not merely a witness, nor even the victim, but actually the defendant in the case, although he had been granted bail in the interval by order of the court.

Compared with those in large towns, the courtroom at Cahors was small, but it was filled by a considerable and select crowd. Quiet greetings and talk were freely exchanged, but there was an air of melancholy about every person present, and it was obvious that they were drawn there by no mere curiosity or desire for horrid details, but by legitimate interest in the development of great drama.

One of the leading heroines in the case was pointed out with particular sympathy.

"That's Thérèse Auvernois, over there in the first row! The president of the court gave her that seat; the officer who took the card of admission over to Querelles told me so."

"That's where Mme. de Vibray lives, isn't it?"

"Yes, she is sitting next to Thérèse now—that pretty woman in gray. Since Mme. de Langrune's death she has kept the child with her, thinking, quite rightly, that it would be too painful for her to be at Beaulieu. The family council has appointed President Bonnet temporary guardian of Thérèse. He is that tall, thin man over there, talking to the steward, Dollon."

The Baronne de Vibray turned affectionately to Thérèse, who was looking dreadfully pale in her long mourning veil.

"Are you sure this won't tire you too much, dear? Shall we go outside for a little while?"

"Oh, no, please do not worry about me," Thérèse replied. "Indeed, I shall be all right."

President Bonnet sat with the two ladies. He had been engaged solemnly exchanging bows with everyone in the courtroom whom he considered worth knowing; now he took part in the conversation and displayed his special knowledge by explaining the constitution of the court and pointing out where the clerk sat, and where the public prosecutor sat, and where the jury sat, all at great length and much to the interest of the people near him—with, however, one exception; a man dressed entirely in black, with his head half buried in the huge collar of a long overcoat and dark glasses over his eyes, appeared to be vastly bored by the old magistrate's disquisition. Juve—for it was he—knew too much about legal procedure to require explanations from President Bonnet.

Suddenly a thrill ran through the room and conversation stopped abruptly. M. Etienne Rambert had just walked down the gangway in the court to the seat reserved for him, just in front of the witness box and close to a kind of rostrum on which Maître Dareuil, an old member of the Cahors bar, immediately took his place. M. Etienne Rambert was very pale, but it was obvious that he was by no means overwhelmed by the death hanging over him. He was, indeed, a fine figure as he took his seat and mechanically passed his hand through his long white curls, flinging them back and raising his head almost as if in defiance of the inquisitive crowd that was gazing at him.

Almost immediately after he had taken his seat a door was thrown open and the jury filed in, and then a black-gowned usher came forward and shrilly called for silence.

"Stand up, gentlemen! Hats off, please! Gentlemen, the court!"

With solemn, measured steps and heads bent as if absorbed in profoundest meditation, the judges slowly proceeded to their seats. The president formally declared the court open, whereupon the clerk rose immediately to read the indictment.

The clerk of the court at Cahors was a most excellent man, but modesty was his distinguishing characteristic and his chief desire appeared to be to shun responsibility, figure as little prominently as possible, and even escape observation altogether. Court sessions were not often held at Cahors, and he had had few occasions to read an indictment as tragic as this present one, with the result that he lacked confidence now. He read in a toneless, monotonous voice, so nervously and softly that nobody in the audience of the court could hear a word he said, and even the jury members were obliged to lean their elbows on the desk before them and strain their ears to find out what it was all about.

Etienne Rambert, however, was only a few feet from the clerk; he did not miss a word and it was evident from his sporadic nervous movements that some passages in the indictment hit him very hard indeed, and even eroded his general air of confidence.

When the clerk had finished, Etienne Rambert sat still with his forehead resting in his hands, as if crushed by the weight of the memories the indictment had evoked. Then the sharp, thin voice of the president of the court snapped the chain of his thoughts.

"Stand up, sir!"

And as pale as death Etienne Rambert rose and folded his arms across his breast. In firm yet somehow muffled tones, he answered the preliminary formal questions. His name was Hervé Paul Etienne Rambert; his age, fifty-nine; his occupation, a merchant, owning and working rubber plantations in South America. Then followed the formal question whether he had heard and understood the indictment that had just been read.

"I understood it all, sir," he replied, with a little gesture to show he understood the gravity of the facts detailed and the weight of the evidence against him, and this won general sympathy for him. "I understood it all, but I protest some of the allegations, and I protest with all my soul against the suggestion that I have failed in my duty as a man of honor and as a father!"

The president of the court checked him irritably.

"Excuse me, I do not intend to permit you to extend the pleadings indefinitely. I shall examine you on the various points of the indictment, and you may protest as much as you please." The unfeeling rudeness provoked no comment from the defendant, and the president proceeded. "Well, you have heard the indictment. It charges you first with having aided and abetted the escape of your son, whom an inquiry held in another place had implicated in the murder of the Marquise de Langrune; and it charges you secondly with having killed your son, whose body has been recovered from the Dordogne, in order that you might escape public scandal."

At this brutal statement of the case Etienne Rambert made a proud gesture of indignation.

"Sir," he exclaimed, "there are different ways of putting things. I do not deny the contents of the indictment, but I object to the summary of it that you present. No one has ever dared to contend that I killed my son in order to escape public scandal, as you have just insinuated. I am entirely indifferent to the world's opinion. What the indictment is intended to allege, the only thing it can allege, is that I wrought justice upon a criminal who ought to have filled me with horror but who, nevertheless, I could not hand over to the public executioner."

This time it was the judge's turn to be astonished. He had expected to make mincemeat of this poor, broken old man whom the law had delivered to his tender mercy. But he discovered that the old man had great courage and had replied with spirit to his malevolent remarks.

"We will discuss your right to take the law into your own hands presently," he said, "but that is not the question now; there are other points which it would be well for you to explain to the jury. Why, in the first place, did you obstinately decline to speak to the examining magistrate?"

"I had no answer to make to the examining magistrate," Etienne Rambert answered slowly, as if he were weighing his words, "because in my opinion he had no questions to put to me! I do not admit that I am charged with anything contrary to the code of honor or that any such charge can be formulated against me. The indictment charges me with having killed my son because I believed him to be guilty of the murder of Mme. de Langrune and would not hand him over to the gallows. I have never confessed to that murder, sir, and nothing will ever make me do so. And that is why I would not reply to the examining magistrate, because I would not admit that there was anything before the court concerning myself; because, since the dreadful tragedy in my private life was exposed to public opinion, I desired that I should be judged by public opinion, which, sir, is not represented by you who are a professional judge, but by the jury here who will shortly say whether I am really a criminal—by the jury, many of whom are fathers themselves and, when they think of their own sons, will wonder what appalling visions must have passed through my mind when I was forced to believe that my boy, my own son, had committed murder! What sort of tragedy will they think that must have been like for a man like me, with sixty years of honor and of honorable life behind him?"

The outburst ended on a sob, and the whole court was moved with sympathy, women wiping their eyes, men coughing, and even the jury striving hard to conceal the emotion that stirred them.

The judge glared around the court and after a pause addressed the defendant again with sarcasm.

"So that is why you stood mute during the inquiry, was it, sir? Odd! Very odd! I admire the interpretation you place upon your duty as an honorable man. It is—quaint!"

Etienne Rambert interrupted the sneering speech.

"I am quite sure, sir, that there are plenty of people here who will understand and endorse what I did."

The declaration was so pointedly personal that the judge took it up.

"And I am quite sure that people of principle will understand me when I have shown them your conduct as it really was. You seem to prefer a heroic interpretation, so it will not be without interest to point out certain things. Your attitude throughout this affair has been this; it is not for me to anticipate the outcome of the inquiry that will be held someday into the murder of Mme. de Langrune. I must recall the fact that the moment you believed your son was the murderer, the moment you discovered the bloodstained towel that furnished the circumstantial evidence of his guilt, you—the man of honor, mind you—never thought of handing over the culprit to the police who were actually in the precincts of the château, but only thought of securing his escape and helping him to get away! You even accompanied him in his flight, and so became in a sense his accomplice. I suppose you do not deny that?"

Etienne Rambert shook with emotion and answered in ringing tones.

"If you are of the opinion, sir, that that was an act of complicity on my part, I will not only not deny it, I will proclaim it from the housetops! I became the accomplice of a murderer by inducing him to run away, did I? You forget, sir, that at the moment when I first believed my son was the culprit—I was not his accomplice then, I suppose?—there was a bond between us already that I could not possibly break; he was my son! Sir, the duty of a father—and I attach the very loftiest meaning to the word 'duty'—can never entail his giving up his son!"

A fresh murmur of sympathy through the court annoyed the judge, who shrugged his shoulders.

"Let us put aside empty rhetoric," he said. "You have plenty of fine phrases with which to defend your action; that, indeed, is your concern, as the jury will doubtless appreciate. But I think it will be more advantageous to clear up the facts a little—not more advantageous to you, perhaps, but that is what I am here to do. So will you please tell me whether your son confessed to having murdered Mme. de Langrune, either during that night when you persuaded him to run away, or afterward? Yes or no, please."

"I can't answer, sir. My son was mad! I will not believe my son was a criminal! There was absolutely no motive to prompt him to the deed, and his mother is in an asylum! That is the whole explanation of the crime! If he committed murder, it was in a fit of temporary insanity! He is dead; I refuse to cover his memory with the stain of infamy!"

"In other words, according to you Charles Rambert did confess, but you don't want to say so."

"I do not say he did confess."

"You leave it to be inferred."

Etienne Rambert made no reply, and the judge passed on to another point.

"What exactly did you do after you left the château?"

"What anyone does, I suppose, when he runs away. We wandered miserably about, going through the fields and woods, I accusing him and he defending himself. We avoided the villages, scarcely venturing out even in the early morning to go and buy food, and walked quickly, wishing to get as far away as possible. We spent the most awful time it is possible to imagine."

"How long was all this?"

"I was with my son for four days, sir."

"So it was on the fourth day that you killed him?"

"Have pity, sir! I did not kill my son. It was a murderer that I had with me, a murderer for whom the police were hunting and for whom the guillotine was waiting!"

"A murderer, if you prefer it so," said the judge, entirely ignoring the unhappy man's protests. "But you had no right to assume the function of executioner. You admit you did kill him?"

"I do not admit it."

"Do you deny that you killed him?"

"I did what my duty told me to do!"

"Still the same story!" said the judge, angrily drumming his fingers on the desk. "You refuse to answer. But even in your own interests you must have the courage to adopt some definite theory. Well, would you have been glad if your son had taken his own life?"

"I beg you to remember that my son is dead!" Etienne Rambert said once more. "I can only remember the one fact that he was my son. I can't say that I desired his death. I don't even know now if he was guilty. Whatever horror I may feel for a crime, I can only remember now that Charles was not in his right mind, and that he was my own son!"

Again a tremor of emotion passed through the court, and again the judge made an angry gesture ordering silence.

"So you decline to answer any of the principal points of the indictment? The jury will no doubt appreciate the reason. Well, can you let us know any of the advice you gave your son? If you did not desire him to take his own life, and if you had no intention of killing him, what did you want?"

"Oblivion," said Etienne Rambert, more calmly this time. "It was not for me to give my son up, and I could only desire for him oblivion, and if that was impossible, then death. I implored him to think of the life that was before him, and the future of shame, and I urged him to disappear forever."

"Ah, you admit you did recommend him to commit suicide?"

"I mean I wanted him to go abroad."

The president pretended to be occupied with his notes, purposely giving time for the importance of the last admission he had wrung from Etienne Rambert to sink into the minds of the jury. Then, without raising his head, he asked abruptly:

"You were very surprised to hear of his death?"

"No," said Rambert dully.

"How did you part from each other?"

"The last night we slept out of doors, under a haystack; we were both worn out and heartsick; I prayed to God for Him to have mercy on us. It was by the bank of the Dordogne. Next morning when I woke up I was alone. He—my son—had disappeared. I know no more."

The judge quelled the emotion in the court by a threatening glance and sprang a new question like a trap on the defendant, to catch him lying.

"If at that time you knew no more, how was it that a few days later you called on Inspector Juve and asked him at once what was known about the dead body of your son? The body had only been recovered within the previous hour or two and had not been absolutely identified; the newspapers, at any rate, only suggested the identity, with the utmost reserve. But you, sir, had no doubt about the subject! You knew that the corpse was your son's! Why? How?"

It was one of the strongest points that could be made in support of the theory that Etienne Rambert had murdered his son, and the defendant immediately saw the difficulty he would have in giving an adequate answer without compromising himself. He turned to the jury, as though he had more hope in them than in the court.

"Gentlemen," he cried, "this is torture! I can bear no more! I cannot answer any more. You know quite enough to form your judgment of me. Form it now! Say if I failed in my duty as a man of honor and a father! I at least can answer no more questions!" and he sank back in his place like a beaten man, crushed by the distress evoked by all these painful memories.

The judge nodded to the jury with the grim complacency of a man who has run down his game.

"This refusal to answer my questions is in itself tantamount to a confession," he said acidly. "Well, we will proceed to call the witnesses. I should like to say that the most interesting witness would undoubtedly be Bouzille, the tramp who recovered the body of Charles Rambert; but unfortunately that individual has no fixed abode and it has not been possible to serve him with a subpoena."

A number of witnesses succeeded one another in the witness box, without, however, throwing any new light on the matter; they were peasants who had met the two Ramberts when they were fleeing the château, village bakers who had sold them bread, and lock keepers who had seen, but been unable to recover, the floating corpse. The people in the court began to weary of the proceedings, the more so as it was confidently rumored that Etienne Rambert had proudly declined to call any witnesses on his behalf, and even to allow his counsel to make any rhetorical appeal to the jury. It might be foolhardy, but there was something admirable in his defiance.

There was, however, one more thrill of interest for the public. The judge had explained that he deemed it unnecessary to call the detective Juve, inasmuch as all the information he had to give was already detailed in the long indictment, but as Mme. de Langrune's granddaughter was present in court, he would exercise his discretion and request her to answer one or two questions. And, much taken aback by this unexpected attention, Thérèse Auvernois followed the usher to the witness box.

"Mademoiselle Thérèse Auvernois, I need hardly ask if you recognize M. Rambert, but do you identify him as the person

whose conversation with young Charles Rambert you overheard on that fatal night at the château of Beaulieu?"

"Yes, sir, that is M. Etienne Rambert," she replied quietly,
and with a long and tender look of pity at the defendant.

"Will you please tell us anything you know that has any
bearing on the charge brought against the defendant, the
charge of having killed his son?"

Thérèse made a visible effort to restrain her distress.

"I can only say one thing, sir: that M. Rambert was talking
to his son in tones of such terrible distress that I knew his heart
was broken by the tragedy. I have heard so much from my dear
grandmother about M. Etienne Rambert that I can only remember that she always declared him to be a man of the very highest principles, and I can only tell him here how dreadfully sorry
I am for him, and that everybody pities him as much as I do."

The judge had expected that Thérèse would be a witness hostile to the defendant. Instead anything she was going to say
would obviously be much to his advantage, so he cut her short.

"That is enough, Mademoiselle. Thank you," and while
Thérèse was going back to her seat, wiping away the tears that
came to her eyes despite her bravest efforts to maintain her self-
control in the presence of so many strangers, the judge announced that there were no other witnesses to be heard, and
called upon the public prosecutor to address the court.

That person rose at once and launched into a harangue that
was eloquent enough, no doubt, but introduced no new features into the case. He relied upon law rather than facts; rapidly recapitulated the defendant's contradictions and pitifully
weak arguments, if arguments they could be called; claimed
that the facts had been proved despite the defendant's steady refusal to answer questions; and insisted on the point that the defendant had no right whatever to take the law into his own
hands, and either kill his son or aid and abet his flight. He con-
cluded by asking for a verdict of guilty and a sentence of life
imprisonment.

Next followed counsel for the defendant, whose speech was
brevity itself. He declined to make any appeal *ad misericordiam*
but simply asked the jury to decide whether the defendant had

not acted as any high-principled father would when he discovered that his son had committed a crime during a fit of insanity. He asked only for an impartial decision on the facts, from men of high principle, and he sat down confident of having focused the issue on the proper point and secured the sympathy of the public.

The judges withdrew to their chambers, the jury retired to consider its verdict, and Etienne Rambert was accompanied out by two prison guards. Juve had not stirred during the whole trial, or displayed the least sign of approval or disapproval at any of the exchange. He sat now unobtrusively listening to the conversation that was taking place around him about the outcome of the case.

President Bonnet thought that Etienne Rambert had blundered in refusing to put up any defense; he had shown contempt of court, which was always unwise, and the court would show him no mercy. Dollon was of another opinion—according to him Etienne Rambert was a victim of fate, deserving pity and the court would be very lenient. Another man declared that Etienne Rambert had been between a rock and a hard place. However fondly he loved his son he could not but hope that he might commit suicide. If a friend committed an offense against the laws of honor, the only thing to do was to put a pistol into his hand, and so on. The only point on which all were unanimous was their sympathy with the defendant.

But a bell rang sharply; grave and impassive, the jury returned, the judges filed once more into their seats, Etienne Rambert was led back into court by the guards. In tense silence the foreman of the jury spoke:

"In the presence of God and of man, and upon my honor and my conscience I declare that the answer of the jury is 'no' to all the questions put, and that is the answer of them all."

It was acquittal!

There was no applause, but yet it seemed as if the words that set the defendant free had relieved every heart of an overwhelming dread. The air seemed easier to breathe, and there was no one there who didn't seem physically better and also happier for hearing a verdict that sanctioned the general pity they had felt for the poor defendant, a man of honor and a most unhappy father!

By its verdict the jury had implicitly applauded and commiserated with Etienne Rambert; but he still sat in the dock, broken and prostrated by terrible distress, sobbing unreservedly and making no effort to restrain his immeasurable grief.

PRINCESS SONIA'S BATH

Four months had passed since Etienne Rambert had been acquitted at the Cahors courthouse, and the world was beginning to forget the Beaulieu tragedy as it had already almost forgotten the mysterious murder of Lord Beltham. Juve alone did not allow his daily occupations to put the two cases out of his mind. True, he had ceased to make any direct inquiries and gave no outward signs that he still had any interest in those cases; but the detective knew very well that in both of them he was contending with no ordinary murderer and he was content to remain in the shadows, waiting and watching, seemingly inactive, waiting for some slip to betray the person or persons who had perpetrated two of the most puzzling murders that he had ever had to deal with.

It was the end of June, and Paris was beginning to empty out. But the spring had been late and cold that year, and although July was only a couple of days away, society lingered on in the capital; luxuriously appointed carriages still swept along the Champs Elysées as the audiences poured out of theaters and concert halls, and fashionably attired people still thronged the broad pavements and gathered before the brilliantly lighted cafés on the Rond-Point; even at that late hour the Champs Elysées was as animated as it was during the busiest hours of the day.

At the Royal Palace Hotel the entire staff still hurried about the vast entrance halls and the palatial public rooms on the ground floor; for it was the hour when the guests were returning from their evening's amusements, and the spacious vestibules of the immense hotel were crowded with men in evening dress, young fellows in dinner jackets, and women in low-cut gowns.

A young and fashionable woman got out of a perfectly appointed victoria, and M. Louis, the manager of the staff, came forward and bowed deeply, as he did only to clients of the very highest distinction. The lady responded with a gracious smile, and the manager called a servant: "The elevator for Madame la Princesse Sonia Danidoff," and the next moment this beautiful vision, who had created a sensation merely by passing through the hall, had disappeared within the elevator and was borne up to her apartments.

Princess Sonia was one of the most important clients that the Royal Palace Hotel possessed. She belonged to one of the greatest families in the world, being, by her marriage to Prince Danidoff, cousin to the emperor of Russia and, so, connected to many people of royal blood. Still barely thirty years of age, she was not pretty but remarkably lovely, with wonderful blue eyes that formed a strange and bewitching contrast to the heavy masses of black hair that framed her face. A woman of immense wealth, and sophistication, the princess spent six months of the year in Paris, where she was a well-known and much liked figure in the most exclusive circles; she was clever and cultivated, a first-rate musician, and her reputation was impeccable, although only very seldom was she accompanied by her husband, whose duties as grand chamberlain to the czar kept him almost continuously in Russia. When in Paris she occupied a suite of four rooms on the third floor of the Royal Palace Hotel, a suite identical in its layout and luxuriousness with that reserved for sovereigns who came there incognito.

The princess passed through her drawing room, a vast, round room with a superb view over the Arc de Triomphe, and went into her bedroom where she switched on the electric light.

"Nadine," she called, in her grave, melodious voice, and a young girl, almost a child, sprang from a low divan hidden in a corner. "Nadine, take off my cloak and unfasten my hair. Then you can leave; it is late, and I am tired."

The little maid obeyed, helped her mistress to put on a silk dressing gown, and loosened the masses of her hair. The princess passed a hand across her brow, as if to brush away a headache.

"Before you go, get a bath ready for me; I think that would relax me."

Ten minutes later Nadine crept back like a shadow and found the princess standing dreamily on the balcony, inhaling deep breaths of the pure night air. The child kissed the tips of her mistress's fingers. "Your bath is ready," she said, and then withdrew.

A few more minutes passed, and Princess Sonia, half undressed, was just going into her dressing room when suddenly she turned and went back to the middle of the bedroom which she had been on the point of leaving.

"Nadine," she called, "are you still there?" No answer came. "I must have been dreaming," the princess murmured, "but I thought I heard someone moving about."

Sonia Danidoff was not unusually nervous, but like most people who live mostly alone and in large hotels, she was in the habit of being careful, and wished to make sure that no uninvited person had gotten into her rooms. She made a rapid survey of her bedroom, glanced into the brilliantly lighted drawing room, and then moved to her bed and saw that the electric bell board, which enabled her to summon any of her own or the hotel's servants, was in perfect order. Then, satisfied, she went into her dressing room, quickly slipped off the rest of her clothes, and plunged into the perfumed water of her bath.

She thrilled with pleasure as her limbs, so tired after a long evening, relaxed in the warm water. On a table close to the bath she had placed a volume of old Muscovite folk tales, and she was glancing through these by the shaded light from a lamp above her when a fresh sound made her start. She sat up quickly in the water and looked around her. There was nothing there. Then a little shiver shook her and she sank down again in the warm bath with a laugh at her own nervousness. And she was just beginning to read once more when suddenly a strange voice, with an unmistakable ring of malice in it, sounded in her ear. Someone was looking over her shoulder and reading aloud the words she had just begun!

Before Sonia Danidoff had time to utter a cry or make a movement, a strong hand was over her lips, and another gripped her wrist, preventing her from reaching the button of the electric bell that was fixed among the taps. The princess almost fainted. She was expecting some horrible shock, expecting to feel some weapon that would take her life, when the pressure on her mouth and the grip on her wrist gradually relaxed; and at the same moment the mysterious individual who had taken her by surprise moved around the bathtub and stood in front of her.

He was a man of about forty years of age, and extremely well dressed. A perfectly cut dinner jacket proved that the strange visitor was no lowly dweller of the Paris slums; no thug such as the princess had read terrifying descriptions of in luridly illustrated newspapers. The hands that had held her motionless, and which now restored to her liberty of movement, were white and well manicured and adorned with a few plain rings. The man's face was a distinguished one, and he wore a very fine black beard; slight baldness added to the height of a naturally large forehead. But what struck the princess most, although she had no heart to observe the man very carefully, was the abnormal size of his head and the number of wrinkles that ran right across his temples, following the line of the eyebrows.

In silence and with trembling lips Sonia Danidoff made an instinctive effort again to reach the electric bell, but with a quick movement the man caught her shoulder and prevented her from doing so. There was a cryptic smile on the stranger's lips, and with a furious blush Sonia Danidoff dived back again into the milky water in the bath.

The man stood in perfect silence, and at length the princess mastered her terror and spoke to him.

"Who are you? What do you want? Go at once or I will call for help."

"Above all things, do not call out, or you are a dead woman!" said the stranger harshly. Then he gave a little ironical shrug of his shoulders. "As for ringing—that would not be easy; you would have to leave the water to do so! And, besides, I would object."

"If it is money or jewelry you want," said the princess between clenched teeth, "take them! But please go!"

The princess had laid several rings and bracelets on the table by her side, and the man glanced at them now, but without paying much attention to what the princess said.

"Those trinkets are not bad," he said, "but your signet ring is much finer," and he calmly took the princess's hand in his and examined the ring that she had kept on her third finger. "Don't be frightened," he added as he felt her hand trembling. "Let us chat, if you don't mind! There is nothing especially tempting about jewels apart from their personality," he said after a little pause, "apart, I mean, from the person who habitually wears them. But the bracelet on a wrist, or the necklace round a neck, or the ring upon a finger is another matter!"

Princess Sonia was as pale as death and utterly at a loss to understand what this extraordinary visitor was driving at. She held up her ring finger and made a frightened little apology.

"I cannot take this ring off; it fits too tightly."

The man laughed grimly.

"That does not matter in the least, Princess. Anyone who wanted to get a ring like that could do it quite simply." He felt absent-mindedly in his waistcoat pocket and produced a miniature razor, which he opened. He flashed the blade before the terrified eyes of the princess. "With a sharp blade like this a skillful man could cut off the finger that carried such a splendid jewel in a couple of seconds," and then, seeing that the princess, in fresh panic, was on the very point of screaming, quick as a flash he laid the palm of his hand over her lips, while still speaking in gentle tones to her. "Please do not be so terrified; I suppose you take me for some common hotel thief, but, Princess, can you really believe that I am anything of the kind?"

The man's tone was so earnest, and there was so deferential a look in his eyes, that the princess recovered some of her courage.

"But I do not know who you are," she said half questioningly.

"So much the better," the man replied; "there is still time to make one another's acquaintance. I know who you are, and that is the main thing. You do not know me, Princess? Well, I assure you that on many occasions I have mingled with the blessed company of your adorers!"

The princess's anger rose steadily with her courage.

"Sir," she said, "I do not know if you are joking or if you are talking seriously, but your behavior is extraordinary, hateful, disgusting—"

"It is merely original, Princess, and it pleases me to reflect that if I had wanted to be presented to you in the ordinary way, in one of the many drawing rooms we both frequent, you would certainly have taken much less notice of me than you have taken tonight; from the persistence of your gaze I can see that from this day onward not a single feature of my face will be unfamiliar to you, and I am convinced that, whatever happens, you will remember it for a very long time."

Princess Sonia tried to force a smile. She had recovered her self-possession and was wondering what kind of man she had to deal with. If she was still not quite persuaded that this was not a vulgar thief, and if she had little faith in his professions of admiration for herself, she was considerably alarmed by the idea that she was alone with a lunatic. The man seemed to read her thoughts for he, too, smiled a little.

"I am glad to see, Princess, that you have a little more self-confidence now; we shall be able to arrange things much more easily. You are certainly much calmer, much less uneasy now. Oh, yes, you are!" he added, checking her protest. "Why, it is quite five minutes since you last tried to ring for help. We are getting on. Besides, I somehow can't picture the Princess Sonia Danidoff, wife of the grand chamberlain and cousin of His Majesty the emperor of all the Russias, allowing herself to be surprised alone with a man whom she did not know. If she were to ring, and someone came, how would the princess account for the gentleman to whom she had accorded an audience in the most delightful but certainly the most private of all her apartments?"

"But tell me," pleaded the poor woman, "how did you get in here?"

"That is not the question," the stranger replied. "The problem actually before us is, how am I to get out? For, of course, Princess, I shall not be so indelicate as to prolong my visit unduly. I hope only that you will permit me to repeat it on some other evening soon." He turned his head, and plunging his hand into the bath in the most natural manner possible, took out the thermometer which was floating on the perfumed water. "Thirty degrees centigrade, Princess! Your bath is getting cold; you must get out!"

In her blank astonishment Princess Sonia did not know whether to laugh or cry. Was she alone with a monster who, after having played with her as a cat plays with a mouse, would suddenly turn on her and kill her? Or was this merely some harmless lunatic? Whatever the case might be, the man's last words had made her aware that her bath really was getting cold. A shiver shook her whole frame, and yet—

"Oh, go, please go!" she implored him.

He shook his head, an ironical smile in his eyes.

"For pity's sake," she entreated him again, "have mercy on a helpless woman!"

The man appeared to be considering.

"It is very embarrassing," he murmured, "and yet we must decide on something soon, for I am most anxious you should not take a chill. Oh, it is very simple, Princess; of course you know the arrangement of everything here so well that you could find your dressing gown at once, by merely feeling your way? We will put out the light, and then you will be able to get out of the bath in the dark without the least fear." He was on the very point of turning off the switch of the lamp when he stopped abruptly and came back to the bath. "I was forgetting that exasperating bell," he said. "A movement is so very easily made; suppose you were to ring inadvertently, and regret it afterward?" Putting his idea into action, the man made a quick cut with his razor and severed the two electric wires several feet above the ground. "That is perfect," he said. "By the way, I don't know where these other two wires go that run along the wall, but it is best to be on the safe side. Suppose there were another bell." He lifted his razor once more and was trying to sever the electric wires when the steel blade cut the insulator and an alarming flash of light resulted. The man leaped into the air and dropped his razor. "Good Lord!" he growled. "I suppose that will make you happy, Madame; I have burned my hand most horribly! These must be wires for the light! But no matter;

I have still got one good hand, and that will be enough for me to secure the darkness that you desire. And anyhow, you can press the button of your bell as much as you like; it won't ring. So I am sure of a few more minutes in your company."

Sudden darkness fell upon the room. Sonia Danidoff hesitated for a moment and then half rose in the bath. All her pride as a great lady was in revolt. If she must defend her honor and her life, she was ready to do so, and desperation would give her strength; but in any event she would be better out of the water and on her feet, prepared. The darkness was complete, both in the bathroom and in the adjacent bedroom, and the silence was absolute. Standing up in the bath, Sonia Danidoff swept her arms around in a circle to feel for any obstacle. Her touch met nothing. She drew out one foot, and then the other, sprang toward the chair on which she had left her dressing gown, slipped into it with feverish haste, slid her feet into her slippers, stood motionless for just a second, and then, with sudden decisiveness, moved to the switch by the door and turned on the light.

The man had gone from the bathroom, but taking two steps toward her bedroom Sonia Danidoff saw him smiling at her from the far end of that room.

"Sir," she said, "this—pleasant visit—has lasted long enough. You must go. You must!"

"Must?" the stranger echoed. "That is a word that is not often said to me. But you are forgiven for not knowing that, Princess. I forgot for the moment that I have not been formally introduced to you. But what is on your mind now?"

Between them was a little writing desk, on the top of which was lying the tiny inlaid revolver that Sonia Danidoff always carried when she went out at night. If she could get to it, it would be a potent argument to induce this stranger to obey her. The princess also knew that in the drawer of that desk which she could actually see half open, she had placed, only a few minutes before going in to her bath, a pocketbook filled with bank notes for 120,000 francs, money she had withdrawn from the strongbox of the hotel that very morning in order to meet some bills next day. She looked at the drawer and wondered if the pocketbook were still there, or if this mysterious admirer of

hers was only a vulgar hotel thief after all. The man had followed her eyes to the revolver.

"That is an unusual knickknack to find in a lady's room,
Princess," and he sprang in front of her as she was taking a step
toward the desk, and grabbed the revolver. "Do not be alarmed,"
he added, noticing her little gesture of terror. "I would not do
you an injury for anything in the world. I shall be delighted to
give this back to you in a minute, but first let me render it harmless." He deftly slipped the six cartridges out of the barrel and
then handed the now useless weapon to the princess with a gallant little bow. "Do not laugh at my extreme caution; accidents
happen so easily!"

It was in vain that the princess tried to get near her writing
desk to ascertain if the drawer had been tampered with; the
man stayed between her and it all the time, still smiling, still po-
lite, but watching every movement she made. Suddenly he took
his watch from his pocket.

"Two o'clock! Already! Princess, you will be annoyed with me
for having imposed upon your hospitality to such an extent, I
must go!" He appeared not to notice the sigh of relief that broke
from her but went on in a melodramatic tone, "I shall take my
departure, not through the window like a lover, nor up the chimney like a thief, nor yet through a secret door behind the tapestry
like a bandit in romantic tales, but like a gentleman who has
come to pay his tribute of homage and respect to the most enchanting woman in the world—through the door!" He made a
movement as if to go, and came back. "And what are you thinking of doing now, Princess? Perhaps you will be angry with me?
Possibly some unpleasant discovery, made after my departure,
will inspire your animosity against me? You might even ring as
soon as my back is turned and alarm the staff, merely to embar-
rass me in my exit and without paying any attention to the possible subsequent scandal. That is a complex arrangement of bells
and telephones beside your bed! It would be a pity to spoil such a
pretty thing, and besides, I hate doing unnecessary damage!" The
princess's eyes turned once more to the drawer; it was practically
certain that her money was not there now! But the man again interrupted her thoughts. "What can I be thinking of? Just imagine

my not having presented myself to you even yet! But as a matter of fact I do not want to tell you my name out loud; it is a romantic one, utterly inappropriate to the typically modern environment in which we now stand. Ah, if we were only on the steep side of some mountain with the moon like a great lamp above us, or by the shore of some wild ocean, there would be some glamour in proclaiming my identity in the silence of the night, or in the midst of lightning and thunder as a hurricane swept the seas! But here—in a third-floor suite of the Royal Palace Hotel, surrounded by telephones and electric lights, and standing by a window overlooking the Champs Elysées—it would be positively anachronistic!" He took a card out of his pocket and drew near the little writing desk. "Allow me, Princess, to slip my card into this drawer, left open on purpose, it would seem," and while the princess uttered a little cry she could not repress, he did just that. "And now, Princess," he went on, compelling her to retreat before him as he moved to the door of the anteroom opening on to the corridor, "you are too well bred, I am sure, not to wish to conduct your visitor to the door of your suite." His tone altered abruptly, and in a deep imperious voice that made the princess quake he ordered her: "And now, not a word, not a cry, not a movement until I am outside, or I will kill you!"

Clenching her fists and summoning all her strength to prevent herself from swooning, Sonia Danidoff led the man to the anteroom door. Slowly she unlocked the door and held it open, and the man stepped quietly out. The next second he was gone!

Leaping back into her bedroom Sonia Danidoff set off every bell ringing; with great presence of mind she telephoned down to the hall porter: "Don't let anybody go out! I have been robbed!" and she pressed hard on the special button that set the great alarm bell clanging. Footsteps and voices resounded in the corridor; the princess knew that help was coming and ran to open her door. The night watchman and the manager of the third floor came running up and bellboys appeared at the end of the corridor.

"Stop him! Stop him!" the princess shouted. "He has only just gone out; a man in a dinner jacket with a black beard!"

———

A lad came hurrying out of the elevator.

"Where are you going? What is the matter?" inquired the hall porter, whose office was at the far end of the hall, next to the courtyard of the hotel, the door into which he had just closed.

"I don't know," he answered. "There is a thief in the hotel! They are calling from the other side."

"It's not in your area, then? By the way, what floor are you on?"

"The second."

"All right," said the hall porter, "it's the third floor that they are calling from. Go up and see what is wrong."

The lad turned on his heel, and disregarding the sign forbidding staff to use the guest elevator, hurried back into it and upstairs again. He was a solidly built fellow, with a smooth face and red hair. On the third floor he stopped immediately opposite Sonia Danidoff's suite. The princess was standing at her door, taking no notice of the watchman Muller's efforts to calm her, and mechanically twisting between her fingers the blank visiting card that her strange visitor had left in place of her pocketbook and the 120,000 francs. There was no name whatever on the card.

"Well," said Muller, to the redheaded lad, "where do you come from?"

"I'm the new man on the second floor," the fellow answered. "The hall porter sent me up to find out what was going on."

"Going on!" said Muller. "Somebody has robbed the princess. Here, send someone for the police at once."

"I'll run sir," and as the elevator, instead of being sent down, had carelessly been sent up to the top floor, the young fellow ran down the staircase at full speed.

Through the telephone, Muller was just ordering the hall porter to send for the police when the second-floor servant rushed up and caught him by the arm, dragging him away from it.

"Open the door, for the Lord's sake! I'm off to the police station," and the hall porter made haste to facilitate his departure.

Through the top floor echoed more cries of astonishment. The servants had been alarmed by the uproar and, surprised to see the elevator stop and nobody get out of it, they opened the door and found a heap of clothing, a false beard, and a wig. Two housemaids and a valet gazed in amazement at these extraordinary things and never thought of informing the manager, M. Louis. Meantime, however, that gentleman had hurried through the mazelike service passages of the hotel and had just reached the third floor when he was stopped by the Baronne Van den Rosen, one of the hotel's oldest clients.

"M. Louis!" she exclaimed, bursting into sobs. "I have just been robbed of my diamond necklace. I left it in a jewel case on my table before going down to dinner. When I heard the noise just now, I got up and looked through my jewel case, and the necklace is not there."

M. Louis was too dazed to reply. Muller ran up to him.

"Princess Sonia Danidoff's pocketbook has been stolen," he announced, "but I have had the hotel doors locked and we shall be sure to catch the thief."

The princess came up to explain matters, but at that moment the servants came down from upstairs, bringing with them the articles of disguise that they had found in the elevator. They laid these on the ground without a word, and M. Louis was staring at them when Muller had a sudden inspiration.

"M. Louis, what is the new man on the second floor like?"

Just at that instant a servant appeared at the end of the corridor, a middle-aged man with white whiskers and a bald head.

"There he is, coming toward us," M. Louis replied. "His name is Arnold."

"Good God!" cried Muller. "And the redheaded fellow?" M. Louis shook his head, not understanding, and Muller tore himself away and rushed down to the hall porter. "Has he gone out? Has anyone gone out?"

"No one," said the porter, "except, of course, the servant from the second floor, whom you sent for the police."

"The redheaded fellow?" Muller inquired.

"Yes, that's the one."

Princess Sonia Danidoff lay back in an armchair, receiving

the anxious attentions of Nadine, her Circassian maid. M. Louis was holding salts to her nose. The princess still held the card left by the mysterious stranger who had just robbed her so cleverly of 120,000 francs. As she slowly came to, the princess, fascinated, gazed at the card, and this time her haggard eyes grew wide with astonishment. For upon the card, which until now had appeared immaculately white, letters were gradually becoming visible, and the princess read:

"Fan—tô—mas!"

MAGISTRATE
AND DETECTIVE

M. Fuselier was standing in his office in the courthouse in Paris, meditatively smoothing the nap of his silk hat. His mind was busy with the cases he had been prosecuting during the day, and although he had no reason to be dissatisfied with his day's work he had no clear idea as to what his next steps ought to be.

Three discreet taps on the door interrupted his thoughts.

"Come in," he said, then stepped forward with a hearty welcome as he recognized his visitor. "Juve, by God! What good luck has brought you here? I haven't seen you for ages. Have you been busy?"

"Terribly."

"Well, it's a fact that there's no shortage of sensational crime just now. The calendar is terribly full."

Juve had ensconced himself in a huge easy chair in a corner of the room.

"Yes," he said, "it's true. But unfortunately the calendar won't be a brilliant one for the police. There may be lots of cases, but there are not lots that they have properly solved."

"You've got nothing to complain about," M. Fuselier smiled. "You have been in enough cases lately that were solved. Your reputation isn't in any danger."

"I don't know what you mean," Juve said deprecatingly. "If you're referring to the Beltham and Langrune cases, you must admit that your congratulations are not in order. I have not achieved satisfactory results in either of those cases."

M. Fuselier also dropped into a comfortable chair. He lit a cigarette.

"You have come up with nothing new on the mysterious murder of Lord Beltham?"

"Nothing. I'm beaten. It is an unsolvable mystery to me."

"You seem to feel very sorry for yourself, but really you needn't, Juve. You cleared up the Beltham case, and you solved the Langrune case, although you try to pretend you didn't. And allow me to inform you, those two successes count, my friend."

"You are very kind, but you are rather misinformed. Unfortunately I have not cleared up the Beltham case at all."

"You found the missing peer."

"Well, yes, but—"

"That was an amazing achievement. By the way, Juve, what made you go to the rue Lévert to search Gurn's trunks?"

"That was very simple. You remember the excitement there was when Lord Beltham disappeared? Well, when I was put on the case I saw immediately that all ideas of accident or suicide might be dismissed, and that consequently the disappearance involved some sort of crime. Convinced of that, I naturally suspected every single person who had ever dealt with Lord Beltham, for there was no single individual for me to suspect. Then I found out that the ex-ambassador had been in continuous contact with an Englishman named Gurn whom he had known in the South African war, and who led a very strange sort of life. That of course took me to Gurn's place, if for nothing else than to pick up information. And—well, that's about it. It was just by going to Gurn's place to question him, rather than anything else, that I found the noble lord's remains locked away in the trunk."

"Your modesty is delightful, Juve," said M. Fuselier with an approving nod. "You present things as if they were all matters of course, whereas really you are only further proving your extraordinary instinct. If you had arrived twenty-four hours later the corpse would have been packed off to the Transvaal, and only the Lord knows then if that extraordinary mystery would have ever been cleared up."

"Luck," Juve protested, "pure luck!"

"And were your other remarkable discoveries luck too?" inquired M. Fuselier with a smile. "Your discovery that sulphate of zinc had been injected into the body to prevent it from smelling."

"That was only a matter of using my eyes," Juve protested.

"All right," said the magistrate, "we will admit you did not display any remarkable skill in the Beltham case, if you would rather have it that way. That does not change the fact that you solved the Langrune case."

"Solved it!"

M. Fuselier flicked the ash off his cigarette and leaned forward toward the detective.

"Of course I know you were at the Cahors trial, Juve. What was your impression of the whole case—of the verdict, and of Etienne Rambert's guilt or innocence?"

Juve got up and began to walk up and down the room, followed by the magistrate's eyes. He seemed to be hesitating as to whether he would answer at all, but finally he stopped abruptly and faced his friend.

"If I were talking to anybody but you, M. Fuselier, I would either not answer at all, or I would give an answer that was no answer! But as it is—well, in my opinion, the Langrune case is only just beginning, and nothing about it is known at all for certain."

"You mean to say you think that Charles Rambert is innocent?"

"I didn't say that."

"What are you saying then? I don't suppose you think the father was the murderer?"

"The hypothesis is not absurd! But there you are! What is the real truth of the whole affair? That is what I wonder all the time. That murder is never out of my mind; it interests me more and more every day. Oh, yes, I've got lots of ideas, but they are all totally vague and improbable; sometimes my imagination seems to be running away with me."

He stopped, and M. Fuselier wagged a teasing finger at him.

"Juve," he said, "I charge you formally with attempting to implicate Fantômas in the murder of the Marquise de Langrune!"

The detective replied in the same joking tone.

"Guilty, my lord!"

"Good Lord!" the magistrate exclaimed. "Fantômas is a perfect obsession with you," and as Juve acquiesced with a laugh the magistrate dropped his bantering tone. "Shall I tell you something, Juve? I too am beginning to have an obsession for that fantastic misfit! And what I want to know is why you haven't come to me before to ask me about that sensational robbery at the Royal Palace Hotel!"

"The robbery of Princess Sonia Danidoff?"

"Yes, the Fantômas robbery!"

"Fantômas, eh?" Juve protested. "That remains to be seen."

"Why," M. Fuselier retorted, "you have heard about the card the man left, haven't you? The visiting card that was blank when the princess found it, and on which the name of Fantômas afterward became visible?"

"There's no Fantômas about that, in my opinion."

"Why not?"

"Well, it isn't one of Fantômas's habits to leave clear traces behind him. One might as well picture him committing robbery or murder wearing a cap with a neat little band round it: 'Fantômas and Company.' He might even add 'Discretion Assured!' No, it's most unlikely."

"You don't think Fantômas capable of tantalizing the police with some such material proof of his identity?"

"I always base my arguments on probabilities," Juve replied. "What emerges from this Royal Palace story is that some common hotel thief conceived the ingenious idea of casting suspicion on Fantômas; it was just a trick to mislead the police; at least, that is my opinion."

But M. Fuselier declined to be convinced.

"No, you are wrong, Juve; it was no common hotel thief who stole Madame Van den Rosen's necklace and Princess Sonia's hundred and twenty thousand francs. The loot was big enough to appeal to Fantômas, and the amazing audacity of the crime is indicative too. Just think what presence of mind the man must have had to be able to paralyze the princess's power of resistance when she tried to call for help; and also to get away in spite of the numbers of servants in the hotel and all the precautions taken!"

"Tell me all about the robbery, M. Fuselier," said Juve.

The magistrate sat down at his desk and took up the notes he had made in the course of his official inquiry that day. He told Juve everything he had been able to find out.

"The most amazing thing to me," he said in conclusion, "is the way the fellow, once he got out of Princess Sonia's room, managed to shed his evening clothes, get into uniform, and make his first attempt to escape. When the hall porter stopped him he did not lose his head but got into the elevator again, sent that flying up to the top of the hotel with the clothes that would have given him away, calmly introduced himself to Muller, the night watchman, and managed to be told to go for the police, ran down the stairs again, and took advantage of the night watchman's telephoning to the hall porter to get the latter to open the door for him, and so walked away without a hitch. A man who kept his nerve like that and could make such amazing use of every circumstance, who was so quick and daring, and who was capable of carrying through such an intricate farce in the middle of the general uproar, richly deserves to be taken for Fantômas!"

Juve sat in deep consideration of the whole story.

"That isn't what interests me most," he said at last. "His escape from the hotel might have been accomplished by any clever thief. What I think more remarkable is the means he took to prevent the princess from screaming when he was just leaving her rooms; that really was masterly. Instead of trying to get her as far away as possible and shut her up in her bedroom, he took her with him to the front door itself, opening on to the corridor, where the faintest cry might have involved the worst possible consequences. To be so sure that the terror he had inspired would prevent her from uttering that cry, to be able to assume that the victim was so hysterical that she would make no effort at all and could do nothing—that is really very good indeed; quite admirable."

"So you see there are some unusual features in the case," said M. Fuselier complacently. "This, for instance: Why do you suppose the fellow stayed for so long with the princess and went through all that silly business in the bathroom? Don't forget that she came in late, and he probably could have finished the job before she returned."

Juve passed his hand through his hair, a characteristic gesture when his mind was working.

"I can imagine only one answer to that question, M. Fuselier. But you have inspected the scene of the crime. Tell me first, where do you think the rascal was hidden?"

"Oh, I can answer that definitely. The princess's suite of rooms ends in the bathroom, you know, and the chief things there are the bathtub, some cupboards, and a shower bath; the shower is one of those large models with lateral as well as vertical sprays, and a waterproof curtain hanging from rings at the top down to the tub at the bottom. There were footprints on the enamel of the tub, so it is clear that the thief hid there, behind the curtain, until the princess got into her bath."

"And I suppose the shower is in the corner of the room near the window?" Juve went on. "And the window was partly open, or had been until the maid went in to prepare her mistress's bath? It's quite interesting! The man had just succeeded in stealing the necklace from Madame Van den Rosen, whose rooms are next to Princess Sonia's. For some reason or other he had not been able to escape through the corridor, and so he naturally made up his mind to go into the princess's suite, which he did by the simple act of stepping over the railing on the balcony and walking in through the open window of the dressing room."

"And then Nadine came in, and he had to hide?"

"No, no!" said Juve. "You are going too fast. If that had been so, there would have been no need for all the bath business; besides, the princess was robbed, too, you know. That was not just chance, it was planned; and so if the thief hid in the shower he did so on purpose to wait for the princess."

"But he did not want *her*!" Fuselier retorted. "Very much the opposite. If he was in the room before anybody else, all he had to do was take the pocketbook and go!"

"Not at all!" said Juve. "This robbery took place at the end of the month, when the princess would have her monthly bills to meet, as the thief must have known. He must have found out that she had withdrawn money from the strongbox of the hotel. But he must have been ignorant of where she had put the money; and he waited to ask her—and she told him!"

"That's a pretty tall talc!" M. Fuselier protested. "What on earth is it based on? The princess would never have shown the man the drawer where the money was!"

"Yes, she did!" said Juve. "Look here, this is what happened. The fellow wanted to steal this pocketbook and did not know where it was. He hid in the shower and waited, either for the princess to go to bed or take a bath, either of which would place her at his mercy. When the lady was in the bath he appeared, threatened her until she was terrified, and then calmed her down a bit again and hit on the trick of putting out the electric light—not out of respect for her wounded pride, but simply in order to get a chance to search through her clothes and make sure that the money was not there. I am convinced that if he had found it then he would have bolted at once. But he didn't find it. So he went to the end of the next room and waited for the princess to come to him there, which is precisely what she did. He did not know where the money was, so he watched every movement of her eyes and saw them go automatically toward the drawer and stay there; then he slipped his card into the drawer, extracted the pocketbook, and took his leave, being so confident as to make her see him to the door!"

"My God, Juve, you are a wonder," M. Fuselier said admiringly. "I've spent the entire day cross-examining everybody in the hotel and came to no definite conclusion; and you, who have not seen anything or anybody connected with it, sit in that chair and in five minutes clear up the entire mystery. What a pity you won't believe that Fantômas had a finger in this! What a pity you won't take up the case!"

Juve ignored the compliments and took out his watch and looked at the time.

"I must go," he said; "it's time I did my own work. Well, we may not have been wasting our time, M. Fuselier. I admit I had not paid much attention to the Royal Palace Hotel robbery. You have really interested me in it. I won't make any promises, but I think I shall very likely come again in a day or two for another talk with you about the case. It really interests me now. And once I'm finished with one or two pressing jobs, I might ask your permission to really go into it with you."

A KNOCKOUT BLOW

The staff members of the Royal Palace Hotel were just finishing their dinner, and the greatest animation prevailed in the vast white-tiled servants' hall. The tone of the conversation varied at different tables, for the servants jealously observed a strict hierarchy among themselves, but the topic was the same all over: the recent sensational robbery from Mme. Van den Rosen and the Princess Sonia Danidoff. At one table, smaller than the rest, a party of higher-ranking servants sat: M. Louis was here, the general manager; M. Muller, the superintendent of the second floor; M. Ludovic, chief valet; M. Maurice, head footman; M. Naud, chief cashier; and last but not least Mlle. Jeanne, the young lady cashier whose special duty it was to take charge of all the money and valuables deposited in the custody of the hotel by guests who wished to relieve themselves of the responsibility of keeping these in their own rooms. This small and select company was increased tonight by the addition of M. Henri Verbier, a man of about forty years of age, who had left the branch hotel at Cairo belonging to the same company to join the staff at the Royal Palace Hotel in Paris.

"I am afraid, M. Verbier, you must have a very bad opinion of our establishment," said M. Muller to him. "It is really a pity that you should have left the Cairo branch and come here just when these robberies have given us a bad name."

Henri Verbier smiled.

"You need not be afraid of my attaching too much importance to that," he said. "I've been in hotel life for fifteen years now, in one capacity or another, and, as you may suppose, I've known similar cases before, so they don't surprise me much.

But one thing does surprise me, M. Muller, and that is that no clues have been found yet. I suppose the board has done everything possible to trace the culprit? The reputation of the hotel is at stake."

"You can bet they have looked for him!" said M. Louis, with a pathetic shrug of his shoulders. "Why, they even chewed me out for having let the door be opened for the thief! Luckily I had a good friend in Muller, who admitted that he had been completely tricked and that he had given the order for the fellow, whom he supposed to be the second-floor waiter, to be allowed out. I knew nothing about it."

"And how was I to guess that the man was an impostor?" Muller protested.

"All the same," Henri Verbier retorted, "it is uncommonly annoying for everybody when things like that happen."

"So long as one has not broken any orders, and so can't be made a scapegoat, one shouldn't grumble," M. Muller said. "Louis and I did exactly what we should have, and no one can say anything against us. The magistrate acknowledged that a week ago."

"He does not suspect anybody?" Henri Verbier asked.

"No, nobody," Muller answered.

M. Louis smiled.

"Yes, he did suspect somebody, Verbier," he said, "and that was your charming neighbor Mademoiselle Jeanne there."

Verbier turned toward the young cashier.

"What? The magistrate tried to make out that you were implicated in it?"

The girl had only spoken a few words during the whole dinner, although Henri Verbier had made several gallant attempts to draw her into the general conversation. Now she laughingly protested.

"M. Louis only says that to tease me."

But M. Louis stuck to his guns.

"Not a bit, Mademoiselle Jeanne. I said it because it is the truth. The magistrate was after you: I tell you he was! Why, M. Verbier, he cross-examined her for more than half an hour after the general staff interview, while he finished with Muller and me in less than ten minutes."

"God, M. Louis, a magistrate is a man, isn't he?" said Henri Verbier gallantly. "The magistrate may have enjoyed talking to Mademoiselle Jeanne more than he did to you, if I may suggest it without being rude."

There was general laughter at this on the part of the new superintendent, and then M. Louis continued:

"Well, if he wanted to flirt with her he has a funny way of doing it, for he only made her angry."

"Did he really?" said Henri Verbier, turning again to the girl. "Why did the magistrate cross-examine you so much?"

The young cashier shrugged her shoulders.

"We have been over it so often, M. Verbier! But I will tell you the whole story. The morning of the day when the robbery was committed I returned to Princess Sonia Danidoff the pocketbook containing a hundred and twenty thousand francs which she had put into my custody a few days before; I could not refuse to give it to her when she asked for it, could I? How was I to know that it would be stolen from her the same evening? Customers deposit their valuables with me and I hand them a receipt. They give me back the receipt when they want their valuables back. And all I do is comply with their request, without asking questions. Isn't that so?"

"But that was not what puzzled the magistrate, I suppose," said Henri Verbier. "If you only complied strictly with your orders."

"Yes," M. Muller broke in, "but Mademoiselle Jeanne has only told you part of the story. Listen to this. Only a few minutes before the robbery Madame Van den Rosen had asked Mademoiselle Jeanne to take charge of her diamond necklace, and Mademoiselle Jeanne had refused!"

"That really was bad luck for you," said Henri Verbier to the girl with a laugh, "and I quite understand why the magistrate thought it was rather odd."

"From the way they put it, M. Verbier," she protested, "you might think that I refused to take charge of Madame Van den

Rosen's jewelry in order to make things easy for the thief, which is as much as to say that I was his accomplice."

"That is precisely what the magistrate did think," M. Louis interpolated.

The girl took no notice of the interruption but went on with her explanation to Henri Verbier.

"What happened was this. The rule is that I am at the disposal of customers, to take charge of deposits or to return them to the owners, until nine P.M., and until nine P.M. only. After that, I am free to lock my safe and go. I come back at nine o'clock the next morning. You know that it does not do to make exceptions in a position like mine. So when Madame Van den Rosen came with her diamond necklace at half past nine, I was perfectly within my rights in refusing to accept the deposit."

"That's right," said M. Muller, who, having finished his dessert, was now sipping coffee into which he had put so much sugar that it was as thick as syrup. "But you were rather uncooperative, my dear young lady, and that was what struck the magistrate; it really would not have been much trouble to register the new deposit and take charge of Madame Van den Rosen's necklace for her."

"No, it wouldn't," the girl replied, "but when there is a rule it seems to me that it ought to be obeyed. My shift is over at nine o'clock, and I am not supposed to accept any deposits after nine o'clock, and that's why I refused. I was perfectly right; and I should do the same again, if the same thing happened."

Henri Verbier was manifestly anxious to conciliate the young cashier. He expressed his approval of her conduct now.

"I quite agree with you, it never does to interpret orders freely. It was your duty to close your safe at nine o'clock, and you did it, and no one can say anything against you. But, joking apart, what did the magistrate want?"

The girl shrugged her shoulders in a gesture of indifference.

"You see, I was right: M. Louis is only trying to tease me by saying that the magistrate cross-examined me harshly. As a matter of fact, I was simply asked what I just told you, and when I gave this explanation, no more questions were asked." As she spoke, Mlle. Jeanne folded her napkin carefully, pushed back her chair, and shook hands with her two neighbors at the table. "Good night," she said. "I am going up to bed."

Mlle. Jeanne had hardly left the room when Henri Verbier also rose from the table and prepared to do the same.

M. Louis gave M. Muller a friendly poke in his comfortable paunch.

"I'll bet you anything," he said, "that our friend Verbier means to make a pass at Mademoiselle Jeanne. Well, I wish him luck! But that young lady is not a very easy catch!"

"You didn't succeed," M. Muller replied unkindly, "but it doesn't follow that nobody else will!"

M. Louis was right. Henri Verbier evidently did find his neighbor at the dinner table a very charming young woman.

Mlle. Jeanne had hardly reached her room on the fifth floor of the hotel, and flung open her window to gaze over the magnificent panorama spread out below her and inhale the still night air, when she heard a gentle tap at the door and called to come in. Henri Verbier entered the room.

"My room is next to yours," he said, "and as I saw you standing at your window I thought perhaps you might like to smoke an Egyptian cigarette. I brought some back from Cairo; it is very mild tobacco—real ladies' tobacco."

The girl laughed and took a dainty cigarette from the case that Henri Verbier offered her.

"It's very kind of you," she said. "I don't make a habit of smoking, but I occasionally let myself be tempted."

"I'd be just grateful," Henri Verbier replied, "if you'd allow me to stay here a few minutes and smoke a cigarette with you."

"By all means," said Mlle. Jeanne. "I love to get a little air before going to bed. You will prevent me from getting bored with my own company. Please tell me all about Cairo."

"I'm afraid I know very little about Cairo," Henri Verbier replied; "you see, I spent almost all my time in the hotel. But as you seem so kind and so friendly I wish you would tell me a few things."

"But I hardly know anything."

"I am a newcomer here and am quite aware that my arrival,

and my position, will make me some enemies. Now, whom ought I to be on my guard against? Who is there, among the staff, I should watch out for? I ask all the more because I will tell you frankly that I had no personal introduction to the board. I have not got the same advantage that you have."

"How do you know I had any introduction?" the girl inquired.

"God, I'm sure of it," Henri Verbier answered; he was leaning his elbows on the windowsill and gradually drawing closer to the young cashier. "I don't suppose that an important position like the one you hold, requiring absolute integrity and competence, is given without a full investigation."

"You are quite right, M. Verbier. I did have an introduction to the board, and I had first-rate testimonials too."

"Have you been working long? Two years—three years?"

"Yes," Mlle. Jeanne replied, purposely refraining from being explicit.

"I only asked because I thought I'd seen you before somewhere. I recognize your eyes!" Henri Verbier smiled and looked meaningfully at the girl. "Mademoiselle Jeanne, on summer nights like this, when you are looking at a lovely view like this, don't you have a strange sort of feeling?"

"No. What do you mean?"

"Oh, I don't know. But you see, I'm a sentimental person unfortunately, and I really suffer a lot from always living by myself, without any affection. There are times when I feel as if love were an absolute necessity."

The cashier looked at him ironically.

"That's ridiculous. Love is idiotic and ought to be guarded against as the worst possible mistake. Love always means misery for working people like us."

"You are the one who's being foolish," Henri Verbier protested gently, "or else you are mischievous. No, love is not stupid for working people like us; on the contrary, it is the only means we have of attaining perfect happiness. Lovers are rich!"

"A wealth that lets them die of hunger," she scoffed.

"No, no," he answered, "no. Look here, all today you and I have been working hard, earning our living. Well, suppose you were not laughing at me but we were really lovers, would not this be the time to enjoy the fruits of our hard work?" And as the girl did not reply, Henri Verbier, like an experienced lady's man, drew closer to her all the time until his shoulder was touching hers, and he took her hand. "Would not this be wonderful?" he said. "I would take your little fingers into mine—like this, I would look at them so tenderly and raise them to my lips—"

But the girl pulled herself away.

"Let me go! I won't have it! Do you understand?" And then, to mitigate the sharpness of her rebuke, and also to change the conversation, she said, "It is beginning to get chilly. I am going to put a coat over my shoulders," and she moved away from the window to unhook a coat from a peg on the wall.

Henri Verbier watched her without moving.

"How unkind you are!" he said reproachfully, disregarding the angry gleam in her eyes. "Can it really be wrong to enjoy a kiss on a lovely night like this? If you are cold, Mademoiselle Jeanne, there is a better way of getting warm than by putting a wrap over your shoulders, and that is by resting in someone else's arms."

He put out his arms as he spoke, ready to catch the girl as she came across the room, and was on the very point of taking her into his arms as he had suggested when she broke from his grasp with a sudden turn and, furious with rage, dealt him a tremendous blow right on the temple. With a stifled groan, Henri Verbier dropped unconscious to the floor.

Mlle. Jeanne stared at him for a moment, dumbfounded. Then with amazing speed the young cashier sprang to the window and hurriedly closed it. She took down her hat from a hook on the wall and put it on with a single gesture, opened a drawer and took out a little bag; and then, after listening for a minute to make sure that there was nobody in the hallway outside her room, she opened her door, went out, rapidly turned the key behind her, and ran down the stairs.

Two minutes later Mlle. Jeanne passed the porter on duty with a smile and wished him good night.

"Bye-bye," she said. "I'm going out to get a little fresh air!"

———

Slowly, as if emerging from some extraordinary dream, Henri Verbier began to recover from his brief unconsciousness; he could not understand at first what had happened to him, why he was lying on the floor, why his head ached so much, or why his bloodshot eyes saw everything through a mist. He gradually struggled into a sitting posture and looked around the room.

"Nobody here!" he muttered. Then as if the sound of his own voice had brought him back to life, he got up and hurried to the door and shook it furiously. "Locked!" he growled angrily. "And I can scream till I'm blue in the face! No one has come upstairs yet. I'm trapped!" He turned toward the window, with some idea of calling for help, but as he passed the mirror over the mantelpiece he caught sight of his own reflection and saw the bruise on his forehead, with a tiny stream of blood beginning to trickle from a cut in the skin. He went up to the mirror and looked at himself in dismay. "Juve," he murmured, "you've let yourself be knocked out by a woman!" And then Juve, for it was Juve, cleverly disguised, uttered a sudden oath, clenching his fists and grinding his teeth in rage. "Damn it all, I swear that blow was not dealt by any woman!"

THÉRÈSE'S FUTURE

M. Etienne Rambert was in the study of the house that he had purchased a few months previously in the Place Pereire, rue Eugène-Flachat, smoking and chatting with his old friend Barbey, who also was his banker. The two had been discussing investments, but the wealthy merchant was indifferent to the banker's recommendation of various gilt-edged securities.

"To tell you the truth," he said at length, "these things don't interest me much; I'm used to big enterprises—am almost what you would call a gambler. Of course you know that nothing is as risky as the development of rubber plantations. No doubt the industry has prospered amazingly since the boom in automobiles began, but you must remember that I went into it when no one could possibly foresee the immense market that the new means of locomotion would open for our product. That's enough to prove to you that I'm no coward when it's a question of risking money." The banker nodded; his friend certainly did display extraordinary energy and willpower for a man of his age. "As a matter of fact," M. Rambert went on, "any business of which I am not actually a director does not interest me. You know I'm not boasting when I say that I'm rich enough to justify incurring a certain amount of financial risk without having to fear any serious consequences if the ventures should happen to turn out badly. I have a sporting instinct."

"It's a fine one," M. Barbey said with some enthusiasm. "And I don't mind telling you that if I were not your banker, and did not have a certain responsibility in your case, I should not hesitate to put a scheme before you that has been running around in my head for a year or two now."

"A scheme of your own, Barbey?" said M. Rambert. "Why haven't you ever told me about it? I thought we were close enough friends for that."

The hint of reproach in the words pricked the banker, and also encouraged him to proceed.

"It's rather a delicate matter, and you will understand my hesitation when I tell you—for I'll burn my bridges now—that it isn't any ordinary speculation, such as I usually recommend to my customers. It is a speculation in which I am interested personally; in short, I want to increase the capital of my bank and convert my house into a really large concern."

"Oh-ho!" said M. Etienne Rambert, half to himself. "Well, you are quite right, Barbey. But if you are suggesting that I help finance it, you had better put all the cards on the table and let me know exactly what shape you're in; of course if nothing comes of it, I will regard any information you give me as absolutely confidential."

The two men plunged into the subject, and for a good half-hour discussed all its aspects, making endless calculations and contemplating all contingencies. At last M. Rambert threw down his pen and looked up.

"I'm accustomed to the American method of hustle, Barbey. In principle I like your proposition, but I won't be *one* of your financial partners; if the thing goes through I'll be the only one, or not at all. I know what's on your mind," he went on with a smile, as he noticed the banker's surprise; "you know what my fortune is, or rather you think you do, and you are wondering where I shall get the million or so that you want. Well, put your mind at ease about that; if I talk like this, it's because I've got it." The banker's bow was very deferential, and M. Rambert continued: "Yes, the last year or two have been good, even very good, for me. I've made some lucky speculations and my capital has further been increased by some gambles that have worked out lately. Well!" he broke off with a sigh. "I suppose one can't always be unlucky in everything, though money can't cure the wounds in one's heart."

The banker made no answer; he could think of nothing to

say about the sad memories that were still fresh in the old man's mind. But M. Rambert soon reverted to his business tone.

"I'm quite interested in a financial venture like yours, Barbey. But you must understand you will have a good deal more than a silent partner in me. Will that suit you? I should not ask you to abdicate your authority, but I tell you frankly I should follow all the operations of your house very carefully indeed."

"There will be no secrets from you, my dear friend, my dear partner, if I may call you that," said M. Barbey, rising. "Quite the contrary!"

The banker looked toward the mantelpiece, as if expecting to see a clock there; M. Rambert understood the instinctive action and drew out his watch.

"Twenty minutes to eleven, Barbey; it's late for you. So off with you." He cut short the banker's halfhearted apologies for not prolonging the evening. "I am turning you out quite unceremoniously, and besides, as you know, I'm not as lonely tonight as I usually am. I have a young and very charming companion for whom I have the greatest affection, and I am going to join her."

M. Etienne Rambert conducted his friend to the hall door, heard the sound of his automobile die away in the distance, and then walked across the hall. But, instead of going back to the study, he turned into the adjoining drawing room. He paused for a moment in the doorway, tenderly contemplating the charming spectacle that met his eyes.

The shaded light from an electric lamp fell upon the bent head, oval face, and delicate features, of Thérèse Auvernois, who was lost in a book. The girl was emerging from childhood into young womanhood now, and sorrow had emphasized her natural distinction by giving her a stamp of seriousness that was new. Her figure was slight and supple, delicate and graceful, and her long, tapering fingers turned the pages of the book with a slow and regular movement. Thérèse looked around toward Etienne Rambert when she heard him coming in, and laying down her book she got up to meet him, moving with easy grace.

"I am sure I am keeping you up terribly late, dear M. Rambert," she said apologetically, "but what am I to do? I must wait for the Baronne de Vibray, and the dear woman is so often late!"

The tragedy at the château of Beaulieu had had the effect of knitting together all the friends of the Marquise de Langrune in close friendship. Prior to that event Etienne Rambert had scarcely known the Baronne de Vibray; now the two were intimate friends. The baronne had not desisted from her first generous efforts until she had persuaded the family council to appoint her guardian of the orphaned Thérèse Auvernois. At first she had moved the child to Querelles and remained there with her, leading the quietest possible life, partly out of respect for Thérèse's grief and partly because she herself was also much upset by the tragedy. She had even enjoyed the rest, and her new vocation of playing mother, or rather elder sister, to Thérèse. But as the weeks passed and time accomplished its healing, Paris called to the baronne once more, and yielding to the solicitations of her many friends she brought her new ward to the capital and settled in a little apartment in the rue Boissy-d'Anglais. At first she protested that she would go out nowhere, or at most pay only absolutely necessary visits, but by degrees she accepted first one and then another invitation, though always deploring the necessity of leaving Thérèse for hours at a time.

Fortunately there was always Etienne Rambert, who was also staying in Paris just now. It had gradually become the custom of the Baronne de Vibray, when she was dining out, to entrust Thérèse to Etienne Rambert's care, and the young girl and the old man got on together perfectly. Their hearts had met across the awful chasm that fate had tried to put between them.

To Thérèse's last words now Etienne Rambert replied:

"You need not apologize for staying late, dear; you know how glad I am to see you. I wish the house were yours."

The girl glanced around the room that had grown so familiar to her and with a sudden rush of feeling slipped her arm around the old man's neck and laid her lovely head on his shoulder.

"I should love to stay here with you, M. Rambert!"

The old man looked oddly at her for a moment, repressing

the words that he perhaps wished to say, and then gently released himself from her affectionate embrace and led her to a sofa, on which he sat down by her side.

"That is one of the things that we must not allow ourselves to think about, my dear," he said. "I would have loved to receive you in my home, and your presence would have brought happiness to my lonely fireside; but unfortunately those are vain dreams. We have to reckon with the world, and the world would not approve of a young girl like you living in the home of a lonely man."

"Why not?" Thérèse inquired in surprise. "Why, you might be my father."

Etienne Rambert winced at the word.

"Ah," he said, "you must not forget, Thérèse, that I am not your father, but—his, the father of the man who—" But Thérèse's soft hand laid upon his lips prevented him from finishing what he would have said.

To change the conversation Thérèse feigned concern about her own future.

"When we left Querelles," she said, "President Bonnet told me that you would tell me something about my affairs. I gather that my fortune is not a brilliant one."

It was indeed the fact that after the murder of the marquise the unpleasant discovery had been made that her fortune was by no means as large as had generally been supposed. The estate was mortgaged, and President Bonnet and Etienne Rambert had had long and anxious debates as to whether it might not be well for Thérèse to renounce her inheritance to Beaulieu, so doubtful did it seem whether the assets would exceed the liabilities.

Etienne Rambert made a vague but significant gesture when he heard the girl raise the point now, but Thérèse had all the carelessness of youth.

"Oh, I shall not be downhearted," she exclaimed. "My poor grannie always set me an example of industriousness and hard work; I've got plenty of pluck, and I will work too. Suppose I become a governess?"

M. Rambert looked at her thoughtfully.

"My dear child, I know how brave and earnest you are, and

that gives me confidence. I have thought about your future a great deal already. Someday, of course, some nice and wealthy young fellow will come along and marry you—Oh, yes, he will, you'll see. But in the meantime it will be necessary for you to have some occupation. I am wondering whether it will not be necessary to let, or even to sell, Beaulieu. And, on the other hand, you can't stay forever with the Baronne de Vibray."

"No, I realize that," said Thérèse, who, with the tact that was one of her best qualities, had quickly seen that it would not be long before she would become a difficulty in the way of the independence of the kind baronne. "That is what troubles me most."

"Your birth and your upbringing have been such that you would certainly suffer in taking up the difficult and delicate, and sometimes painful, position of governess in a family; and, without wishing to be offensive, I must remind you that you need to have studied very hard to be a governess nowadays, and I am not aware that you are exactly an intellectual. But I have an idea, and this is it; for a great many years now I have been on good terms with a lady who belongs to the very best English society: Lady Beltham; you may have heard me speak of her." Thérèse opened her eyes wide in astonishment, and Rambert went on: "A few months ago Lady Beltham lost her husband in strange circumstances, and since then she has been good enough to confide in me more than before. She is immensely rich and very charitable, and I have frequently been asked by her to look after some of her many financial interests. Now, I have often noticed that she has with her several young English ladies who live with her, not as companions, but, shall I say, secretaries? Do you understand the difference? She treats them like friends or relatives, and they all belong to the very best social class, some of them even being daughters of English peers. If Lady Beltham, to whom I could speak about it, would admit you into her little circle, I am sure you would be in a most delightful *milieu*, and Lady Beltham—who, I know, would adore you—would almost certainly take an interest in your future. She knows what unhappiness is as well as you do, my dear," he added, bending fondly over the girl, "and she would understand you."

"Dear M. Rambert!" murmured Thérèse, much moved. "Do that. Speak to Lady Beltham about me; I would be so grateful!"

Thérèse did not finish what she would have said because a loud ring at the front doorbell broke in upon her words, and Etienne Rambert rose and walked across the room.

"That must be the Baronne de Vibray," he said.

MADEMOISELLE JEANNE

After she had so roughly disposed of Henri Verbier, whose unseemly advances had so greatly scandalized her, Mlle. Jeanne took to her heels; as soon as she was out of sight of the Royal Palace Hotel, she ran like one possessed. She stood for a moment in the brilliantly lit, crowded avenue Wagram, shaking with excitement, and then mechanically hailed a passing cab and told the driver to take her toward the Bois. There she gave another heedless order to go to the boulevard Saint-Denis, but as the cab approached the place de l'Etoile she realized that she was once more near the Royal Palace Hotel, and stopping the driver by the tram lines she dismissed him and got into a tram that was going to the Auteuil station. It was just half past eleven when she reached the station.

"When is the next train for Saint-Lazaire?" she asked.

She learned that one was leaving almost at once, and hurriedly buying a second-class ticket she jumped into a ladies' carriage and went as far as Courcelles. There she got out, went out of the station, looked around her for a minute or two to get her bearings, and then walked slowly toward the rue Eugène-Flachat. She hesitated a second and then walked firmly toward a particular house and rang the bell.

"A lady to see you, sir," the footman said to M. Rambert.

"Bring her in at once," said M. Rambert, supposing that the man had kept the Baronne de Vibray waiting in the anteroom.

The drawing room door was open a little ways, and someone came in and stepped quickly into the shadow by the door. Thérèse, who had risen to hurry toward the visitor, stopped short when she perceived that it was not her guardian. Noticing her action, M. Etienne Rambert turned and looked at the person who had entered.

It was a lady.

"To what am I indebted—" he began with a bow; and then, having approached the visitor, he broke off short. "Good heavens—!"

The bell rang a second time, and on this occasion the Baronne de Vibray hurried into the room, a radiant incarnation of gaiety.

"I am most dreadfully late!" she exclaimed. She was hurrying toward M. Etienne Rambert with outstretched hands, full of some amusing story she had to tell him, when she too caught sight of the strange lady standing stiffly in the corner of the room with downcast eyes.

Etienne Rambert repressed his first emotion, smiled to the baronne, and then went toward the mysterious lady.

"Madame," he said, not a muscle of his face moving, "may I trouble you to come into my study?"

"Who is that lady, M. Rambert?" said Thérèse when M. Rambert came back into the drawing room. "And how white you are!"

M. Rambert forced a smile.

"I am rather tired, dear. I have had a great deal to do these last few days."

The Baronne de Vibray was full of instant apologies.

"It is all my fault," she exclaimed. "I am dreadfully sorry to have kept you up so late," and in a few minutes more the baronne's car was speeding toward the rue Boissy-d'Anglais.

M. Rambert hurried back to his study, shut and locked the door behind him, and almost leaped toward the unknown lady, his fists clenched, his eyes popping out of his head.

"Charles!" he exclaimed.

"Papa!" the girl replied, and sank upon a sofa.

There was silence. Etienne Rambert seemed utterly dumbfounded.

"I won't, I can't remain disguised as a woman any longer.

I'm through with it. I cannot bear it!" the strange creature murmured.

"You must!" said Rambert harshly, imperiously. "I insist!"

The phony Mlle. Jeanne slowly took off the heavy wig that concealed her real features and tore away the corsage that compressed her bosom, revealing the strong and muscular frame of a young man.

"No, I will not," replied the strange individual, to whom M. Rambert had unhesitatingly given the name of Charles. "I would rather die."

"You have got to pay for your actions," Etienne Rambert said with the same harshness.

"The torture is unendurable," the young fellow answered.

"Charles," said M. Rambert very gravely, "are you forgetting that legally you are dead?"

"I would rather be really dead!" the unhappy lad exclaimed.

"My God!" his father murmured, speaking very fast. "I thought your mind was more unhinged than it really is. I saved your life, regardless of any risk, because I thought you were insane, and now I know you are a criminal! Oh, yes, I know things, I know your life!"

"Father," said Charles Rambert with so stern and determined an expression that Etienne Rambert felt a moment's fear, "I want to know how you managed to save my life and make out that I was dead. Was that just chance, or was it planned deliberately?"

Confronted with this new firmness of his son's, Etienne Rambert dropped his peremptory tone; his shoulders dropped in distress.

"Can one anticipate things like that?" he said. "When we parted, my heart bled to think that you, my son, must fall into the hands of justice, and that you must tread the path that led to the scaffold or, at least, to jail. I wondered how I could save you; then chance, chance, mind you, brought that poor drowned body my way. I saw the fortunate coincidence of a faint resemblance and resolved to pass it off as you; I buried the dead man's clothes and put yours on the corpse. Do you know, Charles, that I have suffered too? Do you know what agony and torture I, as a man of honor, have endured? Have you not heard the story of my appearance in court and of my humiliation there?"

"You did all that!" Charles Rambert murmured. "Strange, indeed!" Then his tone changed and he sobbed. "Oh, my poor father, what an awful mess it all is!" Suddenly he sprang to his feet, "But I committed no crime, Papa! I never killed the Marquise de Langrune! Oh, believe me! Why, you have just this minute said that you know I am not mad!"

Etienne Rambert looked at his son with distress.

"Not mad, my poor boy? Yet perhaps you were mad—then?" Then he stopped abruptly. "Don't let us go over all that again! I forbid it absolutely." He leaned back on his writing table, folded his arms, and asked sternly: "Have you come here only to tell me that?"

The curt question seemed to have a strange effect on the lad. All his former audacity dropped from him. Nervously he stammered:

"I can't remain a woman any longer!"

"Why not?" snapped Etienne Rambert.

"I can't."

The two men looked at each other in silence, as if trying to read one another's thoughts. Then Etienne Rambert seemed to see the real meaning of the words his son had just said.

"I see!" he answered slowly. "I understand. . . . The Royal Palace Hotel, where Mademoiselle Jeanne held a trusted post, has been the scene of a sensational robbery. Obviously, if anyone could prove that Charles Rambert and the new cashier were one and the same person—"

But the young fellow understood the insinuation and burst out:

"I did not commit that robbery!"

"You did!" Etienne Rambert insisted. "You did. I read the newspaper accounts of the robbery, read them with all the agony that only a father like me with a son like you could feel. The detectives and the magistrates were at a loss to find the key to the mystery, but I saw right away what the solution was. And I knew and understood because I knew it was—you!"

"I did not commit the robbery," Charles Rambert shouted.

"Do you mean to begin all your horrible accusations again, as you did at Beaulieu?" he demanded in almost threatening tones. "What evil spirit possesses you? Why will you insist that your poor son is a criminal? I had nothing to do with those robberies at the hotel; I swear it, Father!"

M. Rambert shrugged his shoulders and clasped his hands.

"What have I done," he muttered, "to deserve a terrible fate like this?" He turned again to his son. "Your defense is childish. What is the use of merely denying it? Words don't mean anything without proof to support them." The lad was silent, seeming to decide it was useless to attempt to convince a father so certain of his guilt, and also crushed by the thought of all that had happened at the hotel. His father now became uneasy at a new thought that had come into his mind. "I told you not to come to me again except as a last resort, when the law was actually overtaking you, or when you had proved your innocence. Why are you here now? Has something happened that I do not know about? What has happened? What else have you done? Speak!"

Charles answered in a toneless voice, as if hypnotized:

"There has been a detective in the hotel for the last few days. He called himself Henri Verbier and was disguised, but I knew him, for I had seen him lately, and in circumstances too vivid in my mind for me to be able to forget him, although I only saw him then for a few minutes."

"What do you mean?" said the elder man uneasily.

"I mean that Juve was at the Royal Palace Hotel."

"Juve?" exclaimed Etienne Rambert. "And then—go on!"

"Juve, disguised as Henri Verbier, subjected me to a kind of examination, and I don't know what conclusion he came to. Then, this evening, barely two hours ago, he came up to my room and had a long talk, and while he was trying to get some information from me about a matter that I know nothing about—for I swear, Papa, that I had nothing whatever to do with the robbery—he came up to me and tried to kiss me. And I lost my head! I felt that in another minute the game would be up with me—that he would establish my identity, which he maybe suspected already—and I thought of all you had done to save my life by pretending that I was dead, and—"

Charles paused for breath. His father's fists were clenched and his face stricken.

"Go on!" he said. "Go on, but speak lower!"

"As Juve came close," Charles went on, "I dealt him a terrific blow on the forehead, and he fell like a stone. And I got away!"

"Is he dead?" Etienne Rambert whispered.

"I don't know."

For ten minutes Charles Rambert remained alone in the study where his father had left him, thinking deeply. Then the door opened and Etienne Rambert came back carrying a bundle of clothes.

"There you are," he said to his son. "Here are some men's clothes. Put them on, and go!"

The young man hastily took off his woman's garments and dressed himself in silence, while his father walked up and down the room, plunged in deepest thought. Twice he asked, "Are you quite sure it was Juve?" and twice his son replied, "Quite sure." And once again Etienne Rambert asked, in tones that betrayed his keen anxiety, "Did you kill him?" and Charles Rambert shrugged his shoulders and replied, "I told you before, I don't know."

And now Charles Rambert stood upon the threshold of the house, about to leave his father without a word of farewell or a parting embrace. M. Etienne Rambert stayed him, holding out a wallet full of bank notes.

"There. Take that," he said, "and go!"

THE MAD WOMAN'S PLOT

When Dr. Biron built his famous private asylum in the very heart of Passy, intended, according to his prospectus, to provide a retreat for people suffering from nervous breakdown or from overwork or overexcitement, and to offer hospital treatment for the insane, he took the wise precaution to hire several residents from the hospitals. The idea was a shrewd and a successful one, and his establishment thrived.

Perret and Sembadel were having breakfast, and also grumbling.

"I wouldn't curse the management quite so much if they didn't give us so many jobs," said Sembadel. "Damn it all, man, we are both qualified, and when we agreed to assist Dr. Biron we did so, I presume, in order to top off our theoretical training with some practical clinical experience."

"Who's stopping you?" Perret inquired.

"How can we find the time when besides all our real work with the patients we have to do all this administrative work, writing to people to say how the patients are, and all that? That ought to be done by clerks, not by us."

"Isn't one job as good as another?" Perret retorted. "Besides, we are the only people who know how the patients really are, so isn't it just common sense that we should write to their friends?"

"They might let us have a secretary, anyhow," Sembadel growled.

Perret saw that his friend was in a bad temper, so he did not try to carry on the argument.

"Say," he said, "you ought to make a special note of that case in number twenty-five, for your thesis. She was in your ward for about six months, wasn't she?"

"Number twenty-five?" said Sembadel. "Yes, I know: a woman named Rambert, about forty years old; hallucinations that people are persecuting her; anemic, with alternate crises of excitement and melancholia, punctuated by fits of passion. Treatment was rest, nourishment, tranquilizers."

"You evidently remember the case pretty well."

"She interested me; she has marvelous eyes. Well, what about her?"

"Why, when she was moved into my pavilion the diagnosis was bad and the prognosis very bad; she was supposed to be incurable. Just go and see her now; her brain is restored; she's a new woman." He came to the table and picked up some notepaper. "I wrote to her husband a day or two ago and told him he might expect to hear that his wife had recovered, but I imagine he didn't get my letter because he hasn't answered. I have a good mind to write to him again and ask for permission to send her to the convalescent ward. The bad part is that this Etienne Rambert may want to remove her altogether, and that would mean one less paying patient, which would put our worthy director in a bad mood for a month."

He turned to his correspondence, and for some minutes the silence in the room was only broken by the scratching of pens on paper. Then an attendant came in, bringing a number of letters. Perret picked them up and began to sort them out.

"None for you," he said to Sembadel. "Not even one of those little mauve envelopes that you wait for every day and that determines what kind of a mood you'll be in."

"I won't even have time to complain today," Sembadel growled again. "You forget that Swelding pays us an official visit today."

"The Danish professor? Is he coming this morning?"

"So it seems."

"Who is the fellow?"

"Just one of those foreign scholars who haven't succeeded in becoming famous at home and so go abroad to bother other people under a pretext of research. That's why he wants to come here. Wrote some awful little pamphlet on the ideontology of the hyperimaginative. Never heard of it myself."

The conversation flagged, and presently the two men went off to their wards to see their patients and warn the attendants to have everything in shipshape order for the official inspection.

Meantime, in the great reception room, elaborate greetings were being exchanged between Dr. Biron and Professor Swelding.

Dr. Biron was a man of about forty, with a highly colored face and an active, vigorous frame. He gesticulated freely and spoke in an unctuous, fawning tone.

"I am delighted at the great compliment you pay me by coming here, sir," he said. "When I started this institution five years ago I certainly did not dare to hope that it would so soon gain a good enough reputation to entitle it to the honor of a visit by men so eminent in the scientific world as yourself."

The professor listened with a courteous smile but evinced no hurry in replying.

Professor Swelding was certainly a remarkable figure. He might have been sixty, but he bore lightly the weight of the years that laid their snows upon his thick and curly but startlingly white hair. It was this hair that one noticed first; it was extraordinarily thick and joined on to a heavy mustache and a long and massive beard. He was like a man who had taken a vow never to cut his hair. It covered his ears and fell down on his forehead, so that hardly a vestige of his face could be seen, while, further, his eyes were concealed behind large blue spectacles. The professor was enveloped in a heavy cloak in spite of the bright sunshine; evidently he was one of those men from the cold North who do not know what real warmth is and have no idea of what it means to be overdressed. He spoke French correctly, but with a slight accent and a slow enunciation that betrayed his foreign origin.

"I was really anxious, sir, to observe for myself the measures you have taken which have set your institution in the forefront of establishments of the kind," he replied. "I have read with the very greatest interest your various communications to the learned societies. It is a great advantage for a practitioner like myself to be able to profit by the experience of a scholar of your high standing."

A few further compliments were exchanged and then Dr. Biron suggested a visit to the various wards and led his guest out into the grounds of the institution.

If Dr. Biron did not possess that theoretical knowledge of insanity that has made French psychiatrists famous throughout the world, he was certainly a first-rate organizer. His sanatorium was a model one. It was situated in one of the wealthiest, quietest, and most pleasant quarters of Paris, and stood in a vast enclosure behind high walls; within this enclosure were a number of small pavilions, all attractive in design and connected by broad flights of steps with a beautiful garden studded with trees and shrubs, but further subdivided into a series of little gardens separated from one another by white picket fences.

"You see, Professor, I rely entirely on the isolation principle. A single block would have involved a deleterious arrangement of various types of insanity, so I built this series of small pavilions, where my patients can be segregated according to their type of alienation. The system has great therapeutic advantages, and I am sure it is the explanation of my high percentage of cures."

Professor Swelding nodded approval.

"We apply the system of segregation in Denmark," he said, "but we have never carried it so far as to divide the general grounds. I see that each of your pavilions has its own private garden."

"I regard that as indispensable," Dr. Biron declared. He led his visitor to one of the little gardens, where a man of about fifty was walking about between two attendants. "This man is a megalomaniac," he said; "he believes that he is the Almighty."

"What is your treatment here?" Professor Swelding inquired. "I am aware that the books prescribe isolation, but that is insufficient by itself."

"I nurse the brain by nursing the body," Dr. Biron replied. "I build up my patient's system by careful attention to hygiene, diet, and rest, and I pretend to ignore his mental alienation. There is always a spark of sense in a diseased brain. This man imagines he is the Almighty, but when he is hungry he has to ask for something to eat, and then we pretend to wonder why he has any need to eat if he is the Almighty; he has to concoct some explanation, and very gradually his reasoning power is restored. A man ceases to be insane the moment he begins to comprehend that he is insane."

The professor followed the doctor, casting curious glances at the various patients who were walking in their gardens.

"Have you many cures?"

"That is a difficult question to answer," said Dr. Biron. "The statistics are very different in the different categories of insanity."

"Of course," said Professor Swelding, "but take some particular type of dementia, say, persecution complex. What percentage of cures can you show there?"

"Twenty percent absolute recoveries, and forty percent definite improvements," the doctor replied promptly, and as the professor evinced noticeable astonishment at so high a percentage, Dr. Biron took him familiarly by the arm and drew him along. "I will show you a patient who actually is to be sent home in a day or two. I believe that she is completely cured, or on the point of being completely cured."

A woman of about forty was sitting by the side of an attendant in one of the gardens and quietly sewing. Dr. Biron paused to point her out.

"That lady belongs to one of our great merchant families. She is Madame Alice Rambert, wife of Etienne Rambert, the rubber merchant. She has been under my care for nearly ten months. When she came here she was in the final stages of debility and anemia and suffered from the most characteristic hallucination of all; she thought that assassins were all around her. I have built up her physical health, and now I have cured her mind. Now she is not mad at all, in the proper sense of the term."

"She never shows any symptoms of reverting to her morbid condition?" Professor Swelding inquired with interest.

"Never."

"And would not, even if violently upset?"

"I do not think so."

"May I talk to her?"

"Certainly," and Dr. Biron led the visitor toward the seat on which the patient was sitting. "Madame Rambert," he said, "may I present Professor Swelding to you? He has heard that you are here and would like to pay his respects."

Mme. Rambert put down her needlework and rose and looked at the Danish professor.

"I am delighted to make the gentleman's acquaintance," she said, "but I should like to know how he was aware of my existence, my dear doctor."

"I regret that I cannot claim to know you, Madame," said Professor Swelding, replying for Dr. Biron, "but I know that you are an inmate of this institution who will testify most warmly to the scientific skill and the devotion of Dr. Biron."

"In any case," Mme. Rambert replied coldly, "he carries his kindness to the extent of wishing his patients never to be dull, by bringing unexpected visitors to see them."

The phrase was an implicit reproach of Dr. Biron's too ready inclination to exhibit his patients as so many rare and curious wild animals, and it stung him all the more because he was convinced that Mme. Rambert was perfectly sane. He pretended not to hear what she said, giving some order to the attendant Berthe, who was standing respectfully by.

"I understand, Madame," Professor Swelding replied gently. "You object to my visit as an intrusion?"

Mme. Rambert had picked up her work and already was sewing again, but suddenly she sprang up, so abruptly that the professor recoiled, and exclaimed sharply:

"Who called me? Who called me? Who—"

The professor was attempting to speak when the patient interrupted him.

"Oh!" she cried. "Alice! Alice! His voice—his voice! Go away! You frighten me! Who spoke? Go away! Oh, help! Help!"

and she fled screaming toward the far end of the garden, with the attendant and Dr. Biron running after her. With all the cleverness of the insane she managed to elude them and continued to scream. "Oh, I recognized him! Do go away, I implore you! Go! Murder! Murder!"

The attendant tried to reassure the doctor.

"Don't be frightened, sir. She is not dangerous. I expect the visit from that gentleman has upset her."

The poor demented creature had taken refuge behind a clump of shrubs and was standing there with eyes dilated with anguish, fixed on the professor and pointing to him, shaking like a leaf.

"Fantômas!" she cried. "Fantômas! There—I know him! Oh, help me!"

The scene was horribly distressing, and Dr. Biron put an end to it by ordering the attendant to take Mme. Rambert to her room and to send at once for M. Perret. Then he turned to Professor Swelding.

"I am greatly distressed by this incident, Professor. It proves that the cure of this poor creature is by no means as certain as I led you to believe. But there are other cases that will restore your faith in my judgment, I hope. Shall we go on?"

Professor Swelding tried to comfort the doctor.

"The brain is a pathetically frail thing," he said. "You could not have more striking evidence to prove it; that poor lady, who you believed to be cured, suddenly having a typical crisis provoked by—what? Neither you nor I look particularly like assassins, do we?" And he followed Dr. Biron, who was still rather upset, to be shown other matters of interest.

"Better now, Madame? Are you going to be all right?"

Mme. Rambert was reclining on a sofa in her room, watching her attendant Berthe moving about and tidying up the slight disorder caused by her recent attempts to calm the patient. The patient made a little gesture of despair.

"Poor Berthe!" she said. "If you only knew how unhappy I am, and how sorry I am for having panicked just now!"

"Oh, that was nothing," said the attendant. "The doctor won't attach any importance to that."

"Yes, he will," said the patient with a weary smile. "I think he will attach importance to it, and in any case it will delay my discharge from this place."

"Not a bit of it, Madame. Why, you know they have written to your home to say you are cured?"

Mme. Rambert did not reply for a minute or two. Then she said:

"Tell me, Berthe, what do you understand by the word 'cured'?"

The attendant was rather nonplussed.

"Why, it means that you are better, that you are quite well."

Her patient smiled bitterly.

"It is true that my health is better now, and that my stay here has done me good. But that is not what I was talking about. What is your opinion about my insanity?"

"You mustn't think about that," the attendant remonstrated. "You are no more crazy than I am."

"Oh, I know the worst symptom of insanity is to declare you are not crazy," Mme. Rambert answered sadly, "so I will be careful not to say it, Berthe. But, apart from this last panic, the reason for which I cannot tell you, have you ever known me to do or say anything that was utterly without reason, in all the time that I have been in your charge?"

Struck by the remark, the attendant, in spite of herself, was obliged to confess:

"No, I never have—that is—"

"That is," Mme. Rambert finished for her, "I have sometimes protested that I was the victim of an abominable persecution, and that there was a tragic mystery in my life; in short, that if I was shut up here, it was because someone wanted me to be shut up. Come now, Berthe, has it ever occurred to you that perhaps I was telling the truth?"

The attendant had been shaken for a minute by the calm self-possession of her patient; now she resumed her professional manner.

"Don't worry anymore, Mme. Rambert, for you know as well as I do that Dr. Biron acknowledges that you are cured now. You are going to leave the place and resume your ordinary life."

"Ah, Berthe," said Mme. Rambert, twisting and untwisting her hands, "if you only knew! Why, if I leave this sanatorium, or rather if the doctor sends me back to my family, I shall certainly be put in some other sanatorium within two days! No, it isn't merely an idea that I have gotten into my head," she went on as the attendant protested. "Listen! During the whole ten months that I have been here, I have never once protested that I was not insane. I was glad to be in this place! I felt safe here. But now I am not even sure of that. I must go, but not merely to return to my husband! I must be free, free to go to those who will help me escape the horrible trap in which I have spent the last few years of my life!"

Mme. Rambert's earnest tone convinced the attendant in spite of her own instinct.

"Yes?" she said inquiringly.

"I suppose you know that I am rich, Berthe?" Mme. Rambert went on. "I have always been generous to you, and higher fees are paid for me here than for any other patient. Would you like to make sure of your future forever, and quite easily? I have heard you talk about getting married. Shall I give you a dowry? You might lose your job here, but if you trust me I will make it up to you a hundred times over, if you will help me escape from this place! And it cannot be too soon! I have not got a minute to lose!"

Berthe tried to get away from her patient, but Mme. Rambert held her back, almost by force.

"Tell me your price," she said. "How much do you want? A thousand? Two thousand?" And as the attendant, bewildered by the mere suggestion of such fabulous sums, was silent, Mme. Rambert slipped a diamond ring off her finger and held it out to the young woman. "Take that as proof of my sincerity," she said. "If anybody asks me about it I will say that I lost it. And from now, Berthe, begin to plan a way for me to escape! The very night I am free I swear you will be a rich woman!"

Berthe got up, swaying, hardly knowing if she were awake or dreaming.

"A rich woman!" she murmured. "A rich woman!" And suddenly a horrible expression of cupidity and desire crept over the girl's face.

AMONG THE
MARKET PORTERS

"Boulevard Rochechouart," said Berthe, the young asylum nurse, to the conductor as she sprang into the tram just as it was starting.

It was a September afternoon, one of the last fine days of the dying summer, and the girl had just gotten her fortnightly leave for forty-eight hours. She had gone off duty at noon and now had until noon two days hence to resume her own personality and shake off the anxieties common to those who are charged with the constant care of the insane, the most difficult kind of patient that exists. As a general rule Berthe spent her days off with her old grandparents in their cottage outside Paris, but on this occasion she decided to remain in the city, the reason being the long conversation she had had with the patient assigned to her particular care, number twenty-five, Mme. Rambert. Since that first talk with her, on the day of Professor Swelding's visit to the asylum, she had had others, and Berthe had now concocted a plan to enable the supposed lunatic to escape and had decided to spend her short holiday in preparing for the plan's execution.

At the boulevard Rochechouart Berthe got out of the tram, looked around to get her bearings in the somewhat unfamiliar neighborhood, and then turned into the rue Clignancourt and stood on the left-hand side of the street, looking at the shops. The third one was a bar, only the first of many on the street.

Berthe pushed the door of this establishment a little way open and looked at the rather rowdy company gathered around the zinc counter, all with flushed faces and all talking loudly. She did not venture inside but in a clear voice asked, "Is M. Geoffroy here?" No definite answer was forthcoming, but the men turned around, hearing her question, and seeing her pretty figure began to nudge one another and joke and laugh coarsely. "Come in, miss," said one of them, but already Berthe had quickly closed the door and gone on her way.

A few yards further on there was another bar, and into this, also, Berthe peeped and once more asked, "Is M. Geoffroy here?" adding by way of further explanation, "Hogshead Geoffroy, I mean." This time a roar of laughter followed, and the girl fled, flushed with indignation.

Yet she did not abandon her strange search, and at last, at the sixth shop, her question was answered by a deep bass voice from the far end of a smoke-clouded den. "Hogshead Geoffroy? Here!" And heaving a sigh of relief Berthe went inside the shop.

When you want to see M. "Hogshead" Geoffroy, the procedure is simplicity itself. As he has no known address, all you have to do is to start at the bottom of the rue Clignancourt on the left-hand side, look into every tavern, and ask, in tones loud enough to be heard above the clatter of conversation, whether Hogshead Geoffroy is there, and it will be very bad luck if, at one or other of the bars, you do not hear the answer, "Hogshead Geoffroy? Here," followed immediately by that gentleman's order to the *patronne*; "Half a pint, please; the gentleman will pay!" It is a safe order; the *patronne* knows from past experience that she can serve the half-pint without anxiety; Hogshead Geoffroy rapidly drains it and then holds out a huge and hairy hand to the visitor and asks, "Well, what is it?"

If, as often happens, the Hogshead finds himself confronted by a stranger, he feels no surprise; he knows his own popularity and is a modest soul, so he calls his visitor by his Christian name at once, taps him amicably on the shoulder, calls him "old boy" and invites him to stand a drink. The Hogshead is an artist in his line; he hires himself out to public halls to announce in his powerful voice, reinforced by a trumpet, the various items on the program. He also harangues the crowd on behalf of showmen or hurls threats at overexcited demonstrators at public demonstrations. Between times he rolls hogsheads down into cellars, or bottles wine and even drinks it when he is among friends who have money to pay for it.

At the sight of Berthe, Hogshead Geoffroy so far departed from custom as not to give an order to the *patronne* at the bar; instead, he rose and went toward the girl and unceremoniously embraced her.

"Ah-ha, little sister, there you are! Why, I was just this moment thinking of you!" He drew her to the back of the shop, toward a bunch of sturdy, square-shouldered fellows drinking there, to whom he introduced her. "Now then, boys, try to behave yourselves; I'm bringing a charming young lady to see you, my sister Berthe, little Bob—Bobinette, as we called her when we lived with the old folks." The girl blushed, a little uneasy at finding herself in such mixed company, but Hogshead Geoffroy put everyone at ease; he put his great hand under Berthe's chin and tilted her head back. "Don't you think she is pretty, this little sister of mine? She's the spitting image of her brother!" There was a general roar of laughter. The contrast between the two figures could hardly have been greater and it seemed impossible there could be any relationship between them: the graceful, slender, tiny *Parisienne* looking tinier still beside the huge colossus of a man six feet high, with the chest of a bull and the shoulders of an athlete. "We don't seem to be built on quite the same lines," M. Geoffroy admitted, "but all the same there is a family likeness!"

The men made room for the girl, and after she had yielded to the general insistence and accepted a glass of white wine, Geoffroy bent forward and spoke in a lower tone.

"Well, what do you want?"

"I want to talk to you about something that will interest you, I'm sure," Berthe answered.

"Anything to be got out of it?" was the giant's next inquiry.

Berthe smiled.

"I guess so, or I wouldn't have troubled you."

"Whenever there's any money to be picked up the Hogshead's always on," he replied, "especially just now when

things aren't so great, though I may tell you I think there's going to be an alteration in that respect."

"Have you got a job?" Berthe asked in surprise.

Hogshead Geoffroy laid a finger on his lip.

"It's still a secret," he said, "but there's no harm in talking it
over, for everybody here knows all about it," and at interminable length, and with many pauses for drinking, he explained that he was a candidate for market porter. He had been
cramming for two weeks, in order to emerge triumphantly
from the examination to which candidates were always subjected, and that very morning he had sat in the Hôtel de Ville
wrestling with nothing less than a problem in arithmetic. As
proof, he produced from his pocket a crumpled, greasy, and
wine-stained sheet of paper scrawled all over with childish writing and figures, and showed it to his sister, immensely proud of
the effect he was producing on her. "A problem," he repeated.
"See here; two taps fill a tank at the rate of twenty liters a
minute, and a third tap empties it at the rate of fifteen hundred
liters an hour. How long will it take for the tank to get full?"

A friend of Geoffroy's broke in; it was Mealy Benoît, his
most formidable competitor for the appointment.

"Not as long as it will take you to get full," he said with a
loud laugh.

Hogshead Geoffroy banged his fist on the table.

"This is a serious conversation," he said, and turned again to
his sister, who wanted to know if he had succeeded in finding the
answer to the problem. "Maybe," he replied. "I worked by rule
of thumb, for, as you know, arithmetic isn't exactly my forte. To
sit for an hour, writing at a table in the great hall of the Hôtel de
Ville made me sweat more than carrying four hundred pounds!"

But the company was preparing to leave. It was getting late,
and at six o'clock the second part of the examination, the physical test, was to be held in the fish market. Mealy Benoît had
paid his bill already, and Hogshead Geoffroy's deferential es-
cort of friends was getting restless. Berthe won fresh favor in
her brother's eyes by paying for their refreshments with a ten-
franc piece and leaving the change to be placed to his credit,
and then they left the tavern.

The annual competition for an appointment as market porter is held at the end of September. It is a great event. There are generally many candidates, but only two or three, and sometimes fewer, are picked. The posts are few and good, for the number of porters is limited. The examination is in two parts: one purely intellectual, consisting of some simple problem and a little dictation, the other physical, in which the candidates have to carry a sack of meal weighing three hundred pounds a distance of two hundred yards in the shortest time.

At six o'clock punctually the market women were in their places along the pavement by their respective stalls. The hall was decorated with flags; the salesmen and regular merchants were provided with chairs, and their assistants were behind them, with the sweepers and criers; at the back stood three or four rows of the general public, all eager to witness the impressive display.

The two-hundred-yard course was carefully cleared, every obstacle having been scrupulously swept off the asphalt, especially pieces of orange-peel, lettuce leaves, and bits of rotten vegetable matter, which might have caused a competitor to slip when trying to break the record for carrying the sack. A high official of the Hôtel de Ville and three of the senior market porters formed the jury, and there were also two officials of the cyclists' union, expert in the use of stopwatches, armed with tested chronometers, to take the exact time of each contestant.

The crowd of onlookers was as odd and eclectic and excited as can possibly be imagined. Berthe, who knew that demure behavior is quite out of place in popular gatherings, mingled freely. Among other picturesque types she had noticed one particularly extraordinary individual who, although he was in the last row, towered over the rest by at least half of his body, being perched on an antiquated tricycle, which provoked the hilarity of the mob.

"What ho, Bouzille!" somebody called out, for the man was a well-known and popular figure, and everybody knew his name. "Is that Methuselah's tricycle you've pinched?" And to some of the sallies the fellow replied with a smile that was almost lost in his matted beard, and to others with a joke uttered in the purest dialect of Auvergne.

Someone spoke softly in Berthe's ear, and she turned and saw a sturdy fellow of about twenty-five, wearing a blue shirt, a red handkerchief around his neck, and a drover's cap; he was a well-built, powerful man and, in spite of his humble dress, had an intelligent face and an almost distinguished manner. Berthe responded amiably, and a few commonplace remarks were exchanged between the two.

"In case you care to know, my name's Julot," said the man.

And Berthe replied frankly, but without otherwise compromising herself.

"And I am Bob, or Bobinette, whichever you like. I am Hogshead Geoffroy's sister," she added with a little touch of pride.

A murmur ran around the crowd. Mealy Benoît was beginning his turn. The great fellow came along with rapid, rhythmical step, with supple limbs and chest hunched forward. Surely balanced on his broad shoulders and the nape of his neck was an enormous sack of meal, accurately weighed to scale three hundred pounds. Without the least hesitation or slackening of pace, he covered the two hundred yards, reaching the goal perfectly fresh and fit; he stood for a moment or two in front of the judges, displaying the mighty muscles of his naked chest over which the perspiration was running and showing off his genuine delight in not unloading his heavy burden at the earliest possible moment. The applause was enthusiastic and immediate, but silence quickly fell again and all eyes turned toward the starting post. It was Hogshead Geoffroy's turn.

The giant was really a splendid sight. Instead of walking as his rival had done, he began to run like an athlete, and the crowd yelled its delight. It seemed he would beat his rival's time easily, but all at once the great sack on his shoulders began to shake, and Geoffroy almost stopped, uttering a heavy groan before he got going again. The crowd looked on in surprise; there was a wet mark upon the asphalt; Geoffroy had slipped on a piece of orange peel. But he managed to restore the equilibrium of the

sack, and, using greater caution, he finished the course with
measured steps.

Two hours later the result of the competition was announced.
Hogshead Geoffroy and Mealy Benoît were tied, having taken
exactly the same time to cover the course; the result would depend on the written examination, and the matter was all the
more important because this year there was only one vacancy
for a market porter.

Berthe, or Bobinette, was vehemently discussing with her
neighbors the mishap that had happened to Geoffroy during his
trial. A man dressed in a shabby black overcoat buttoned up to
the chin, and wearing a kind of jockey cap on his greasy hair,
was watching her intently, seeming to agree with all she said
while really being interested in something else. Berthe, who was
very intent upon the matter in hand, did not notice this individual; it was Julot, her faithful squire for the last two hours, who
got her away.

"Come," he said, taking her by the sleeve, "you know your
brother is waiting for you." As she yielded to his insistence he
whispered in her ear, "That guy's a dirty-looking type. I don't
think too much of him!"

"He certainly is unusually ugly," the girl admitted. Then, like
the trained nurse she was, she added, "And did you notice his
complexion? The man must be ill; he is absolutely green!"

AT THE
SAINT-ANTHONY'S PIG

"Buy me a drink and I'll listen to you," said Hogshead Geoffroy to his sister.

After numerous stops at the many bars and taverns that surround the markets, they had finally gone for a late supper into the Saint-Anthony's Pig, the most popular tavern in the neighborhood, Geoffroy having reconciled himself to waiting for the result of the examination, which would not be announced until the following day.

A new and original attraction had been stationed outside the Saint-Anthony's Pig for the last few days. After the formal inquiries following his discovery of the drowned body in the river, Bouzille had come to Paris to see the Eiffel Tower. He had experienced only a week's delay in his itinerary, having been locked up for that time at Orléans for some trifling misdemeanor.

On entering the capital, Bouzille's extraordinary equipage had caused quite a sensation, and as the worthy fellow, with utter disregard for the heavy traffic in the city, had careered about in it through the most crowded streets, he had very soon been run in to the nearest lockup. His train had been confiscated for forty-eight hours, but as there were no real charges against the tramp, he had merely been requested to make himself scarce and not to do it again.

Bouzille did not quite know what to make of it all. But while he was towing his two carriages behind his tricycle toward the Champ-de-Mars, from which point he would at last be able to contemplate the Eiffel Tower, he had fallen in with the editor of the *Auto,* to whom, in exchange for a bottle of wine at the next café, he had ingenuously confided his story. A sensational article about the globe-trotting tramp appeared in the next issue of that famous sporting journal, and Bouzille awoke to find himself famous. The next thing that happened was that François Bonbonne, the proprietor of the Saint-Anthony's Pig, shrewdly foreseeing that this remarkable character would furnish a singular attraction, engaged him to station himself outside the establishment with his train from eleven to three every night, in return for his board and lodging and a salary of five francs a day.

It hardly need be said that Bouzille accepted the offer. But getting tired of cooling his heels on the doorstep, he had gradually taken to leaving his train on the pavement and going down into the hall, where he generously returned his five francs every night to the proprietor in exchange for libations to that amount.

In the basement of the Saint-Anthony's Pig the atmosphere was steadily getting smokier, and the noise louder. The time was about a quarter to two. The socialites, and the young men about town who went to have a bowl of onion soup at the popular café because that was the latest fashionable thing to do had withdrawn. The few pale and shabby dancers had performed, and in another ten minutes, when the wealthy customers had departed, the dining room would resume its normal appearance and everybody would be at home. François Bonbonne had just escorted the last of them up the narrow winding staircase that led from the basement to the ground floor, and now he stood, his stout body entirely filling the only exit, unctuously suggesting that perhaps somebody would like to order a hot wine "salad."

Berthe was sitting in a corner beside her brother, who was drowsy from the warmth of the room and several drinks. Thinking it an opportune moment to tell him of her scheme, before he became talkative or quarrelsome, she began to explain.

"There's nothing much to do, but I want a strong man like you."

"Any barrels to roll anywhere?" he asked in a thick voice.

Berthe shook her head, her glance meanwhile resting, without thinking, on a small young man with a budding beard and a pale face, who had just taken a seat opposite her and was timidly ordering a portion of sauerkraut.

"I want some bars removed from a window, iron bars set in stone, but the stone is worn and the bars are rusty, and anybody with a little muscle could wrench them out."

"And that's all?" Geoffroy inquired suspiciously.

"Yes, that's all."

"Then I shall be very glad to help you. I suppose it will be worth something, won't it?" He broke off short, noticing that a man sitting close by seemed to be listening attentively to the conversation. Berthe followed his eyes and then turned with a smile to her brother.

"That's all right, don't mind; I know that man." And in proof of the statement she held out a friendly hand to the individual who seemed to be spying upon them. "Good evening again, M. Julot; how are you? I didn't notice you were here."

Julot shook hands with her and, without taking any further interest in her, went on with the conversation he was having with his own companion, a clean-shaven fellow.

"Go on, Billy Tom," he said in low tones. "Tell me what has happened."

"Well, there has been hell to pay at the Royal Palace, owing to that—accident, you know; of course I wasn't mixed up in it in any way. I stick to my own job. But three weeks later, Muller was suddenly kicked out, because the door was opened for the guy who worked the robbery."

"Muller, Muller?" said Julot, seeming to be searching his memory. "Who is Muller?"

"Why, the watchman on the second floor."

"Oh, ah, yes; and who turned him out?"

"I think his name is Juve."

"Oh—ho!" Julot muttered to himself. "I thought as much!"

There was a noise at the entrance of the hall, and down the winding staircase came two people who, judging by the greeting they received, were very popular: Ernestine, a well-known figure, and Mealy Benoît, who was very drunk.

Benoît lurched from one table to another, leaning on every head and pair of shoulders that came his way, and reached an empty seat on a bench onto which he collapsed, half squashing the pale young man with the budding beard. The lad made no protest, seeming to be afraid of his neighbor's bulk, but merely wriggled sideways and tried to give the newcomer all the room he wanted. Benoît did not seem even to notice the humble little fellow, but Ernestine took pity on him and assured him that she would look after him.

"All right, son," she said, "Mealy won't squash you, and if he tries any of his tricks on you, Ernestine will look after you." She took his head between her two hands and kissed his forehead affectionately, ignoring Mealy Benoît's angry protests. "He's a dear little fellow. I like him," she said to the company at large. "What's your name, dear?"

The boy blushed to the tips of his ears.

"Paul," he murmured.

But François Bonbonne the proprietor, with his usual eagle eye for business, arrived just then and set down before Mealy Benoît the famous hot wine salad of which he had spoken before. Behind Bonbonne came Bouzille, who had come down into the dining room to eat and drink his five francs' worth, and more if credit could be gotten.

Benoît caught sight of Hogshead Geoffroy and immediately offered to clink glasses with him; he pushed a glass toward him, inviting him to dip it with the rest into the steaming bowl, but Geoffroy was heating up under the influence of alcohol, and broke into sudden fiery wrath at the sight of Mealy Benoît. If Benoît should be given the first place, it would be a rank injustice, he reflected, for he, Geoffroy, was most certainly the stronger man. And besides, the sturdy Hogshead was beginning to wonder whether his rival might not have devised an odious plot against him and put the famous piece of orange peel upon the track, but for which Geoffroy would have won hands down. So Geoffroy, very drunk, offered Benoît, who was not a whit more sober, the gross affront of refusing to clink glasses with him!

"Why, it's you!" exclaimed Bouzille, in ringing tones of such glad surprise that everybody turned around to see whom he was addressing. Julot and Berthe looked with the rest.

"Why, it's the green man from before," said the asylum nurse to her companion, and he assented, moodily enough.

"Yes, it's him all right."

Bouzille took no notice of the attention he had aroused, and did not seem to notice that the green man appeared to be anything but pleased at having been recognized.

"I've seen you before, I know," he went on. "Where have I met you?"

The green man did not answer; he affected to be engrossed in a most serious conversation with the friend he had brought with him into the dining room, a shabby individual who carried a guitar. But Bouzille was not to be put off, and suddenly he exclaimed, with perfect indifference to what his neighbors might think:

"I know; you are the tramp who was arrested with me down there the day of that murder—you know—the murder of the Marquise de Langrune!"

Bouzille in his excitement had caught the green man by the sleeve, but the green man impatiently shook him off, growling angrily.

"Well, and what about it?"

For some minutes now Hogshead Geoffroy and Mealy Benoît had been exchanging threatening glances. Geoffroy had given voice to his suspicions, and kind friends had not failed to report his words to Benoît. Inflamed with drink as they were, the two men were bound to come to blows before long, and a dull murmur ran through the room in anticipation of the approaching altercation. Berthe, anxious on her brother's behalf and a little frightened on her own, did all she could to induce Geoffroy to come away, but even though she promised to pay for any number of drinks elsewhere, he refused to budge from the bench where he was sitting hunched up in a corner.

When at length he got rid of Bouzille and his exasperating chatter, the green man resumed his conversation with his friend with the guitar.

"It's rather odd that he hasn't a trace of accent," the latter remarked.

"Oh, it's nothing for a fellow like Gurn to speak French like a Frenchman," said the green man in a quiet voice; then he stopped nervously. Ernestine was walking about among the company, chatting to this one and that and getting drinks, and he fancied that she was listening to what he said.

But another dialogue became audible in another part of the room.

"If the gentleman would like to show his muscle there's someone who's ready to take him on."

Hogshead Geoffroy had thrown down his glove!

Silence fell upon the room. It was Mealy Benoît's turn to answer. At that precise moment, however, Benoît was draining the salad bowl. He slowly swallowed the last of the red liquid—one can't do two things at once—laid the bowl down empty on the table, and in thundering, dignified tones demanded another. Wiping his lips on the back of his sleeve, he turned his huge head toward the corner where Geoffroy was hunched up, saying, "Will the gentleman kindly repeat his last remark?"

Ernestine moved furtively to Julot's side and, affecting to be interested only in the argument going on between Geoffroy and Benoît, said without looking at him:

"The pale man with the greenish complexion said to the man with the guitar, 'It's him, all right, because of the burn mark on the palm of his hand.' "

Julot choked back an oath and instinctively clenched his fist, but Ernestine already had moved on and was huskily bantering with the young man with the budding beard. Julot sat with somber face and angry eyes, replying only in curt monosyllables to the occasional remarks of his neighbor, Billy Tom. Marie the waitress was passing by him, and he signaled to her to stop.

"Say, Marie," he said, nodding toward the window behind him, "where does that window open on to?"

The girl thought for a moment.

"On to the cellar," she said; "this hall is in the basement."

"And the cellar," Julot went on, "how do you get out of that?"

"You can't," the servant answered, "there's no door; you have to come through here."

Momentarily becoming more uneasy, Julot scrutinized the long tunnel of a room at the extreme end of which he was sitting; there was only one means of getting out, up the narrow winding staircase leading to the ground floor, and at the very foot of that staircase was the table occupied by the green man and the man with the guitar.

A plate aimed by Hogshead Geoffroy at Mealy Benoît crashed against the opposite wall. Everyone jumped to his feet, the women screaming, the men swearing. The two would-be market porters stood confronting one another, Hogshead Geoffroy brandishing a chair, Benoît trying to wrench the marble top from a table to serve as a weapon. The melee exploded, plates smashing on the floor and dinner utensils flying toward the ceiling.

Suddenly a shot rang out, but as soon as it had been fired, the green man and the man with the guitar saw who fired it. For the last few minutes indeed these two mysterious individuals had never taken their eyes off Julot.

Julot, who Berthe had supposed from his appearance to be an honest cattle drover, was undoubtedly a crack shot. Having observed that the room was lit by a single chandelier composed of three electric bulbs, and that the current was supplied by only two wires running along the cornice, Julot had taken aim at the wires and cut them clean in two with a single shot!

Immediately following, the room was plunged into absolute darkness. A perfectly incredible uproar ensued, men and women struggling together and shouting and trampling one another, and china and dinner things crashing down from the sideboards and tables on to the floor.

Above the din a sudden hoarse cry of pain rang out, "Help!" Simultaneously Berthe, who was lost in the mob, heard a muttered exclamation in her ear and felt two hands groping all over her body as if someone were trying to identify her. The young nurse was the only woman in the room wearing a hat. Half swooning with terror, she felt herself picked up and thrust upon a bench, and then someone whispered in a voice laced with wine: "You are not to help number twenty-five—the Rambert woman—to escape."

Berthe was so utterly astonished that she overcame her fright sufficiently to stammer out a question:

"But what—but who—?"

Lower still, but yet more peremptorily, the voice became audible again.

"Fantômas forbids you to do it! And if you disobey, you will die!"

The nurse dropped back upon the bench half fainting with fright, and the row in the dining room grew worse. Three men were fighting now, the green man taking on two at once. The green man did not seem to feel the blows rained on him, but with a strength that was superhuman he grabbed an arm and slid his hands along the sleeve, never letting go of the arm, until he reached the wrist, when wrenching open the clenched fist, he slipped his fingers on to the palm of the hand. A little exclamation of triumph escaped him, and simultaneously the owner of the hand uttered an exclamation of pain, for the green man's fingers had touched a still raw wound upon the hollow of the palm.

But at that instant the green man's leg was caught between two powerful knees, and the slightest pressure more would have broken it. The green man was forced to let go of the hand he held; he fell to the ground with his adversary upon him, and for a moment it looked as if he was lost. But at the same moment his adversary let go of him, having been taken by surprise by yet a third combatant who joined in the fray and separated the first two, devoting himself to a furious assault upon the man whom the green man had tried to capture. The green man passed a rapid hand over the face of the individual who had just rescued him from the fierce assault and felt a shock of surprise as he identified the young man with the budding beard; thereupon he grabbed him firmly by the neck and did not let him go.

In the crush the fighters had been forced toward the staircase, and at this narrow entrance into the hall bodies were being trampled underfoot and screams pierced the air. François Bonbonne had not made the least attempt to interfere. He knew exactly what to do when trouble of this sort broke out, and he had gone to the corner of the street and sent the policeman on duty there to the nearest police station for help. As soon as the first gendarmes arrived, François Bonbonne led them behind the counter in the shop and showed them the fire hose; with skill acquired by long practice, they rapidly unrolled the hose, introduced it into the narrow mouth of the staircase, turned on the faucet, and proceeded to drench everybody in the dining room below.

The unexpected sousing stopped the combatants short, separated all the champions, and drove the shrieking mob back to the far end of the room.

The operation lasted for a good five minutes, and when the gendarmes considered that the customers of the Saint-Anthony's Pig were sufficiently cooled down, the sergeant threw the light of a lantern, which the proprietor obligingly had ready for him, over the dining room and authoritatively ordered the company to come up, one by one.

Seeing that resistance would be futile, everyone obeyed. As they slowly emerged at the top of the winding staircase, meek and subdued, the gendarmes at the top arrested them, slipped handcuffs on them, and sent them off in twos to the station. When the sergeant assumed that everyone had come out, he went down, just to make sure that nobody was still hiding there. But the room was not quite empty. One unfortunate man was lying on the floor, bathed in his own blood. It was the man with the guitar, and a knife had been driven through his chest!

The green man and the young man with the budding beard, of whom his companion had never once let go since identifying him during the fight, were taken to the station. The clerk, who was taking down the names of the prisoners, with difficulty repressed an exclamation of surprise when the green man produced an identification card and whispered a few words in his ear.

"Release that gentleman at once," said the clerk. "With regard to the other—"

"With regard to the other," the green man broke in, "kindly release him too. I want to keep him with me."

The clerk bowed in consent, and both men were immediately released from their handcuffs. The young man stared in astonishment at the individual who a minute before had been his companion in bonds and was about to thank him, but the other grasped him firmly by the wrist, as though to warn him of the impossibility of flight, and led him out of the police station. In the street they met the sergeant with a gendarme bringing in the unfortunate man with the guitar, who was barely breathing and in whom the officials had recognized a police detective. Without letting go of the youth, the green man bent forward to the sergeant and had a brief but animated conversation with him.

"Yes, sir, that's all," the sergeant said respectfully, "I haven't got anyone else."

The green man stamped his foot in wrath.

"Good Lord! Gurn has got away!"

Toward the rue Montmarte the green man rapidly dragged his companion, who was trembling all over and utterly at a loss to guess what the future held in store for him. Suddenly the green man halted, just under the light of a street lamp outside the church of Saint-Eustache. He stood squarely in front of his prisoner and looked him full in the eyes.

"I am Juve," he said, "the detective!" and as the young man stared at him in silent dismay, Juve went on, emphasizing each of his words and with a sardonic smile flickering over his face. "And you, Mademoiselle Jeanne—you are Charles Rambert!"

A PRISONER
AND A WITNESS

Juve had spoken in a tone of authority that precluded any reply. His keen eyes seemed to pierce through Paul and read his innermost soul. The light of the street lamp shed a wan halo around the lad, who began to move away from it. Juve held him fast.

"Come now, answer! You are Charles Rambert, and you were Mademoiselle Jeanne?"

"I don't understand," Paul declared.

"Really!" sneered Juve. He hailed a passing cab. "Get in," he ordered, and pushing the lad in before him he gave an address to the driver, entered the cab and shut the door. Juve sat there rubbing his hands as if pleased with his night's work. For several minutes he remained silent, and then turned to his companion.

"You think it is clever to deny it," he remarked, "but do you imagine it isn't obvious to everyone that you are Charles Rambert, and that you were disguised as Mademoiselle Jeanne?"

"But you are wrong," Paul insisted. "Charles Rambert is dead."

"So you know that, do you? Then you admit that you know what I am talking about?"

The lad blushed and began to tremble. Juve looked out of the window, pretending not to notice him, and smiled gently. Then he went on in a friendly tone. "But you know it's stupid to deny what can't be denied. Besides, you should remember that if I know you are Charles Rambert I must know something else as well, and therefore—"

"Well, yes," Paul acknowledged, "I *am* Charles Rambert, and

I was disguised as Mademoiselle Jeanne. How did you know it? Why were you at the Saint-Anthony's Pig? Did you come to arrest me? And where are you taking me now—to prison?"

Juve shrugged his shoulders.

"You want to know too much, my boy. Besides, you ought to know Paris, and so ought to be able to guess where I told the driver to go merely by looking at the streets we are passing through."

"That is exactly what frightens me," Charles Rambert replied. "We are on the quays, near the courthouse."

"And the police station, my son. It's useless to make a scene; you will gain nothing by attempting to get away. You are in the hands of justice, or rather in my hands, which is not quite the same thing, so come quietly. That is really good advice!"

A few minutes later the cab stopped at the Tour Pointue which has such melancholy associations for so many criminals. Juve got out and made his companion get out as well, paid the driver, and walked up the staircase to the first floor of the building. It was daylight now, and the men were coming on duty; all of them saluted Juve as he walked along with his trembling captive. The detective went down one long passage, turned into another and opened a door.

"Go in there," he ordered curtly.

Charles Rambert obeyed and found himself in a small room the nature of which he recognized immediately from the furniture it contained. It was the measuring room. So what he feared was about to happen; Juve was going to lock him up!

But the detective called out in a loud voice: "Hector, please!" And one of the men still on duty in case the police detectives needed to find the records of any previously convicted criminal came hurrying in.

"Ah, M. Juve, and you bagged one too! So early? You think he has been here before?"

"No," said Juve in a dry tone that put a stop to further indiscreet questions. "I don't want you to look up my companion's record but to take his measurements, and very carefully too."

The man was somewhat surprised at the order, for it was not usual to be asked to do this at so early an hour. He was rather irritable too at being disturbed from the rest he was enjoying, and he spoke very curtly to Charles Rambert.

"Get over here, please. Your height first; take off your boots."

Charles obeyed and stood under the measuring stick, and then, as the assistant ordered him, he submitted to having his fingers smeared with ink so that his fingerprints could be taken; to being photographed, full face and in profile; and finally to having the width of his head, from ear to ear, measured with a special pair of caliper compasses.

Hector was surprised by his docility.

"I must say your friend is not very talkative, M. Juve. What has he been up to?" And as the detective merely shrugged his shoulders and did not reply, he went on: "That's done, sir. We will develop the negatives and take the prints, and recopy the measurements, and the record will be filed in the register in a couple of hours."

Charles was more scared than ever. He felt that he was definitely arrested now. But Juve left the armchair in which he was sitting, and, coming up to him, laid his hand upon his shoulder, speaking with a certain gentleness.

"There are some other points I'd like to question you about." He led him from the room along a dark corridor and, taking a key from his pocket, opened a door and pushed the boy in before him. "Go in there," he said. "This is where we make the dynamometer tests."

A layman looking around the room might have almost supposed that it was merely some carpenter's shop. Pieces of wood of various shapes and sizes and sorts were arranged along the wall or on the floor; in glass cases were heaps of strips of metal, five or six inches long, and of varying thickness.

Juve closed the door carefully behind him.

"For God's sake, Monsieur Juve, tell me what you are going to do with me," Charles Rambert implored.

The detective smiled.

"Well, there you ask a question that I can't answer yet. What am I going to do with you, eh? That still depends upon a few things."

As he spoke Juve tossed his hat aside and, looking at a high

little table, proceeded to take off of it a gray cloth that pro-
tected it from dust. He moved it into the middle of the room.
This article was composed of a metal body screwed on to a
sturdy tripod, with a lower tray that moved backward and forward, and two lateral buttresses with a steel crosspiece firmly
bolted on to them above. On top of this were two dynamome-
ters operated by an ingenious piece of mechanism. Juve looked
at Charles Rambert and explained.

"This is Dr. Bertillon's effraction dynamometer. I am going
to use it to find out once and for all whether you warrant further interest. I don't want to tell you more just right now." Juve
slipped a thin strip of wood he had selected with particular care
from one of the heaps of material arranged along the wall into
a specially prepared notch. From a chest he took a tool that
Charles Rambert, who had had some intimate acquaintance of
late with the light-fingered community, immediately recognized
as a jimmy. "Take hold of that," said Juve, and as Charles took
it in his hand he added: "Now put the jimmy into this groove,
and press with all your strength. If you can move that needle to
the point that I want, which is difficult but not impossible, you
can congratulate yourself on being in luck."

Thus encouraged by the detective, Charles exerted all his
might upon the lever, afraid only that he might not be strong
enough. Juve stopped him quite soon.

"That's all right," he said, and substituting a strip of sheet
iron for the strip of wood, he handed another tool to the lad.
"Now try again."

A few seconds later Juve took a magnifying glass and closely
examined both the strip of metal and the strip of wood. He gave
a little satisfied click with his tongue and seemed to be pleased.

"Charles Rambert," he remarked, "I think we are going to
do a good morning's work. Dr. Bertillon's new apparatus is a
marvelously useful invention."

The detective might have gone on with his congratulatory
monologue had not an attendant come into the room at that
moment.

"Ah, there you are, M. Juve, I have been looking for you

everywhere. Someone is asking for you who says he knows you will receive him. I told him this was not a good time, but he was so insistent that I promised to bring you his card. Besides, he says you gave him an appointment."

Juve took the card and glanced at it.

"That's all right," he said. "Ask the gentleman in and tell him I will be with him in a minute." The attendant went out, and Juve looked at Charles with a smile. "You are worn out," he said; "before we do anything else we've got to let you get some rest. Follow me; I'll take you to a room where you can sack out on a sofa and sleep for an hour or so while I go and see this visitor." He led the boy into a small waiting room, and as Charles obediently stretched himself out on the sofa, Juve looked at the pale, nervous, and completely silent boy, and said with even greater gentleness: "There, go to sleep, sleep quietly, and in a little while—"

Juve left the room, and called a man to whom he gave an order in a quiet voice.

"Stay with that gentleman, please. He is a friend of mine, but a friend, you understand, who must not leave this place. I am going to see someone, but I will come up again in a while," and Juve hurried downstairs.

The visitor rose as the door opened, and Juve made a formal bow.

"M. Gervais Aventin?" he said.

"M. Gervais Aventin," that gentleman replied. "And you are Detective Juve?"

"I am, sir," the detective answered, and pointing his visitor to a chair he took a seat himself at a small table littered with official documents.

"Sir," Juve began, "I urgently asked you to come to Paris today, because from inquiries I had made about you, I was sure that you were a man with a sense of duty, who would not resent being inconvenienced when it was a question of advancing the causes of justice and of truth."

The visitor, a man of perhaps thirty, of somewhat fashionable appearance and careful though understated dress, was rather surprised.

"Inquiries about me, sir? Why? I must confess that I was astonished when I received your letter informing me that the famous Detective Juve wanted to see me, and at first I suspected some practical joke. On second thought, I decided to come here without worrying, but I had no idea that you had made any inquiries about me. How do you know me, may I ask?"

Juve smiled.

"Is it a fact," he asked, instead of replying directly, for like the good detective he was, he enjoyed mystifying people with his skill, "is it a fact that your name is Gervais Aventin? A civil engineer? Considerably well off? About to be married? And that lately you made a short trip to Limoges?"

The young man nodded and smiled.

"Your information is perfectly correct. But I do not yet understand what crime I have committed to warrant these inquiries on your part."

Juve smiled again.

"I wondered, sir, why you didn't answer the local inquiries that have been made at my instance, or the advertisements that I have had put in the papers, in which I discreetly made it known that the police wanted to get in touch with all passengers who traveled first-class on the slow train from Paris to Luchon on the night of the twenty-third of December last."

This time the young man looked anxious.

"Good God!" he exclaimed. "Are you working for my future father-in-law?"

Juve burst into a roar of laughter.

"First acknowledge that you did travel by that train on that night; that you got into it at Vierzon, where you live and where you are going to be married; and that you were going to Limoges to see a lady—and that you did not want your fiancée's family to know anything about it."

Gervais Aventin pulled himself together.

"I had no idea that the police undertook espionage of that sort," he said rather dryly. "But it is true, sir, that I went to Limoges—my last post before I was appointed to Vierzon—to make a final farewell to a lady. But since you are so accurately informed about all this, since you even know what train I went by, a train I deliberately chose because in little places like Vierzon so much notice is taken of people who travel by the express, you must also know—"

Juve checked him with a wave of the hand.

"A truce to this prank," he said; "excuse me, sir, I was only amusing myself by observing once more how quickly decent people, who have a little sin on their conscience, are disturbed when they think they have been caught. Your love affairs do not interest me, sir; I don't want to know if you have a lady friend or not. The information I want from you is of a very different nature. Tell me simply this: In what circumstances did you make that journey? What carriage did you get into? Who traveled with you in that carriage? I am asking you because, sir, I have every reason to believe that you traveled that night with a murderer who committed a particularly terrible crime, and I think you may be able to give me some interesting information."

The young man who had been looking grave smiled once more.

"I would rather answer that than questions about my defunct love affairs. Well, sir. I got into the train in Vierzon, into a first-class carriage—"

"What kind of carriage?"

"One of the old-fashioned corridor carriages, that is to say, not a corridor communicating with the other carriages, but a single carriage with four compartments, two in the middle opening onto the corridor, and two at the ends opening onto the corridor by a small door."

"I know," said Juve; "the lavatory is in the center, and the end compartments are like the ordinary noncorridor compartments, except that they have only seven seats and also have the little door that opens onto the narrow passage down one side of the carriage."

"That's it. I got into the smoking compartment at the end."

"You're going too fast," said Juve. "Tell me whom you saw in the various compartments. Let us go even farther back. You were on the platform, waiting for the train; it came in. What happened then?"

"To be very precise," Gervais Aventin remarked, "when the train pulled in I looked for the first-class carriage; it was a few

yards away from me, and the corridor was alongside the platform. I got in and was about to choose my compartment. I remember clearly that I went first to the rear compartment, the
last one in the carriage. I could not get into that, for the door
opening into it from the corridor was locked."

"That is correct," Juve nodded. "I know from the guard that
that compartment was empty. What did you do then?"

"I turned back and, passing the ladies' compartment and the
lavatory, decided to take my seat in the one next to it opening
on to the corridor. But no luck; a pane of glass was broken and
it was bitterly cold there, so I had to resort to the only compartment left, the smoking one toward the front of the train."

"Were there many of you there?"

"I thought at first that I was going to have a fellow traveler,
for there was some luggage and a rug arranged on the seat. But
the passenger must have been in the lavatory, for I didn't see
him. I lay down on the other seat and went to sleep. When I got
out of the train at Limoges, my companion must have been in
the lavatory again, for I remember quite distinctly that he was
not on the opposite seat. I thought at the time how easy it
would have been for me to steal his luggage. Nobody would
have seen me."

Juve had listened intently to every word of the story. He
asked for one further detail with a certain anxiety in his voice.

"Tell me, sir, when you woke up did you have any impression that the baggage arranged on the seat opposite yours had
been disturbed at all? Might the traveler, whom you did not
see, have come in for a sleep while you yourself were asleep?"

Gervais Aventin made a little gesture of uncertainty.

"I can't answer, M. Juve. I did not notice; and, besides, when
I got into the compartment, the shade was pulled down over the
lamp and the curtains were drawn across the windows. I hardly
saw how the things were arranged. And then when I got out at
Limoges I was in a hurry, and only thought about finding my
ticket and jumping on to the platform. But I don't think the
other fellow did take his place while I was asleep. I did not hear
a sound, and yet I did not sleep at all heavily."

"So you traveled in a first-class compartment in the slow

train from Paris to Luchon on the night of the twenty-third of December, and in that compartment there was the luggage of a traveler whom you did not see—who may not have been there?"

"Yes," said Gervais Aventin, and when the detective was silent for a moment, he asked: "Is my information too vague to be of any use to you?"

Juve was wondering inwardly why in God's name Etienne Rambert was not in that compartment when, according to the depositions of the guard, he must have been there; but he said nothing about this. Instead, he said:

"Your information is most valuable, sir. You have told me everything I wanted to know."

Gervais Aventin displayed still more surprise.

"Well," he said, "to show your gratitude, Monsieur Juve, tell me something that puzzles me. How did you know I traveled by that train that night?"

The detective drew out his wallet and from an inner pocket produced a first-class ticket, which he held out to the engineer.

"That is very simple," he replied. "Here is your ticket. I wanted to know exactly who everyone was who traveled in that first-class compartment, so I sent for all the first-class tickets that were given up by passengers who left the train at the different stations. That's how I got yours. It had been issued at Vierzon, the station where you got in, so I interrogated the clerk at the booking office who gave me a description of you; then I sent down an inspector to Vierzon to make discreet inquiries, and he got me all the information I needed. All I had to do then was to write and ask you to come here today; and the unfortunate story of your broken affair with the lady guaranteed you would be on time for the appointment!"

JÉRÔME FANDOR

Whistling, a sure sign with him of a good mood, Juve opened the door of the little room where he had left Charles Rambert and looked at the sleeping lad.

"It's wonderful to be young," he remarked to the man he had left on guard; "that boy plunges into the wildest adventures and comes within an inch of the scaffold, and yet after one late night he sleeps as peacefully as any chancellor of the Legion of Honor!" He shook the lad with a friendly hand. "Get up, lazy-bones! It's ten o'clock, high time for me to take you away."

"Where to?" the unhappy boy asked, rubbing his eyes.

"There's no doubt that inquisitiveness is your fatal flaw," Juve replied cryptically. "Well, we've got a quarter of an hour's drive ahead of us. But you're not going to prison; I'm going to take you home with me!"

Juve had taken off his collar and tie and put on an old jacket, had set some bread and milk in front of Charles Rambert, and was leisurely enjoying his own breakfast.

"I didn't want to answer any questions before," he said, "because I hate talking in cabs where I have to sit by a man's side and can't see him or hear half of what he says. But now that we are comfortable here, I've no right to keep you waiting any longer, and I'll give you some good news."

"Comfortable" was the right word with which to describe Juve's private abode. The detective had attained a respected and well-paid position in his profession, and, exposed as he was in the course of his work to all sorts of danger and deprivation, he compensated himself by making a cozy, if not luxurious, nest where he could relax from the work.

When he finished his breakfast he lit a big cigar and sank into an easy chair, crossing his hands behind his head. He turned a steady gaze upon Charles Rambert, who was still completely puzzled and half frightened by this sudden friendliness, and did not know whether he was a prisoner or not

"I will give you a bit of good news; that is, you are innocent in the Langrune affair when you were Charles Rambert, and innocent also in the Danidoff affair, when you were Mademoiselle Jeanne. I need not say anything about that brawl last night, in which you played a more distinguished part."

"What are you telling me?" asked Charles nervously. "Of course I know I did not rob Princess Sonia Danidoff; but how did you recognize me last night, and how did you find out that I was Mademoiselle Jeanne?"

Juve smiled and shook back a lock of hair that was falling over his eyes.

"Listen, my boy, do you suppose that knockout blow you dealt Henri Verbier when he was making love to Mademoiselle Jeanne could fail to make me determined to find out who that young lady was with the strength of a man?"

The allusion made Charles very uneasy.

"But that does not explain how you recognized me tonight. I recognized you when you were Henri Verbier at the hotel, but I had no idea that it was you last night."

"That's nothing," said Juve with a shake of the head. "And you may as well understand once and for all that when I have looked anybody square in the face, he needs to be a pretty clever fellow to fool me afterward by means of any disguise. You don't know how to make yourself up, but I do, and that's why I took you in and you did not take me in."

"Why do you believe I didn't rob Princess Sonia Danidoff?" Charles asked after a pause. "Everything points to my having been the thief."

"Not quite everything," Juve answered gently. "There are one or two things you don't know, and I'll tell you one of them. The princess was robbed by the same man who robbed Madame Van den Rosen, wasn't she? Well, Madame Van den Rosen was the victim of a burglary; some of the furniture in her room was broken into, and the tests I made this morning with the dynamometer proved to me that you are not strong enough to have caused that damage."

"Not strong enough?" Charles exclaimed.

"No. I told you at the time that your innocence would be proved if you were strong enough, but I said that to prevent you from playing any tricks and not using all your strength. As a matter of fact, it was your comparative weakness that saved you. The dynamometer tests and the figures I obtained just now prove absolutely that you are innocent of the Van den Rosen robbery and, consequently, of the robbery of Sonia Danidoff."

Again the lad reflected for a minute or two.

"But you didn't know who I was when you came to the hotel, did you? And therefore had no suspicion that I was Charles Rambert? That's true, isn't it? How did you find out? I was supposed to be dead."

"That was child's play," Juve replied. "I got the anthropometric records of the body that had been buried as yours, and I planned to get symmetrical photographs of you in your character of Mademoiselle Jeanne, as I did of you today at headquarters. My first job was to find Mademoiselle Jeanne, but I very soon found her, as I expected. She had turned into a man again, and was living in the most disreputable company. I made any number of inquiries, and when I went to the Saint-Anthony's Pig last evening I knew that some unknown person had been buried in your place, that Paul was Mademoiselle Jeanne, and that Mademoiselle Jeanne was Charles Rambert. It was my intention to arrest you and to ascertain definitely by means of the dynamometer that you were innocent of the Langrune and the Danidoff crimes."

"Well, perhaps the dynamometer explains how you know I am not the man who committed the robbery at the hotel, but what clears me of the Langrune murder?"

"Bless my soul!" Juve retorted. "You are arguing as if you wanted to prove you were guilty. Well, my boy, it's the same story. The man who murdered the Marquise de Langrune smashed things, and the dynamometer has proven that you are not strong enough to have been the man."

"And suppose I had been mad at the time," Charles said, his hesitation and his tone betraying his anxiety about the answer, "could I have been strong enough then? Might I have committed these crimes without knowing anything about it?"

But Juve shook his head.

"I know; you are referring to your mother, and are haunted by an idea that through some hereditary insanity you might be a somnambulist and have done these things in your sleep. Come, Charles, finish your breakfast and put all that out of your head. To begin with, you would not have been strong enough, even then; and in the next place there is nothing at present to show that you are mad, nor even that your poor mother— But I need not go on; I've got some rather odd notions on that subject."

"Then, M. Juve—"

"Drop the 'monsieur'; call me 'Juve.' "

"Then if you know that I am innocent, you can go and tell my father? I have nothing to fear? I can reappear in my own name?"

Juve looked at the lad with an ironical smile.

"How you go on!" he exclaimed. "Please understand that although I do believe you are innocent, I am almost certainly the only person who does. And unfortunately I have not yet got any evidence that would be sufficiently convincing to put the idea of your guilt out of your father's head, or anybody else's. This is not the time for you to reappear; it would simply mean that you would be arrested by some detective who knows less than I do and thrown into prison, as you confidently expected to be this morning."

"Then what is to become of me?"

"What do you think you should do yourself?"

"Go to see my father."

"No, no," Juve protested once more. "I'm telling you not to go. It would be stupid and utterly useless. Wait a few days, a few weeks if need be. When I have put my hand on Fantômas's shoulder, I will be the very first to take you to your father and proclaim your innocence."

"Why wait until Fantômas is arrested?" Charles asked, the mere sound of the name seeming to awaken all his former enthusiasm on the subject of that famous criminal.

"Because if you are innocent of the charge brought against you, it is extremely likely that Fantômas is the guilty party. When he is nabbed you will be able to proclaim your innocence without any fear."

Charles sat silent for some minutes, musing on the odds that made his own return to normal life contingent on the arrest of a mysterious criminal, who was merely suspected of existing, and had never even been seen.

"What do you advise me to do?" he asked presently.

The detective got up and began to pace the room.

"Well," he began, "the first thing is that I am interested in you, and the next is, that while I was fighting last night with that scoundrel in the bar, I thought for a minute or two that it was all up with me; your help saved my life. On the other hand, I may now be said to have saved your life by ascertaining your innocence. So we are even in a way. So it's up to me to start a new exchange and not turn you out into the street where you would inevitably get into fresh trouble. So this is what I propose: Change your name and go and take a room somewhere; get some proper clothes and then come back to me, and I'll give you a letter to a friend of mine who is on one of the big evening papers. You are well educated, and I know you are energetic. You are interested in everything connected with the police, and you'll make a splendid reporter. Would you like to try that?"

"I can't thank you enough," Charles said gratefully. "I should love to be able to earn my living working at a job like that."

Juve cut his thanks short and held out some bank notes.

"There's some money; now get out of here; it's high time we both got a little sleep. Get busy finding some rooms, and in two weeks I shall expect you to be editor of *La Capitale.*"

"What name will you use to introduce me to your friend?" Charles asked, after a nervous little pause.

"H'm!" said Juve with a smile. "It will have to be an alias, of course."

"Yes, and as it will be the name I'll write under it ought to be an easy one to remember."

"Something arresting, like Fantômas!" said Juve teasingly, amused by the curious immaturity of this boy, who could take so keen an interest in such a trifle when he was in so critical a situation. "Choose something not too common for the first name, and something short for the other. Why not keep the first syllable of Fantômas? Oh, I've got it—Fandor; what about Jérôme Fandor?"

Charles murmured it over and over.

"Jérôme Fandor! Yes, you are right, it sounds good."

Juve pushed him out the door.

"Well, Jérôme Fandor, leave me to my rest, and go and get ready for the new life that I'm going to open up for you!"

Bewildered by his amazing adventures, Charles Rambert, or Jérôme Fandor, walked down Juve's staircase wondering, "Why should he take so much trouble about me? What interest or what motive can he have? And how on earth does he find out so many incredible things?"

A CUP OF TEA

After the tragic death of her husband, Lady Beltham—whose previous life had already inclined to the austere—withdrew into almost complete seclusion. The world of society and fashion knew her no more. But in the world where poverty and suffering reign, in hospital wards and squalid streets, a tall and beautiful woman might often be seen, dressed all in black, with distinguished bearing and serene and grave eyes, distributing alms and consolation as she moved. It was Lady Beltham, kind, good, bent on the work of charity to which she had vowed her days.

Yet she had not allowed herself to be crushed by sorrow; after the tragedy that left her a widow, she had assumed the effective control of her husband's estate and, helped by faithful friends, had carried on his interests and administered his fortune, spreading a halo of kindness all around her.

To help her in the heavy correspondence entailed by these affairs, she found three secretaries, and that was none too many. On M. Etienne Rambert's recommendation, Thérèse Auvernois was now one of these, and the young girl was perfectly happy in her new surroundings; time was helping her to forget the tragedy that had taken her grandmother from her at Beaulieu, and she enjoyed the company of the well-born, well-bred Englishwomen.

Lady Beltham was reclining on a sofa in the great hall of her house at Neuilly. It was a spacious room, furnished half as a lounge and half as an office, and Lady Beltham liked to receive people there. A large glass-enclosed balcony commanded a view of the garden and the boulevard Richard Wallace beyond, with the Bois de Boulogne beyond that. A few minutes before, a footman had brought in a table and set out tea things, and Lady

Beltham was reading while Thérèse and the two young English girls were chattering among themselves.

The telephone bell rang and Thérèse answered it.

"Hullo? Yes . . . yes, you want to know if you may call this evening? The Reverend—oh, yes, you have just come from Scotland? Hold on a minute." She turned to Lady Beltham. "It is Mr. William Hope, and he wants to know if you will see him tonight. He has just come from your place in Scotland."

"The dear man!" exclaimed Lady Beltham. "Of course he may come." And as Thérèse turned lightly to convey her permission to the clergyman waiting at the other end of the line, she caught a smile on the face of one of the other girls. "What is the joke, Lisbeth?" she asked.

The girl laughed brightly.

"I think the worthy parson must have smelled the tea and toast, and wanted to make up for the miserable dinner he got on the train."

"You are incorrigible," Lady Beltham replied. "Mr. Hope is above such material matters."

"Indeed he isn't, Lady Beltham," the girl persisted. "Why, only the other day he told Thérèse that a badly cooked steak was a kind of sacrilege."

"A badly cooked pheasant," Thérèse corrected her.

"You are both wicked little slanderers," Lady Beltham protested gently, "and don't know the blessing a good appetite is. You do, Susannah, don't you?"

Susannah, a pretty Irish girl, looked up from a letter she was reading and blushed.

"Oh, Lady Beltham, I've been much less hungry since Harry's ship sailed."

"I don't quite see the connection," Lady Beltham answered. "Love is good nourishment for the soul, but not for the body. However, a good appetite is nothing to be ashamed of, and you ought to keep healthy for your future husband and qualify in every way to be an excellent mother of a family."

"With lots and lots of children," Lisbeth went on wickedly, "seven or eight daughters at the very least, all of whom will marry nice young clergymen when their time comes and—"

She stopped speaking and the chatter died away as a footman entered and announced the Reverend William Hope, who followed him immediately into the room, an elderly man with a full, clean-shaven face and a comfortable portliness of figure.

Lady Beltham offered him her hand.

"I am delighted you are back," she said. "Will you have a cup of tea with us?"

The parson made a general bow to the girls gathered about the table.

"I got a wretched dinner on the train," he began, but Lisbeth interrupted him.

"Don't you think this tea smells delicious?" she asked.

The parson put out his hand to take the cup she offered to him, and bowed and smiled.

"Precisely what I was going to say, Miss Lisbeth."

Thérèse and Susannah turned away to hide their laughter, and Lady Beltham adroitly changed the subject. She moved toward her writing table.

"Mr. Hope must have much to tell me, girls, and it is getting late. I must get down to business. Did you have a good journey?"

"As good as usual, Lady Beltham. The people at Scotwell Hill are very courageous and good, but it will be a hard winter; there is snow on the hills already."

"Have the women and children gotten all their woolen things?"

"Oh, yes, twelve hundred garments have been distributed according to a list drawn up by the understeward; here it is." And he handed a paper to Lady Beltham, who passed it on to Susannah.

"I will ask you to check the list," she said to the girl and turned again to the clergyman. "The understeward is a good fellow, but he is a rabid politician. He may have omitted some families that are openly radical, but I think charity should be given equally to all, for poverty makes no political distinctions."

"That is the true Christian view," the clergyman said approvingly.

"And what about the sanatorium at Glasgow?" Lady Beltham went on.

"It is very nearly finished," the good man answered. "I have got your lawyers to cut down the contractor's accounts by something like fifteen percent, which means a saving of nearly three hundred pounds."

"Excellent," said Lady Beltham, and she turned to Thérèse. "You must add that three hundred pounds to the funds of the Scotwell Hill coal charity," she said. "They will need all of it if the winter is going to be a hard one." Thérèse made a note of the instruction, full of admiration for Lady Beltham's simple generosity.

But Mr. Hope was fidgeting in his chair. He seized an opportunity when Lady Beltham was busy making notes and had turned her deep and steady eyes away from him to say in a low tone:

"Have I your permission just to mention—poor Lord Beltham?"

Lady Beltham started, and her face betrayed an emotion which she bravely controlled. Hearing the name pronounced, the three girls withdrew to the far end of the room, where they began to talk among themselves. Lady Beltham signified her assent, and Mr. Hope began.

"You know, dear friend, this has been my first visit to Scotland since Lord Beltham's death. I found your tenants still terribly upset by the tragedy that occurred nearly a year ago. They know by heart all the newspaper accounts of the mysterious circumstances attending Lord Beltham's death, but those are not enough to satisfy the sympathetic curiosity of these excellent people, and I was obliged to tell them over and over again in full detail—all we knew."

"I hope no scandal has gathered around his name," said Lady Beltham quickly.

"You need have no fear of that," the clergyman replied in the same low tone. "The rumor that got about when the crime was first discovered, that Lord Beltham had been surprised in an intrigue and killed in revenge, has not been believed. Local opinion has it that he was decoyed into a trap and killed by the man Gurn, who meant to rob him but who was either surprised or thought he was going to be, and fled before he had time to take the money from the body of his victim. They know that the murderer has never been caught, but they also know that there is a price on his head, and they all hope the police— Oh, forgive me for recalling all these painful memories!"

While he had been speaking, Lady Beltham's face had expressed almost every shade of emotion and distress; it seemed to be drawn with pain at his concluding words. But she made an effort to control herself and spoke resignedly.

"It cannot be helped, dear Mr. Hope. Go on."

But the clergyman changed the topic.

"Oh, I was quite forgetting," he said more brightly. "The understeward has fired the two Tillys, quite on his own authority: you must remember them—two brothers, blacksmiths, who drank a great deal and paid very little, and generally scandalized the place."

"I object to the understeward doing any such thing without asking me first," Lady Beltham exclaimed. "Man's duty is to persuade and forgive, not to judge and punish. Kindness breeds kindness, and it is pity that brings about change. Why should a subordinate, my understeward, presume to do what I would not permit myself to do?"

She had sprung to her feet and was pacing about the room; she had completely dropped the impassive mask she habitually wore to conceal her real personality.

The three girls watched her in silence.

The door opened again and Silbertown came in, the majordomo of Lady Beltham's establishment at Neuilly. He brought the evening letters, and the girls speedily took all the envelopes and newspapers from the tray and began to sort and open them, while the majordomo conversed with his mistress, and the Reverend William Hope seized the opportunity to say good night.

Many of the letters were merely appeals for help or money, but one long letter Lisbeth handed to Lady Beltham. She glanced at the signature.

"Ah, here is news of M. Etienne Rambert," she exclaimed, and as Thérèse instinctively drew near, knowing that she, too, might hear something of what her old friend had written, Lady Beltham put the letter into her hand. "You read it, my dear, and then you can tell me what he has to say."

Thérèse read the letter eagerly. M. Etienne Rambert had left Paris a week before, on a long and important journey. The energetic old fellow was to make a trip to Germany first, and then go from Hamburg to England, where he had some business to attend to on behalf of Lady Beltham, with whom he was on more confidential terms than ever. Then he meant to sail from Southampton and spend the winter in Colombia, where he had important interests of his own to look after.

While Thérèse was reading, Lady Beltham continued her conversation with her majordomo.

"I am glad you had the park gate seen to this afternoon," she said. "You know how nervous I am. My childhood in Scotland was very lonely, and ever since then I have had a vague terror of being alone and of the darkness."

The majordomo reassured her.

"There is nothing for your ladyship to be afraid of; the house is perfectly safe and carefully guarded. Walter the porter is a first-rate watchdog and always sleeps with one eye open. And I, too—"

"Yes, I know, Silbertown," the young widow replied, "and when I give myself time to think I am not nervous. Thank you, you can leave now."

She turned to the three girls.

"I am tired, dears; we won't stay up any later."

Lisbeth and Susannah kissed her affectionately and went away. Thérèse lingered a moment, to bring a bible and place it on a table close to Lady Beltham's chair. Lady Beltham laid a hand upon her head as if in blessing and said gently:

"Good night, God bless you, dear child!"

LORD BELTHAM'S
MURDERER

It was on the stroke of midnight, and absolute stillness reigned throughout the house.

But Lady Beltham had not gone to bed. Although she had remained in the great hall where she did her work, she had been unable to settle down. She had read a little and begun a letter, gotten up and sat down, and finally, beginning to feel chilly, she had drawn an easy chair up to the hearth, where a log was just burning out, and stretching out her slippers toward the warmth she had fallen into a daydream.

A sound caught her ear and she sat upright. At first she thought her mind was playing tricks on her, but in another minute the noise grew louder; there was the hurrying of feet and voices, muffled at first but rapidly becoming louder, and at last a regular uproar, doors banging, glass breaking, and shouts from all parts of the house. Lady Beltham jumped up, nervous and trembling; she was just going to the window when she heard a shot and stopped dead where she stood. Then she rushed out into the vestibule.

"Help!" she screamed. "What on earth is the matter?" And remembering the girls for whom she had assumed responsibility, she called out anxiously for them. "Lisbeth! Thérèse! Susannah! Come here!"

Doors upstairs were flung open, and with their hair streaming over their nightdresses Thérèse and Susannah rushed downstairs and crouched by her side, stifling moans of terror.

"Lisbeth? Where is Lisbeth?" Lady Beltham asked sharply.

At the same moment Lisbeth appeared, her face distorted with fright.

"Oh, Lady Beltham, it's awful! There's a man, a burglar in the garden! And Walter is beating him up! They are fighting terribly! They'll kill one another!"

Silbertown, the majordomo, came rushing in. Seeing the three girls in their nightgowns, he made as if to draw back, but Lady Beltham called him in and demanded an explanation.

"We had just finished our rounds," he answered breathlessly, "when we caught sight of a man hiding in the shadows, a thief probably. When we shouted to him he ran away, but we ran after him and grabbed him; he resisted and there was a fight. But we have got him, and the police will be here in a few minutes."

Lady Beltham listened, with set jaw and hands clenched.

"A thief?" she said, controlling her emotions. "How do you know he is a thief?"

"Well," stammered the majordomo, "he is very poorly dressed, and besides, what was he doing in the garden?"

Lady Beltham was recovering her calm.

"What excuse did he give for being there?" she asked coldly.

"We didn't give him time to invent one," said the majordomo. "We collared him almost as soon as we saw him. And you know, Madame, how strong Walter is. Walter really gave it to him." And the majordomo clenched his fists and vividly demonstrated the porter's reception of the stranger.

Lisbeth was still overcome by what she had seen.

"Oh, the blood!" she muttered hysterically. "It was all over the place!"

Lady Beltham spoke angrily to the majordomo.

"I hate brutality; is the man seriously hurt? I hope not. You ought to have questioned him before assaulting him. No one in my house has a right to use violence. 'Whoso smites with the sword shall perish by the sword'!"

The majordomo heard her in silent astonishment; it was not at all what he expected, in view of all the circumstances.

Lady Beltham went on more gently:

"I suppose I shall have to apologize to this man for your wrong and thoughtless behavior."

"Apologize?" exclaimed Silbertown in amazement. "Surely your ladyship will not do that?"

"One must not shrink from humiliation when one has been in the wrong," said Lady Beltham, in the pulpit manner she affected. "Tell Walter to come here."

A few minutes later the porter, a muscular giant of a man, came into the room and made a clumsy bow.

"How was it possible for anyone to get into the house at this time of night?" his mistress inquired coldly.

Walter dropped his eyes and twisted his cap nervously.

"I hope your ladyship will forgive me. I caught the fellow, and as he was struggling, I hit him. Then two of the footmen came, and they are looking after him in the kitchen."

"Has he given any explanation of his presence here since you assaulted him—and I am very angry about that," said Lady Beltham.

"He hasn't said anything, at least—"

"Well?"

"I don't want to tell you."

"Please do!" said Lady Beltham irritably.

"Well," Walter replied, overcoming his nervousness with an effort, "he says your ladyship is well known for your charity to everybody, and—he wants to see you."

There was a moment's pause.

"I will see him," said Lady Beltham at last, in a stifled voice.

"Will your ladyship allow me to point out the danger of doing any such thing?" Silbertown exclaimed. "Very likely the man is a lunatic! Or it may be a trick; Lord Beltham was murdered, and perhaps—"

Lady Beltham looked intently at the majordomo, as if trying to read his thoughts. Then she answered slowly:

"I will see him. I will have more pity on him than you did," and as the majordomo and the porter made a gesture of futile protest, she added peremptorily: "I have given my orders; kindly obey."

When the two men had reluctantly left the room, Lady Beltham turned to the three girls.

"You had better leave, darlings," she said, kindly but firmly. "Go back to bed. Excitement is bad for you. No, I assure you I am in no danger whatever." And for a few minutes she was left alone.

"Speak," said Lady Beltham in a toneless voice.

The majordomo and the porter had led in a man with un-kempt hair and ragged beard; he was dressed entirely in black, and his face was tired and haggard. Lady Beltham, ghastly pale, was leaning for support against the back of an armchair. The man did not raise his eyes to her.

"I will not speak unless we are alone," he answered dully.

"Alone?" said Lady Beltham, fighting down her emotions. "Then it is something serious you have to tell me?"

"If you know anything of people in misfortune, Madame," the man answered gently, "you know that they do not like to humiliate themselves before—before those who cannot under-stand." And he nodded toward the majordomo and the porter.

"I do know something of misfortune," Lady Beltham replied, in firmer tones, "and I will hear you alone." She looked at her two servants. "Leave us, please."

The majordomo started.

"Leave you alone with him? It's crazy!" And as Lady Beltham merely looked at him in haughty surprise, he began to withdraw in confusion but still protesting. "It's—it's— Your la-dyship has no idea what this fellow wants; do please—"

But Lady Beltham curtly cut him short.

"That is enough!"

A heavy velvet curtain fell over the door, and in the room, dimly lighted by a small electric lamp, Lady Beltham was alone with the strange individual to whom she had so readily, so oddly, consented to see in private. She followed her servants to the door and locked it after them. Then with a sudden move-ment she ran toward the man, who was standing motionless in the middle of the room following her with his eyes, and flung herself into his arms.

"Oh, Gurn, my darling, my darling!" she cried. "I love you! I love you, darling!" She looked up at him and saw blood on his forehead. "Good God! They've hurt you! You must be in pain. Give me your lips!" With kisses she stanched the blood that was trickling down his cheeks, and with her fingers she smoothed his hair. "I am so happy!" she murmured, and broke off again.

"But you must be crazy! Why, why come here like this and let yourself be caught and beaten up?"

Moodily Gurn answered, returning each kiss of hers with one of his own.

"It's been torture without you! And this evening I was prowling around and saw a light. I thought that everyone would be asleep—except you, of course. And so I came straight to you, over walls, and gates—drawn to you like a moth to the flame!"

With shining eyes and heaving breast Lady Beltham clung to her lover.

"I love you so! How brave you are! Yes, I am completely yours, only yours. But this is madness! You might have been arrested and subjected to God knows what horrors, without my knowing it!"

Gurn seemed to be hypnotized by the fierce and passionate love of this great lady.

"I never gave it a thought," he murmured. "I only thought of you!"

Silence fell upon these tragic lovers as they stood beaming love at each other and recalling memories; utterly unlike as they were outwardly, yet they were linked by the strongest bond of all, the bond of love.

"What happy hours we spent together out there!" Lady Beltham whispered. Her thoughts had wandered to the far Transvaal and the battlefield where first she had set eyes on Gurn, the sergeant of artillery with powder-blackened face; and then to the homeward voyage on the mighty steamer that bore them across the blue sea, toward the dull white cliffs of England.

Gurn's thoughts followed hers.

"Out there! Yes, and then on the vast ocean, on the ship bound for home! The peace and quiet of it all! And our meetings every day; our long, long talks, and longer silences—in the clear starlight of those tropical skies! We were learning to know each other—"

"We were learning to love each other," she said. "And then—London, and Paris, and all the tumult of daily life threatening our love. But it is stronger than anything in the world;

and—do you remember? Oh, the ecstasy of it all! But do you remember too what you did for me—through me—thirteen months ago?"

She had risen and, with white lips and haggard eyes, held Gurn's hands with her own even more tightly. Emotion choked her words.

"Yes, I remember," Gurn went on slowly; "it was in our little room in the rue Lévert, and I was on my knees beside you when the door opened quietly, and there stood Lord Beltham, insane with rage and jealousy!"

"I don't know what happened then," Lady Beltham whispered in a hopeless undertone, dropping her head again.

"I do," muttered Gurn. "His eyes were riveted on you, and a pistol was pointed at your heart! He would have fired, but I sprang and knocked him down! And then I strangled him!"

Lady Beltham's eyes were fixed on the man's hands that she still held between her own.

"And I saw the muscles in these hands tense up beneath the skin as they tightened on his throat!"

"I killed him!" groaned the man.

But Lady Beltham, swept by a surge of passion, looked up and sought his lips.

"Oh, Gurn!" she sobbed. "My darling!"

"Listen," said Gurn harshly, after a pause of anxious silence. "I had to see you tonight, for who knows if tomorrow—" Lady Beltham shrank at the words, but Gurn went on regardless. "The police are after me. Of course I have almost made myself unrecognizable, but lately I have almost been caught twice."

"Do you think the police have any idea of what really happened?" Lady Beltham asked abruptly.

"No," said Gurn after a moment's hesitation. "They think I killed him with the mallet. They did not find out that I had to strangle him. As far as I know, they found no hand marks on his throat. In any case, they could not have been certain, for his collar—you understand." The man spoke of his crime without the least sign of remorse or repugnance now; he dreaded only getting caught. "But nonetheless they have identified me. That detective Juve is very clever."

"We did not think it through," Lady Beltham said despairingly. "We ought to have led them to suspect someone else, have made them think that it was someone like Fantômas."

"Not that!" said Gurn nervously; "don't talk about Fantômas! We did all we could. But the main thing now is that I should get away. I had better go—across the channel—across the Atlantic—anywhere. But—would you come too?"

Lady Beltham did not hesitate. She flung her arms around the neck of the man who had murdered her own husband and yielded to a fit of wild passion.

"You know that I am yours, wherever you go. Will it be to-morrow? We can meet—you know where—and arrange everything for your escape."

"*My* escape?" said Gurn, with reproachful emphasis on the pronoun.

"For our escape," she replied, and Gurn smiled again.

"Then it's settled," he said. "I am happy! Good-bye."

He took a step toward the door, but Lady Beltham stopped him gently.

"Wait," she said. "Walter will let you out of the house. Do not say anything. I will explain; I will invent some story to satisfy the servants."

They clung to one another in a parting caress. Lady Beltham tore herself away.

"Till tomorrow!" she whispered.

She stole to the door and unlocked it noiselessly, then crossed the room and rang the bell placed near the fireplace. Resuming her impassive mask, and the haughty air and attitude of cold indifference that were in such utter contrast to her real character, she waited, while Gurn stood still in the middle of the room.

The porter, Walter, came in.

"Take that man to the door, and let no harm come to him," said Lady Beltham proudly and authoritatively. "He is free."

Without a word or sign or glance, Gurn went out of the room, and Walter followed to obey his mistress's command.

Once more alone in the great hall, Lady Beltham waited nervously to hear the sound of the park gate closing behind Gurn.

She did not dare go out on the balcony to follow her departing lover with her eyes. So, shaken by her recent emotions, she stood waiting and listening, agonizing to know that he was safe. Then all of a sudden the noises that she had heard an hour before came again: hurrying feet and broken shouts, and words, vague at first but rapidly growing clearer. She crouched forward listening, filled with a horrible fear, her hand laid upon her scarcely beating heart.

"There he is, hold him!" someone shouted. "That's him all right! Look out, officer!"

"This way! Yes, it's him, it's Gurn."

Paler than death, Lady Beltham cowered upon a sofa.

"Good God! Good God!" she moaned. "What are they doing to him!"

The uproar in the garden quieted down some, then voices sounded in the corridor, Silbertown's shouts rising above the frightened cries of the three young girls.

"Gurn! Arrested! The man who murdered Lord Beltham!" Lisbeth called out in anxious terror.

"But Lady Beltham? Dear God, perhaps he has murdered her too!"

The door was flung open and the girls rushed in. Lady Beltham, by a tremendous effort of will, had risen to her feet and was standing by the end of the sofa.

"Lady Beltham! Alive! Yes, yes!" And Thérèse and Lisbeth and Susannah rushed sobbing to her, and smothered her with hugs and kisses.

But the agonized woman motioned them away. With hard eyes and set mouth she moved toward the window, straining her ears to listen. From the park outside Gurn's voice rang distinctly; the lover wished to let his mistress know what had happened and to take a last farewell.

"You've got me, you've got me! Yes, I am Gurn."

The fatal words were still ringing in Lady Beltham's ears when the majordomo Silbertown came bursting into the room, with radiant face and shining eyes and smiling lips, and hurried to his mistress.

"I thought as much!" he exclaimed excitedly. "It was him, all right. I recognized him from the description, in spite of his beard. I called the police! As a matter of fact, they have been watching for the last two days. Just imagine, your ladyship, a detective was shadowing Gurn—and when he was going out of the house I gave him the signal!"

Lady Beltham stared at the majordomo in mute horror.

"Yes?" she muttered, on the point of swooning.

"I pointed him out to the police, and it's thanks to me, your ladyship, that Gurn the murderer has been arrested at last!"

For just another moment Lady Beltham stared at the man who had given her this horrible news, seemed to try to utter something, then fell to the floor unconscious.

The majordomo and the girls ran to her side to help her.

At that moment the door was pushed a little way open and the figure of Juve appeared.

"May I come in?" said he.

THE SCRAP OF PAPER

It was three o'clock when Juve arrived at the rue Lévert, and he found the concierge of number 147 just finishing her coffee.

Amazed at the results achieved by the detective, the details of which she had learned from the sensational articles in the daily papers, Mme. Doulenques had conceived a most respectful admiration for the detective of the Criminal Investigation Department.

"That man," she constantly declared to Mme. Aurore, "hasn't got eyes in his head, but telescopes, magnifying glasses! He sees everything in a second—even when it isn't there!"

She gave him an admiring "good afternoon, sir," as she came into her quarters. Going to a board on which numbers of keys were hanging, she took one down and handed it to him.

"So there's something new today?" she said. "I've just seen in the paper that Monsieur Gurn has been arrested. So it was my lodger who did it? What a dreadful man! Whoever would have thought it? It turns my blood cold to think of him!"

Juve was never a man for general conversation, and he was still less interested in the nonsense of this loquacious creature. He took the key and cut her short by walking to the door.

"Yes, Gurn has been arrested," he said abruptly; "but he has made no confession, so nothing is known for certain yet. Please go on with your work exactly as though I were not in the house, Madame Doulenques."

It was his usual phrase and a constant disappointment to the concierge, who would have liked nothing better than to go upstairs with the detective and watch him at his wonderful work.

Reflecting somewhat moodily, Juve went up the five floors to the apartment formerly occupied by Gurn. Of course Gurn's arrest was a coup, but in point of fact Juve had learned nothing new from the arrest, and he was obsessed with the idea that this murder of Lord Beltham was an altogether exceptional crime. He did not yet know why Gurn had killed Lord Beltham, and he did not even know exactly who Gurn was; all he could say was that the murder had been planned and carried out with marvelous audacity and skill, and that was not enough.

Juve let himself into the apartment and closed the door carefully behind him. The rooms were a mess, the result of the police searches. The rent had not been paid for some time, and as no friend or relation had come forward to take control of Gurn's interests, the furniture and knickknacks of the little apartment were to be sold at auction.

The detective walked through the rooms, then flung himself into an armchair. He did not know precisely why he had come. He had searched the place a dozen times already since his discovery of the corpse and had found nothing more, no telltale marks or fresh detail, to assist in elucidating the mystery. He would have given anything to be able to identify Gurn as one of the many criminals who had passed through his hands, and still more to be able to identify him as that one most mysterious criminal whose awful deeds had shocked the world so greatly. Somehow the particular way in which this murder was committed, the very audacity of it, led him to think, to "sense," almost to swear that—

Juve got up. It was not in his nature to sit still. Once more he went all around the apartment.

"The kitchen? Let me see, I have been through everything? The stove? The cupboards? The saucepans? I even went so far as to make sure that there was no poison in them, though it seemed like a wild idea. The anteroom? Nothing there; the umbrella stand was empty, and the one interesting thing I did see, the torn curtain, has been described and photographed." He went back into the dining room. "I've searched all the furniture, and I went through all the packages Gurn had made up before he left and would, no doubt, have come back for had I not discovered the body. In one corner of the room was a heap of old newspapers, crumpled and torn and thrown down in disorder. Juve kicked them aside. "I've looked through all that, even read the lonelyhearts columns, but there was nothing there." He went into the bedroom and contemplated the bed—which the concierge had stripped, the chairs set one on top of another in a corner—and the wardrobe that stood empty, its former contents scattered on the floor by the police during their search. There, too, nothing was to be found.

Against the wall, near the fireplace, was a little writing desk with a shelf above it, containing a few battered books.

"My men have been all through that," Juve muttered; "it's unlikely they missed anything, but perhaps I had better look."

He sat down before it and began methodically to sort through the scattered papers; with a quick, trained glance he scanned each document, putting one after another aside with a grimace of disappointment. Almost the last document he picked up was a long sheet of parchment, and as he unfolded it an exclamation escaped his lips. It was an official notice of Gurn's promotion to the rank of sergeant when fighting under Lord Beltham in the South African war. Juve read it through—he knew English well—and put it down, shaking his head.

"It is extraordinary," he muttered. "That seems to be perfectly authentic; it is authentic, and it proves that Gurn was a decent fellow and a brave soldier once; that is a fine record of service." He drummed his fingers on the desk and spoke aloud. "Is Gurn really Gurn then, and have I been mistaken from beginning to end in the little intrigue I have been weaving around him? How do I find the key to the mystery? How do I prove the truth I feel so very close to, but which slips away every time I'm about to grab hold of it?"

He went on with his search and then, looking at the bookcase, took the volumes out and, holding each by its covers, shook it to make sure that no papers were hidden among the pages. But all in vain. He did the same with a large railroad timetable and several shipping schedules.

"The odd thing is," he thought, "that all these timetables do prove that Gurn really was the commercial traveler he professed to be. It's exactly the kind of things one would expect to find in the apartment of a man who traveled a lot."

In the bookcase was a box, made to look like a bound book, and containing a collection of maps. Juve took them out to make sure that no loose papers were included among them and one by one unfolded every map.

Then a sharp exclamation burst from his lips.

"Good Lord! Now there—"

In his surprise he sprang up so abruptly that he pushed back his chair and overturned it. His excitement was so great that his hands were shaking as he carefully spread out upon the desk one of the maps he had taken from the case.

"It's the map of the center district, all right, the map that shows Cahors, and Brives, and Saint-Jaury and—Beaulieu! And the missing piece—it is the missing piece that would give that precise area!"

Juve stared at the map with hypnotized gaze, for a piece had been cut out of it, cut out with a penknife neatly and carefully, and that piece must have shown the exact area where the château stood that had been occupied by the Marquise de Langrune.

"Oh, if I could only prove it, prove that the piece missing from this map, this map belonging to Gurn, is really and truly the piece I found near the Verrières station just after the murder of the Marquise de Langrune—what a triumph that would be! What a damning proof! What astounding consequences this discovery of mine might have!"

Juve made a careful note of the number of the map quickly and nervously, folded it up again, and prepared to leave the apartment.

He had taken but a step or two toward the door when a sharp ring at the bell made him jump.

"What?" he exclaimed softly. "Who can be coming to see Gurn when everybody in Paris knows he has been arrested?" And he felt automatically in his pocket to make sure that his revolver was there. Then he smiled. "What a fool I am! Of course it is only Madame Doulenques, wondering why I was staying up here so long."

He went to the door, flung it wide open, and then recoiled in astonishment.

"You?" he exclaimed, surveying the caller from head to toe. "You? Charles Rambert! Or, I should say, Jérôme Fandor! Now what in God's name does this mean?"

THE WRECK OF THE
LANCASTER

Jérôme Fandor entered the room without a word. Juve closed
the door behind him. The boy was very pale and visibly upset.

"What is the matter?" said Juve.

"Something terrible has happened," the boy answered. "I
have just read some awful news; my poor father is dead!"

"What?" Juve exclaimed sharply. "Monsieur Etienne Rambert dead?"

Jérôme Fandor put a newspaper into the detective's hand.
"Read that," he said, and pointed to an article on the front
page with a huge headline, WRECK OF THE *LANCASTER*: 150
LIVES LOST. There were tears in his eyes, and he had such obvious difficulty in restraining his grief that Juve saw that to read
the article was the speediest way of finding out what had occurred.

The Red Star liner *Lancaster*, sailing between Caracas and
Southampton, had gone down the night before, just off the Isle
of Wight, and at press time only one person was known to have
been saved. There was a good sea running, but it was by no
means rough, and the vessel was still within sight of the light-
house and making for the open sea at full speed when the light-
house men suddenly saw her literally blown into the air and then
disappear beneath the waves. The alarm was given immediately
and boats of all kinds put off to the scene of the disaster, but although a great deal of wreckage was still floating about, only
one man of the crew was seen, clinging to a spar; he was picked
up by the *Campbell* and taken to the hospital, where he was in-
terviewed by *The Times*. However, he was unable to throw any
light upon what was an almost unprecedented disaster at sea.

All he could say was that the liner had just gotten up full speed and was making a perfectly normal beginning of her trip when suddenly a tremendous explosion occurred. He himself was engaged at the moment fastening the tarpaulins over the baggage hold, and he was confident that the explosion had occurred down in the cargo. But he could give absolutely no more information; the entire ship seemed to be torn apart, and he was thrown into the sea, stunned, and knew no more until he recovered consciousness and found himself aboard the *Campbell*.

"It's quite incomprehensible," Juve muttered; "surely there can't have been any explosives aboard? They aren't carried on these great liners; they only take passengers and the mail." He scanned the list of passengers. "Etienne Rambert's name is given among the first-class passengers, true enough," he said. "Well, it's odd!"

Jérôme Fandor heaved a profound sigh.

"It is a death I will never get over," he said. "When you told me the other day that you knew I was innocent, I ought to have gone to see my father, in spite of what you said. I am sure he would have believed me and come to see you; then you could have convinced him, and I would not have this horrible grief of remembering that he had died without learning that his son was not a bad man, but was deserving of his affection."

Jérôme Fandor was making a brave struggle to maintain his self-control, and Juve looked at him without concealing the real sympathy he felt for him. He put his hand kindly on his shoulder.

"Listen, my dear boy; odd as you may think it, you can take my word for it that there is no need for you to get upset; there is nothing to prove that your father is dead; he may not have been on board."

The boy looked up in surprise.

"What do you mean, Juve?"

"I don't want to say anything yet, my boy, except that you would be wrong to get upset yet. If you have any confidence in me, you may believe me when I say that. There is nothing yet to prove that you have lost your father; and, besides, you still have your mother, who is perfectly sure to get well; do you understand—*perfectly sure*!" He changed the subject abruptly. "There is one thing I would like to know; what brought you here?"

"You were the first person I thought of when I found out," Fandor replied. "Directly after I read about the disaster in that paper I came to tell you at once."

"Yes, I quite understand that," Juve answered. "What I do not understand is how you guessed you would find me here, in Gurn's apartment."

The question seemed to perturb the boy.

"It—it was quite by chance," he stammered.

"That is the kind of explanation one offers to fools," Juve retorted. "By what chance did you see me come into this house? What were you doing in the rue Lévert?" The lad showed some inclination to make for the door, but Juve stopped him firmly. "Answer my question, please; how did you know I was here?"

Driven into a corner, the boy blurted out the truth:

"I followed you."

"Followed me?" Juve exclaimed. "Where from?"

"From your rooms."

"You mean, and you may as well confess to it right now, that you were shadowing me."

"Well, yes, Monsieur Juve, it is true," Fandor confessed, all in one breath. "I was shadowing you; I do every day!"

Juve was dumbfounded.

"Every day? And I never saw you! God, you are pretty good! And may I ask why you have been exercising this supervision over me?"

Jérôme Fandor hung his head.

"Forgive me," he faltered, "I have been an idiot. I thought you—I thought you were—Fantômas!"

The idea tickled the detective so much that he fell back into a chair, he was laughing so hard.

"You have some imagination," he said. "And what made you suppose that I was Fantômas?"

"Monsieur Juve," Fandor said earnestly, "I made a vow that I would find out the truth and discover the bastard who has made such an awful mess of my life. But I did not know where to begin. From all you said I realized that Fantômas was an extraordinarily clever man; I did not know anyone who could be cleverer than you, and so I watched you! It was just logical!"

Far from being angry, Juve was rather flattered.

"I am amazed by what you have just told me, my boy," he said with a smile. "In the first place your reasoning is not at all bad. Of course it is obvious that I cannot suspect myself of being Fantômas, but I quite admit that if I were in your place I might make the same supposition, wild as it may seem. And, in the next place, you have shadowed me without my having an inkling of it and that is very good indeed, proof that you are uncommonly smart." He looked at the boy attentively for a few moments and then went on more gravely: "Are you satisfied now that your hypothesis was wrong? Or do you still suspect me?"

"No, I don't suspect you now," Fandor declared, "not since I saw you come into this house. Fantômas certainly would not have come to search Gurn's rooms because—"

He stopped, and Juve, who was looking at him keenly, did not make him finish what he was saying.

"Shall I tell you something?" he said at last. "If you continue to display as much thought and initiative as you just have, you will soon be the best newspaper detective of the day!" He jumped up and led the boy off. "Come with me. I've got to go to the courthouse at once."

"You've found out something new?"

"I'm going to ask them to call an interesting witness in the Gurn affair."

Rain had been falling heavily all morning and afternoon, but within the last few minutes it had almost stopped. Dollon the steward put his hand out the window and found that only a few drops were falling now from the heavy gray sky.

He was an invaluable servant, and a few months after the death of the Marquise de Langrune, the Baronne de Vibray had gladly offered him a situation and a cottage on her estate at Querelles.

He walked across the room and called his son.

"Jacques, would you like to come with me? I am going down to the river to see that the floodgates have been opened properly. The banks are anything but sound, and these rains will flood us out one of these days."

The steward and his son went down the garden toward the stream that formed one boundary of Mme. de Vibray's park.

"Look, Father," Jacques exclaimed, "the postman is calling us."

The postman, a crusty but good-hearted fellow, came hurrying up to the steward.

"You do keep me on the run, Monsieur Dollon," he complained. "I went to your house this morning to take you a letter, but you weren't there."

"You might have given it to anybody."

"Excuse me!" the man retorted, "it's against regulations. I've got an official letter for you, and I can only give it to you yourself." And he held out an envelope which Dollon tore open.

"Magistrates' office?" he said with surprise, as he glanced at the heading of the notepaper. "Who can be writing to me from the courthouse?" He read the letter aloud:

"Sir: As time does not permit a regular summons being sent to you, I beg you to be so good as to come to Paris immediately, the day after tomorrow if possible, and visit my office, where your depositions are absolutely required to conclude a case in which you are interested. Please bring, without exception, all the papers and documents entrusted to you by the clerk of the court at Cahors, at the conclusion of the Langrune inquiry."

"It is signed Germain Fuselier," Dollon remarked. "I've often seen his name in the papers. He is a very well-known magistrate and is employed in many criminal cases." He read the letter through once more and turned to the postman. "Can I offer you a glass of wine, Muller?"

"That's a thing I never say no to."

"Well, go into the house with Jacques, and in the meantime I will write a reply telegram which you can take back to the office for me."

While the man was quenching his thirst Dollon wrote his reply:

"Will leave Verrières tomorrow evening by seven-twenty train, arriving Paris five A.M. Wire appointment at your office to me at Hôtel Francs-Bourgeois, One Fifty-two rue du Bac."

He read the message over, signed it "Dollon," and considered.

"I wonder what they want me for? Oh, if only they have found out something about the Langrune affair, how happy it will make me!"

UNDER LOCK AND KEY

After the preliminary interrogation, Gurn had been transferred to the Santé prison. At first the prisoner seemed to have terrible difficulty in accustoming himself to confinement; he suffered from alternate fits of rage and despair, but by sheer strength of character he overcame these. As a prisoner on remand he was entitled to the privilege of a separate cell, also during the first forty-eight hours he had been able to have his meals sent in from outside. Since then, however, his money had run out, and he was obliged to content himself with the regular prison diet. But Gurn was not fastidious; this man whom Lady Beltham had singled out, accepted as her lover, had often demonstrated he had above-average education and intelligence.

Gurn was walking quickly around the exercise yard when a breathless voice sounded in his ear.

"God, Gurn, you know how to march! I was going to join you for a while, but I could not keep up with you."

Gurn turned and saw old Siegenthal, the guard in charge of his division, in whose custody he had been placed.

"My word," the old fellow panted, "anybody could tell you've been in the infantry. Well, so have I, though that was a while ago. But we never marched as fast as you do. We made a fine march once though—at Saint-Privat."

Out of pity for the decent old fellow Gurn slackened his pace. He had heard the story of the battle of Saint-Privat a dozen times already, but he was quite willing to let Siegenthal tell it again. The guard, however, wandered to another point.

"By the way, I heard you were promoted sergeant out in the Transvaal; is that so?" And as Gurn nodded assent, he went on: "I never rose above the rank of corporal, but at any rate I have always led an honest life." A sudden compassion for his prisoner seized the old man, and he laid a kindly hand on Gurn's shoulder. "Is it really possible that an old soldier like you, who seems to be such a steady, serious kind of man, can have committed such a crime?"

Gurn dropped his eyes and did not reply.

"I suppose there was a woman at the bottom of it?" Siegenthal said tentatively. "You acted on impulse, in a fit of jealousy, eh?"

"No," Gurn answered with sudden bluntness, "I may as well admit that I did it out of anger, because I wanted money—for the sake of robbery."

"I'm sorry," said the old guard simply. "You must have been desperately hard up."

"No I wasn't."

Siegenthal stared at his prisoner. The man must be utterly callous to talk like that, he thought. Then a clock struck and the guard gave a curt order.

"It's time, Gurn! We must go back." And he conducted the unresisting prisoner up the three flights of stairs that led to his cell. "By the way," he remarked as they went, "I forgot to tell you that you and I won't be seeing each other again."

"Oh?" said Gurn. "Am I to be transferred to another prison?"

"No, it's I who am going. Just imagine, I have been appointed head guard at Poissy; I go on leave tonight and take up my new post in a week." Both halted before the door of cell number 127. "In with you," said Siegenthal, and when Gurn had obeyed he turned to go. Then he wheeled around again quickly and put out his hand hurriedly, as if half afraid of being seen. "Put it there, Gurn," he said; "no doubt you are a murderer and, as you have confessed yourself, a thief; but I can't forget that if you had kept out of trouble you would be the sergeant and I would have had to obey you. I'm sorry for you!" Gurn was touched and murmured a word of thanks. "That's all right, that's all right," Siegenthal muttered, not attempting to hide his emotion; "let us hope that everything will turn out all right." And he left Gurn alone in the cell to his meditations.

Twice, Gurn, knowing of the sympathy he had evoked in the old guard's heart, had been on the point of broaching a serious and delicate matter with him; but he had not actually spoken, being deterred by some undefinable scruple, as well as partly suspecting that his application would have been in vain. And now he was glad he had been so cautious, for even if the guard had been amenable, his transfer to a new job would have made the whole thing moot.

A singsong voice echoed in the corridor.

"Number one twenty-seven, you are wanted in the barristers' room. Get ready." And the next minute the door of the cell was thrown open and a cheery-looking guard with a strong Gascon accent appeared. Gurn had noticed him before; he was the second guard in this division, a man named Nibet, and no doubt he would be promoted to Siegenthal's place when the chief guard left. Nibet looked curiously at Gurn with a certain sympathy in his quick brown eyes. "Ready, Gurn?"

Gurn growled an answer and pulled on his coat again. His counsel was Maître Barberoux, one of the foremost criminal lawyers of the day; Gurn had thought it prudent to retain him for his defense, especially as it would cost him nothing personally. But he had no particular desire to talk to him now; he had already told him everything he intended to tell him, and he had no intention of allowing the case to become a sensation. Quite the reverse; in his opinion, the flatter the case fell, the better it would be for his interests, though no doubt Maître Barberoux would not be thinking the same way.

But he said nothing and merely walked in front of Nibet along the corridor toward the barristers' room, the way to which he already knew. On the way they passed some masons who were at work in the prison, and these men stopped to watch him pass, but contrary to Gurn's apprehensions they did not seem to recognize him. He hoped it meant that the murder was already ceasing to be a scandal for the public at large.

Nibet pushed Gurn into the barristers' room, saying respectfully to the person in it already, "You only have to ring, sir, when
you finish," and then withdrew, leaving Gurn in the presence,
not of his counsel as he had expected, but of that person's assistant, a young apprentice in law named Roger de Seras, who was
also a most incredible dandy.

Roger de Seras greeted Gurn with an engaging smile and advanced as if to shake hands with him, but suddenly wondering
whether that action might not suggest undue familiarity, he
raised his hand to his own head instead and scratched it; the
young fellow was still inexperienced in his business and did not
know whether it was proper etiquette for a lawyer, or even an
assistant, to shake hands with a prisoner who was implicated in
a notorious murder.

Gurn felt inclined to laugh and on the whole was glad that it
was the junior whom he had to see; the futile verbosity of this
very young apprentice might possibly be amusing.

Maître Roger de Seras began with civil apologies.

"You will excuse me if I only stay for a few minutes, but I
am terribly busy; besides, two ladies are waiting for me outside
in my carriage. I may say confidentially that they are actresses,
old friends of mine, and, just imagine, they are most anxious
to see you! That's what it means to be famous, Monsieur
Gurn, eh?"

Gurn nodded, not feeling unduly flattered. Roger de Seras
continued. "Just to please them I have begged the governor of
the prison, but nothing doing, my dear friend; that bastard
Fuselier insists on your being kept in solitary confinement. But
nonetheless, I've got some news for you. I know lots; why, my
friends at the courts call me 'the peripatetic paragraph'! Not
bad, eh?" Gurn smiled, and Roger de Seras was encouraged.
"It's given me a real kick with my boss, acting for you, and my
being able to come and see you whenever I like! Everybody asks
me how you are, and what you are like, and what you say, and
what you think. You can congratulate yourself on having
caused a sensation in Paris."

Gurn began to be irritated by all this chatter.

"I must confess I'm not the least interested in what people are saying about me. Is there anything new in my case?"

"Absolutely nothing that I am aware of," Roger de Seras replied serenely, without stopping to think whether there was or not. "But—Lady Beltham—"

"Yes?" said Gurn.

"Well, I know her very well, you know. I go out quite a lot and I have often met her, a charming woman, Lady Beltham!"

Gurn really did not know how to treat the idiot. Never one to suffer fools gladly, he grew irritable and would almost certainly have said something that would have put the garrulous young bungler in his place had not the latter suddenly remembered something, just as he was on the point of getting up to go.

"Oh, by the way," he said with a laugh, "I was nearly forgetting the most important thing of all. Just imagine, Juve, the marvelous detective whom the newspapers rave about, went to your place yesterday afternoon to make another official search!"

"Alone?" inquired Gurn, much interested.

"Quite alone. Now, what do you suppose he found? The place has been ransacked dozens of times, you know; of course I mean something sensational in the way of a find. I bet you a thousand—"

"I never bet," Gurn snapped. "Tell me what it was."

The young fellow was proud of having caught the attention of his boss's notorious client, if only for a moment; he paused and wagged his head, weighing each word to give them greater emphasis.

"He found an ordnance map in your bookcase, my dear friend—an ordnance map with a bit torn out of it."

"Oh! And what then?" said Gurn, a frown upon his face.

The young assistant did not notice the expression on the murderer's face.

"Well, it appears that Juve thought it was very important. Between you and me, my opinion is that Juve tries to be a little too clever and succeeds in looking a fool. How, I ask you, can the discovery of that map affect your case or influence the decision of the jury? By the way, there is no need for you to worry about the verdict; I have had a lot of experience in criminal cases, and so rest assured you are all right: extenuating circumstances, you know. But—oh, yes, there is one thing more I wanted to tell you. A fresh witness is going to be called at the examination; let me see, what's his name? Dollon; that's it, the steward Dollon."

"I don't understand," said Gurn; his head was bent and his eyes cast down.

A glimmer of light dawned in the young apprentice's brain.

"Wait, there is some connection," he said. "The steward Dollon is in the employ of a lady who calls herself the Baronne de Vibray. And the Baronne de Vibray is guardian to the young lady who was staying with Lady Beltham the day, or rather the night, when you—you—well, you know. And that young lady, Mademoiselle Thérèse Auvernois, was placed with Lady Beltham by Monsieur Etienne Rambert. And Monsieur Etienne Rambert is the father of the young man who murdered the Marquise de Langrune last year. I tell you all these things without attempting to figure them out for I haven't the faintest idea why the steward Dollon has been summoned in our case at all."

"Nor have I," said Gurn, and the frown on his brow was deeper.

Roger de Seras hunted all around the little room for his gloves and found them in his pocket.

"Well, my dear sir, I must leave you. We have been chatting for a whole half-hour, and those ladies are still waiting for me. What on earth will they say to me?"

He was about to ring for the guard when Gurn abruptly stopped him.

"Tell me," he said with a sudden air of interest, "when is that man coming—what's his name? Dollon?"

The young apprentice was on the point of saying he did not know when a brilliant recollection came into his mind.

"God, what an idiot I am! Why, I have a copy of the telegram he sent the magistrate in my briefcase here." He opened the briefcase and picked out a sheet of blue paper. "Here it is."

Gurn took it from him and read:

"Will leave Verrières tomorrow evening by seven-twenty train, arriving Paris five A.M. . . . ."

Gurn appeared to be satisfied; in any case, he paid no attention to the rest of the message. Lord Beltham's murderer handed the document back without a word.

A few minutes later Maître Roger de Seras had rejoined his lady friends, and the prisoner was once more in his cell.

AN UNEXPECTED
ACCOMPLICE

Gurn was walking nervously up and down in his cell after this visit when the door was pushed open and the cheery face of the guard Nibet looked in.

"Evening, Gurn," he said; "it's six o'clock, and the restaurant keeper opposite wants to know if he is to send your dinner in to you."

"No," Gurn growled. "I'll have the prison grub."

"Oh-ho!" said the guard. "Funds low, eh? Of course, it's not for you to despise our food, but still, government beans—" He came further into the cell, ignoring Gurn's impatient preference for his solitude, and said in a low tone: "There, take that," and thrust a bank note into the hand of the dumbfounded prisoner. "And if you want any more, it will be forthcoming," he added. He made a sign to Gurn to say nothing and went to the door. "I'll be back in a few minutes. I'll just go and order a decent dinner for you."

Gurn felt as if a tremendous weight had been lifted from his shoulders; the cell seemed larger, the prison walls less high; he had an intuition that Lady Beltham was not deserting him. He had never doubted the sincerity of her feelings for him, but he quite realized how a woman in her delicate position might feel embarrassed trying to intervene in favor of any prisoner, and much more so in the case of the one who the entire world believed to be the sole murderer of her husband. But now Lady Beltham had intervened. She had succeeded in communicating with him through the medium of this guard. And almost certainly she would do much more yet.

The door opened again, and the guard entered, carrying a wicker basket containing several dishes and a bottle of wine.

"Well, Gurn, that's a more agreeable dinner, eh?"

"God, I wanted it after all," said the murderer with a smile. "It was a good idea of yours, Monsieur Nibet, to insist on my getting my dinner sent in from outside."

Nibet winked; he appreciated his prisoner's tact; obviously he was not one to make untimely remarks about the guard's breach of discipline in conveying money to him.

As he ate Gurn chatted with Nibet.

"I suppose it is you who will be promoted into Siegenthal's place?"

"Yes," said Nibet, sipping the wine Gurn had offered him. "I have asked for the job quite a few times, but it never came; I was always told to wait because the job was not open and another one must be found first for Siegenthal, who was my senior. But the old fool would never make any application. However, three days ago, I was sent for to the ministry, and one of the staff told me that someone in the embassy or the government or somewhere was taking an interest in me, and they asked me a lot of questions and I told them all about it. And then all of a sudden Siegenthal was promoted to Poissy, and I was given his position here."

Gurn nodded; he saw light.

"And what about the money?"

"That's stranger still, but I understood all the same. A lady met me in the street the other night and spoke to me by name. We had a chat there on the pavement, for the street was empty, and she shoved some bank notes in my hand—not just one or two but a great bunch—and she told me that she was interested in me—in you—and that if things turned out as she wished there were plenty more bank notes where those came from."

While the guard was talking Gurn watched him carefully. The murderer was an experienced reader of character in faces, and he immediately realized that his lover's choice had fallen on an excellent object. Thick lips, a narrow forehead, and prominent cheekbones suggested a material nature that would stop at nothing to satisfy its carnal appetites, so Gurn decided that further circumlocution was a waste of time and that he might safely come to the point. He laid his hand familiarly on the guard's shoulder.

"I'm getting sick of being here," he remarked.

"I bet," the guard answered uneasily, "but you must use common sense; time is passing, and things arrange themselves."

"They do when you help them," Gurn said peremptorily, "and you and I are going to help them."

"That remains to be seen," said the guard.

"Of course, everything has got to be paid for," Gurn went on. "One can't expect a guard to risk his job merely to help a prisoner to escape." He smiled as the guard made an exclamation of nervous warning. "Don't be frightened, Nibet. We're not going to play any games, but let's talk seriously. Of course, you have another appointment with the worthy lady who gave you that money?"

"I am to meet her tonight at eleven in the boulevard Arago," Nibet said, after a moment's hesitation.

"Good," said Gurn. "Well, you are to tell her that I must have ten thousand francs."

"What?" exclaimed the man, in utter astonishment, but his eyes shone with greed.

"Ten thousand francs," Gurn repeated calmly, "and by tomorrow morning. Fifteen hundred of those are for you; I will leave tomorrow evening."

There was a tense silence; the guard seemed doubtful, and Gurn turned the whole of his willpower upon him to persuade him.

"Suppose they suspect me?" said Nibet.

"Idiot!" Gurn retorted. "All you will have to do is make a little slip in your duty; I don't want you to be an accomplice. Listen, there will be another five thousand francs for you, and if things get awkward, you'll be able to go across to England and live there comfortably for the rest of your life."

The guard was obviously almost ready to comply.

"Who will guarantee it?" he asked.

"The lady, I tell you—the lady of the boulevard Arago. Here, give her this." And he tore a page out of his notebook and, scribbling a few words on it, handed it to Nibet.

"Well," said the guard hesitatingly, "I don't say no."

"You've got to say yes," Gurn retorted.

The two looked steadily in each other's eyes; then the guard blanched.

"Yes," he said.

Nibet was going away and was already almost in the corridor when Gurn calmly called him back.

"You will figure out a plan, and I will start tomorrow. Don't forget to bring me a timetable; the Orléans Company timetable will do."

The murderer was not disappointed in his expectations. The next morning Nibet appeared with a mysterious expression and eager eyes. He took a small bundle from underneath his sweater and gave it to Gurn.

"Hide that in your bed," he said, and Gurn obeyed.

The morning passed without further developments; numerous guards came and went in the corridor, attending to the prisoners, and Gurn could not talk privately with Nibet, who contrived, however, to come into his cell several times on various pretexts and assure him with a nod or a word that all was going well. But soon, while walking in the exercise yard, the two men were able to have a conversation.

Nibet manifested an intelligence of which his appearance gave no indication; but it seems to be an established fact that the inventive faculties, even of men of inferior mental quality, are sharpened when they are engaged in mischief.

"For the last three weeks," he said, "about a dozen masons have been working in the prison, repairing the roof and fixing up some of the cells. Cell number one twenty-nine, the one next to yours, is empty, and there are no bars on the window; the masons go through that cell and that window to get on to the roof. They knock off work soon after six o'clock. The gatekeeper knows them all, but he does not always look closely at their faces when they go by, and you might perhaps be able to go out with them.

"In the bundle that I gave you there is a pair of workman's trousers, and a jacket and a felt hat; put those on. At about a quarter to six, the men who went up on to the roof through the cell come down by way of the skylights to the staircase that leads to the clerk's office, pass the office where they are asked no questions, cross the two yards, and go out by the main gate. I will open the door of your cell a few minutes before six, and you must go into the empty cell next to yours, slip up on to the roof, and take care to hide behind the chimney stacks until the men have finished work. Let them go down in front of you, and follow behind with a pick or a shovel on your shoulder; and when you are passing the clerk, or anywhere where you might be noticed, be careful to let the men go a few feet in front of you. When the gate is just being shut after the last workman, call out quietly but as naturally as you can, 'Hold on, Monsieur Morin, don't lock me in; I'm not one of your lodgers. Let me out after my pals.' Make some joke of that sort, and once you are outside the gate, by George, you'll have to really get going!"

Gurn listened attentively to the guard's instructions. Lady Beltham must indeed have been generous and have made the man perfectly secure about his own future.

"In one of the pockets of the clothes," Nibet went on, "I have put ten hundred-franc notes; you asked for more, but I could not get it; we can settle that some other time."

Gurn made no comment.

"When will my escape be discovered?" he asked.

"I am on night duty," the guard answered. "Arrange your clothes on your bed to make it look as if you were in bed, and then they will think I might have been deceived. I go off duty at five; the next round is at eight. My buddy will open the door of the cage, and by that time you will be miles away."

Gurn nodded. Time did not permit longer conversation. The bell had rung some minutes ago, proclaiming that the exercise period was over. The two men hurried upstairs to cell number 127 on the third floor, and the prisoner was locked in alone, while Nibet went about his duty as usual.

A MYSTERIOUS CRIME

Arriving in plenty of time at the little station at Verrières, where he was about to take the train to Paris to keep his appointment at the courthouse, the old steward Dollon gave his parting instructions to his two children, who had come to see him off.

"I must, of course, call upon Madame de Vibray," he said, "and I don't yet know what time Monsieur Fuselier wants to see me at his office. Anyhow, if I don't come back tomorrow, I will the next day, without fail. Well, I'm off now, so say good-bye and get home as fast as you can. It looks to me as if there is going to be a storm, and I want to know that you are safe at home."

With a heavy creaking of iron wheels and hoarse blowing of steam from the engine, the Paris train drew into the station. The steward gave a final kiss to his little son and daughter and got into a second-class carriage.

In a neighboring village a clock had just struck three in the morning.

The storm had been raging since early evening, but now it seemed infused with a fresh fury; the rain was lashing down more fiercely, and the wind was blowing harder still, making the slender poplars along the railway line bow and bend before the squalls and assume the most fantastic shapes, shadowy forms against the night. The night was inky black. The sharpest eye could make out nothing at all distinctly, even at the distance of a few yards; the darkness was so dense as to seem absolutely solid.

Nevertheless, along the railway embankment a man was

making his way with steady step, seeming not a bit disturbed by the nastiness of the storm.

He was a man of about thirty, rather well dressed in a large waterproof coat, the collar of which, turned up to his ears, hid the lower part of his face, and a big felt hat with brim turned down protecting him fairly well from the worst of the weather. The man fought his way against the wind, which drove into him with such force that sometimes it almost stopped his progress, and he walked the stony track without paying any attention to the sorry state into which it would most surely put the thin boots he was wearing.

"Awful weather!" he growled. "I don't remember such a miserable night for years; wind, rain, everything! But I mustn't complain, for the total absence of a moon will be very useful for my purpose." A flash of lightning streaked the horizon, and the man stopped and looked quickly about him. "I can't be far from the place," he thought, and again went on his way. Soon he heaved a sigh of relief. "Here I am at last."

At this spot the line was completely enclosed between two high slopes, or ran at the bottom of a deep ravine.

"It's better here," the man said to himself; "the wind is passing over my head." He stopped and carefully deposited on the ground a rather bulky bundle he had been carrying under his arm; then he began to pace up and down, stamping his feet in an effort to keep warm. "It has just struck three," he muttered. "From the timetable I can't expect anything for another ten minutes. Well, better too soon than too late!" He contemplated the bundle that he had laid down a few minutes before. "It's heavier than I thought, and in the way, damn it. But it was absolutely necessary to bring it. And down here there is nothing for me to be anxious about; the grass is thick so I can run, and the line is so straight that I shall see the lights of the train a long way off." A thin smile curled his lips. "Who would have thought, when I was in America, that I should ever find it so useful to have learned how to jump a train?"

A dull sound in the distance caught his ear. In a second he had sprung to his bundle, picked it up, and, choosing a spot on the ballast, crouched down listening. At the place where he stood, the line ran up a steep incline. It was from the lower end of this that the noise he had heard proceeded and now was growing louder, almost deafening. It was the heavy, regular puffing of a powerful engine coming up a steep gradient under full steam.

"No mistake; my luck is with me!" the man muttered, and as the train approached he stretched his muscles and, taking a firmer grip of his bundle, he bent forward in the crouching attitude that runners take when starting a race.

With a heavy roar and enveloped in clouds of steam, the train came up, traveling slowly because of the steep gradient, certainly less than twenty miles an hour. The moment the engine had passed him, the man started off, lithe as a cat, and ran at top speed. The train, of course, gained on him; the locomotive, baggage cars, and third-class carriages passed him, and a second-class carriage was just coming up. The pace alone would have deprived almost anyone else of the ability to think clearly, but this man was evidently a first-rate athlete, for the moment he caught sight of the second-class carriage he made his decision. With a tremendous effort he caught hold of the handrail and sprang upon the footboard, where, with extraordinary skill, he managed to remain.

Reaching the summit of the slope the train gathered speed and, with an even louder roar, continued its headlong journey through the darkness and the storm, which seemed to increase in intensity with every passing minute.

For a few seconds the man hung on where he was. Then, when he had gotten his breath back, he pulled up to the upper step and listened at the door of the corridor at which he found himself. "No one there," he muttered. "Besides, everyone will be asleep." And, chancing everything, he opened the door and stepped into the second-class carriage with a grunt of relief.

Making no attempt to conceal himself, he walked boldly into the lavatory and washed his face that was blackened with the smoke from outside, and then, in the most leisurely, natural way possible, he came out of the lavatory and walked along the corridor, talking to himself, not minding whether he were overheard or not.

"It's intolerable! No one can sleep with traveling companions like that!"

As he spoke he went along the corridor, rapidly glancing into every compartment. In one, three men were asleep, obviously unaware that anyone was surveying them from outside. The door of the compartment was ajar, and the stranger noiselessly stepped inside. The fourth corner was unoccupied, and here the man took his seat, laying his bundle down beside him and pretending to sleep. He waited motionless for a good quarter of an hour, until he was quite satisfied that his companions were really sleeping soundly, then he slid his hand into the bundle by his side, seemed to be doing something inside it, then withdrew his hand silently, stepped out of the compartment, and carefully closed the door.

In the corridor he heaved a sigh of relief and took a cigar from his pocket.

"Everything is going perfectly," he said to himself. "I was cursing this terrible storm just now, but it has been extremely useful to me. On a night like this no one would dream of opening the windows." He strolled up and down, holding on to the handrail with one hand to balance himself against the rocking of the train and every now and then taking out his watch with the other to look at the time. "I haven't too much time," he muttered. "I shall have to be quick, or my friend will miss his train!" He smiled, as if amused at the idea, and then, holding his cigar away from him so as not to inhale the smoke, he drew several deep breaths. "There is a faint smell," he said, "but you would have to be told about it beforehand in order to detect it. The trouble is that it so often causes nightmare; that would be awful!" He listened again. There was no sound from within the compartments except the snoring of a few travelers and the monotonous, rhythmical noise of the wheels passing over the joints of the rails. "I've waited twenty minutes; it would be risky to wait longer; let's get to work!"

He stepped briskly back into the compartment, and, furtively glancing into the corridor to make sure that no one was there, he went across to the opposite window and opened it wide. He put his head out into the air for a minute or two and then turned to examine his traveling companions. All three were still sound asleep.

The man could not help a dry chuckle. He drew his bundle toward him, felt until he found something within it, and threw it back on to the seat. Then he walked up to the man opposite him, slipped his hand inside his coat, and abstracted a wallet and began to examine the papers it contained. "Ah!" he exclaimed suddenly, "that was what I was afraid of!" And taking one of the papers, he put it inside his own wallet, chose one from his own and put it into the other man's wallet, and then, having effected this exchange, replaced the man's property and chuckled again. "You do sleep!"

And indeed, although the pickpocket took no particular precautions, the man continued to sleep soundly, as did the other two men in the compartment.

The thief looked once more at his watch.

"Time!"

He leaned out of the open window and slipped back the safety catch. Then he opened the door wide, took the sleeping traveler by the shoulders and picked him up from the seat, and with all his strength rolled him out on to the line!

The next moment he seized from the luggage rack the light articles that evidently belonged to his victim and threw them out after him.

When he had finished his ghastly work he rubbed his hands in satisfaction. "Good!" he said, and, closing the door again but leaving the window down, he left the compartment, not troubling to pick up his belongings, and walked along the corridors to another second-class compartment toward the front of the train, in which he calmly installed himself.

"Luck has been with me," he muttered as he stretched himself out on the seat. "Everything has gone off well; no one has seen me, and those two fools who might have upset my plans will wake up quite naturally when they begin to feel the cold, and they will attribute the headache they will probably feel to their tiring journey."

A train, traveling in the opposite direction, suddenly roared past the window and made him jump. He started up, and smiled.

"God! I said my friend would miss his train, but he'll catch it in another five minutes! In another five minutes, luggage and body both will be mincemeat!" And as if completely reassured by the idea he chuckled again. "Nothing could have gone better; I can have a rest, and in an hour's time I will be at Juvisy, where, thanks to my ingenious plans, I shall be able to whitewash myself—literally." One thing, however, still seemed to worry him; he did not know exactly where on the line he had thrown his unhappy victim, but he had an idea that the train had run through a small station shortly afterward; if that were so, the body might be found sooner than he would have liked. He tried to dismiss the notion from his mind, but he caught sight of the telegraph poles speeding past the windows, and he shook his fist at them malignantly. "That is the only thing that can trip me up now," he muttered.

"Juvisy! Juvisy! Two minutes!"

It was barely half past six, and the porters hurried along the train, calling out the name of the station and rousing sleepy travelers from their dreams. A man jumped nimbly out of a second-class carriage and walked toward the exit from the station, holding out his ticket. "Season ticket," he said, and went out quickly.

"Good idea, that season ticket," he said to himself. "Much less dangerous than an ordinary ticket, which the police could have traced."

He walked briskly, crossed the main road, and took a turn that led down toward the Seine. Taking no notice of the mud, the man went into a field and hid himself in a little thicket on the riverbank. He looked carefully all around him to make sure that he was unobserved; then took off his overcoat, jacket, and trousers; and drawing a bundle from one of the pockets of his large raincoat, proceeded to dress himself in new clothes. As soon as he was dressed, he spread the raincoat out on the ground, folded up in it the clothes and hat he had previously been wearing, added a number of heavy stones, and tied the whole bundle up with a piece of string. He swung it once or twice the full length of his arm and sent it hurtling right into the middle of the river, where it sank at once.

A few minutes later a bricklayer in his working clothes presented himself at the Juvisy booking office.

"A workman's ticket to Paris, please, missus," he said, and having got it, the man went on to the departure platform. "It would have been risky to use my own ticket," he muttered. "This return ticket will put them off the scent." And with a smile he waited for the train that would take him to Paris.

The slow train from Luchon was drawing near its Paris terminus and the travelers were all making hasty preparations and tidying themselves up after their long night journey. Just, however, as it was approaching it slowed down and stopped. The passengers, surprised, put their heads out of the windows to ascertain the reason for the unexpected delay, hazarding various conjectures but unanimous in their condemnation of the company.

Three men were walking slowly along the line, looking carefully at every door. Two were porters, and they were paying very careful attention to everything the third man said; he was a serious individual, very correctly attired.

"Look there, sir," one of the porters exclaimed, "there is a door where the safety catch has either been undone or not fastened; that is the only one on the train."

"That is so," said the gentleman, and grasping the handle he opened the door of the compartment and got in. Two travelers were busy strapping up their bags, and they turned around simultaneously in surprise.

"You will forgive me, gentlemen, when you know who I am," said the intruder, and throwing open his coat he showed his tricolor scarf. "I have to make an inquiry relative to a dead body that has been found on the line near Bretigny; it probably fell from this train, and perhaps from this compartment, for I have just observed that the safety catch is not fastened. Where did you get onto the train?"

The two passengers looked at one another in astonishment.

"What a terrible thing!" one of them exclaimed. "Why, sir, tonight, while my friend here and I were asleep, one of our fellow travelers did disappear. I made a remark about it, but this gentleman very reasonably pointed out that he must have gotten out at some station while we were asleep."

The official was extremely interested.

"What was this passenger like?"

"Quite easily recognized, sir; a man of about sixty, rather stout, and with a beard."

"That tallies with the description. Did he look like a butler or a steward?"

"That is exactly what he looked like."

"Then that must be the man whose body has been found on the line. But I do not know whether it is to be regarded as a case of suicide or murder, for some hand baggage has been picked up as well; a suicide would not have thrown his luggage out, and a thief would not have wanted to get rid of it."

The passenger who had not yet spoken broke in.

"You're wrong, sir, all his luggage was not thrown out onto the line." And he pointed to the bundle left on the seat. "I thought this belonged to the gentleman here, but he has just told me it isn't his."

The official rapidly unfastened the straps and started back.

"What's this? A bottle of liquid carbonic acid! Now what does that mean?" He looked at it. "Did this bundle belong to the man who disappeared?"

The two passengers shook their heads.

"I don't think so," one of them said. "I would certainly have noticed that Scotch rug."

"Was there a fourth passenger in this compartment then?" the official inquired.

"No, we traveled alone," said one of the men, but the other said:

"It is very odd, and I am not sure about it, but I really wonder whether someone did get into our compartment last night while we were asleep. I have a vague impression that someone did, but I can't be sure."

"Do try to remember, sir," the official urged him; "it is of the very highest importance."

But the passenger shook his shoulders doubtfully.

"No, I really can't say anything definite, and, besides, I have a terrible headache."

The official was silent for a minute or two.

"In my opinion, gentlemen, you were uncommonly lucky to escape murder yourselves. I do not quite understand yet how the murder was committed, but I think it proves almost incredible daring. However—" He stopped and put his head out the window. "You can let the train go now," he called to a porter, and resumed: "However, I must ask you to accompany me to the stationmaster's office and give me your names and addresses, and to help me afterward in conducting the legal investigation."

The two travelers looked at one another, both clearly upset.

"It is really frightening," said one of them; "you're not safe anywhere nowadays."

"You really aren't," the other agreed. "So many awful murders and crimes occur every day that you would think not one but a dozen Fantômases were at work!"

THREE SURPRISING
INCIDENTS

Nibet went off duty at five in the morning and returned home to go to bed. As a general rule he slept like a log after a night on duty, but tonight he could not close an eye, being far too nervous about his cooperation in Gurn's escape.

A few minutes before six in the evening he had taken advantage of no one being about to slip Gurn from cell number 127 into number 129, from where he could make his way to the roof. At six, when he actually came on duty, Nibet opened the peephole in the door of number 127, as he did in all the others, and saw that Gurn had made an admirable dummy in the bed; it was so good that it even deceived a head guard who made a single rapid inspection of all the cells where Nibet was on one of his several rounds during the night. Obviously Gurn must have gotten away from the prison, for if he had been caught it would certainly have become general knowledge.

These reflections somewhat comforted the restless man, but he knew that the most difficult part of his task still lay ahead: pretending to be surprised and upset when he got back to the prison and was told by his fellow guards of the prisoner's escape; and answering in a natural manner the close questioning to which he would be subjected by the governor and the police and possibly even M. Fuselier, who would be in a rage when he learned that his captive had escaped. Nibet meant to pretend he was ignorant and stupid. He would far rather be called a fool than found out to be a crook and an accomplice.

About half past eleven Nibet got up; Gurn's escape must certainly be known at the prison by this time. The guard on duty would have gone to the cell about seven to wake the prisoner, and though nothing might have been detected then, the cell would, without doubt, have been found to be empty at eight o'clock when the morning food was taken around. And then—

As he walked from his home to the prison, Nibet met the gang of masons coming out for dinner; he crossed the street toward them, hoping to hear some news, but they passed by him in silence, one or two of them giving a careless nod or word of greeting. At first Nibet took their silence as a bad sign, thinking they might have been warned not to tell him, but he reflected that if Gurn's escape were discovered, as it surely was, the authorities would probably prefer to keep the matter a secret.

As he reached the porter's lodge his heart beat violently. What would old Morin have to tell him? But old Morin was busy trying to make his kitchen fire burn properly instead of sending all the smoke pouring out into the room; the old man's slovenly figure was just visible in a gap in the smoke, and he returned Nibet's greeting with nothing more than a silent nod.

"That's funny!" thought Nibet, and he passed through the main courtyard toward the clerks' offices at the end. Through the windows he could see the staff, some bending over their work, others reading newspapers, none of them obviously interested in anything special. Next he presented himself before the guards' turnkey, and again he was allowed to pass on without a word.

By this time Gurn's accomplice was in a state of such nervous tension that he could hardly restrain himself from grabbing hold of one or other of the guards he saw at work and asking them questions. How could the escape of so important a prisoner as the man who had murdered Lord Beltham create so little excitement? Nibet longed to rush up the flights of stairs to number 127 and interrogate the guard who had gone on duty after himself, and whom he was now about to relieve. He must surely know all about it. But it would not do to create suspicion, and Nibet had sufficient self-control to go upstairs at his usual leisurely pace. Outwardly calm and steady, he reached his post just as the clock was striking twelve; he was always punctuality itself, and he was on duty at noon.

"Well, Colas," he said to his colleague, "here I am; you can go now."

"Good!" said the guard. "I'll be off right away. I'm on again at six tonight." And he moved away.

"Everything all right?" Nibet inquired in a tone he tried to make as casual as possible, but that trembled a little nevertheless.

"Quite," said Colas, perfectly naturally, and he went away.

Nibet could contain himself no longer, and the next second he threw caution to the winds; rushing to Gurn's cell he flung the door open.

Gurn was there, sitting on the foot of his bed with his legs crossed and a notebook on his knees, making notes with quiet concentration; he scarcely appeared to notice Nibet's violent invasion.

"Oh! So you are there?" stammered the astonished guard.

Gurn raised his head and looked at him with a cryptic gaze.

"Yes, I'm here."

Every imaginable idea crowded through Nibet's brain, but he could not find words for any of them. Had the plot been discovered before Gurn had time to get away, or had the whole plot merely been a trap to test his own incorruptibility? Nibet went white and leaned against the wall for support. At last Gurn spoke again, reassuring him with a smile.

"Don't look so miserable," he said. "I am here. That is a matter of absolutely no importance. We will suppose that nothing passed between us yesterday, and—that's the end of it."

"So you haven't gone, you didn't go?" said Nibet again.

"No," Gurn replied; "since you are so interested, all I can say is that I was afraid to risk it at the last minute."

Nibet cast a careful and experienced eye all over the cell; under the washstand he saw the little bundle of clothes that he had brought the prisoner the previous day. He rightly decided that the first thing to do was to remove these dangerous articles, whose presence in Gurn's cell would appear very suspicious if they happened to be discovered. He took the bundle and was hurriedly stowing it away under his own clothes when he uttered an exclamation of surprise; the things were wet, and he knew that the rain had never ceased throughout the whole of the previous night.

"Gurn," he said reproachfully, "you are up to something! These things are soaked. You must have gone out last night or these things would not be like this."

Gurn smiled sympathetically at the guard.

"Not bad!" he remarked; "that's pretty good reasoning for a mere prison guard." And as Nibet was about to press the matter, Gurn anticipated his questions and made a frank confession. "Well, yes, I did try to get out—got as far as the clerk's office last evening, but at the last minute I lost my courage, and went back on to the roof. But when I got into number one twenty-nine again I found I could not get back into my own cell, for, as you know, one twenty-nine was locked outside. So to avoid getting caught I returned to the roof and spent the night there; at daybreak I took advantage of the little disturbance caused by the workmen coming in and slipped down from the roof just as they were going up. As soon as I found myself on this floor I ran along this corridor and slipped into my cell. When your friend Colas brought me my breakfast he did not notice that my cell was unlocked— and there you are!"

The explanation was not altogether convincing, but Nibet listened to it and pondered the situation. On the whole, it was much better that things should be as they were, but the guard was wondering how the great lady who paid so well might take the matter. She most certainly had not promised so large a sum of money, nor paid ten thousand francs in advance, merely in order that Gurn might have a breath of fresh air. What was to be done with regard to that? With much ingenuousness Nibet confided his anxiety to the prisoner, who laughed.

"It's not over yet," he declared. "Actually, it is only just beginning. What if we only wanted to test you? Relax, Nibet. If Gurn is in prison at the present moment it is because he has his own reasons for being there. But who is able to predict the future?"

It was time for Gurn to go to the exercise yard, and Nibet, reassuming the uncompromising attitude that all guards ought to maintain when holding custody of prisoners, led the murderer down to the courtyard.

———

In his office at the courthouse, M. Fuselier was having a private conversation with Juve and listening with much interest to what the clever detective inspector was saying to him.

"I tell you again, sir, I attach great importance to the finding of this ordnance map in Gurn's rooms."

"Yes?" said M. Fuselier, with a touch of skepticism.

"And I will tell you why," Juve went on. "About a year ago, when I was engaged on the case of the murder of the Marquise de Langrune at her château down in Lot, I found a small piece of a map showing the district in which I was at the time. I took it to M. de Presles, the magistrate who was conducting the inquiry. He attached no importance to it, and I myself could not see at the time that it gave us any new evidence."

"Quite so," said M. Fuselier. "There is nothing particularly remarkable in finding a map, or a piece of a map, showing a district, in the district itself."

"Those are M. de Presles's very words to me," said Juve with a smile. "And I will give you the same answer I gave him, namely, that if someday we could find the other portion of the map that completed the first piece we found, and could identify the owner of the two portions, there would then be a formal basis on which to proceed to build a hypothesis."

"Proceed to build it," M. Fuselier suggested.

"That's very easy," said Juve. "The fragment of map numbered one, found at Beaulieu, belongs to X. I do not know who X is, but in Paris, in Gurn's rooms, I find the fragment of map numbered two, which belongs to Gurn. If it turns out as I expect that the two fragments of map, when pieced together, form a single and complete whole, I shall conclude logically that X, who was the owner of fragment number one, is the same as the owner of fragment number two, to be specific, Gurn."

"How are you going to find out?" inquired M. Fuselier.

"That's why we have sent for Dollon," Juve replied. "He was steward to the late Marquise de Langrune and has all the circumstantial evidence relating to that case. If he has still got the fragment of map, it will be easy to prove what I have suggested, and perhaps to make the identification I suggest."

"Yes," said M. Fuselier, "but if you do succeed, will it be of

really great importance, in your opinion? Will you be able to infer from that one fact that Gurn and the man who murdered the
Marquise de Langrune are the same person? Isn't that going
rather far? Especially as, if I remember rightly, it was proved that
the murderer in that case was the son of a Monsieur Rambert,
and this young Rambert committed suicide after the crime."

Juve evaded the issue.

"Well, we shall see," was all he said.

The magistrate's clerk came into the room and unceremoniously
interrupted the conversation.

"It is two o'clock, sir," he said. "There are some prisoners to
examine and a whole lot of witnesses." And he placed two
bulky bundles of papers before the magistrate and waited for a
sign to call the various persons whom the magistrate had to see.

The first bundle caught Juve's attention. It was tagged
"Royal Palace Hotel Case."

"Anything new about the robbery from Madame Van den
Rosen and Princess Sonia Danidoff?" he asked. And when the
magistrate shook his head, he added, "Are you going to examine Muller now?"

"Yes," said the magistrate.

"And after that you are to question Gurn, aren't you, in connection with the Beltham case?"

"It's true."

"I wish you would do me a favor by letting the two men con-
front each other while I am still here."

M. Fuselier looked up in surprise; he could not see what connection there could be between the two utterly dissimilar cases.
What object could Juve have in wanting the man who had murdered Lord Beltham to be confronted with the unimportant little
hotel worker who had really been arrested more as a concession
to public opinion than because he was actually considered capable of burglary or attempted burglary? Might not Juve, with his
well-known obsession for associating all crimes with each other,
be going just a little too far in the present instance?

"Have you got some idea in the back of your head?" said
M. Fuselier.

"I've got a—a scar in the palm of my hand," Juve answered with a smile, and as the magistrate confessed that he failed to understand, Juve enlightened him. "We know that the man who pulled off that robbery at the Royal Palace Hotel burned his hand badly when he was cutting the electric wires in the princess's bathroom. Well, a few weeks ago, while I was on the lookout for someone with a scar from such a wound, I was told of a man who was prowling in the slums. I had the fellow followed up, and the very night the hunt began I was going to arrest him when, to my great surprise, I discovered that he was no other than Gurn. He escaped me that time, but when he was caught later on I found that he has an unmistakable scar inside the palm of his right hand; it is fading now, for the burn was only superficial, but it is there. Now do you see my idea?"

"Yes, I do," the magistrate exclaimed, "and I am glad to hear it, since I am having both the men here now. Shall I bring Muller in first?"

Juve assented. . . .

"So you still refuse to confess?" said the magistrate at last. "You still maintain that your—extraordinary—order to let the red-haired waiter out was given in good faith?"

"Yes, yes, yes, sir," the night watchman answered. "That very evening a new employee had joined the staff. I had not even set eyes on him. When I saw this—stranger—I took him to be the one who had been engaged the day before, and I told them to open the door for him. That is the real truth."

"And that is all?"

"That is positively all."

"We are only charging you with complicity," the magistrate went on, "for the man who touched the electric wires burned his hand; that is a strong point in your favor. And you also say that if the thief were put before you, you could recognize him?"

"Yes," said the man confidently.

"Good!" said M. Fuselier, and he signaled to his clerk to call in another man.

The clerk understood, and Gurn was brought in between two municipal guards and was followed by the young apprentice in law, Maître Roger de Seras, who represented his boss at most of these preliminary examinations. As Gurn came in, with the light from the window falling full on his face, M. Fuselier gave a curt order.

"Muller, turn around and look at this man!"

Muller obeyed and surveyed with some bewilderment, and without the least comprehension, the bold head and the well-built, muscular frame of Lord Beltham's murderer. Gurn did not flinch.

"Do you recognize that man?" the magistrate demanded.

Muller ransacked his brains and looked again at Gurn, then shook his head.

"No, sir."

"Gurn, open your right hand," the magistrate ordered. "Show it." And he turned again to Muller. "The man before you seems to have burned the palm of his hand, as that scar shows. Can you not remember having seen that man at the Royal Palace Hotel?"

Muller looked steadily at Gurn.

"On my honor, sir, although it would be in my interest to recognize him, I am bound to acknowledge that I really and truly don't."

M. Fuselier had a brief conversation aside with Juve, and then, the detective appearing to agree with him, turned once more to the night watchman.

"Muller," he said, "the court is pleased with your frankness. You will be set free provisionally, but you are to keep yourself at the disposal of the court." And he signaled to the municipal guards to lead the grateful man away.

Meanwhile Gurn's case appeared to him to be becoming much more serious and much more interesting. He had the prisoner placed in front of him, while Juve, who had withdrawn into a dark corner of the room, never took his eyes off the murderer.

"Gurn," he began, "can you give me an account of your time during the second half of December of last year?"

Gurn was unprepared for the point-blank question and made a

gesture of doubt. M. Fuselier, probably anticipating a sensation, was just on the point of ordering Dollon to be called when he was interrupted by a discreet tap on the door. His clerk went to answer it and saw a gendarme standing at the door. At almost the first words he said, the clerk uttered an exclamation and wheeled around to the magistrate.

"Oh, Monsieur Fuselier, listen! They have just told me—"

But the gendarme had come in. He saluted the magistrate and handed him a letter, which M. Fuselier hastily tore open and read.

> To M. Germain Fuselier, Examining Magistrate, the Law Courts, Paris
>
> The special commissioner at Brétigny station has the honor to report that this morning at eight A.M. the police informed him of the discovery on the railway line, five kilometers from Brétigny on the Orléans side, of the dead body of a man who must either have fallen accidentally or been thrown intentionally from a train bound for Paris. The body had been mutilated by a train traveling in the other direction, but papers found on the person of the deceased, and in particular a summons found in his pocket, show that his name was Dollon, and that he was on his way to Paris to meet with you.
>
> The special commissioner at Brétigny Station has, quite late, been informed of the following facts: passengers who left the train on its arrival at the Austerlitz terminus at five A.M. were examined by the special commissioner at that station and subsequently allowed to go. Possibly you have already been informed. We have, however, thought it our duty, after having searched the body, to report this identification to you and have therefore requisitioned an officer of the police at Brétigny to convey to you the information contained in this communication.

M. Fuselier had turned pale as he read this letter. He handed it to Juve. With feverish haste the famous detective read it through and wheeled around to the gendarme.

"Tell me, do you know if this man's papers, all his papers, were found and have been kept?"

The man shook his head in ignorance. Juve clasped the magistrate's hand. "I'm off to Brétigny this minute," he said in a quiet voice.

Throughout this incident Maître Roger de Seras had remained in a state of blank incomprehension.

Gurn's face was more expressionless and impenetrable than ever.

THE COURT

"Call Lady Beltham!"

It was a perfect May day, and everyone who could pretend on any conceivable ground to be entitled to it had schemed and intrigued to obtain admission to a trial that promised to be a public sensation: the trial of Gurn for the murder of Lord Beltham, exambassador and foremost man of fashion.

The preliminary formalities had furnished nothing to tickle the palates of the sensation-loving crowd. The indictment had been almost inaudible, and, besides, it contained nothing that had not already been made public by the press. Nor had the examination of the prisoner been any more interesting; Gurn sat, strangely impassive, in the dock between two municipal guards and hardly listened to his counsel, the eminent Maître Barberoux, who was assisted by a galaxy of juniors, including young Roger de Seras. Moreover, Gurn had frankly confessed his guilt almost immediately after his arrest. There was not much for him to add to what he had said before, although the president of the court pressed him as to some points that were still not satisfactorily clear with respect to his own identity and the motives that prompted him to commit his crime, and, subsequently, to pay that most risky visit to Lady Beltham, at the close of which Juve had effected his arrest.

But Lady Beltham's evidence promised to be much more interesting. Rumor had been busy for a long time with the great lady and her feelings, and odd stories were being whispered. She was said to be beautiful, wealthy, and charitable; people said, under their breath, that she must know a good deal about the murder of her spouse, and when she made her appearance in the box a sudden hush fell upon the crowded court. She was indeed a most appealing figure, robed in long black cloths, young, graceful, and very pale, so sympathetic a figure that all rumors were forgotten in the general tense desire to hear her answers to the president of the court.

Following the usher to the witness box, she took off her gloves as desired and, in a voice that trembled slightly but was beautifully modulated, repeated the words of the oath with her right hand raised. Noticing her agitation, the president mitigated somewhat the harshness of the tone in which he generally spoke to witnesses.

"Please compose yourself, Madame. I am sorry to have to subject you to this examination, but the interests of justice require it. Now, you are Lady Beltham, widow of the late Lord Beltham, of English nationality, residing in Paris, at your own house in Neuilly?"

"Yes."

"Will you kindly turn around, Madame, and tell me if you know the prisoner in the dock?"

Lady Beltham obeyed mechanically; she glanced at Gurn, who paled a little, and answered the president.

"Yes, I know the prisoner; his name is Gurn."

"Very good, Madame. Can you tell me first of all how you came to be acquainted with him?"

"When my husband was in South Africa, at the time of the Boer War, Gurn was a sergeant in the regular army. It was then that I first met him."

"Did you know him well at that time?"

Lady Beltham seemed to be unable to prevent herself from casting long glances at the prisoner; she appeared to be almost hypnotized and frightened by his close proximity.

"I saw very little of Gurn in the Transvaal," she answered. "It was just by chance that I learned his name, but of course the difference between his own rank and my husband's position made the relations that I could have with a mere sergeant very limited indeed."

"Yes, Gurn was a sergeant," the president said. "And after the war, Madame, did you see the prisoner again?"

"Yes, immediately after the war; my husband and I went to England by the same boat on which Gurn went home."

"Did you see much of him on board?"

"No, we were first-class passengers, and he, I believe, went second. It was just by accident that my husband caught sight of him soon after the boat sailed."

The president paused and made a note.

"Were those all the relations your husband had with the prisoner?"

"They are at any rate all the relations I had with him," Lady Beltham replied in tones of some distress; "but I know that my husband employed Gurn on several occasions, to help him in various affairs and matters of business."

"Thank you," said the president, "we will return to that point presently. Meanwhile, there is one question I should like to ask you. If you had met the prisoner in the street a few months ago, would you have recognized him?"

Lady Beltham hesitated, then answered confidently.

"I am sure I should not have recognized him, and the proof of this is, that just before his arrest I conversed with the prisoner for several minutes, without having the faintest idea that the poor man was no other than the man Gurn, for whom the police were looking."

The president nodded, and Maître Barberoux leaned forward and spoke eagerly to his client in the dock. But the president continued immediately.

"You must forgive me, Madame, for putting a question that may seem rather harsh, and also for reminding you that you are under oath. Did you love your husband?"

Lady Beltham quivered and was silent for a moment, as though endeavoring to frame a correct answer.

"Lord Beltham was much older than myself—" she began, and then, perceiving the meaning implicit in her words, she added: "I had the very highest esteem for him, and a very real affection."

A cynical smile curled the lip of the president, and he glanced at the jury as though asking them to pay still closer attention.

"Do you know why I put that question to you?" he asked, and as Lady Beltham confessed her ignorance he went on: "It has been suggested, Madame, by a rumor that is very generally current in the newspapers and among people generally that the prisoner may possibly have been in love with you; that perhaps—well, is there any truth in this?"

As he spoke the president bent forward, and his eyes seemed to pierce right through Lady Beltham.

"It is a wicked lie," she protested, turning very pale.

Throughout the proceedings Gurn had been sitting in an attitude of absolute indifference, almost of scorn, but now he rose to his feet and uttered a defiant protest.

"Sir," he said to the president of the court, "I want to say publicly here that I have the most profound respect for Lady Beltham. Anyone who has given currency to the foul rumor you refer to is a liar. I have confessed that I killed Lord Beltham, and I do not retract that confession, but I never made any attempt upon his honor, and no word, look, or deed has ever passed between Lady Beltham and myself that might not have taken place in front of Lord Beltham's own eyes."

The president looked sharply at the prisoner.

"Then tell me what your motive was in murdering your victim."

"I have told you already! Lady Beltham is not to be implicated in any way! I had constant business dealings with Lord Beltham; I asked him, over the telephone, to come to my place one day. He came. We had a heated discussion; he got angry and I answered angrily; then I lost control of myself and in a moment of madness I killed him! I am profoundly sorry for my crime and stoop to beg pardon for it; but I cannot tolerate the suggestion that the murder I committed was in the remotest way due to personal relations with a lady who is, I repeat, entitled to the very highest respect from the whole world."

A murmur of sympathy ran through the court at this chivalrous declaration, by which the jury, which had not missed a word, seemed to be entirely convinced. But the president was trained to look for truth in detail, and he turned again to Lady Beltham who still stood in the witness box, very pale and swaying with distress.

"You must forgive me if I attach no importance to a mere

assertion, Madame. The existence of some relations between yourself and the prisoner, which delicacy would prompt him to conceal, and honor would compel you to deny, would alter the whole tone of this case." He turned to the usher. "Recall Madame Doulenques, please."

Mme. Doulenques considered it a tremendous honor to be called as a witness in a trial that the press was full of and was particularly excited because she had just been requested to pose for her photograph by her own favorite paper. She followed the usher to where Lady Beltham stood.

"You told us just now, Madame Doulenques," the president said suavely, "that your lodger Gurn often received visits from a lady friend. You also said that if this lady were placed before you, you would certainly recognize her. Now will you kindly look at the lady in the box? Is this the same person?"

Mme. Doulenques, crimson with excitement and nervously twisting in her hands a huge pair of white gloves which she had bought for this occasion, looked curiously at Lady Beltham.

"God help me, I can't be sure that this is the lady," she said after quite a long pause.

"But you were so certain of your facts just now," the president smiled encouragingly.

"But I can't see the lady very well, with all those veils on," Mme. Doulenques protested.

Lady Beltham did not wait for the request that the president would inevitably have made but haughtily pulled back her veil.

"Do you recognize me now?" she said coldly.

The scorn in her tone upset Mme. Doulenques. She looked again at Lady Beltham and turned instinctively as if to ask help from Gurn, whose face, however, was expressionless, and then replied:

"It's just what I told you before, Your Worship: I can't be sure, I couldn't swear to it."

"But you think she is?"

"You know, Your Worship," Mme. Doulenques protested, "I took an oath just now to tell the truth and nothing but the truth; so I don't want to tell any stories; well, this lady might be the same lady; and again she might not be."

"In other words, you cannot give a definite answer."

"That's it," said the concierge. "I don't know, I can't swear. This lady is like the other lady—there's a sort of family resemblance between them—but at the moment I do not exactly recognize her; it's much too serious!"

Mme. Doulenques would willingly have continued to give evidence forever and a day, but the president cut her short.

"Very well, thank you," he said, and dismissed her with the usher, turning again to Lady Beltham.

"Will you kindly tell me now what your personal opinion is as to the relative guilt of the prisoner? Of course you understand that he has confessed to the crime, and your answer will bear chiefly on the motive that may have inspired him."

Lady Beltham appeared to have recovered some of her confidence.

"I cannot say anything definite, can only express a very vague feeling about the matter. I know my husband was quick-tempered, very quick-tempered, and even violent; and his aggressiveness predisposed him to believe he was always right. He maintained what he considered his rights at all times and over all others; if, as the prisoner says, there was a heated discussion, I should not be surprised if my husband did make use of arguments that might have provoked anger."

The president gently gave a clearer turn to the phrase she used.

"So in your opinion the prisoner's version of the story is quite possible? You admit that Lord Beltham and his murderer may have had a heated discussion, as a consequence of which Gurn committed this crime? This is your honest belief?"

"Yes," Lady Beltham answered, trying to control her voice, "I believe that that may be what took place. And then it is the only way in which I can find the least excuse for the crime this man Gurn committed."

The president picked up the word in astonishment.

"Do you want to find excuses for him, Madame?"

Lady Beltham stood erect and looked at the president.

"It is written that to pardon is the first duty of good Christians. It is true that I have mourned my husband, but the punishment of his murderer will not dry my tears; I ought to forgive

him, bow underneath the burden that is laid upon my soul, and
I do forgive him!"

Ghastly pale, Gurn was staring at Lady Beltham from the
dock; and this time his emotion was so visible that all the jury
noticed it. The president held a brief conference with his colleagues, asked the prisoner's counsel whether he desired to put
any questions to the witness, and, receiving a reply in the nega-
tive, dismissed Lady Beltham with a word of thanks and announced that the court would adjourn.

Immediately a hum of conversation broke out in the warm
and sunny court; lawyers in their robes moved from group to
group, criticizing, explaining, prophesying; and in their seats the
world of beauty and fashion bowed and smiled and gossiped.

"She's uncommonly pretty, this Lady Beltham," one young
lawyer said, "and she's got a way of answering questions without compromising herself, and yet without throwing blame on
the prisoner, that is uncommonly clever."

"You are all alike, you men," said a pretty, perfectly dressed
woman in mocking tones; "if a woman is young and decent-
looking and has a charming voice, your sympathies are with her
at once! Oh, yes, they are! Now, shall I tell you what your Lady
Beltham really is? Well, she is nothing more nor less than a flirt!
She knew well enough how to get on the soft side of the judge,
who was quite ridiculously nice to her, and to capture the sympathy of the court. I think it was outrageous to declare that she
had married a man who was too old for her, and to say that she
felt nothing but esteem for him!"

"There's an admission!" the young barrister laughed. "*Vive
l'amour*, eh? And *mariages de convenance* are placed out, eh?"

On another bench a little further away, a clean-shaven man
with a highly intelligent face was talking animatedly.

"Baloney! Your Lady Beltham is anything you like. Who
cares about Lady Beltham? But Gurn, now! There's a type, if
you like! What an interesting, characteristic face! He has the
head of the assassin of genius, with perfect mastery of self, implacable, cruel, malignant, a Torquemada of a man!"

"Your excitement is running away with you," someone
laughed.

"I don't care! It is so seldom one comes across people in a city who really are prototypes. That man is not an assassin; he is *the assassin*—the *type*!"

Two ladies sitting close to this enthusiast had been listening closely to this diatribe.

"Do you know who that is?" one whispered to the other. "That is Valgrand the actor," and they turned their lorgnettes on the actor who was getting more excited every moment.

A bell rang, and, heralded by the usher proclaiming silence, the judges returned to the bench and the jury to its box. The president cast an eagle eye over the court, compelling silence, and then resumed the proceedings.

"Next witness; call Monsieur Juve!"

VERDICT AND SENTENCE

Once more a wave of excitement ran through the court. There was not a single person who had not heard of Juve and his marvelous exploits, or who did not regard him as a kind of hero. All leaned forward to watch him as he followed the usher to the witness box, wholly unaffected in manner and not seeking to exploit his popularity. Indeed, he seemed rather to be uneasy, almost nervous, as one of the oldest newspaper reporters present remarked audibly.

He took the oath, and the president of the court addressed him in friendly tones.

"You are quite familiar with procedure, Monsieur Juve. Which would you prefer: that I should interrogate you, or that I should leave you to tell your story in your own way? You know how important it is, for it is you who are, so to speak, the originator of the trial today, inasmuch as it was your great detective skill that brought about the arrest of the criminal, after it had also discovered the crime."

"Since you are so kind, sir," Juve answered, "I will make my statement first, and then be ready to answer any questions that may be put to me by yourself or by counsel for the defense."

Juve turned to the dock and fixed his piercing eyes on the impassive face of Gurn, who met it unflinchingly. Juve shrugged his shoulders slightly and, turning half toward the jury, began his statement. He did not propose, he said, to recite the story of his search, which had resulted in the arrest of Gurn, for this had been set forth fully in the indictment, and the jury had also seen his depositions at the original examination. He had nothing to add to or to subtract from his previous evidence. He merely asked for the jury's particular attention, for, although he was adducing nothing new in the case actually before them, he had some unexpected disclosures to make about the prisoner's personal guilt. The first point that he desired to emphasize was that human intelligence should hesitate before no improbability, however improbable, provided that some explanation was humanly conceivable and no definite material object rendered the improbability an impossibility. His whole statement would be based on the principle that the probable is incontestable and true, until proof of the contrary has been established.

"Gentlemen," he went on, "lately the police have been helpless before a number of serious crimes, still unsolved. Let me recall these cases to your memory: They were the murder of the Marquise de Langrune at her château of Beaulieu; the robberies from Madame Van den Rosen and the Princess Sonia Danidoff; the murder of Dollon, the former steward of the Marquise de Langrune, on his way from the neighborhood of Saint-Jaury to Paris to obey a summons sent to him by Monsieur Germain Fuselier; and, lastly, the murder of Lord Beltham, which occurred prior to the cases just enumerated and for which the prisoner in the dock is at this moment standing trial. Gentlemen, I have to say that all these cases, the Beltham, Langrune, and Dollon murders, and the Rosen-Danidoff burglaries, are absolutely and indisputably to be attributed to one and the same individual, to that man standing there—Gurn!"

Having made this extraordinary assertion, Juve again turned around toward the prisoner. That mysterious person appeared to be keenly interested in what the detective said, but it would have been difficult to say whether he was merely surprised, or perturbed and excited as well. Juve hushed, with a wave of his hand, the murmur that ran through the court and resumed his address.

"My assertion that Gurn is the sole person responsible for all these crimes has surprised you, gentlemen, but I have proof that must, I think, convince you. I will not go into the details of each of those cases, for the newspapers have made you quite familiar with them, but I will be as brief and as lucid as I can.

"My first point, gentlemen, is this: The murderer of the Marquise de Langrune and the man who robbed Madame Van den Rosen and Princess Sonia Danidoff are one and the same person.

"That is shown beyond a doubt by tests made in the two cases with a Bertillon dynamometer, an instrument of the highest precision, which proved that the same individual operated in both cases; that is one point made good. And next, the man who robbed Madame Van den Rosen and Princess Sonia is Gurn. That is proved by the fact that the burglar burned his hand while engaged in this crime, and that Gurn has a scar on his hand that betrays him as the criminal. The scar is faint now perhaps, but I can testify that it was very obvious at the time of a disturbance that occurred at a seedy café named the Saint-Anthony's Pig, where, accompanied by Detective Lemaroy—who is still in the hospital for treatment of injuries received on that occasion—I attempted, and failed, to arrest this man Gurn.

"Thus, gentlemen, I prove that the Langrune and Danidoff cases are the work of but one man, and that man is Gurn.

"I come to my next point. As you know, the murder of the Marquise de Langrune was accompanied by some strange circumstances. At the inquest it was proved that the murderer most probably got into the house from outside, opening the front door with a skeleton key; and that he obtained admission into the bedroom of the marquise, not by criminal means—I stress that—but by the simple means of her having opened the door to him, which she did on the strength of his name; and, finally, that if robbery was the motive for the crime, the nature of the robbery remained a mystery.

"Now I have ascertained, gentlemen, and—if, as I shall ask you presently, you decide to have an adjournment and a supplementary investigation—I shall be able to prove two important facts. The first is that the marquise had in her possession a lottery ticket that had just won a large first prize; this ticket had been sent to her by Monsieur Etienne Rambert. This ticket was not found at the time, but it was subsequently traced to a person who for the moment has utterly disappeared, who declared that it was given to him by Monsieur Etienne Rambert. And it is further noteworthy that Monsieur Etienne Rambert seemed to have increased his fortune during that time. The second fact I have ascertained is that, although Monsieur Etienne Rambert pretended to get into a first-class carriage of a slow train at the Gare d'Orsay, he most certainly was not in that train between Vierzon and Limoges. I can, if you wish, call a witness who inspected all the compartments of that carriage and can prove that he was not there.

"The probable—almost certain—inference is that Monsieur Etienne Rambert got into that slow train at the Gare d'Orsay for the definite purpose of establishing an alibi, and then got out of it on the other side and entered an express that was going in the same direction and in front of the slow train.

"You may remember that it was shown that all trains stopped at the mouth of the Verrières tunnel, near Beaulieu, and that it was possible for a man to get out of the express, commit the crime, and then return—I would remind you of the footprints found on the embankment—and get into the slow train that followed the express at an interval of three hours and a half, and get out of that train at Verrières Station. The passenger who did that was the criminal, and it was Monsieur Etienne Rambert.

"As I have already proved that it was Gurn who murdered the Marquise de Langrune, it seems to follow necessarily that Monsieur Etienne Rambert must be Gurn!"

Juve paused to make sure that the jury had followed his deductions and understood all his points. He proceeded; the courtroom was profoundly hushed and tense.

"We have just identified Gurn as Rambert and proved that Rambert-Gurn is guilty of the Beltham and Langrune murders, and the robbery of Madame Van den Rosen and Princess Sonia Danidoff. There remains the murder of the steward Dollon.

"Gentlemen, when Gurn was arrested on the single charge of the murder of Lord Beltham, you may readily believe that his one fear was that all these other crimes, for which I have just shown him to be responsible, might be brought up against him. I was just then on the very point of finding out the truth, but I had not yet done so. A single link was missing in the chain that would connect Gurn with Rambert, and identify the murderer of Lord Beltham as the person who committed the other crimes.

That link was some common clue, or better still, some object belonging to the murderer of Lord Beltham, which had been forgotten and left on the scene of the Langrune murder.

"That object I found. It was a fragment of a map, picked up in a field near the château of Beaulieu, in the path that Etienne Rambert must have followed from the railway line; it was a fragment cut out of a large map, the rest of which I found in Gurn's rooms, thereby identifying Gurn with Rambert

"Gentlemen, the fragment of map that was picked up in the field was left in the custody of the steward Dollon. That unfortunate man was summoned to Paris by Monsieur Germain Fuselier. There was only one person who had any interest in preventing Dollon from coming, and that person was Gurn, or it would be better to say Rambert-Gurn. And you know that Dollon was killed before he reached Monsieur Germain Fuselier. Is it necessary to declare that it was Gurn, Rambert-Gurn, who killed him?"

Juve said the last words in tones of such earnest and solemn denunciation that the truth of them seemed beyond all doubt. And yet he read incredulous surprise in the attitude of the jury. From the body of the court, too, a murmur rose that was not sympathetic. Juve realized that the sheer audacity of his theory must come as a shock, and he knew how difficult it would be to convince anyone who had not followed every detail of the case as he himself had done.

"Gentlemen," he said, "I know that my assertions about the multiple crimes of this man Gurn must fill you with amazement. That does not dismay me. There is one other name that I must mention, perhaps to silence your objections, perhaps to show the vast importance I attach to the deductions that I have just been privileged to detail to you. This is the last thing I have to say.

"The man who has been capable of assuming in turn the guise of Gurn, and of Etienne Rambert, and of the man of fashion at the Royal Palace Hotel; who has had the genius to devise and to accomplish such terrible crimes in incredible circumstances, and to combine audacity with skill, and a conception of evil with a pretense of respectability; who has been able to play the Proteus eluding all the efforts of the police—this man, I say, ought not to be called Gurn! He is—and can be—no other than Fantômas!"

The detective suddenly broke off his long statement, and the syllables of the melodramatic name seemed to echo through the court and, taken up by all those present, to swell again into a dread murmur.

"Fantômas! He is Fantômas!"

For several minutes judges and jury seemed to be absorbed in their own reflections, and then the president of the court made an abrupt gesture of violent dissent.

"Monsieur Juve, you have just enunciated some astounding facts and elaborated an appalling indictment against this man Gurn. I have no doubt the public prosecutor will ask for a supplementary examination, which this court will be happy to grant, if he concludes your arguments are worth consideration. But are they? I will submit three objections." Juve bowed coldly. "First of all, Monsieur Juve, do you believe that a man could assume disguises with the cleverness that you have just represented? Monsieur Etienne Rambert is a man of sixty; Gurn is thirty-five. Monsieur Rambert is an elderly man, who has trouble moving, and the man who robbed Princess Sonia Danidoff was a nimble, active man."

"I have anticipated that objection, sir," Juve said with a smile, "by saying that Gurn is Fantômas! Nothing is impossible for Fantômas!"

"Suppose that is true," said the president with a wave of his hand, "but what do you say to this: You charge Etienne Rambert with the murder of Madame de Langrune, but do you not know that Etienne Rambert's son Charles Rambert, who, according to the generally received and most plausible theory, was the real murderer of the marquise, committed suicide from remorse? If Etienne Rambert was the guilty party, Charles Rambert would hardly have taken his own life."

Juve's voice shook a little.

"You would be quite right, sir, if again it were not necessary to add that Etienne Rambert is Gurn—that is to say, Fantômas! Is it not a possible hypothesis that Fantômas might have affected the mind of that boy; have suggested to him that it was he who committed the crime in a moment of insanity, and at last have urged him to commit suicide? Haven't you ever heard of the power of suggestion?"

"Suppose that also is true," said the president with another vague wave of his hand. "I will put two incontestable facts before you. You accuse Etienne Rambert of being Gurn; Etienne Rambert was lost in the wreck of the *Lancaster*. You also accuse Gurn of having murdered Dollon: At the time that murder was committed, Gurn was in solitary confinement in the Santé prison."

This time the detective made a sign as if to admit defeat.

"If I have waited until today to make the statement you have just listened to, it was obviously because I still have no absolute proof, but merely a chain of certainties. I spoke today because I could not keep silent any longer; if I still cannot explain in detail, I am sure I will be able to someday. Everything comes to light sooner or later. And as to the two facts you have just put before me, I would reply that there is no proof that Monsieur Rambert was lost in the wreck of the *Lancaster:* It has not been legally established that he ever was on board that ship. Of course, I know his name was on the list of passengers, but a child could have contrived a device of that sort. Besides, all the circumstances attending that disaster are still a total mystery. My belief is that a Fantômas would be perfectly capable of causing an explosion on a ship and blowing up a hundred and fifty people, if by doing it he could dispose of one of his identities, especially such a terribly compromising identity as that of Etienne Rambert."

The president dismissed the theory out of hand.

"Pure speculation!" he said. "And what about the murder of Dollon? I should like further to remind you that the fragment of map that, according to you, was the real reason for this man's death was found on his body and does not correspond in the least with the hole cut in the map you found in Gurn's rooms."

"As for that," Juve said with a smile, "the explanation is obvious. If Gurn, whom I charge with the murder of Dollon, had been content merely to steal the real fragment, he would have drawn suspicion to the crime. But he was much too clever for that. He was subtle enough to take the compromising fragment and substitute another fragment for it—the one found on the body."

"Perhaps," said the president, "that is possible, but I repeat, Gurn was in prison at the time."

"True! True!" said Juve, throwing up his hands. "I am prepared to swear that it was Gurn who committed the murder, but I cannot yet explain how he did it, since he was in solitary confinement in the Santé."

Silence fell upon the court; Juve refrained from saying anything more, but a sarcastic smile curled his lip.

"Have you anything else to say?" the president asked after a pause.

"Nothing, except that anything is possible to Fantômas."

The president turned to the prisoner.

"Gurn, have you anything to say, any confession to make? The jury will listen to you."

Gurn rose to his feet.

"I do not understand a word of what the detective has just been saying," he said.

The president looked at Juve again.

"You suggest that there will be a supplementary investigation?"

"Yes."

"Mr. Solicitor-General, have you any application to make on that subject?" the president asked the public prosecutor.

"No," said the official. "The witness's allegations are altogether too vague."

"Very well. The court will deliberate forthwith."

The judges gathered around the president of the court and held a short discussion. Then they returned to their places and the president announced their decision. It was that after consideration of the statement of the witness Juve, their opinion was that such statement rested merely upon hypotheses, and their decision was that there was no occasion for a supplementary inquiry.

And the president immediately called upon the public prosecutor to address the court.

Neither in his lengthy address nor in the ensuing address of Maître Barberoux on behalf of the defendant was the slightest allusion made to the fresh facts adduced by the detective. The theories he put forward were so unexpected and so utterly astonishing that nobody paid the least attention to them! Then the session was adjourned while the jury considered its verdict. The judges retired and guards removed the prisoner, and Juve, who had accepted the dismissal of his application for a further inquiry with perfect equanimity, went up to the pressbox and spoke to a young journalist sitting there.

"Shall we go out for a quarter of an hour, Fandor?" And when they were presently in the corridor, he slapped the young fellow in a friendly way on the shoulder and asked: "Well, my boy, what do you say to all that?"

Jérôme Fandor seemed to be overwhelmed.

"You accuse my father? You really accuse Etienne Rambert of being Gurn? I must be dreaming!"

"My dear young idiot," Juve growled, "do pray understand one thing: I am not accusing your father, your real father, but only the man who pretended to be your father! Just think: If my contention is right—that the Etienne Rambert who killed the Marquise is Gurn—it is perfectly obvious that Gurn is not your father, for he is only thirty-five years of age! He has merely disguised himself as your father."

"Then who is my real father?"

"I don't know anything about that," said the detective. "That's a matter we will look into one of these days! Take it from me that we are only just at the beginning of all these things."

"But the court has refused a supplementary inquiry."

"God!" said Juve. "I quite expected it would! I have not got enough proof to satisfy the legal mind; and then, too, I had to hold my tongue about the most interesting fact that I knew."

"What was that?"

"Why, that you are not dead, Charles Rambert! I had to conceal that fact, my boy, for the unfortunate reason that I am a poor man and depend on my job. If I had let out that I had known for a long time that Charles Rambert was alive when he was supposed to be dead, and that I had known him first as Jeanne and then as Paul, and yet had said nothing about it, I would have been dismissed from the service as sure as my name is Juve—and it is equally certain that you would have been arrested; which is precisely what I do not wish to happen!"

In tense silence the foreman of the jury rose.

"In the presence of God and man, and upon my honor and my conscience, I declare that the answer of a majority of the jury is 'yes' to all the questions submitted to them."

Then he sat down, making no mention of extenuating circumstances.

The words of the fatal verdict fell like a stone in the silent courtroom, and many faces went white.

"Have you anything to say before sentence is passed?"

"Nothing," Gurn replied.

In rapid tones the president read the formal pronouncement of the court. It seemed horribly long and unintelligible, but presently the president's voice became slower as it arrived at the fatal words. There was a second's pause, and then he reached the point:

"—the sentence on the prisoner Gurn is death."

And almost simultaneously he gave the order.

"Guards, take the condemned away!"

Juve, who had returned to court with Fandor, spoke to the young journalist.

"God!" he exclaimed. "Now I know what self-confidence is. That man is truly remarkable; he never even turned a hair!"

AN ASSIGNATION

The final curtain had fallen on the first performance of the new drama at the Grand Treteau.

The night had been one long triumph for Valgrand, and although it was very late the Baronne de Vibray, who prided herself on being the great tragedian's dearest friend, had made her way behind the scenes to praise and congratulate him, and to have a little triumph of her own by presenting her friends to the hero of the hour. In vain had Charlot, the old dresser, tried to prevent her invasion of his master's dressing room. He was no match for her perseverance, and before long she had swept into the room with the proud smile of a general entering a conquered town. The Comte de Baral, a tall young man with a monocle, followed close in her wake.

"Will you please announce us," he said to the dresser.

Charlot hesitated a moment in surprise, then broke rapidly into explanations.

"Monsieur Valgrand is not here yet. What, didn't you know? At the end of the performance the minister of public instruction sent for him to congratulate him! That's a tremendous honor, and it's the second time it has been paid to Monsieur Valgrand."

Meanwhile the other two ladies in the party were roaming about the dressing room: Mme. Simone Holbord, wife of a colonel of the marines who had just distinguished himself in the Congo, and the Comtesse Marcelline de Baral.

"How thrilling an actor's dressing room is!" exclaimed Mme. Holbord, inspecting everything in the room through her lorgnette. "Just look at these darling little brushes! I suppose he uses those in making up? And, oh, my dear! There are actually three kinds of rouge!"

The Comtesse de Baral was fascinated by the photographs adorning the walls.

" 'To the admirable Valgrand from a comrade,' " she read in awestruck tones. "Come and look, dear, it is signed by Sarah Bernhardt! And listen to this one: 'At Buenos Aires, at Melbourne, and New York, wherever I am I hear the praises of my friend Valgrand!' "

"A real globe-trotter!" said Mme. Holbord; "I expect he belongs to the Comédie Française."

Colonel Holbord interrupted, calling to his wife.

"Simone, come and listen to what our friend De Baral is telling me; it is really very interesting."

The young woman approached, and the comte began again for her benefit.

"You haven't been back long enough from the Congo to be up-to-date on all our Paris happenings, and so you won't have noticed this little touch, but in the part that he created tonight Valgrand made himself up exactly like Gurn, the man who murdered Lord Beltham!"

"Gurn?" said Mme. Holbord, to whom the name did not convey much. "Oh, yes, I think I read about that; they never caught him, did they?"

"Well, they took a long time," the comte de Baral replied. "As usual, the police were giving up all hope of finding him, when one day, or rather one night, they did find him and arrested him; and where do you suppose that was? Why, with Lady Beltham! Yes, really—in her own house at Neuilly!"

"Impossible!" cried Simone Holbord. "Poor woman! What an awful shock for her!"

"Lady Beltham is a brave, dignified, and truly charitable woman," said the Comtesse de Baral. "She simply worshiped her husband. And yet she pleaded sincerely for mercy for the murderer—though she did not succeed in getting it."

"What a dreadful thing!" said Simone Holbord perfunctorily;

her attention was wandering to all the other attractions in this attractive room. A pile of letters was lying on a writing table, and the reckless young woman began to look at the envelopes. "Just look at this pile of letters!" she cried. "How funny! Every one of them in a woman's hand! I suppose they're all throwing themselves at his feet."

Colonel Holbord went on talking to the Comte de Baral in a corner of the room.

"I am enormously interested in what you are telling me. What happened then?"

"Well, this wretch Gurn was recognized by the police as he was leaving Lady Beltham's, and was arrested and put in prison. The trial was held about six weeks ago. All Paris went to it, of course including myself! This man Gurn is a monster, but a strange one, rather difficult to define; he swore that he had killed Lord Beltham after a quarrel, practically for the sake of robbing him, but I got the impression that he was lying."

"But why else would he have committed the murder?"

The Comte de Baral shrugged his shoulders.

"Nobody knows," he said. "Politics, perhaps, nihilism, or perhaps—love. There was one fact—or coincidence—worth noting: When Lady Beltham came home from the Transvaal after the war—during which, by the way, she did wonderful work among the sick and wounded—she sailed by the same boat that was taking Gurn to England. Gurn also was a bit of a popular hero just then; he had volunteered at the beginning of the war, and came back with a sergeant's stripes and a medal for distinguished conduct. Can Gurn and Lady Beltham have met and gotten to know each other? The Lady's behavior during the trial was commented upon, if not exactly a scandal. She had odd collapses in the presence of the murderer, collapses that were accounted for in various ways. Some people said that she was half out of her mind with grief at the loss of her husband; others said that if she were mad, it was over someone else, this vulgar criminal perhaps. They even went so far as to allege that Lady Beltham had an affair with Gurn!"

"Come, come!" the colonel protested, "a great lady like Lady Beltham, so religious and so austere? Absurd!"

"People say all sorts of things," said the Comte de Baral vaguely. He turned to another subject. "Anyhow, the case caused a tremendous sensation; Gurn's getting sentenced to death was very popular, and the case was so typically Parisian that our friend Valgrand, knowing that he was going to create the part of a murderer in this tragedy tonight, followed every phase of the trial closely, studied the man in detail, and literally identified himself with him in this character. It was a shrewd idea. You noticed the sensation he caused when he came on the stage?"

"Yes, I did," said the colonel; "I wondered what the shouts from all over the house meant."

"Try to find a portrait of Gurn in one of the illustrated papers," said the comte, "and compare it with— Ah, I think this is Valgrand coming!"

The Baronne de Vibray had tired of her conversation with the old dresser Charlot and had left him to take up her stand outside the dressing room, where she greeted with nods and smiles the other actors and actresses as they hurried by, and listened to the sounds coming from the end of the passage. Soon she heard the voice of Valgrand singing a refrain from a musical comedy. The Baronne de Vibray hurried to meet him, with both hands outstretched, and led him into his dressing room.

"Let me present Monsieur Valgrand!" she exclaimed, and then presented the two young women to the bowing actor. "Comtesse Marcelline de Baral, Madame Holbord."

"Pardon me, ladies, for keeping you waiting," the actor said. "I was deep in conversation with the minister. He was so charming, so kind!" He turned to the Baronne de Vibray. "He did me the honor to offer me a cigarette! A treasured souvenir! Charlot! Charlot! You must put this cigarette in the little box where all my treasures are!"

"It is very full already, Monsieur Valgrand," said Charlot deprecatingly.

"We must not keep you long," the Baronne de Vibray murmured. "You must be very tired."

Valgrand passed a weary hand across his brow.

"Positively exhausted!" Then he raised his head and looked at the company. "What did you think of me?"

A chorus of eulogies sprang from every lip.

"Splendid!" "Wonderful!" "The apex of art!"

"No, but really?" protested Valgrand, swelling with satisfied vanity. "Tell me candidly; was it really good?"

"You really were wonderful; could not have been better," the Baronne de Vibray exclaimed enthusiastically, and the crowd of worshipers endorsed every word until the artist was convinced that their praise was quite sincere.

"How I have worked!" he exclaimed. "Do you know, when rehearsals began—ask Charlot if this isn't true—the piece simply didn't exist!"

"Simply didn't exist!" Charlot corroborated him, like an echo.

"Didn't exist," Valgrand repeated, "not even my part. It was insignificant, flat! So I took the author aside and I said: 'Frantz, my boy, I'll tell you what you must do. You know the lawyer's speech? Absurd! What am I to do while he is delivering it? I'll make the speech for my own defense and I'll get something out of it!' And the prison scene! Just fancy, he had written a parson into that! I said to Frantz: 'Cut the parson, my boy. What the hell am I to do while he is preaching? Simply nothing at all; it's absurd. Give his speech to me! I'll preach to myself!' And there you are. I don't want to boast, but really I did it all! And it was a success, eh?"

Again the chorus broke out, to be stopped by Valgrand, who was contemplating his reflection in a mirror.

"And my makeup, Colonel? Do you know the story of my makeup? I hear they were talking about it all over the house. Do I look like Gurn? What do you think? You saw him close up at the trial, Comte. What do you think?"

"The resemblance is amazing," said the Comte de Baral with perfect truth.

The actor stroked his face mechanically; a new idea struck him.

"My beard is real," he exclaimed. "I let it grow on purpose.

I hardly had to make myself up at all; I have the same build, the same coloring, the same profile; it was ridiculously easy!"

"Give me a lock of hair from your beard for a locket," said the Baronne de Vibray impudently.

Valgrand looked at her and heaved a profound sigh.

"Not yet, not yet, dear lady; I am terribly sorry, but not yet; a little later on, perhaps; wait for the hundredth performance."

"I must have one too," said Simone Holbord, and Valgrand with great dignity replied:

"I will put your name down for one, Madame!"

But the Comte de Baral had looked furtively at his watch and uttered an exclamation of surprise.

"My good people, it is terribly late! And our great artist must be overcome with fatigue!"

And so they all prepared to depart, in spite of the actor's courteous protests that he could not hear of letting them go so soon. They lingered at the door for a few minutes in eager, animated conversation, shaking hands and exchanging farewells, thanks, and congratulations. Then the sound of their footsteps died away along the corridors, and the Baronne de Vibray and her friends left the theater. Valgrand turned back into his dressing room and locked the door, then dropped into the low and comfortable chair that was set before his dressing table.

He remained there resting for a few minutes, and then sat up and threw a whimsical glance at his dresser who was laying out his ordinary clothes.

"Damn it all, Charlot! What's exhaustion? The mere sight of such enchanting women would wake a man from the dead!"

Charlot shrugged his shoulders.

"Will you never be serious, Monsieur Valgrand?"

"God, I hope not!" exclaimed the actor. "I hope not, for if there is one thing of which one never tires, it is Woman, the peerless rainbow that illuminates this vale of tears!"

"You are very poetical tonight," the dresser remarked.

"I am a lover—in love with love! Oh, love, love! And in my time, you know—" He made a sweeping, comprehensive gesture and came back abruptly to mundane affairs. "Come, help me dress."

Charlot offered him a bundle of letters, which Valgrand took carelessly. He looked at the envelopes one after another, hugely amused.

"Violet ink and monograms and coronets and—perfume. Say, Charlot, is this a proposal? What do you want to bet?"

"You never get anything else," the dresser grumbled "—except bills."

"Do you bet?"

"If you insist, I'll bet it is a bill; then you will win," said Charlot.

"Done!" cried Valgrand. "Listen," and he began to declaim the letter aloud: "Oh, wondrous genius, a flower but now unclosing— Got it, Charlot? Another of them!" He tore open another envelope. "Ah-ha! Photograph enclosed, and will I send it back if the original doesn't appeal to me." He flung himself back in his chair to laugh. "Where is my collar?" He picked up a third envelope. "Want to bet that this violet envelope contains another tribute to my fatal beauty?"

"I bet it is another bill," said the dresser; "but I'm sure you'll win."

"I have," Valgrand replied, and again declaimed the written words: " 'If you promise to be discreet and true, you shall never regret it.' Does one ever regret it—even if one does not keep one's promises?"

"At lovers' perjuries—" Charlot quoted.

"Drunken promises!" Valgrand retorted. "By the way, I'm dying for a drink. Give me a whiskey and soda." He got up and moved to the table on which Charlot had set decanters and glasses, and was about to take the glass the dresser offered him when a tap on the door brought the conversation to a sudden stop. The actor frowned; he did not want to be bothered by more visitors. But curiosity got the better of his annoyance, and he told Charlot to see who it was.

Charlot went to the door and peered through a narrow opening at the thoughtless intruder.

"Imagine making all this fuss over a letter!" he growled. "Urgent? Of course, they always are urgent." And he shut the door on the messenger and gave the letter to Valgrand. "A woman brought it," he said.

Valgrand looked at it.

"H'm! Mourning! Want to bet, Charlot?"

"Deep mourning," said Charlot; "then I bet it is a declaration. I expect you will win again, for very likely it is a pleading letter. Black edges stir compassion."

Valgrand was reading the letter, carelessly to begin with, then with deep attention. He reached the signature at the end, and then read it through again, aloud this time, punctuating his reading with flippant comments: " 'In creating the part of the criminal in the tragedy tonight, you made yourself up into a most incredible likeness of Gurn, the man who murdered Lord Beltham. Come tonight, at two o'clock, *in your costume*, to Twenty-two rue Messier. Take care not to be seen, but come. Someone who loves you is waiting for you there.' "

"And it is signed—?" said the dresser.

"That, my boy, I'm not going to tell you," said Valgrand, and he put the letter carefully into his wallet. "Now what are you up to?" he added, as the dresser came up to him to take his clothes.

"Up to?" the servant exclaimed. "I am only helping you get your things off."

"Idiot!" laughed Valgrand. "Didn't you understand? Give me my black tie and villain's coat again."

"What on earth is the matter with you?" Charlot asked with some uneasiness. "Surely you are not thinking of going?"

"Not going? Why, in the whole of my career as lover, I have never had such an opportunity before!"

"It may be a hoax."

"Take my word for it, I know better. Things like this aren't hoaxes. Besides, I know the—the lady. She has often been pointed out to me, and at the trial— By Jove, Charlot, she is the most enchanting woman in the world: strangely lovely, infinitely distinguished, absolutely fascinating!"

"You are raving like a schoolboy."

"So much the better for me! Why, I was half dead with fatigue, and now I am myself again. Hurry up! My hat! It's getting late. Where is it?"

"Where is what?" the bewildered Charlot asked.

"Why, this address," Valgrand answered irritably, "this rue Messier. Look it up in the directory."

Valgrand stamped impatiently up and down the room while Charlot hurriedly turned over the pages of the directory, muttering the syllables at the top of each as he ran through them in alphabetical order.

"J . . . K . . . L . . . M . . . Ma . . . Me . . . Why, Monsieur Valgrand—"

"What's the matter?"

"Why, it is the street where the prison is!"

"The Santé? Where Gurn is—in the condemned cell?" Valgrand cocked his hat rakishly on one side. "And I have an assignation at the prison?"

"Not exactly, but not far off; right opposite, yes, number Twenty-two must be right opposite."

"Right opposite the prison!" Valgrand exclaimed gaily. "The choice of the spot and the desire to see me in my costume as Gurn are evidence of a positive refinement in erotic delight! See? The lady and I—the double of Gurn—and right opposite the real Gurn in his cell! Quick, man, my cloak! My cane!"

"Do think about it, sir," Charlot protested; "it is absolutely absurd! A man like you—"

"A man like me," Valgrand roared, "would keep an appointment like this if he had to walk on his hands to get there! Good night!" And singing gaily, Valgrand strode down the corridor.

Charlot was accustomed to these wild escapades on his master's part, for Valgrand was the most incorrigible rake it is possible to imagine. But while he was tidying up the room after Valgrand had left, the dresser shook his head.

"What a pity! And he such a great actor! These women make an absolute fool of him! Why, he hasn't even taken his gloves or his wallet!" There was a tap at the door, and the doorman looked in.

"Can I turn out the lights?" he asked. "Has Monsieur Valgrand gone?"

"Yes," said the dresser absently, "he has gone."

"A great night," said the doorman. "Have you seen the last edition of *The Capitale*, the eleven o'clock edition? There's a notice of us already. The papers don't lose any time nowadays. They say it is a great success."

"Let's look at it," said the dresser. Glancing through the notice, he added, "Yes, that's quite true: 'M. Valgrand has achieved his finest triumph in his last creation.'" He looked casually through the newspaper and suddenly gasped. "Good heavens, it can't be possible!"

"What's the matter?" the doorman asked.

Charlot pointed a shaking finger to another column.

"Read that, Jean, read that! I must be mistaken."

The doorman peered over Charlot's shoulder at the passage he was pointing at.

"So what? It's that Gurn affair again. Yes, he is to be executed at daybreak on the eighteenth."

"But that is this morning—the one coming up," Charlot exclaimed.

"Maybe," said the doorman indifferently; "yes, last night was the seventeenth, so it is the eighteenth now! Are you ill, Charlot?"

Charlot pulled himself together.

"No, it's nothing, I'm only tired. You can put out the lights. I shall be out of the theater in five minutes; I only want to do one or two little things here."

"All right," said Jean, turning away. "Shut the door behind you when you leave if I have gone to bed."

Charlot sat on the arm of a chair and wiped his brow.

"I don't like this at all," he muttered. "Why the hell did he want to go? What does this woman want with him? I may be only an old fool, but I know what I know, and there have been too many weird stories about this case already." He sat there meditating till an idea took shape in his mind. "Dare I go around there and just see what's happening? Of course he will be furious, but suppose that letter was a decoy and he is walking into a trap. One never can tell. An assignation on that particular street with that prison opposite and Gurn to be guillotined within the next hour or so?" The man made up his mind, hurriedly put on his coat and hat, and switched off the electric lights in the exquisitely appointed dressing room. "I'll go!" he said aloud. "If I see anything suspicious, or if at the end of half an hour I don't see Monsieur Valgrand leaving the house—well!" Charlot turned the key in the lock. "Yes, I will go. It'll put my mind at ease."

TREACHERY

Number Twenty-two rue Messier was a wretched one-story house that belonged to a country vintner who seldom came to Paris. It was damp, dirty, and dilapidated, and would have had to be rebuilt from top to bottom if it were to be rendered livable. There had been a long succession of so-called tenants of this hovel, shady, disreputable people who, for the most part, left without paying any rent, the landlord being only too glad if occasionally they left behind them a little miserable furniture or worn-out kitchen utensils. He was finding it more and more difficult to rent the wretched house, and for weeks at a time it had remained unoccupied. But one day, about a month ago, he had been astonished to receive an application to take it from someone who vaguely signed himself Durand; and still further astonished by finding in the envelope money representing a year's rent in advance. Delighted with this windfall, and congratulating himself on not having gone to the expense of putting the place into something like repair—unnecessary now since he had secured a tenant, and a good one, for at least twelve months— the landlord promptly sent a receipt to this Durand, with the keys, and thought no more about it.

In the living room, on the first floor of this hovel, some poor furniture had been put: a shabby sofa, an equally shabby armchair, a few cane-bottomed chairs, and a card table. On the table was a teapot, a small kettle over a kerosene stove, and a few cups and small cakes. A smoky lamp shed a dim light over this depressing interior, and a handful of coal was smoldering in the cracked grate.

And here, in these miserable surroundings, Lady Beltham had installed herself on this eighteenth day of December.

The great lady was even paler than usual, and her eyes shone with curious brilliance. That she was suffering from the most acute and feverish nervous excitement was obvious from the way in which she kept putting her hands to her heart as though its violent throbbing were unbearable and from the restless way in which she paced the room, stopping at every other step to listen for some sound to reach her through the silence of the night. Once she stepped quickly from the middle of the room to the wall opposite the door that opened on to the staircase; she pushed ajar the door of a small cupboard and murmured "Hush," making a warning movement with her hands, as if addressing someone concealed there; then she moved forward again and, sinking on to the sofa, pressed her hands against her throbbing temples.

"No one yet!" she murmured. "Oh, I would give ten years of my life to—! Is all really lost?" Her eyes wandered around the room. "What a squalid place!" And again she sprang to her feet and paced the room. Through the grimy panes of the window she could just see a long row of roofs and chimneys outlined against the sky. "Oh, those black roofs, those horrible black roofs!" she muttered. The already wretched light in the wretched room was burning dimmer, and Lady Beltham turned up the wick of the lamp. As she did so she heard a sound and stopped. "Can that be he?" she exclaimed, and hurried to the door. "Footsteps—and a man's footsteps!"

The next moment she was sure. Someone stumbled in the passage below, came slowly up the stairs, was on the landing.

Lady Beltham recoiled toward the sofa and sank down on it, turning her back to the door and hiding her face in her hands.

"Valgrand!"

Valgrand was a man with a passion for adventure. But invariable success in his flirtations had made him blasé, and now only the absolutely novel could appeal to him. And there could certainly be no question that the woman who had sent him the present invitation was anything but commonplace! Moreover, it was not just any woman who had asked him to keep this assignation in the outward guise of Gurn, but the one woman in whose heart the murderer ought to inspire the greatest abhorrence, the widow of the man whom Gurn had murdered. What should his behavior be when he came face to face with her? That was what preoccupied the actor as he left the theater and made him get out of his taxi before he reached his destination.

Valgrand came into the room slowly, knowing how to make a strong impression. He flung his cloak and hat theatrically on the armchair and moved toward Lady Beltham, who still sat motionless with her face hidden in her hands.

"I have come!" he said in deep tones.

Lady Beltham uttered a little exclamation as if of surprise and seemed even more anxious to hide from him.

"Odd!" thought Valgrand. "She seems to be really upset; what can I say to her, I wonder?"

But Lady Beltham made a great effort and sat up, looking at the actor with strained eyes, yet forcing a smile.

"Thank you for coming, sir," she murmured.

"It is not from you, Madame, that the thanks should come," Valgrand answered magnificently. "Quite the reverse; I am infinitely grateful to you for having summoned me. Pray believe that I would have been here even sooner but for the delay inevitable with a first performance. But you are cold," he broke off, for Lady Beltham was shivering.

"Yes, I am," she said almost inaudibly, automatically pulling a scarf over her shoulders. Valgrand was standing, taking in every detail of the squalid room in which he found himself with this woman, whose wealth and taste and sumptuous home at Neuilly were famous.

"I must clear up this mystery," he thought, while he moved to the window to see that it was shut and searched about, in vain, for a little coal to put on the fire. While he was doing this Lady Beltham also rose and, going to the table, poured two cups of tea.

"Perhaps this will warm us up, in the absence of anything better," she said, making an effort to seem more amiable. "I am afraid it is rather strong, Monsieur Valgrand; I hope you do not mind?" And, with a hand that trembled as if it held a heavy weight, she brought one of the cups to her guest.

"Tea never upsets me, Madame," Valgrand replied as he took the cup. "Indeed, I like it." He came to the table and picked up the bowl filled with sugar, making first as if to put some in her cup.

"Thanks, I never take sugar in tea," she said.

Valgrand made a little grimace. "I admire you, but I will not imitate you," he said, and unceremoniously tipped a generous helping of the sugar into his own cup.

Lady Beltham watched him with haggard eyes.

While they were sipping their tea there was silence between them. Lady Beltham went back to the sofa, and Valgrand sat in a chair quite close to her. The conversation was certainly less than sparkling, he reflected whimsically. Would the lady succeed in reducing him to the level of a callow schoolboy? And she most certainly did seem to be horribly upset. He raised his eyes to her and found that she was gazing into infinity.

"One has got to use psychology here," Valgrand mused. "It is not I in whom this lovely creature takes any interest, or she would not have desired me to come in this outfit that makes me look like Gurn. I have to really get into Gurn's skin! But how should I behave? Sentimentally? Or brutally? Or shall I appeal to her proselytizing mania and do the repentant sinner act? I'll chance it, here goes!" And he rose to his feet.

As he moved, Lady Beltham looked around, uneasy, frightened, almost anguished; it seemed as though she realized that the moment had come for extraordinary things to happen.

Valgrand began to speak as he did on the stage, restraining his effects at first and draining his voice of any set purpose; to save the full effect for later on.

"At your summons, Madame, the prisoner Gurn has burst his bonds, broken through the door of his cell, and scaled his prison walls, triumphing over every obstacle with the single object of coming to your feet. He comes—" And he took a step nearer to her.

Lady Beltham stayed him with a gesture of terror.

"Don't! Don't! Please say no more!" she murmured.

"I've got a nibble," Valgrand said to himself. "Let's try another bait." And, as if reading his part, he said dramatically: "Has your charitable heart turned toward the guilty soul that you would rescue from transgression? Men say you are so great a lady, so good, so near to heaven!"

Again Lady Beltham put up a protesting hand.

"Not that! Not that!" she said imploringly. "Oh, this is torture, go away!"

In her distress she was really superbly beautiful, but Valgrand knew too much about women of every temperament—neurotic, hysterical, and many other kinds—not to suppose that here he was merely taking part in a sentimental comedy. He made a rough gesture and laid his hand on Lady Beltham's arm.

"Do you not know me?" he said harshly. "I am Gurn! I will crush you to my heart!" And he tried to draw her to him.

But this time Lady Beltham threw him off with the violence of despair. "Stand back! You brute!" she cried in tones that could not be mistaken.

Valgrand recoiled in real dismay and stood silent in the middle of the room, while Lady Beltham went to the wall farthest from him and leaned for support against it.

"Listen, Madame," Valgrand began presently, in dulcet tones that had the effect of making Lady Beltham try to control her emotion and murmur some faint words of apology. "Of course you know I am Valgrand, Valgrand the actor; I will apologize for having come to you like this, but I have some small excuse in your note!"

"My note?" she murmured. "Oh, yes, I forgot!"

Valgrand went on, seeming to pick and choose his words.

"You have overestimated your strength, and now perhaps you find the resemblance too startling? Do not be frightened. But your letter came to me like healing balm upon a quivering wound. For weeks, long weeks—" The actor stopped and rubbed his eyes. "It's odd," he thought to himself, "but I feel more inclined to go to sleep than to make love." He shook off his drowsiness and began again. "I have loved you since the first day I saw you. I love you with such intensity—"

For some moments Lady Beltham had been looking at him

with a calmer air and eyes that were less hostile. The old lady's man observed it and made a tremendous effort to overcome his most inopportune sleepiness.

"How can I be silent when at last kind heaven is about to grant the fondest desire of my heart? When, all afire with love, I am kneeling at your feet?"

Valgrand dropped to his knees, Lady Beltham drew herself up, listening. In the distance a clock struck four.

"Oh, I can't bear it any longer!" she cried stammeringly. "Listen, four o'clock! No, no! It is too much, too much for me!" The woman seemed absolutely frantic. She paced up and down the room like a caged animal. Then she came close to Valgrand and looked at him with an immense pity in her eyes. "Go, sir; if you believe in God, go away! Go as quickly as you can!"

Valgrand struggled to his feet. His head was heavy, and he had an irresistible desire to hold his tongue and just stay where he was. Partly from gallantry and partly from his desire not to move, he murmured, not without a certain aptness: "I believe only in the god of love, Madame, and he bids me remain!"

In vain did Lady Beltham make every effort to rouse the actor and induce him to go away; in vain were all her frantic appeals to him to flee.

"I will stay," was all he said, and he dropped heavily on the sofa by Lady Beltham's side and mechanically tried to put his arm around her.

"Listen!" she began, freeing herself from him. "In heaven's name, you must— And yet I cannot tell you! Oh, it is horrible! I am going mad! How am I to choose! What am I to do! Which—? Oh, go—go—go! There is not a minute to lose!"

"I will stay!" said Valgrand again; this amazing drowsiness was gaining on him so fast that he had but one desire left—for sleep! Surely a strange assignation, this, and not much of a lover, either!

Lady Beltham stopped her torrent of appeal and looked at the actor crumpled up beside her. Suddenly she started and listened; a slight noise became audible, coming from the staircase. Lady Beltham stood erect and rigid, then dropped to her knees on the floor.

"Oh! It is all over!" she sobbed.

In spite of his overwhelming longing for sleep, Valgrand suddenly started. Two heavy hands fell on his shoulder, and then his arms were pulled behind him and his wrists rapidly bound together.

"Good God!" he cried, in stupefied surprise, turning quickly around. Two men stood before him, soldiers by the look of them, in dark uniforms relieved only by the gleam of metal buttons. He was going to say more, but one of the men laid his hand over his lips.

"Hush!" he said.

Valgrand made frantic efforts to prevent himself from falling.

"What does this mean? Let me go! What right—"

The two men began to drag him gently away.

"Come along," said one of them in his ear. "Time's up. Don't be stubborn."

"Besides, you know it's useless to resist, Gurn," the other added, not unkindly. "Nothing in the world could—"

"I don't understand," Valgrand protested feebly. "Who are you? And why do you call me Gurn?"

"Let me finish," growled one of the men irritably. "You know we are running an awful risk in getting you out of the prison and bringing you here when you were supposed to be with the chaplain; you swore you would behave and go back when you were told. Now you've got to keep your promise."

"The lady paid us well to give you an hour with her," the other man put in, "but you've had more than an hour and a half, and we've got our reputations and our jobs to look after. So now, come along, Gurn, and don't let us have any nonsense."

Valgrand, fighting hard against his overpowering sleepiness, began to have some vague comprehension of what was happening. He recognized the uniforms and guessed that the men were prison guards.

"Good God!" he exclaimed thickly. "The fools think I am Gurn! But I am not Gurn! Ask—" He cast a despairing eye at Lady Beltham who throughout the awful scene remained on her knees in a corner of the room, dumb with anguish, apparently deaf and turned to stone. "Tell them, Madame," he implored her. "Oh, God save me!" But still the guards dragged him toward the door. By a Herculean effort he swayed them back with him into the middle of the room. "I am not Gurn, I tell you," he shouted. "I am Valgrand, Valgrand the actor. Everybody in the world knows me. You know it too, but— Search me, I tell you." And he made a sign with his head toward his left side. "Look in my wallet; my name's inside. And you'll find a letter too, proof of the trap I've been led into; the letter from that woman over there!"

"Better look and see, Nibet," one guard said to the other, and to Valgrand he added: "Not so much noise, man! Are you trying to get us all caught?"

Nibet quickly looked through Valgrand's pockets; there was nothing there. He shrugged his shoulders.

"Besides, what about it?" he growled. "We brought Gurn here, didn't we? Well, we've got to take Gurn back again. That's all I know. Come on!"

Beaten down by the drowsiness that was quite irresistible, and worn out by his violent but futile efforts to resist the guards, Valgrand was half dragged, half carried out by the two men, his head drooping on his chest, his consciousness failing. But still as they were getting him down the stairs his voice could be heard in the half-dark room above, bleating more weakly and at longer intervals:

"I am not Gurn! I am not Gurn!"

Once more silence reigned in the room. After the three men had gone, Lady Beltham rose to her feet, tottered to the window, and stood there listening. She heard their footsteps crossing the street and stopping by the door into the prison. She waited for a few minutes to make sure that they had escaped unnoticed from their amazing adventure, then turned again to the sofa, struggled to unfasten the collar of her dress to get more air, drew a few deep sighs, and swooned.

The door opposite the staircase opened slowly, and noiselessly Gurn emerged from the darkness and went toward Lady Beltham. The murderer flung himself at her feet, covered her face with kisses, and pressed her hands in his.

"Maud!" he called. "Maud!"

She did not answer, and he hunted about the room for something to revive her. Presently, however, she recovered consciousness without any help and uttered a faint sigh. Her lover hurried to her.

"Oh, Gurn," she murmured, laying her white hand on the wretch's neck, "it's you, dear! Come close to me and hold me in your arms! It was too much for me! I almost broke down and told them everything! I could not take any more. Oh, what a terrible time!" She sat up sharply, her face drawn with terror. "Listen, I can hear him still!"

"Try not to think about it," Gurn whispered, caressing her.

"Did you hear him, how he kept saying, 'I am not Gurn! I am not Gurn!' Oh, heaven grant they may not find that out!"

Gurn himself was shaken by the horror of the plot he had contrived with his mistress to effect this substitution of another for himself; it surpassed in ghastliness anything that had gone before, and he had not dared to give the least hint of it to Nibet.

"The prison guards were well paid," he said to reassure her now. "They would deny everything." He hesitated a second, and then asked: "He drank the drug, didn't he?"

Lady Beltham nodded.

"It will take effect. It was acting already, so rapidly, that I thought for a moment he would fall unconscious there at my feet!"

Gurn drew a deep breath.

"Maud, we are saved!" he exclaimed. "See," he went on, "as soon as it is light and there are enough people in the street for us to mix with them unobserved, we will go away from here. While you were with—him—I burned my other clothes, so I will take these to get away in." He picked up the hat and cloak which Valgrand had thrown on the chair and wrapped the heavy cloak around himself. "This will disguise me effectively."

"Let us go at once!" Lady Beltham exclaimed, but Gurn stopped her.

"I must get rid of this beard and my mustache," he said, and he took a pair of scissors from his pocket and was walking toward a mirror when suddenly they both heard the distinct sound of footsteps coming slowly and steadily up the stairs. Gurn had no time to get back to his former hiding place; all he could do was to sink into the one armchair in the room and conceal his features as well as he could by turning down the brim of the hat and turning up the collar of the cloak that the actor had forgotten. The man went as white as a sheet, but Lady Beltham appeared to recover her presence of mind and strength and daring at the approach of danger, and she hurried to the door. Although she tried to keep it shut, it slowly turned on the hinges, and a timid, hesitating figure appeared in the doorway and advanced toward the retreating woman.

"Who are you? What do you want?" Lady Beltham faltered.

"I beg you excuse me, Madame," the man began, "I came to—" He caught sight of Gurn and pointed to him. "Monsieur Valgrand knows me well. I am Charlot, his dresser at the theater, and I came to—I wanted to have a word—wait—" He took a small square parcel from his pocket. "Monsieur Valgrand went off so hastily that he forgot his wallet, and so I came to bring it to him." The dresser was trying to get near the murderer, whom he supposed to be his master, but Lady Beltham, most anxiously, kept between the two men. Charlot misunderstood her intention. "I also came to—" He stopped again and whispered to Lady Beltham. "He does not speak; he is very angry with me for coming? I didn't come out of curiosity or to cause you any trouble, Madame; will you ask him not to be very angry with his poor old Charlot?"

Lady Beltham felt like swooning again; she could endure very little of this old man's garrulity.

"Go, for goodness sake, go," she said distantly.

"I am going," Charlot said. "I know I am in the way, but I must explain to him." He raised his voice and spoke to Gurn, who sat quite still, sinking as far as he could into the shadow of the chair. "You are not very angry with me, Monsieur Valgrand, are you?" Getting no reply, he looked apologetically at Lady Beltham. "It was all these stories, and then the street, and the prison opposite; but perhaps you do not know. You see, I read in the paper yesterday—or rather tonight, a couple of hours ago—that that man Gurn, who murdered the rich English gentleman, was to be executed this morning. And so I was rather what you might call uneasy; at first I only meant to follow Monsieur Valgrand and wait for him down below, but I lost my way and I have only just arrived. I found the door open, and as I did not know whether he had gone or was still here, I took the liberty to come upstairs. But I am going now, quite reassured since he is quiet and happy here with you. And I beg your pardon, Madame." He threw a last appeal to where Gurn sat. "I hope you will forgive me, Monsieur Valgrand?" He sighed as no answer was forthcoming and made a pathetic little appeal to Lady Beltham. "You will explain to him, Madame, won't you? He is a kind master, and he will understand. One does get crazy ideas like that, you know. But now I will go away easy, quite easy in my mind, since I have seen him."

Charlot turned away slowly, with bent shoulders. As he passed the window he glanced outside and stopped short. Day was just beginning to break, making the wan light of the street lamps still more wan. From the window one could see a kind of platform at the corner of the boulevard Arago which was bounded by the high wall of the Santé prison. This spot, usually deserted, was crowded with people, a mob, swarming and struggling behind some hastily erected barriers. Charlot stretched a trembling hand toward the spectacle in sudden comprehension.

"Good heavens!" he cried. "That must be where they are putting up the scaffold. Yes, I can see the planks; it is the guillotine! The exe—"

The old man's words ended in a sudden cry, and almost simultaneously there was a heavy thud.

Struck from behind, Charlot fell like a log to the floor, while Lady Beltham recoiled in terror, clenching her fists to prevent herself from screaming.

Seizing the opportunity presented by Valgrand's faithful servant standing motionless, hypnotized by the gruesome spectacle being prepared outside, Gurn had drawn a knife from his pocket and, springing on the unfortunate old man, had driven the blade in all the way behind his neck.

Charlot fell prone and rigid, the weapon remaining in the wound and stopping the flow of blood.

Lady Beltham was staring at the victim in horror, but Gurn seized her roughly by the arm.

Without troubling to alter the appearance of his face—or to comfort Lady Beltham, who was horrified by the tragedies that had succeeded one another in such appalling and rapid succession during this awful night—Gurn drew the half-fainting woman to him and hurried her away.

"Come quickly!" he muttered hoarsely. "Let's get out of here!"

ON THE SCAFFOLD

It was still dark.

In the keen morning air a crowd came hurrying along the sidewalks, flowing over into the streets. The boulevards were black with people, all marching briskly toward one common goal. And it was a light-hearted, singing crowd, chanting the choruses of popular songs and swarming into the open restaurants and bars and taverns.

And it was noticeable that all these late-night owls belonged to one of two sharply divided classes. They were either rich or miserably poor; they came either from the night clubs, or they were the poor devils with no homes or hearths who roam about the city from one month to another. There were crooks whose faces shone with the evil excitement of alcohol, bums of all kinds, beggars, and young men—all young men—with sleek oiled hair and shiny boots, in whose eyes and behavior theft and crime could be seen.

By a curious coincidence the great news seemed to have reached all, socialites and crooks alike, at exactly the same time. About midnight the rumor had run through the town; it was certain, definite this time; the official steps had been taken, and the guillotine was going to raise her bloodstained arms toward the sky. At earliest dawn, Gurn, the man who had murdered Lord Beltham, was to undergo the supreme punishment and expiate his murder with his life.

No sooner had the great news become known than all prepared, as for a holiday, to go to see the man's head fall. At Montmartre carriages were requisitioned and taxicabs were at a premium. Women in gorgeous gowns and sparkling with jewels streamed from the open doors into the carriages which would bear them swiftly toward the Santé prison and the place of execution. In the suburbs likewise, the bars were emptied of their customers, and men and women, linked arm-in-arm, set forth on foot with songs and jokes on their lips for the spectacle of blood and the boulevard Arago.

Around the Santé prison an atmosphere of pleasure reigned as the people, massed together in tight ranks, produced bottles of wine and ate sausages and gaily enjoyed an improvised supper in the open air, while speculating about the details of the sight they had come to see. And so the crowd amused itself, for Gurn's head was going to fall.

Worming his way through the crowd, François Bonbonne, the landlord of the Saint-Anthony's Pig, led a little company of friends who took advantage of his greater stature to find the best path.

The landlord was half drunk already in honor of the occasion.

"Come along, Billy Tom," he shouted. "Catch hold of the tail of my coat and then you won't lose us. Where is Hogshead Geoffroy?"

"He's coming along with Bouzille."

"Good! Just fancy if Bouzille had tried to get through here with his train! There are a few people about, eh?"

Two men passed the landlord of the market inn just then.

"Come along," said one of them, and as the other caught up with him, Juve added: "Didn't you recognize those fellows?"

"No," said Fandor.

Juve told him the names of the men whom they had passed.

"You will understand that I don't want them to recognize me," he said, and as Fandor smiled Juve went on: "It's a queer thing, but it is always the future customers of the guillotine, crooks and fellows like that, who make a point of seeing this ghastly spectacle." The detective stopped and laid a hand on the journalist's shoulder. "Wait," he said, "we are right in front now; only the men who are holding the line are ahead of us. If we want to get through and avoid the crush we must make ourselves known at once. Here is your pass."

Jérôme Fandor took the card that Juve held out to him and had gotten for him as a special favor.

"What do we do now?" he asked.

"Here come the municipal guards," Juve replied. "I can see their sabers flashing. We will get behind the newspaper stands and let them drive the crowd back, and then we will go through."

Juve had correctly anticipated the maneuver that the officer in command of the squadron immediately proceeded to execute. Grave and imposing, and marvelously mounted on magnificent horses, a large number of municipal guards had just arrived on the boulevard Arago, by the side of the Santé prison and just where the detective and the journalist were standing. A sharp order rang out, and the guards deployed fanwise and, riding knee to knee, drove the crowd back irresistibly to the end of the avenue, utterly disregarding the angry murmur of protest and the general crush that ensued.

The municipal guards were followed by troops of infantry, and these by gendarmes who, holding hands, moved on all who by some means or other had managed to worm their way between the horses of the guards and the infantry, determined at any cost to stay in the front row of spectators.

Juve and Fandor, armed with special passes that admitted them to the enclosure where the guillotine actually stood, had no difficulty in getting through the triple line. They found themselves in the center of a large portion of the boulevard Arago, entirely clear of spectators, and bounded on one side by the walls of the prison and on the other by those of a convent.

In this clear space about a dozen individuals in black coats and silk hats were walking about, affecting complete indifference to what was going to happen, although really profoundly affected by it.

"Chief detectives," Juve said, pointing them out, "my colleagues. Some of yours too. Do you see them? Chief reporters of the big dailies. Are you aware that you are uncommonly lucky to have been selected, at your extremely youthful age, to represent your paper at this lugubrious function?"

Jérôme Fandor made an odd grimace.

"I don't mind admitting to you, Juve, that I am here because

I, like you, want to see Gurn's head fall; you have satisfied me beyond all doubt that Gurn is Fantômas, and I want to be sure that Fantômas is really dead. But if it were not the execution of that one particular villain—the only thing that can make society safe—I should certainly have declined the honor of reporting this event."

"It upsets you?"

"Yes."

Juve bent his head.

"So it does me! Just think: For more than five years I have been fighting Fantômas! For more than five years I have believed in his existence, in spite of all ridicule and sarcasm! For more than five years I have been working for this wretch's death, for death is the only thing that can put a stop to his crimes!" Juve paused a moment, but Fandor made no comment. "And I am rather sorry, too, because, although I have become certain that Gurn is Fantômas and have succeeded in convincing intelligent people, who were ready to study my work in good faith, I have nevertheless not succeeded in establishing legal proof that Gurn is Fantômas. Deibler and the public prosecutor, and people generally, think that it is merely Gurn who is going to be decapitated now. I may have secured this man's condemnation, but nonetheless he has beaten me and deprived me of the satisfaction of having brought him, Fantômas, to the scaffold! I have only consigned Gurn to the scaffold, and that is a defeat!"

The detective stopped. From the boulevard Arago, where the crowd had been driven back, cheers and applause and joyous shouts broke out; it was the mob welcoming the arrival of the guillotine.

Drawn by an old white horse, a heavy black van arrived at a fast trot, escorted by four mounted police with drawn swords. The van stopped a few yards from Juve and Fandor; the police rode off, and a shabby brougham came into view, from which three men in black proceeded to get out.

"Monsieur de Paris and his assistants," Juve informed Fandor, "Deibler and his men." Fandor shivered, and Juve continued to explain. "That van contains the timbers and the blade. Deibler and his men will get the guillotine up in half an hour, and in an hour at the outside Fantômas will be no more!"

While the detective was speaking, the executioner had stepped briskly to the officer in charge of the proceedings and exchanged a few words with him. He signified his approval of the arrangements, saluted the superintendent of police of that division, and turned to his men.

"Come along, boys, get to work!" He caught sight of Juve and shook hands with him. "Good morning," he said, adding, as though his work were of the most commonplace kind: "Excuse me, we are a bit late this morning!"

The assistants took out of the van some long cases, wrapped in gray canvas and apparently very heavy. They laid these on the ground with the utmost care; they were the timbers and frame of the guillotine and could not be warped or strained, for the guillotine is a precisely accurate machine!

They swept the ground thoroughly, careful to remove any gravel that might have affected the equilibrium of the framework, and then set up the red uprights of the scaffold. The floor timbers fit one into another and were joined by stout metal clamps fastened together by a bolt; next the men set the grooved slides, down which the knife must fall, into holes cut for the purpose in the middle of the floor. The guillotine now raised its awful arms to the sky.

Hitherto Deibler had merely watched his men at work. Now he helped out himself.

With a level he ascertained that the floor was absolutely horizontal; next he arranged the two pieces of wood, from each of which a segment is cut so as to form the lunette into which the victim's neck is thrust; then he tested the lever, to make sure that it worked freely, and gave a curt order.

"The knife!"

One of the assistants brought a case, which Deibler opened, and Fandor instinctively shrank as a flash from the bright steel struck his eyes, that sinister triangular knife that presently would do the work of death.

Deibler leaned calmly against the guillotine; fit the shank into the grooves in the two uprights; and, setting the mechanism to work, hoisted up the knife, which glittered strangely. He looked the whole thing over and turned again to his assistants.

"The hay!"

A truss was arranged in the lunette, and Deibler faced the instrument and pressed a spring. Like a flash the knife dropped down the uprights and severed the truss in two.

The rehearsal was finished. Now for the real drama!

While the guillotine was being set up Juve had stood by Fandor, nervously chewing on a cigarette.

"Everything is ready now," he said to the boy. "Deibler has only got to put on his coat and wait for delivery of Fantômas."

The assistants had just arranged two baskets filled with hay along each side of the machine; one was destined to receive the severed head, the other the body when that was released from the plyer. The executioner pulled on his coat, rubbed his hands mechanically, and then strode toward a group of officials who had arrived while the guillotine was being erected and were now standing by the entrance to the prison.

"Gentlemen," said Deibler, "it will be sunrise in a quarter of an hour. We can proceed to awaken the prisoner."

Slowly, in single file, the officials went inside the prison.

There were present the attorney general; the public prosecutor, his deputy, the governor of the prison; and behind these, M. Havard, Deibler, and his two assistants.

The little company passed through the corridors to the third floor, where death row is.

The guard Nibet came forward with his bunch of keys in his hand.

Deibler looked at the public prosecutor.

"Are you ready, sir?" And as the gentleman, who was very white, made a sign of assent, Deibler looked at the governor of the prison.

"Unlock the cell," the Governor ordered.

Nibet turned the key silently and pushed open the door.

The public prosecutor stepped forward. He had hoped to find the condemned man asleep and so have had a moment's respite before announcing the fatal news. But he drew back; the man was awake and dressed, sitting ready on his bed with mad, haggard eyes.

"Gurn," said the public prosecutor. "Be brave! Your appeal has been rejected!"

The others, standing behind him, were all silent, and the words of the public prosecutor fell like a death knell. The condemned man, however, had not stirred, had not even seemed to understand; his attitude was that of a man hypnotized. The public prosecutor was surprised by this strange impassivity and spoke again, in strangled tones.

"Be brave! Be brave!"

A spasm crossed the face of the condemned man, and his lips moved as though he were making an effort to say something.

"I'm not—" he murmured.

But Deibler laid his hands upon the man's shoulders and cut the horrid moment short.

"Come now!"

The chaplain came forward in his turn.

"Pray, my brother," he said; "do you wish to hear mass?"

At the touch of the executioner the prisoner had trembled; he rose, like an automaton, with dilated eyes and twitching face. He understood what the chaplain said and took a step toward him.

"I—not—"

M. Havard intervened and spoke to the chaplain.

"Really, sir, no; it is time."

Deibler nodded approval.

"Let us be quick; we can proceed; the sun has risen."

The public prosecutor was still bleating, "Be brave, be brave!"

Deibler took the man by one arm, a guard took him by the other, and between them they half carried him to the office to prepare for the end. In the little room, dimly lighted by a winking lamp, a chair had been set close to a table. The executioner and his assistant pushed the condemned man into the chair, and Deibler took up a pair of scissors.

The public prosecutor spoke to the prisoner.

"Would you like a glass of rum? Would you like a cigarette? Do you have any last wish?"

Maître Barberoux, who had not arrived in time for the awakening of the prisoner, now approached his client; he, too, was ghastly white.

"Is there anything else that I can do for you? Have you any last wish?"

The condemned man made another effort to rise from the chair, and a hoarse groan escaped from his throat.

"I—I—"

The prison doctor had joined the group and now drew the public prosecutor's deputy aside.

"It is appalling!" he said. "The man has not articulated a single word since he was awakened. It's as though he's sunk in a stupefied sleep. There is a technical word for his condition; he is in a state of inhibition. He is alive, and yet he is a corpse. Anyhow he is utterly unconscious, incapable of any clear thought or of saying a word that makes any sense. I have never seen such complete stupefaction."

Deibler waved aside the men who were pressing around him.

"Sign the jail book, please, M. Havard," he said, and while that gentleman affixed a shaky signature to the warrant authorizing the delivery of Gurn to the public executioner, Deibler took the scissors and cut a segment out of the prisoner's shirt and cut off a wisp of hair that grew down on his neck. Meanwhile an assistant bound the wrists of the man who was about to die. Then the executioner looked at his watch and made a little bow to the public prosecutor.

"Come! Come! It is the time fixed by law!"

Two assistants took the wretch by the shoulders and raised him up. There was a horrible, deep, unintelligible rattle in his throat.

"I—I—"

But no one heard him, and he was dragged away. It was practically a corpse that the servants of the guillotine took down to the boulevard Arago.

Outside, the first rosy tints of early dawn were waking the birds and reflecting off the great triangular knife, drawing gleams from it. The time was ten minutes past five. And now the supreme moment was at hand.

The crowd, all the time growing denser, was crushed behind the cordon of troops that had difficulty keeping it at a distance from the guillotine. The soldiers, ignoring the oaths and curses and entreaties with which they were assailed, carried out their orders and permitted no one to take up his stand anywhere near the guillotine, except the few special individuals who had special passes.

A sudden murmur ran through the crowd. The mounted police, stationed opposite the guillotine, had just drawn their sabers. Fandor gripped Juve's hand nervously. The detective was very pale.

"Let's get over there," he said, and led Fandor just behind the guillotine, to the side where the severed head would fall into the basket. "We shall see the poor devil get out of the carriage, and be fastened on to the bascule and pulled into the lunette." He went on talking as if to take his own mind off the thing before him. "That's the best place for seeing things. I stood there when Peugnez was guillotined, a long time ago now, and I was there again in 1909 when Duchémin, the parricide, was executed."

But he came to an abrupt stop. From the great door of the Santé prison a carriage came rapidly out. All eyes were fixed, and a deep silence fell upon the crowded boulevard.

The carriage passed the journalists and the detective at a gallop and pulled up with a jerk just opposite them, on the other side of the guillotine and at the very foot of the scaffold. M. Deibler jumped down from the box and, opening the door at the back of the vehicle, let down the steps. Pale and nervous, the chaplain got out backward, hiding the scaffold from the eyes of the condemned man, who the assistants managed somehow to help out of the carriage.

Fandor was shaking with nervousness and muttering to himself.

But things moved quickly now.

The chaplain, still walking backward, hid the dreaded vision for still a few seconds more, then stepped aside abruptly. The assistants seized the condemned man and pushed him on to the bascule.

Juve was watching the unhappy wretch and could not restrain a word of admiration.

"That man is a brave man! He has not even turned pale! Generally condemned men are livid."

The executioner's assistants had bound the man upon the plank; it tilted upward. Deibler grasped the head by the two ears and pulled it into the lunette, despite one last convulsive struggle of the victim.

There was a click of a spring, the flash of the falling knife, a spurt of blood, a dull groan from ten thousand mouths, and the head rolled into the basket!

But Juve had flung Fandor aside and sprang toward the scaffold. He thrust the assistants away, and plunging his hands into the hay that was soaked with blood, he seized the severed head by the hair and stared at it.

Horrified by this scandalous action, the assistant ran to the detective.

Deibler forced him backward.

"You must be crazy!"

"Get away!"

Fandor saw that Juve was staggering and seemed about to faint. He rushed toward him.

"Good God!" he cried in tones of anguish.

"It isn't Gurn who has just been put to death!" Juve panted brokenly. "This face has not gone white because it is painted! It is made up—like an actor. Oh, curse him! Fantômas has escaped! Fantômas has gotten away! He has had some innocent man executed in his stead! I tell you, Fantômas is alive!"

CLICK ON A CLASSIC
www.penguinclassics.com

The world's greatest literature at your fingertips

Constantly updated information on more than a thousand titles
from Icelandic sagas to ancient Indian epics, Russian drama to
Italian romance, American greats to African masterpieces

•

The latest news on recent additions to the list, updated
editions, and specially commissioned translations

•

Original essays by leading writers

•

A wealth of background material, including biographies
of every classic author from Aristotle to Zamyatin, plot
synopses, readers' and teachers' guides, useful web links

•

Online desk and examination copy assistance for academics

•

Trivia quizzes, competitions, giveaways, news on
forthcoming screen adaptations

FOR THE BEST IN PAPERBACKS, LOOK FOR THE

In every corner of the world, on every subject under the sun, Penguin represents quality and variety—the very best in publishing today.

For complete information about books available from Penguin—including Penguin Classics, Penguin Compass, and Puffins—and how to order them, write to us at the appropriate address below. Please note that for copyright reasons the selection of books varies from country to country.

In the United States: Please write to *Penguin Group (USA), P.O. Box 12289 Dept. B, Newark, New Jersey 07101-5289* or call 1-800-788-6262.

In the United Kingdom: Please write to *Dept. EP, Penguin Books Ltd, Bath Road, Harmondsworth, West Drayton, Middlesex UB7 0DA.*

In Canada: Please write to *Penguin Books Canada Ltd, 90 Eglinton Avenue East, Suite 700, Toronto, Ontario M4P 2Y3.*

In Australia: Please write to *Penguin Books Australia Ltd, P.O. Box 257, Ringwood, Victoria 3134.*

In New Zealand: Please write to *Penguin Books (NZ) Ltd, Private Bag 102902, North Shore Mail Centre, Auckland 10.*

In India: Please write to *Penguin Books India Pvt Ltd, 11 Panchsheel Shopping Centre, Panchsheel Park, New Delhi 110 017.*

In the Netherlands: Please write to *Penguin Books Netherlands bv, Postbus 3507, NL-1001 AH Amsterdam.*

In Germany: Please write to *Penguin Books Deutschland GmbH, Metzlerstrasse 26, 60594 Frankfurt am Main.*

In Spain: Please write to *Penguin Books S. A., Bravo Murillo 19, 1° B, 28015 Madrid.*

In Italy: Please write to *Penguin Italia s.r.l., Via Benedetto Croce 2, 20094 Corsico, Milano.*

In France: Please write to *Penguin France, Le Carré Wilson, 62 rue Benjamin Baillaud, 31500 Toulouse.*

In Japan: Please write to *Penguin Books Japan Ltd, Kaneko Building, 2-3-25 Koraku, Bunkyo-Ku, Tokyo 112.*

In South Africa: Please write to *Penguin Books South Africa (Pty) Ltd, Private Bag X14, Parkview, 2122 Johannesburg.*

Printed in the United States
by Baker & Taylor Publisher Services